RHAPSODY OF HEARTBEATS

COLLIDE

ALANNAH ROBERTS

BOOK ONE

First Edition

Paperback ISBN: 978-1-7641252-0-8

Hardback ISBN: 978-1-7641252-1-5

eBook ISBN: 978-1-7641252-2-2

Cover Design by Manlangit Digital Studios & Alannah Roberts

Editing by Laura at The Hummingbird Editing & Vicky at Neon Galaxy Books

Formatting by Grace Elena Formatting

Published independently by Alannah Roberts

For permissions and inquiries, please contact: author.alannah.roberts@gmail.com

Connect with the author: Instagram & TikTiok: @author.alannah.roberts

Trigger Warnings

Collide is intended for mature audiences and is not suitable for younger readers. This novel contains themes and content that may be distressing to some, including:

- Profanity
- Sexually explicit scenes
- Emotional manipulation & Gaslighting
- Mention of cancer and death of a parent (off-page)
- Familial conflict and abandonment
- Grief and depression
- References to past infidelity and divorce
- Alcohol and drug use
- Mention of pregnancy, pregnancy loss, and infertility

Your mental health is a priority. Reader discretion is advised —please take care of yourself while reading.

Language Translation

Älskling (pronounced ELL-skling)
noun. Darling or beloved one; a Swedish term of endearment, similar to "babe" or "honey."
Anak (pronounced ah-NAHK)
noun. Son or daughter; child; children. Often used as a term of endearment by Filipino parents.
Bogan (pronounced BOH-guhn)
noun. Australian slang used to describe a person perceived as uncultured, unsophisticated, or having poor taste. Often associated—humorously or affectionately—with stereotypically "Aussie" behaviors, interests, or appearances.
Mestiza (pronounced mes-TEE-zah)
noun. A Tagalog term used to describe a woman of mixed ancestry, typically Filipino and European. Often associated with lighter skin, mixed cultural identity, and a blending of Filipino and Western traits. Can be used affectionately, descriptively, or admiringly.

Soundtrack of Collide

Each chapter of *Collide* is titled after a song that mirrors Elena's emotional journey—capturing the highs, lows, and everything in between.

Scan the QR code below to listen along to the official *Collide* playlist on Spotify and immerse yourself fully in her world.

The Sound of Rise

These are the songs that carried me through the darkness—when my heart felt too full, too broken, too alive to put into words.

It's a collection of every ache, every spark, every breath.

As Hans Christian Andersen once said:

"Where words fail, music speaks."

Elena Montgomery

Author Preface

The *Rhapsody of Heartbeats* series is not your typical romance story—it embodies the true essence and addictive drama of telenovelas.

Telenovelas are deeply woven into Filipino and Latin American cultures, known for their captivating storytelling and irresistible dramatic flair. What sets the *Rhapsody of Heartbeats* series apart from conventional contemporary romance is its heartfelt embrace of classic telenovela tropes and tension-filled narratives.

Some of my personal favorites include *Jane the Virgin*, *Ugly Betty*, *Marimar*, and so many more. The *Rhapsody of Heartbeats* series is like all of those—blended with a dash of *Dynasty* and *Gossip Girl*.

Expect dramatic plots rich with themes of love, betrayal, social class divides, hidden pasts, and complex family dynamics —all delivered with emotional intensity. Your fingers will grip your Kindle tighter with heart stopping cliffhangers and captivate you with romantic scenes that will leave you swooning.

It's the intoxicating blend of drama, tension, comedic relief, surprising revelations, and raw emotional depth, paired with characters whose passions leap vividly from the pages that will have you falling in love with *Collide*.

Collide, the first installment in this series, will follow Elena's gripping journey across three immersive books. Because if there's one undeniable truth about telenovelas—they are unapologetically epic, perfectly designed to leave you craving more. Buckle up and enjoy the ride

Chapter 1

Homecoming

Every song begins with a note, every journey with a step, and mine? Mine begins with two flights, three gate changes, and a deathbed promise that landed me here, in the security line at JFK Airport, surrounded by the hum of chaos. I stretch my legs, finally relieved to be on my feet. Between a child kicking my seat for hours on end, to the drunk man snoring next to me, the trip was brutal.

I could have been in first class. But I couldn't accept that.

Not from *him*.

I wait for my turn, scrunching my nose at the smell of tired, unwashed bodies mingled with stale airplane air. I fidget, patience hanging by a thread. With barely any sleep and already in a foul mood, all I want is a hot shower, something to eat, and a nap.

Attendants in navy uniforms wear expressions of thinly veiled impatience, their eyes scanning for the next traveler to process. The energy in the room is one of exhaustion and anticipation, the pressing need to escape the airport's fluorescent-lit purgatory. It isn't the grand welcome one might hope for after a long absence, but it's better than being trapped in the sky. At least now, I can breathe.

The last time I was here was Christmas, five years ago. A short, unpleasant visit that ended in a huge fight and an intense flight. I shudder at the thought.

"Next," calls the security officer.

Stepping forward, I hand her my passport. I can almost taste freedom. Without much fuss, she scans it, stamps it, and hands it back with a polite smile. "Welcome home, ma'am."

Home.

It seems like such a foreign word for this place. Sure, I was born here, but I grew up half a world away, in Australia, after my mother packed us up and left *him* behind.

Sydney to New York. Twenty grueling hours in the air, and now I'm here—like it or not. I don't know if this place will ever feel like mine. But I made a promise.

A freshly signed contract to pursue my dreams again, and make up for lost time with my sister. Mend things with *him*. And maybe—just maybe—learn how to live life without my mother.

There's no going back. Not yet anyway.

I lug twenty-two years' worth of baggage—emotional and otherwise—in two roller bags, a backpack, a duffle, and my guitar, probably looking more like a pack mule than a woman. Weaving through the crush of bodies, I scan the crowd for a familiar face. At my height, seeing over the sea of strangers isn't exactly easy.

Where is she?

The terminal buzzes with reunions. Strangers melt into each other's arms, flowers exchange hands, voices lift in joy and relief. I reach into my pocket for my phone, but before I can fish it out, a voice—sharp and unmistakable—cuts through the din.

"Elena!"

I turn in time to see Philippa waving as she walks toward me.

Relief washes over me.

"Elena," she calls out again, gliding effortlessly through the crowd. She's wearing white capri pants, mint wedges matching her flowing blouse, and a designer handbag dangling from her wrist, perfectly capping off the whole polished look. Her hazel eyes take me in. Chestnut curls fall in neat waves, framing a face so much like our mother's, it makes my chest ache.

Philippa is the spitting image of Mom, who was the former Miss Universe, the Filipino beauty queen who once captivated the world. Though, as Mom used to say, Philippa was the mestiza version of her. Beautiful. Poised. Always composed. Sometimes she makes me feel like a total *bogan* in comparison. She moves with the kind of grace that comes from growing up certain of who she was and is, while I've always felt like I was winging it, making it up as I went.

She stands a little taller than me. I'm five-foot-two on a good day—though Mom used to joke that what I lacked in height, I made up for in attitude. I've got thick, dark, wavy hair falling halfway down my back that refuses to cooperate, no matter how many products I throw at it. My skin is pale and only tans if I'm lucky. And my eyes? They're unusually blue, which is often the first thing people comment on. It's frustrating. They're a constant reminder of *him*.

I guess I'm the perfect mix of my parents—not quite Caucasian, not quite Filipino. People say I'm striking. Maybe. But I think I look like me—someone still trying to figure life out, messy bun and all.

"Hey." I lift my hand in a quick wave, dropping my bags at my feet.

The crowd seems to part for her, as if she commands the surrounding space. I envy the way she carries herself with all the confidence in the world. It seems so easy for her.

Before that bitter thought can take hold, she wraps her arms around me in a tight embrace, nearly knocking me off my feet. The scent of lilacs floods my senses, a reminder of spring, of home, of her—our mother.

It's been two years since I last saw Philippa, and for a moment, I let myself sink into the hug.

Only for a moment.

Squirming free, I find myself at arm's length as her eyes scan every inch of me.

"Oh, my goodness, look at you," she gushes, brushing her hair over her shoulder, grinning ear to ear. "You look great!"

"Considering I spent twenty hours on a plane?" I tease, stretching my stiff neck.

She winks. "You're surviving it well."

"Thanks, Pip."

She gasps. "Oh, God, no one's called me that in years."

Laughing, she reaches for one of my roller bags.

"Thanks," I say, slinging my guitar case over one shoulder as we make our way toward the exit.

"Dad is so delighted to have you back home."

Oh, I bet he is.

The bastard finally got his way—his two 'jewels' back in his possession.

The terminal's sliding doors part, and the June heat rushes in, thick and suffocating. I'd left winter behind, and now the humid air clings to my skin like a second layer. Outside, yellow cabs honk, drivers load bags, and passengers climb into their cars.

Philippa leads me toward a sleek black town car parked at the far end of the curb. I brace myself, hoping—praying—he's not inside. I'll have to face him eventually, but I'm not ready.

"So," Philippa chirps, glancing at me as the driver approaches, "if you don't want to get jet-lagged, you need to stay up as late as possible. What do you want to do today?"

"Sleep," I groan, wiping the condensation forming on my brow.

Philippa's smile falters into a pout. For a second, she looks like her twelve-year-old self who never took no for an answer. Exactly like *him*.

She's used to getting what she wants. The daughter of a tycoon, raised in the lap of generational wealth, every bit the Manhattan heiress. He doted on her—an Ivy League education, a place in his company right after graduation, vacations around the world during holiday breaks.

None of it ever interested me.

My mom and I were happy in our slice of paradise on the other side of the world, far from *him*.

The driver greets us with a nod. "Miss Montgomery."

He grabs my bags with ease and loads them into the trunk before I can protest.

"Oh, I can take those," I offer, heat creeping up my neck.

"Miss Montgomery, it's my pleasure." He smiles, shutting the trunk.

I'm not used to this—people waiting on me. It's not a thing back home.

With a sigh, I slide into the car, the cool leather soothing my sticky skin.

"Pip, it's been a long day. Can't we chill at home?"

She sighs dramatically, rolling her eyes. "I thought we could do a little shopping. Sister bonding time."

"Another time. Maybe tomorrow."

She grins. "Well, that's not a no."

I shake my head, glancing out the window as the car pulls away from the curb. The city blurs past—towering concrete giants, sunlight bouncing off building windows, the constant motion of people threading the sidewalks. The city is alive, electric, untamed.

"Dad will be over today," Philippa mutters, barely looking up from her phone.

Great.

Think of the devil, and he shall appear.

I keep my expression neutral, eyes on the skyline. She doesn't deserve my animosity.

He does.

Him. Father. One and the same.

Before my last visit to New York, I did a short stint in LA, chasing a dream that slipped through my fingers. A failure—one he never missed a chance to remind me of.

Best behavior, kiddo. My stepfather Jack's voice echoes in my head.

I exhale hard, the kind of breath you let go of when you know the next one might take more effort.

"You'll be staying with Andrew and me. Unfortunately, *your* place isn't ready." Philippa's words stop me short.

"Wait? What place?" I sit up, turning my attention to her.

She looks up at me with a huge grin.

"Oh," she says, looking amused.

A cold weight settles in my stomach, and my jaw tightens.

He didn't.

"Whoops, I've ruined the surprise," she quips mockingly, placing her manicured hand over her mouth.

"Phillipa," I bite out, my warning tone prompting her to explain.

"Okay, you've twisted my arm! I'm so excited." She beams animatedly, her smile alone would be enough to cool the burning irritation brewing inside, but this had Mortimer Montgomery written all over it.

She continues, "Dad thought it best for you to have a place of your own now that you're home. Consider it a homecoming gift."

"Of course, he did." I narrow my eyes at her. My sister is

lucky looks don't kill because she's in danger of spontaneously combusting.

No doubt an apartment in a building he owns, which is close enough to Philippa or him so that he can keep tabs on me. It's as if he knows nothing about me. Grand gestures like this, his money and greed, make me sick. A constant reminder of his power and need to control everyone around him.

While I was technically born into wealth, my mom went to great lengths to keep me from becoming a spoiled rich kid, including mailing back any checks my father sent. Back home, I went to a local public school and drove a rundown Honda Civic until it finally gave out on the side of the road.

"The apartment is…a few blocks down from us, and I'm having it renovated," Philippa adds, clapping her hands together, showing her giant sparkling engagement ring. And there it is. Yet another reminder of something missing in my life.

Someone.

I spent over two years drowning in grief after my mother died, and before that…I was already grieving, losing her piece by piece, the moment they diagnosed her. Dating? Love? None of it mattered. I had enough excuses to steer clear of relationships, especially the kind of guys back home who were only interested in a quick thrill before moving on.

I wasn't jealous of Philippa, only jealous she didn't have to carry the burden I did. The burden of knowing the truth.

"Thanks, Pip, I'm sure it's beautiful," I murmur, turning my head and leaning back into the seat to look out at the window, sinking into the storm cloud brewing inside me.

———··———

The walls were thin, but even if they weren't, I

would have heard every word. I was five, maybe six, sitting on the floor with my back pressed against the door, fingers curled into the hem of my dress.

"Make your decision. I will not let you take both girls, Vida. So, decide—one or none!"

Papa's voice was sharp, unwavering, each syllable like the crack of a whip. The air was thick with tension, the kind a child doesn't fully understand but still feels deep in their bones. Though muffled by the door, his voice hit me like a fist to the chest.

"Mortimer, you cannot make me choose!" Mama's plea cracked, raw with desperation. "Please, let me have my girls. We will share them evenly."

"Vida, you're the one who wants to leave. If you can't decide, take Eleanor. She's younger. She'll need you more." His words echoed in my mind like a painful, unrelenting mantra. I remember it stinging, the way my tiny hands clenched into fists, my nails digging into my palms. I felt a hollow ache inside, as if someone had scooped me out and left me empty. My breath hitched, but I swallowed the sobs, refusing to cry, I won't let him know how this breaks me. The cold realization settled in, deep and unforgiving—Papa didn't want me.

"Philippa needs me, too, Monty. You cannot make me choose!" Mama's voice was faint and trembling.

And then...silence. My father's cold, final response came. "It's decided."

——— ..———

"Elena," a soft voice murmurs. I blink, my mind snapping back to the present. Philippa's gentle hand on my shoulder, her worried gaze searching mine. "We're here. Are you okay?"

I must have dozed off. My hand instinctively reaches up to wipe my face, realizing then I've been crying, though I can't remember when I started. How pathetic.

"Yeah," I croak, my throat tight, choking back tears. "I'm fine. Just tired."

But I'm not. Not really. My fingers curl against my palms, my breath unsteady as I push the memory back down where it belongs. The ache in my chest lingers, heavy and suffocating, a dull reminder of wounds never quite healed.

I haven't thought about that day in years. About how he made Mom choose between us, like we were possessions, something to be divided. She didn't deserve that, especially when it wasn't her fault. It was *his*.

And I...I didn't deserve to be overlooked like I always was.

But it wasn't just that moment. It was everything that came after. His cold, indifferent gestures of 'love'—expensive gifts, business deals, all the ways he tried to win me over without actually seeing me. I wanted so badly to matter to him. To not be an afterthought. But all I ever got was the distant, indifferent side of him, like I was a shadow in his life. Philippa was the one he could control, the one who fit into his perfect little world.

And yet here I am, a bundle of daddy issues—mad, sad, and angry, carrying years of insecurity and feeling like I was never enough.

He has a special way of making my blood boil at the mere thought of him. How can I even begin to rebuild a relationship with him?

I promised my mom I would try—a promise I'm really struggling with and now regretting.

MY SISTER AND HER FIANCÉ, Andrew, live in a restored 1920s building—one of many owned by Father, no doubt.

The lobby is all sand-colored marble, deep oak architraves, opulent furnishings, and in the back, a pair of golden elevators. It drips old-world charm, the very definition of *Old Money*. I wouldn't expect anything less from the pretentious Upper East Side of Manhattan.

Though even I have to admit—it's beautiful.

"It's a gorgeous building, isn't it?" Philippa remarks as she presses 'PH3' on the elevator.

I nod.

"Father and I bought this condemned building and restored it to its former glory, with some upgrades. It was my first project," she continues proudly.

I can't help the flicker of jealousy. She was the daughter he wanted—I wasn't. She followed his path and stepped right into the family business. And me? I was the reminder of everything he didn't approve of, a disappointment he hadn't figured out what to do with.

Walking into Philippa's home feels like stepping into a magazine spread. The penthouse is extravagant—sleek lines, soft lighting, everything perfectly in place. It looks like something straight out of *Architectural Digest*.

The elevator doors open into a private foyer with an ornate oak door. Inside, the open living space stretches wide, two grand glass windows framing the city and Central Park. The walls are a soft cream, matching the furniture, contrasted by oak trim throughout. Everything is soft, plush, and thoughtfully arranged, with tall green plants peppered across the space.

Fresh flowers sit in crystal vases—pieces I recognize from our parents' wedding set—adorning the tables. Understated artwork hangs on the walls, offering small bursts of color. The entire place glows under the afternoon sun pouring in through the windows.

It feels like another world up here, high above the noise. Everything seems delicate and untouchable. Nothing like the chaos below.

My temporary bedroom is just as beautiful. The theme flows seamlessly from one room to the next, every detail intentional.

This room has a large window, too, flooding everything with warm light, a perfect view of Central Park stretched below—lush and green, a cinematic oasis tucked inside a concrete maze.

I feel out of place.

It's nothing like the modest home we had back in Australia.

"Hope this room is okay," says Philippa, dropping my duffle on the bed.

"Pip, it's more than okay, it's incredible." I smile, sitting on the bed. "Thank you for letting me crash here." I really do appreciate her and Andrew letting me stay. Sometimes I feel like a stranger to her, even though she's never made me feel like one.

We were forced to grow up apart, spending only weeks together at a time, shuttled back and forth across the ocean, missing out on milestones. As soon as we settled into a comfortable understanding, we'd be ripped apart, and the cycle would start again. Year after year.

"It's our pleasure." She smiles, emphasizing *our* as she toys with her ring again.

I swallow the feeling before it shows. Philippa has someone special—Andrew. She has the security of love, the warmth of companionship. And she has our father. It's hard not to compare our circumstances. I've never been in love, never really had a boyfriend serious enough to be considered a relationship.

"Are you excited about the wedding?" I ask, trying to push those thoughts out of my head.

A huge grin erupts on her face, her cheeks rosy.

"Yes," she gushes, and begins poring over the details she's yet to finalize, all in one breath. She's giddy over their honeymoon plans to the Caribbean on an island owned by one of Father's associates.

Surprisingly, she had asked me to be her maid of honor, but I guess it would be a poor look if I weren't. It's set to be the biggest event of the social calendar, as she has reminded me on more than one occasion.

I'm happy for my sister, truly. She has love and a future mapped out with someone who adores her. And me? I'm sure I know what love is *supposed* to feel like.

"It'll be beautiful." Half smiling, I brush those thoughts away as quickly as they creep back in, knowing it will do nothing to help my dampened mood.

"Anyway, you settle in, I have lunch to prepare. If you need anything, let me know," she says, moving toward the door.

"I'm good. Thanks again," I murmur, pushing off the bed and pulling her into a genuine hug. "I've missed you."

The last time I saw my sister was at Mom's funeral. After that, it was supposed to be my turn to visit, but I couldn't do it. Couldn't board a plane. Couldn't face the world. Time passed. People moved on. I didn't.

Now I'm here. And for the first time in a long while, I want to be. A chance to make up for the time we've lost.

"I've missed you too," she whispers into my ear, her hold lingering a little longer than expected. When she pulls away, she clears her throat, as if shaking off the moment. "Get freshened up. Dad's coming over soon."

"Great." I sigh sarcastically. I'm not ready. But maybe it doesn't matter.

Five years of silence didn't disappear with a flight and a packed suitcase. Still, I am here. In his city. In his world. And whether I like it or not, there is no avoiding him now.

I don't know what I'll say. Or if I'll say anything at all. But I'll show up.

This is me trying.

Trying not to flinch.

Trying not to run.

Trying to be the daughter he never really saw.

And like a silent prayer, I hope trying will be enough.

Chapter 2

Because of You

I reach out to the fogged-up mirror and swipe a clean streak down the center. My reflection stares back—pale, hollow-eyed, worn thin from the flight.

The shower helped. Sort of. At least I didn't smell like *plane* anymore. I'd hoped the steam would take the edge off my nerves, maybe soften the tightness in my chest. Instead, I spent ten minutes replaying old fights, rewriting every word I *should* have said, every truth I bit back.

But time doesn't rewind. And nothing I say now will change what is already broken.

I squeeze toothpaste onto my brush, shoving it into my mouth.

Christmas. Five years ago. That was the last time.

I'd found out the truth—why Mom left, why she cried in the kitchen when she thought I wasn't listening. He didn't even flinch when I confronted him. He launched into a speech about Yale and how I needed to 'start thinking seriously about my future,' like singing was some childish fantasy I'd grow out of.

He called it a pipe dream. A waste of time.

What he meant was, I won't bankroll your life unless it fits the image I want.

Even now, the thought of seeing him again fills me with dread.

The father who didn't want me.

The man who thought gifts could replace love, throwing money at me like I was a scratch he couldn't quite buff out.

The more I think about it, the hotter it burns. My jaw tightens.

Let him try and play nice.

He can take his fancy apartment and shove it straight up his pretentious ass.

I spit out the toothpaste and rinse my mouth, teeth grinding as my frustration simmers beneath the surface. Determined not to let it consume me, I grab my brush and dryer, methodically working through the tangled waves of my hair. If I don't, I'll wake up looking like I crawled out of the Amazon.

Once satisfied, I throw on my favorite pair of distressed denim shorts and an old, oversized band shirt. A quick swipe of tinted lip gloss, a few strokes of mascara to frame my eyes—*his eyes*.

I'm ready.

I know he'll hate this. The way I dress, the way I carry myself —it's everything he disapproves of. Unlike my sister, his polished Manhattan princess, I am the unruly, untamed disappointment. Maybe it's childish, but I don't care. Let him see what he missed out on. Let him choke on it.

When I emerge, I hear two voices. I pause, listening—then breathe a sigh of relief. It's not my father. Has to be Andrew.

Even though he's engaged to my sister, we've never met. They got together two years ago, shortly before Mom died. While their relationship bloomed, I was drowning in grief. I pushed everyone away. Frozen in place while life moved on without me. Standing here now, I feel like an outsider in my own family's story.

I walk into the living space and spot him sprawled across the lounge, sweaty in gym clothes, auburn hair damp and sticking to his forehead. I'd seen a few photos Philippa sent—good-looking, nerdy investment banker type. Not unattractive. Just…expected.

His eyes light up when he sees me. "Oh, hey!" he says, pushing himself upright. "Nice to finally meet you."

I force a smile. "You too."

Philippa walks in a beat later and stops cold. Her eyes land on Andrew, narrowing slightly. A flicker of disapproval crosses her face. Her lips press into a tight line as she takes in the full picture —sweaty gym clothes, his back against the pristine white sofa like it was made for him. Her grip tightens around the tea towel in her hand. Classic Philippa—never one to raise her voice when passive-aggressive silence would do.

Andrew, sensing the shift in the air, lifts his head and grins, completely unfazed, as if he's used to this exact reaction from Philippa. There's an easy confidence about him, the kind that suggests he enjoys pushing her buttons just enough to amuse himself. It's a dynamic I recognize instantly—one built on teasing, on knowing how far to go before she snaps. Exactly like my stepfather would do to my mother.

"What? I ran five miles," he says, stretching lazily as if daring her to scold him further.

Philippa exhales sharply through her nose, her tone clipped yet laced with familiarity. "Andrew…Get cleaned up," she orders, her voice carrying the same authoritative warmth our mother used with Jack. A bittersweet pang settles in my chest.

He chuckles and rolls his eyes, peeling himself up off the lounge.

"I won't be too long." He kisses Philippa's forehead, making his way down the hall. She whips his backside with the tea towel she was holding, reminding me again of something my mother did with Jack.

"Wow, you're exactly like Mom." I smile.

"Hmm, I miss her." Philippa's face softens, echoing my sentiment. "Feeling better?" she adds.

I miss her too.

"Yeah."

"Nothing a good shower can't fix. He should be here soon." She offers a kind smile, reassuring me.

"Cool, what are we eating?" I ask, patting my stomach.

"Lemon herb chicken with a summer salad." She beams, silently mouthing the word *yum*.

Her excitement is adorable.

I look at her in mock horror. "I'm a vegetarian."

Her face drops.

"Kidding!" I snicker, shaking my head. *Oh, Pip, you're too easy.*

Rolling her eyes, she tuts as she makes her way back into the kitchen, shaking her head with a fond exasperation, reminding me of when we were kids. It's a small moment, but it tugs at something deep inside me—something warm, something that reminds me we are sisters, even if it doesn't always feel like it.

"Make yourself comfortable. Do you want anything to drink?" she calls out as she walks away.

"Coffee, please!"

I settle into the white plush lounge, gazing out at the stretch of Central Park below—its green canopy seems out of place against the towers of concrete giants surrounding it. The park and I have that in common. I've never felt at home here, always out of place beneath the weight of the Montgomery name, especially beside my sister, who always knows exactly what to say and how to behave. It isn't her fault—she's just as much a victim of our circumstances, she just happened to handle it better than I did.

The weight of my thoughts nests deep in my chest, pressing hard against my ribs.

My eyelids grow heavy, and exhaustion finally wins.

I let it pull me under.

Surrendering to the quiet.

"Eleanor," calls a voice. My thoughts are blurry. Wait, no one calls me *Eleanor*. My eyes shoot open, and I realize I drifted off on the couch.

"Sorry," I mutter automatically, wiping drool off my face before rubbing my eyes.

Shit. Mascara.

"Don't be sorry. You've had a long day. I'd be exhausted too after flying coach." He chuckles, and my eyes finally meet his.

"Father." I frown. His not-so-subtle jab at my choice to fly coach doesn't go unnoticed.

"Hello, Eleanor." He smiles softly. I roll my eyes. I haven't been called Eleanor in years. I don't know why he persists with such formalities.

"It's EL-EY-NAH," I respond petulantly, pronouncing each syllable of my preferred name. Everyone calls me Elena.

"Sorry, Elena. Look at you—you've changed so much. It's been far too long," he says, shaking his head like he's brushing off the memory of our last encounter.

"Yup."

"You still look so much like your mother," he adds with a smile, the corners of his eyes crinkling. For a second, I'm struck by how much older he looks. Those five years carved lines into his face that I don't remember being there.

"Please don't." I raise a hand to stop him. He has no right to bring her up.

I shift, sitting up straighter from where I'd half-dozed on the couch, suddenly alert. I've been told all my life I looked like her, but I don't see it. She was a beauty queen. I'm not a crown-wearing, pageant-perfect kind of girl.

"Well...except for those beautiful eyes." His grin is full of smug self-importance, leaning back into the armchair like that little genetic match makes me his property. His eyes—the same blue—hold a familiar glint of amusement.

I grip the edge of the couch, resisting the urge to roll mine, already irritated, unsure what game he's playing. *Compliments? Really?* What, butter me up before the slaughter?

"I assume Philippa's told you about my gift," he says, rubbing his hands together, brows arching like this was some exciting reveal.

"Yeah. About that—" I square my shoulders, already shifting into negotiation mode.

"Is something wrong?" he asks, rubbing his forefinger against his lip like he's about to launch into some patronizing monologue.

Yes! The fact that he can't see what's wrong with gifting someone an entire apartment is beyond me! He knows exactly how I feel about him showering me with lavish gifts, like a convertible Mercedes on my sixteenth birthday! What sane person does that?

"You didn't have to do that," I say, keeping my voice even through gritted teeth. "I have my own money, and I'd rather find a place that suits me."

"This isn't up for discussion," he snaps, completely bulldozing me, and there it is, the sweet, calm façade cracking. "It's already done."

You don't say no to Mortimer Montgomery.

"No, it's not. You don't get to tell me what to do. I'm an adult." I sit up, leveling the playing field.

"Elena, I don't want to argue with you." He sighs, lifting his hands in surrender.

I stop mid-step. That—*that*—throws me. Since when does he switch gears? Since when does he call me Elena? Since when does he *not* want to argue? We usually fight until he's blue in the face, and I'm seeing red.

Choose your battles, my mother's voice whispers.

I shake it off.

Not this one.

I'm not backing down.

I open my mouth to pivot, try another approach—

"I'd feel much better if you lived somewhere safe," he cuts in. "Close to your sister…closer to me."

That last part hits weird. Loaded. I don't know if it's guilt or control—or both—but it makes my insides twist.

"Why can't you respect my choices?"

"There are parts of the city that simply aren't safe for a young woman," he warns, slipping back into his usual tone. "And since you refuse to access your trust fund, whatever money you've squirrelled away might get you a cockroach-ridden hovel in Queens or Harlem. If you end up with strange roommates, I won't stand for it. I refuse to let a daughter of mine live like that. Please, Elena, *humor me.*"

He reaches into his jacket pocket and pulls out a small gift box, placing it in my hands like it's supposed to fix everything.

I click my tongue, irritated, and flip open the lid.

Inside, a silver key hangs on a key ring. My initials—*EJM*—are engraved.

"A homecoming gift," he proclaims, rubbing his hands together like this was all part of some grand gesture.

I glance down at the key. A studio in Brooklyn is probably the best I can afford on my own, and he knows that. Queens or Harlem? Please. He always imagines the worst. He always has to have the last say.

This isn't a gift.

It's a cage.

Our eyes meet—his are warm, full of hope. He looks older, grayer. For a second, guilt flickers. So much time has passed since we were last in the same room.

"Aww, you gave it to her without me?" Philippa whines, pouting as she sets a glass of scotch in front of him.

My skepticism kicks in. Just as quickly as the walls started to lower, I haul them back up.

My eyes flick up to her. He smiles at her—soft, familiar. She returns it, easy and natural.

My heart lurches.

The sight of them, so at ease with each other, slices right through me. It's seamless between them—this unspoken bond built on years I wasn't part of. Shared dinners. Inside jokes. A rhythm I never learned.

The ache tightens in my chest—sharp, sudden. Just because I share their blood doesn't mean I share their world.

I place the box on the table between us. "Excuse me for a moment," I mutter, standing up and storming off to my room.

I don't belong here. The truth is, these people are my family, but I don't *know* them.

Not really.

"Elena," Philippa calls after me, her voice tight, panicked.

I shut the door on her.

Exhaling slowly, I press my back against the wood. Frustration simmers beneath the surface. His gift doesn't undo silence. It doesn't explain why he was never there, or why he failed to show up when it mattered.

He doesn't know me.

Never did.

And maybe—maybe—he never wanted to.

That thought loops in my head like a song stuck on repeat. I press my palms into my forehead, digging my fingers into my scalp like I can force the thoughts out.

I collapse onto the bed, head spinning, chest tight. I stare up at the ceiling. Tears threaten, but I fight them. Not now. Not here.

I'm so mad at him. Still mad. What I need isn't a condo or a key. It's *why*. I want him to *say it*. Admit what he did. Tell me why I was never enough.

I breathe in. Out. Again.

I'm trying to hold it together.

And then her voice echoes—faint, warm—Mom's voice: *Anak, choose your battles. Your father...he loves you in his own way. He loves you.*

I cling to it. Because right now? I feel alone.

Here.

Everywhere.

Letting out a long groan, I get up off the bed, knowing deep down the only way forward is if I *try*. And right now, I'm not. Not really. Not for myself. But maybe for Philippa, for Jack, for Mom, I can try harder.

Back in the living room, they're seated, talking quietly. Philippa's brows are furrowed, lips tight. My father's face is drawn with concern. The sight of them makes me hesitate.

"I'm sorry," I murmur, voice low. "I'd blame jet lag, but really...I was being a bitch." I hang my head, the shame creeping in, hot and slow. "This is all...a lot. I'm overwhelmed."

The words leave my mouth, and I feel a little lighter.

"Oh, Elena..." Philippa stands. Her voice cracks, and the pain on my face must hit her full force.

My father rises too. "Elena, I know I've made mistakes," he falters, voice more fragile than I've heard it in years, "but I'll try my best to make them right."

Sadness shadows his eyes, and for a second, I falter. My instinct is to retreat, to armor up again. But the look he gives me —soft, regretful—makes it harder.

My throat tightens. I'm not ready to let it all go.

Not yet.

I've got my own sadness to wade through first.

"Thank you both for the apartment," I mutter, glancing

between them. "And I'll try, too." It's not a promise. Not really. But it's something.

After an incident-free lunch, I find out that Andrew and Philippa both work for my father—so predictable.

She's one of his executive directors, managing his endless property portfolios, and Andrew works in the finance division. As expected.

They met at work when their secretaries accidentally booked the same meeting room. Hell of a meet-cute.

I figure if I'd ended up staying with my father, I probably would've become a corporate drone too, with a position in his company, one I likely didn't earn. Dating someone my father approved of, who would be of an advantage to him and his empire. With a trust fund, of course.

Though technically, I too, am the beneficiary of an unwanted, sizeable trust fund. It remains untouched. I cringe at the thought.

In my hotel-suite-like room, I settle in, unpacking and playing music low through my phone.

I check my messages: two from Riley, my best friend, sending photos and chaotic tales from her adventures in Peru; one from my manager; and a few appointments dropped into my calendar.

I quickly draft an email to my stepdad, letting him know I'm safe.

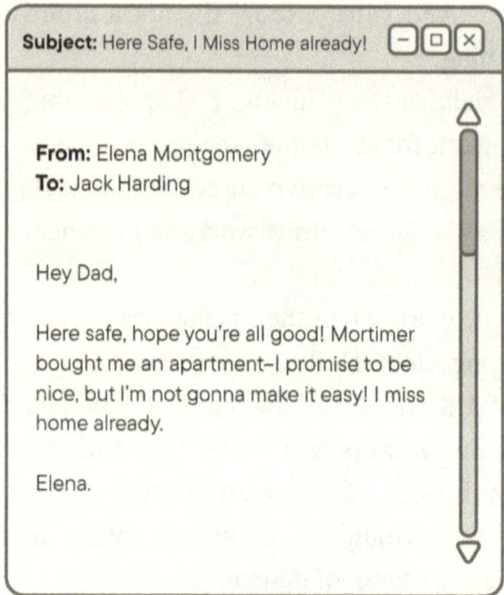

Emailing feels so ancient, but Jack still refuses to get a mobile phone. We lived in a part of the world where cell service barely existed anyway, so I couldn't convince him to get one, no matter how hard I tried.

I sigh, thinking of home—the ocean, the warm, balmy afternoons in Jervis Bay. Walking Bundy, our family dog, along the sand. Partying with friends and singing in grungy pubs that reeked of beer and sweat.

And mostly…

Mom.

I'm about to finish stuffing the last pair of jeans into the bottom dresser drawer when I hear a soft knock at the door.

It's Philippa. "Hey, Mark's here," she announces, peeking her head through the door.

Mark Shepherd is my manager, keeper of my calendar, steering the ship of my career—sharp, reliable and knows how to get shit done.

Getting up from the floor, I make my way to the door. Mark is in the foyer, fiddling with his phone, dressed in a crisp suit, clean-shaven, his salt-and-pepper hair styled to perfection. He's quite good-looking, but I would never mix business with pleasure. Not that I know what *that* kind of pleasure is. I've never been in love before, much less physically intimate with a man.

"Hey, Elena." He looks up from his phone, acknowledging me with a nod.

"Hey, what's up?" I ask, cocking my head to the side.

"Chloe," he calls. A small blonde-haired woman standing beside him, dressed in an equally crisp suit, scuttles toward me with a huge floral arrangement—white orchids, white peonies, and freesias. It smells divine. She places the flowers on the small table beside me and hands me a wicker gift basket wrapped in clear cellophane with a big pink ribbon. The tag says, "Welcome."

My eyes widen as I skim through its contents. A tablet. Workout clothes. Membership key cards for a gym and yoga studio. Jewelry. Skincare products. A bunch of other luxury items. I'm speechless.

"Thank you. You really didn't have to," I murmur, still in awe, holding up the basket to inspect it further.

"The flowers are from me," Mark says with a smile. "The basket's from the label and your endorsers down under."

He turns to the girl, still smiling. "Chloe, this is Elena, my newest and most promising artist." His voice swells with pride. My heart swells, too. Mark really is the best.

Chloe shyly smiles. "Hi," she mumbles. I can't help but wonder if she's his girlfriend. She looks young—possibly younger than me.

Definitely younger than me.

"Chloe's my daughter," Mark smiles, draping an arm around her shoulder. "She's interning with me for the summer."

"Nice to meet you. And thanks for bringing this stuff in." I smile, trying to ease the tension from my earlier, inappropriate thoughts.

We quickly discuss our schedules and exchange dates for our upcoming engagements. As Mark and Chloe are about to leave, he turns to me at the threshold.

"Here." He hands me a small white envelope. "It's an invitation to a small gathering for a fellow artist. It's on Friday night. I've scheduled a stylist, hair, and makeup crew to come to you if you're up for it."

A party.

"Absolutely! Can I bring a plus one?"

"Yes, of course." He nods, then takes his leave.

If I'm going to a party in the city for the first time, I'm not going alone.

"Pip!" I call out as I shut the door behind me.

Chapter 3

Who's that Chick?

A buzzing awakens me. The distant hum of the city filters through the walls, blending with the faint scent of jasmine from last night's bath. My body feels heavy, cocooned in the warmth of the blankets, but the persistent vibration pulls me from sleep. I reach out to the side table for my phone. The room is dim, with rays of sunlight peeking through the curtains. I answer without looking.

"Hello?"

"Elena. Mark. The team will arrive at three, the courier should have already brought over some outfits for you."

"Thanks."

"See you tonight," he says, ending the call.

Well, good fucking morning to you, too, mate.

I check the clock on the nightstand as the weight of the day settles over me—anticipation, nerves, the thrill of stepping further into this new life. A deep breath steadies me, but the flutter in my chest remains, a mix of excitement and uncertainty about what lies ahead. It's ten a.m., and right on cue, there's a knock at the door. Philippa walks in, taking a seat on the end of my bed and crossing her arms. I smile weakly at her.

"Morning." She beams, straightening her huge pear-cut diamond engagement ring, perfectly propped on her freshly manicured hand.

"The stylist?" I ask, running my hands through my tangled hair.

"Yes, there are clothes and shoes all over my lounge room!" she exclaims, shaking her head. Poor little neat freak.

"Thankfully, they're all stunning, so you're forgiven."

"I'm sorry?" I chuckle, shrugging my shoulders.

"Thought I'd take you around to your apartment this morning, but the contractors are behind schedule, so it's not quite ready." She sounds annoyed.

"That's fine. We can go another time if you want to show me once it's all 'perfect,'" I say, doing air quotes with my fingers.

"So, about tonight." Her face drops. I know she's bailing.

"No, no," I groan, dropping my shoulders in frustration and facing her with a pout. "You suck!"

"I know I promised we would hang out, but Father drafted me to do this work engagement. He had to pull out last minute, and we need someone to be there, but..." She pauses, grinning like a Cheshire cat.

"But what?" I narrow my eyes at her.

"I've pulled some strings and got someone even better," she teases, clapping her hands together diabolically.

I find myself secretly wishing it's not a blind date with one of her preppy friends.

"Who?" I hear her scream before I see her. *AHHH*. "Riley!"

Philippa bursts into a fit of giggles as Riley comes barreling into the room like an animal set loose, wild curly red hair and eyes full of excitement.

"Surprise, bitch!" she shouts, jumping on the bed. I wrap my arms around her in shock, nearly knocking my sister to the ground.

"What are you doing here?!"

Excitement frazzles my thoughts. A moment ago, I slept soundly, and now, I'm caught in a wild hug, a tornado of red and black hair.

Riley is my best friend from back home. I haven't seen her in months, since she's been backpacking around South America after graduating from art school.

"Well, I came here to party, like we said—you and me!" She laughs. "We're going to fuck New York up!"

I can't help the flicker of suspicion curling in my gut. The timing feels too perfect. Too convenient. A part of me wonders if my father is behind this—if he pulled strings to bring Riley here, thinking it would win me over.

New York has always been our dream.

Every other summer, I would be shipped here for weeks, and I promised Riley that one day, I'd bring her too.

I wouldn't put it past my father to use that promise against me.

"I'll leave you guys to it," Philippa laughs, heading out of the room.

"When did you get here?" I ask, my brain still buzzing with excitement.

"I've been in town about two weeks." She shrugs.

Oh.

"Why didn't you say anything?"

"Figured I'd give you a few days to settle in before shaking shit up." She winks. "Plus, Philippa wanted to surprise you."

Maybe it *was* to surprise me…But I can't help that my earlier thoughts linger.

"I brought cream cheese blueberry bagels," Riley announces, holding up a paper bag like it's a trophy.

I shake the thoughts away. Riley's here, and it doesn't matter if it's my father's doing.

I grin, scooting over on the bed as she plops down beside me. "My hero."

We settle in, catching up on everything we've missed. Having Riley here feels like a piece of home dropped into my lap, wrapped in unruly red curls and the kind of laughter that makes your sides hurt.

We met back in school after I moved to Australia—me, the bug-eyed Yank, and her, teased for being a 'soulless ginger.' I punched Cody Richards square in the nose for dumping paint in her hair, and that was it. We clicked. She saw the lyrics scrawled in my notebook; I saw the sketches filling hers. She was the artist, I was the musician, and from then on, we were inseparable. She dragged me out of my shell, out of my comfort zone, into trouble and joy in equal measure. The best and worst influence I've ever had, and I love her for it.

"So, you did it! New York!" She beams, her eyes bright with excitement. "I'm so damn proud of you."

I exhale, shaking my head. "Yeah…it was dark there for a bit."

"I know, babe." Her voice softens, the teasing dropping away. "It was hard seeing you like that."

Her words stir something deep inside me, pulling me back to those lost years after my mother died. Riley missed the funeral because she was off the grid at some shaman retreat in the mountains. The moment she found out, she got the first flight home, but by then, I was a ghost of myself. A comatose couch zombie who barely left the house, barely ate, barely washed my hair. I couldn't even listen to music, let alone create it.

Jack had let me be, at first. He was dealing with his own grief, and maybe he thought I'd figure it out eventually. But I didn't.

Days bled into months, and the light I once carried dimmed into nothing.

Until Riley came crashing in.

She refused to let me disappear. Between her and Jack, they nudged me—inch by inch, moment by moment—back to life. A morning walk here, a song on the radio there. Riley would blast music through the house until, one day, I found myself humming along. Then came the moment I sat at the piano, only for a second, pressing a single key. The sound was foreign, but something in me flickered awake. It took time, but music slowly seeped back in—hesitant at first, then louder, until I could finally breathe again.

A reminder that I was still here, that my mother wanted me to live, not just exist. They pieced me back together when I didn't have the strength to do it myself.

"It's okay, Riley," I murmur, grounding myself in the moment. "You're here now."

She squeezes my hand, a wicked grin spreading across her face. "Damn right I am. And we're going to have so much fun!"

I burst out laughing, knowing what her idea of fun means.

Boys.

Booze.

And a whole lot of dancing!

"So, how was Peru? Did you meet the love of your life?"

"Well," she drawls, stretching out dramatically. "There was Juan."

My brows lift. "Juan?"

She grins. "Yeah, guy *one*, two, and three."

"Riley!" I snort, shaking my head as she cackles, her curls bouncing with every movement.

She playfully slaps my arm. "What? The world is a buffet, babe. Taste the rainbow."

"I'll take your word for it," I laugh, shaking my head.

"You should have seen me—one girl, three guys, it was magical. I was a goddess to be worshipped," she gushes, her voice dripping with nostalgia as she recounts her escapade in graphic detail.

If I had pearls, they would well and truly be clutched. I'm not sure whether to be shocked, concerned, or proud, but Riley loves life, and it's infectious.

Laughing even harder, warmth spreads through my chest. This is what she does—brings light into the darkest places. And for the first time in a long time, it feels really, truly good to have her here. I don't feel so alone.

When I step out of my room, I notice someone has neatly placed rows of shoes under the window in the lounge; each pair practically begging to be worn. The buffet table is draped in black velvet, adorned with beautiful accessories gleaming like treasures. A rack filled with outfits for the night stands proudly in the center, ready to transform me into someone else—someone more glamorous.

Promptly at three p.m., the doorbell rings. I walk down the hallway, trying to shake off the lingering jetlag. When I open the door, a short man with a striking purple and blond mohawk stands in front of me. From the color of his eyebrows and skin, blond is definitely not his natural color. Next to him is a woman dressed head-to-toe in black, her thick-framed black glasses and sleek brown bun making her look like a chic librarian with a secret.

"The ravishing Elena Montgomery!" the man announces with a flourish. "I'm Rio, your stylist, and this is Inga Price, your makeup and hair artist. We're here to make you look fabulous!" he sings, shimmying his shoulders almost as if he were performing for a crowd.

I gesture them inside, rolling my eyes fondly at his flamboyance. "Come on in."

Rio is fabulous, or so he keeps saying. With his ever-present silk scarf and a spritz of expensive cologne trailing him wherever he goes, he's impossible to ignore. Though small in stature, he carries himself like a giant, his personality as bold as his wardrobe. He gestures wildly as he speaks, his rings catching the light with every exaggerated movement, ensuring all eyes stay on him.

"Sweetie, you'll look divine in these!" He holds up a pair of nude pumps. Then he presents a shimmering, skintight navy-blue dress, which looks like the night sky. "We'll pair these with this! You'll look so fabulous! I'm a genius!"

I can't help but giggle at his enthusiasm. It's completely contagious, and even though I'm not usually into designer goods, I know the drill. I need to look the part if I want to make it as a recording artist.

"And for you, Miss Riley." Rio sifts through the rack.

"You may call me Miss Fisher," Riley declares in an exaggerated fancy British accent as she curtseys.

Rio throws his head back in laughter, and I can't help but giggle, the energy in the room abuzz with excitement.

Rio dramatically pulls out an emerald bodycon dress with geometric cut-outs. He holds it up and runs his hand up and down the fabric like he's on a cheesy game show, delivering an exaggerated, "Ooh, fabulous! For thee, Miss Riley *Fishah*, I envision this," he announces in an equally exaggerated British accent, rolling the last syllable of her name with panache.

I clap my hands in approval. "Oh, Rio, I love that!" His taste is impeccable.

"Miss Montgomery," Inga calls from the dining room, her voice a soothing contrast to Rio's theatrics. Riley stands from the makeup chair, looking smoking hot. Her usually messy red hair is now tamed into a sleek straight do, framing her oval face. Her green eyes are lined with black kohl, with green glitter catching the light in the inner corners. She looks like a sultry version of herself, more glam than I've ever seen.

"Do you like?" she giggles, striking a *vogue* pose.

I nod, laughing, and take a seat. "You look amazing."

Inga opens another of her metal cases, revealing an arsenal of beauty products: powders, blushes in pinks and rouges, eye shadows of every color, and brushes that could probably double as paintbrushes. It's an artist's dream.

"Miss Montgomery, close your eyes, and we'll begin." Inga beckons, gently placing her hand under my chin. I close my eyes, letting the soothing motions take over, drifting off as she works her magic.

———··———

I stared out at the shadows of the crowd, the bright lights scorching my face. The roar of the audience hummed in my ears, a distant echo beneath the rush of my pounding heart. My hand was slick with sweat, gripping Bella Hunt's hand—my fellow competitor in the grand finale of Starstruck.

Just moments ago, I had been standing in the wings, waiting, my breath shallow as the world around me slowed to a crawl. And now, here I was, standing under the glaring spotlights, waiting for my fate to be sealed.

My dreams could begin here, right now.

The audience fell into a hushed silence, hanging on Dax's last words. My heart thundered in my chest, my stomach thick with knots. I glanced at the judges—they were all as tense as I was.

Dax took a long, deliberate breath, stretching out the suspense. He repeated the sentence, drawing it out longer than felt necessary.

"And the winner is..." He paused. "Elena Montgomery!"

A wave of shock and disbelief rushed through me as the crowd erupted in applause. Jai Silas, my mentor, leapt from his chair, a broad grin splitting his face. He grabbed me into a fierce hug, lifting me off my feet as if I had just won the world. My knees were weak, my whole body trembling with the rush of emotion.

"I won," I whispered to myself, the words almost too surreal to believe.

"You won!" Jai shouted, his voice nearly drowned by the deafening roar of the crowd. He spun me around in his arms as the applause continued to thunder.

"Oh my God, I won!" I whispered again, my breath coming in shallow gasps. My knees buckled, and I collapsed back into Jai's arms, overwhelmed by the sheer weight of the moment.

I scanned the front row, searching for a familiar face. And then—I saw her.

My mom.

Her face was streaked with tears, but her eyes shone with excitement, her grin stretching from ear to *ear. She raised her arms in celebration, and beside her, Jack held her close, his expression filled with pride as they both cheered for me.*

The sight of them—proud, emotional, here—sent a fresh wave of tears streaming down my face.

In that moment, everything I had ever wanted felt like it had come true. A hefty cash prize, a recording contract with Pacific Records Australia, and eventually, a deal with Pacific Records USA.

MY HAIR IS thick with clip-in extensions, and I'm wearing way too much lip gloss. I glance at myself in the mirror, trying not to cringe at the reflection staring back at me. Inga's work is impressive, I'll give her that. I scrub up alright. My long raven hair is styled in luscious, voluminous waves, layers of silky curls that could probably sell shampoo. My bright blue eyes are winged with black liquid liner, a hint of glittery shadow on the lids, and heavy lashes that make my eyes look like they're about to fly off my face. My cheeks are pink and rosy, complementing my nude glossy lips. I look innocent—sweet, even—but with a bit of an attitude problem; looks like a doll, will slit your throat.

Riley and I are dressing together, and she looks hot.

"Your hair is amazing." Helping her with her zipper, I notice how sleek and straight her normally wild curls are. It's a total transformation.

"You excited for tonight?" she asks, her fingers fussing with her hair, probably not used to how smooth and flat it is.

"Nervous." I sigh, shoving my phone and ID into my borrowed designer clutch. The butterflies in my stomach feel more like an actual swarm, and I can't shake the thought of how unprepared I feel for everything that's about to happen.

The car pulls up in front of Bungalow 8, its headlights briefly blinding as the driver makes his way through the crowd that's formed out front, hoping to catch a glimpse of their favorite artists.

Riley links her arm through mine as we make our way inside, discreetly sneaking past the crowd. It's surprisingly open once we're in, with lush potted plants framing the striped booths. There are a fair few famous faces here tonight, along with some selected media representatives and some bigwigs from Pacific Records. I spot Mark standing around with a few others, and the only familiar faces are those of Kylie Turner, my Public Relations Manager, and Sonia and Michelle, my album co-producers.

After a round of pleasantries and some brief introductions to a few *key players*, as Mark calls them, Riley and I grab some champagne from the passing waiters, clinking glasses with strangers who probably won't even remember our names by tomorrow.

"We need to talk about your social media presence as well as a bit of media training for interviews," Kylie practically yells over the booming music.

I nod, taking another gulp of bubbly. It tastes sweet but sharp, warming me from within.

Bleh, social media.

A concept I haven't fully jumped on board with. Comes with the territory, I suppose.

"Kylie, easy with the shop talk, let Elena have some fun and network." Mark winks, taking a sip of his drink. "We'll talk strategy another time."

The night rolls on—casual, easy banter, and a constant stream of drinks. Riley and I have long moved on from champagne to hard liquor cocktails. I will regret this in the morning, but for now, I'm doing my best to forget about my gnawing anxiety.

We mingle with a few fellow artists, most of them new to me, but all signed to the same label. Mark insists on introducing me to people, so that I can network for future collaborations and producing opportunities, as if I don't already have a million things on my mind.

"Have a good night. We'll talk soon, okay?" Kylie beams, her face slick with perspiration from the heat of the club. She hugs me, and then she's gone.

I head to the ladies' room, hoping for a moment of peace, but when I come back, I see Riley getting way too cozy with Mark. Oh, this is not good.

"Riley!" I say a little too loudly, trying to grab her attention. "Want to hit up The Avenue?" I ask, trying to drag her away from the scene before things get too uncomfortable.

Her eyes widen with excitement. "Heck yeah! I'm ready to dance and shake my thing!" She laughs, wiggling her hips dramatically.

Mark laughs too and shoots us a look. "You ladies have a great night. It was lovely to meet you, Riley." His voice drips with smooth charm.

Riley giggles and almost melts into the ground.

I roll my eyes, but Riley—of course—grins and flirts back. "Call me." She winks, holding her hand to her ear like she's taking a phone call.

"Riley!" I hiss, pushing her out of his line of sight. "Really?!"

"What? He's hot in a silver fox kind of way." She snickers, taking my arm and leading me out of the club before things get more awkward.

The night air is cool as we step outside, the sounds of the city alive and buzzing around us. It's late in the night—or early morning, whichever side of the clock you look at—and the city that never sleeps is proving its point. Riley and I are notorious for pulling all-nighters, so this is another night of many, now in New York.

<hr>

THE AVENUE IS JAM-PACKED. The car pulls up to the front, and I see the massive line snaking around the corner. Riley groans beside me, but we step out of the car anyway, the familiar smell of alcohol, cheap perfume, cologne, and cigarettes greeting us like an old friend.

We start heading toward the back of the line when a bouncer calls my name.

"Elena Montgomery!" he shouts after me, his voice cutting through the noise.

I turn, squinting, and see a tall, dark-skinned man with a bald head and earrings in both ears.

"Yes?" I ask, a little confused.

"You don't need to line up. Mr. Shepherd called ahead," he says, stepping forward to usher us past the velvet ropes. "Please, come on in." A few patrons waiting in the line protest at the preferential treatment.

I give Riley a wry smile, rolling my eyes.

"Shepherd?" she asks, clearly confused.

"Mark." I laugh. Typical—she flirts with him all night and doesn't even bother to get his full name.

The Avenue is in full swing. The energy is electric, bodies swaying in the pulsing neon haze. The music thrums in my chest, heavy bass reverberating through the floors, and the air is thick with the scent of sweat, perfume, and spilled liquor. I take a slow breath, letting the atmosphere sink in. Nights like these remind me why I both love and loathe the chaos of this city—thrilling, intoxicating, and an overload for the senses. Go-go dancers in plastic neon tubes and black leather outfits gyrate and dance to the thumping beat of the music, the flashing lights making everything feel like a fever dream. A waitress approaches, handing us two glowing cocktails in test tubes, their color almost as bright as the club lights.

"Oh!" Riley squeals, taking one eagerly. I chuckle, mostly because her enthusiasm is infectious, even if I'm not quite sure what I'm about to drink.

We dance through the night, moving to the rhythm, letting the music pulse through our veins. After the seventh song, Riley wraps her arms around me like a vine, her grip tight and playful.

"Want more drinks?" she yells over the bass, her breath warm and thick with alcohol. The bass rattles my ribs as I nod, already a little unsteady. She disappears into the blur of bodies, and I'm left dancing with a tawny-skinned hottie who's a little too handsy. His mouth moves, but the music's a wall of sound. I just nod and laugh, pretending to hear.

My vision starts to blur as I continue dancing, and after a while, the man disappears into the crowd.

Okay, bye, I guess.

I can't help but giggle at myself. Thanks for the dance, mystery man.

Riley is back in no time, handing me a purple drink. I take a sip, immediately realizing it's more alcohol than cocktail mix.

Great.

Tomorrow's gonna suck.

"*The* hottest guy I have ever seen was at the bar and was totally watching you dance." Riley giggles, leaning in a little too close, practically yelling into my ear.

I shake my head, not believing her. "No way."

"I'm serious! He was like, 'The petite brunette in the dark dress. Watch her.'" Her voice is full of excitement, and then, as if performing, she repeats what the guy allegedly said. "*Look how she moves. She's sexy.*"

I roll my eyes in disbelief, laughing, but I can't help but feel a little flattered. "Okay, sure."

Riley grabs my hand and pulls me toward a quieter spot on a raised platform near the stairs. My legs feel like jelly in these heels, but I keep moving.

"No, I swear," she continues, taking a swig of her drink.

I shake my head, but there's a small part of me that's intrigued. "Okay. Which one is he?"

She scans the bar, then points straight at them—one with dark skin and close-cropped hair, standing just shorter than the man who catches my eye. Tall. Blond. A white shirt clinging to his body in all the right ways.

Oh, wow. I can't really see his face from this far, not with the lights dancing around, but there is something about him. An energy. The kind that makes someone stand out in a crowd.

He's definitely worth the chase.

Liquid courage making me brave, and maybe a little too frisky for my own good, I decide to find out if he really was watching me dance.

I push through the crowd again, most bodies towering over me, but by the time we make it to the bar, the two men are no longer there.

"Aww, he's gone!" I whine, louder than I meant to, trying to keep my cool over the blaring Rihanna track.

Riley laughs, grabbing my arm and pulling me back into the throng of bodies. "Plenty of those around," she announces, clearly more amused by my failure than sympathetic.

After a few hours, I decide I've had enough. I pry Riley off a man with his shirt half open and drag her toward the exit. Pushing the doors open, I'm desperate to escape the thick nightclub air, a toxic mix of sweat, booze, and lust.

The cool, early morning breeze greets me like a breath of fresh air, a whisper of summer on my skin.

As we step outside, I spot a swarm of paparazzi huddled around a group of people. Flashbulbs erupt in chaotic bursts, illuminating their faces in sharp, blinding flashes.

And then, I see him—sort of. My vision is blurred by too much liquor. The tall blond man steps into a sleek black car, the crowd of photographers clamoring after him like a tidal wave.

My breath catches, a strange sense of recognition prickling at the back of my mind.

Was that the guy from the bar?

I squint, trying to focus, but my height works against me, the shifting bodies in front of me blocking my view.

A fleeting pang of frustration twists in my chest. Something about him feels…intriguing. The back of my neck tingles, but before I can piece it together, the car door slams shut, and he's gone, swallowed by the night.

"Don't they ever sleep?" I mutter, rolling my eyes.

As I'm about to walk away, Riley stops in her tracks. Before I can react, she heaves the contents of her stomach toward the curb in front of me.

"Ugh!" I protest, dodging the near miss.

"Oh, God," she gasps, clutching her body. The color drains from her face, and she turns greener than her dress. I hold her once-straight hair, now a frizzy, matted mess, back, watching her empty the liquor from her body into the streets of New York.

Wow, Riley, classy.

I hail a cab, shoving Riley's limp body into the backseat before we make our way home.

My phone buzzes aggressively on the nightstand, jolting me out of my haze. Everything in me sinks as I reach for it, my fingers hesitant, dreading what I'll find. The harsh glow makes my already throbbing head worse. The screen is flooded with notifications, but one message stands out.

KYLIE

Call me. Now.

I don't even have the energy to roll my eyes before tapping her contact. She answers on the first ring.

"You're all over *Page Six*," she blurts out without preamble.

I groan, rubbing my temple. "That bad?"

"They're calling you 'The Long-lost Heiress.' And, the airport photos? Not your best. Also, apparently, some anonymous source thinks it's hilarious that you flew coach despite being 'worth millions.'"

I let out a dry laugh, but it doesn't reach my eyes. A bitter knot twists in my gut. It's not like I asked to be born into wealth. As far as I'm concerned, I'm not worth anything. Yet here I am— reduced to a punchy headline.

They don't know about the rejected demos, the failure that was LA. They didn't see the years I spent away, carving out a life of my own, trying to be more than my last name. Trying to be more than a constant disappointment. And now, with one drunken night, I'm back under their magnifying glass, scrutinized and dismissed in the same breath.

"Great." I shift under the blankets.

Riley rolls over beside me. "Babe, you're famous again."

"Perfect. Just what I ordered—public humiliation with a side of hangover." I sigh, sitting up.

"We need to strategize our next steps. We need to control this narrative STAT. Do you have time today?" Kylie asks, not mucking around. I groan mentally.

"Sure," is all I can muster, my head pounding like an elephant is tap dancing on my temples.

"See you at eleven." Kylie ends the call.

After we sluggishly get ready, Riley staggers to the bathroom and, with a groan, empties what's left of last night into the toilet. I wince at the sound, shaking my head.

"You good?" I call out. A weak thumbs-up emerges from the doorway before she disappears back inside.

Riley and I emerge disheveled but showered and dressed. Philippa, bless her sweet heart, is in the kitchen making bacon, eggs, and pancakes. The smell alone makes my mouth water, despite the lingering hangover fog. I watch her, moving between the stovetop and the counter, humming to herself as if she didn't spend the night out like the rest of us. I shake my head, both impressed and slightly envious of her ability to function like a normal human being.

"You woke up half the building with your cackling. Figured you'd need the hangover cure," she says, preparing us a plate.

Riley presses her head to the cool countertop and mumbles, "My bad."

"Coffee?" I ask, and Philippa points to the rather fancy coffee machine.

"Grab a cup and press the button, it will make whatever you want." Philippa places the plates in front of us on the kitchen island.

I take an empty cup, placing it under the machine as it whirls and beeps, the smell of coffee instantly filling my nose. Clutching my cup like I'm Gollum from *Lord of the Rings*, I take a sip of the sweet precious nectar, letting the warmth fill me.

"How was last night?" Philippa asks, sipping her coffee.

"Awesome," quips Riley with a mouth full of pancakes.

"It *was* great." I snort, less than enthused, already dreading the eleven a.m. crisis meeting. The thought of sitting through another round of damage control makes my gut knot.

It brings me back to the contract renegotiations. After I bailed on promoting my first album, the label was less than thrilled. At the time, I didn't care. Most of it was a blur. I was promptly abandoned by my previous manager before Mark swooped in.

But the idea of being dissected, packaged, and sold as a palatable version of myself doesn't sit right.

"Except I'm on *Page Six*." I sigh, taking another long sip of coffee. "And it doesn't look good. Kylie's coming over today to strategize."

Andrew steps into the kitchen, still flushed from his early morning run, the newspaper tucked under his arm. He shakes his head, tossing it onto the island between us.

"You're famous!" he announces, grabbing a bottle of water from the fridge. "Congratulations."

Philippa, ever curious, snatches the paper before I can react, unfolding it with dramatic flair. "Let's see what the vultures have to say this time," she muses.

She clears her throat and begins reading aloud. "The long-lost heiress returns to claim her rightful place within the Montgomery Dynasty, though our sources say this little songstress has her sights on something a little different, much to the chagrin of the Montgomery Patriarch. Our sources also report that she flew in coach when her father sits on the board of said airline. Was Daddy displeased?"

She pauses to glance at me from above the paper with a raised brow, her eyes full of mirth, before continuing, "The heiress was spotted partying it up with an unidentified friend at Bungalow 8 at the Pacific Records album wrap party for rapper J Jones. She's rumored to have signed a three-album record deal with Pacific Records USA after some success back in Australia, where her single 'Ignite' topped the Hottest Hits Australia charts for five weeks in a row, receiving numerous illustrious Australian Music Awards for the pop hit. However, she was mysteriously absent at the ceremony before disappearing into obscurity for years, only now emerging. Is there more to this disappearance than meets the eye? Why did she vanish at the height of her success? Was she recovering from a secret drug problem in rehab? We've reached out to her representatives for a statement, but so far, silence speaks volumes."

I groan, rubbing my temple. "Of course, they had to throw in the 'drug problem' speculation. Wouldn't be a proper hit piece without it."

Philippa folds the paper, placing it down gently. "They're going to twist everything, Elena. You know that."

Andrew shrugs, taking a long sip of water. "At least they mentioned your deal. Press is press, right?"

I scowl at him. "Not when it makes me sound like some washed-up scandal magnet with a mystery drug problem trying to claw my way back into the spotlight."

Philippa sighs, tapping her nails against her coffee cup. "Do you need our PR team to handle it?"

I shake my head. I trust Kylie. She'll be able to smooth things over. *I hope.*

KYLIE ARRIVES PROMPTLY at eleven a.m., laptop in hand, her expression all business. She's dressed in crisp business casual, a stark contrast to my oversized sweatshirt and leggings. It sucks that she has to work on a Saturday morning, but then again, the press never sleeps.

She doesn't waste time with pleasantries, dropping her bag onto the counter and flipping open her laptop. "Alright, let's get ahead of this before it spirals. We need to craft a statement that acknowledges it without adding fuel to the fire."

I rub my temples, still nursing the lingering effects of last night's choices. "Can't we ignore it?"

Kylie shoots me a look. "Not if you want to control the narrative. The 'Long-lost Heiress' angle is already running wild, and if we don't steer it in the right direction, they'll make up their own version of events."

She types quickly, the rhythmic tapping of her keys filling the kitchen. "We need something casual but confident. Something that says, 'Yes, I'm back. Yes, I'm focused on my career. No, I was not secretly in rehab.'"

I snort at that last part. "Fine. What do you suggest?"

"How do you feel talking about your mom? We need to squash this 'drug problem' narrative. We could frame it in a way that highlights your resilience, how you channeled your grief into your music, and the importance of raising awareness for cancer research. Maybe even donate to a cancer charity in her name? It could show a deeper, more personal side of you, but only if you're comfortable with that."

The thought of giving any of this information out to the press makes my stomach churn. It feels invasive, like I'm exposing a piece of her legacy to be scrutinized by people who might never understand. But I also know my mother. If she were here, she would fight tooth and nail to protect me. And maybe, in some way, this is my way of fighting for myself.

"I'm okay with that, so long as it's tasteful. I don't want her death to be sensationalized." My heart aches, but is resolved in my decision.

Kylie turns the laptop toward me. "Here's a draft social media post: 'Feels good to be back in NYC! Excited for what's ahead and grateful for all the love. New music coming soon. #Back-AtIt'—short, confident, and leaves no room for speculation."

I read over the words, chewing on my lip. It's safe, maybe too safe, but I know she's right. The last thing I need is to add fuel to the gossip fire. I nod. "Fine. Post it."

Kylie then works on drafting a formal statement that I'm happy with for *Page Six*, addressing the rumors head-on. She

keeps it professional yet firm, refuting the baseless drug allega-
tions and emphasizing my dedication to my career. At the same
time, she arranges for Pacific's legal department to issue a notice
warning against further defamatory claims, making it clear that
any continued speculation without evidence will have conse-
quences.

Kylie smiles, already clicking away. "Done." She exhales,
stretching her neck. "Now, let's talk damage control for your next
appearance."

I sink back into my chair. The weight of it all settles in—how
exhausting it is to constantly manage perceptions, to mold myself
into whatever version the world expects. "Do we really have to?"
I mutter, half-joking.

Kylie raises a brow. "Unless you want to keep being a tabloid
magnet, then yes."

Chapter 4

Working for the Weekend

A few days later, Rio is back at Philippa's penthouse, fussing over me as if I'm a porcelain doll about to shatter. I suppress the urge to roll my eyes—*honestly*, I can dress myself.

But Mark was adamant. Cultivating a carefully curated image is part of this glamorous yet suffocating world, particularly after those less-than-flattering airport photos landed unceremoniously on *Page Six*. Thankfully, Kylie's scheme worked its magic, swiftly turning me into yesterday's news. For once, being forgotten feels like a blessing.

Today is important. So, here I am, letting Rio work his magic, as usual. He's got me dressed in a pair of vintage acid-wash jeans, a flowing black tee, lined with gold stitching, finished off with a charcoal blazer, combat boots, and oversized sunglasses with gold accessories. It's a stylish look with enough rock and roll edge. I look well-styled, polished, *and* like I could be on the cover of a magazine.

"Perfect," Rio chirps, stepping back to admire his work.

I give myself one last glance in the mirror, adjusting the collar of the blazer. "Thanks, Rio." I smile, my voice soft but genuine.

I grab my purse and guitar case, heading for the door. I slip into the back of the car, feeling the soft leather of the seat beneath me, settling into the moment. I say a quiet prayer, thankful that no paparazzi were camped outside Philippa's building.

New York is buzzing outside, alive as always. Yellow cabs zoom by in a blur, and businesspeople in suits dart in and out of buildings. The city moves at a speed that makes my head spin, but I've learned to appreciate it, to *become* part of it.

I sink into my seat, pulling out my phone to check my emails. My thumb scrolls across the screen, flicking past work messages and reminders. One email catches my eye. It's from my stepdad.

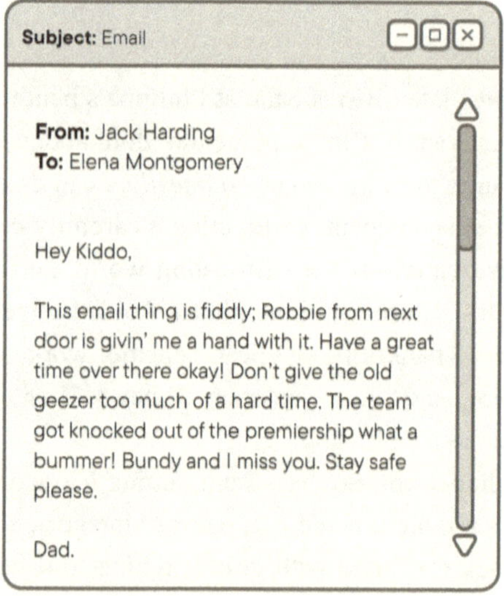

I smile, missing our family dog, Bundy, and laugh at his football update, then draft a quick response.

After the meeting with the executives at Pacific Records, Mark and I head downtown to Ocean Studios.

The room hums with quiet intensity, softly lit with warm

amber lights casting cozy shadows across the room. Sonia leans forward, her sharp eyes focused on the monitor as she adjusts levels, her fingers moving deftly over the mixing console. Michelle sits beside her, headphones snug over her ears, nodding gently in rhythm, occasionally pausing to make careful notes.

I've been in the booth for over an hour, laying down tracks piece by painstaking piece. My throat is scratchy from recording endless layers—harmonies, ad-libs, backing vocals—each take blending into the next as we chase perfection.

This is it, the final touches to my debut U.S. album, the culmination of months spent pouring every ounce of myself into music that I hope will resonate with the world.

Standing in the center of the soundproof room, I close my eyes, listening as the latest track fills the space through the studio speakers. The melody wraps around me, warm and familiar yet fresh, like an extension of my own heartbeat, resonating deep in my chest. When the final notes fade into silence, I open my eyes slowly to see Mark leaning against the sofa in the control room, tablet glowing softly in his hands as he scribbles notes for marketing.

"I feel like we're still missing something," I call from inside the booth, tapping a restless finger against the mic stand. "What do you think?"

"You could definitely use something a little more upbeat," Sonia agrees, sliding her headphones off and shaking out her sleek, platinum bob. Her sharp eyes study me through the glass, sensing my frustration. "How's the writing going?"

"Okay," I lie, forcing a smile. Truthfully, writing isn't *going* at all. Most of these songs are resurrected from notebooks I filled years ago—lyrics that didn't quite fit my first album but have finally found their moment. Michelle and Sonia have worked their magic, transforming my raw words into polished melodies. Yet I haven't written anything new since my mom died; grief drained me dry, and I've spent all my energy clawing back from the pit, leaving little room for creativity.

"Maybe something deeper, more seductive. Something sexy and edgy," Michelle suggests thoughtfully, twirling a pencil between her fingers as she leans back in her chair.

As if I have genuine experience with that. My love life consists of failed dates as a teenager with boys who quickly lost interest. My songs speak of love in wistful metaphors, inspired by secondhand stories from friends or characters in novels, never my own tangled heart.

"I don't know." I sigh softly, glancing down at the scuffed wooden floor, avoiding their hopeful gazes.

"Elena, you're in New York City, one of the most inspiring places on the planet," Michelle urges gently. "Step outside, breathe it in. Let the city inspire something in you."

"Exactly," Sonia chimes in, her voice confident. "The big L— it sells!"

Love.

The eternal muse, a theme universal yet painfully personal. I've sung about it countless times, but always from a distance, a safe observer rather than an active participant. Dread seeps out of me.

"We could bring in some guys from Nashville," Michelle adds casually, flipping through contacts on her phone. My eyes widen sharply.

She laughs lightly, shaking her head. "Not like that, girl, relax. Writers. Nashville has some of the best songwriters in the business. I know a few who'd love to collaborate, help you flesh things out."

I hesitate, uncertainty knotting in my throat. "I'll think about it," I stammer, exhaling heavily. "For now, let's run through a few more ad-libs on 'Sparks.'"

Michelle and Sonia nod simultaneously, headphones slipping

back over their ears, fingers dancing quickly across the sound-board. Taking a deep breath, I steady myself in front of the micro-phone, chasing one more perfect take. Hoping somewhere within these four padded walls, I'll rediscover the spark I've lost.

Mark glances up, smiling reassuringly. "Initial feedback is looking really good on the first few tracks," he shares, scrolling through comments from the advance listening session. "They especially love 'Rise' and 'Sparks'—strong contenders for singles."

I take another deep breath, absorbing the information. "What about 'Nightfall'? That one's personal."

Mark nods knowingly. "Mixed reactions. Some think it's too introspective for a single, but others say it could become your signature track."

Michelle removes her headphones, tilting her head thought-fully. "I agree with Mark. 'Midnight' is my vote—it's fun and meaningful. 'Nightfall' might not appeal to everyone, but if you're comfortable sharing it widely, it could resonate deeply."

"Or it could become a hidden gem," Sonia adds, swiveling in her chair. "Something your true fans discover and hold on to."

Mark stands, placing a comforting hand on my shoulder. "Whatever you decide, we trust your instincts. This is *your* story to tell."

Warmth blooms in my chest. The studio feels less like a work-space and more like a haven where creativity flourishes among trusted friends. "Let's listen one more time," I suggest, smiling at each of them. "Then I'll know for sure."

Sonia grins, turning back to her board. Michelle offers me an encouraging thumbs up, while Mark resumes his position, ready to capture any final thoughts. The music fills the room again, every note confirming that, no matter the decisions ahead, my vision is being honored, supported, and celebrated.

"A few more tweaks and we're on track for the digital album

drop on the 10th of September," Mark starts, scrolling through his phone and flicking through his laptop as Kylie walks in.

"You're also set to perform 'Ignite' from your previous album on *Rise and Shine America*, plus an interview segment as Australia's darling, and promoting the upcoming album," she announces nonchalantly.

"*Rise and Shine America*?" I ask, my mouth dry as I gape at Kylie and Mark.

"Yes." He nods, grinning from ear to ear. "They've asked for you."

"Lara Spencer is a huge *Starstruck* fan," Kylie chimes in, clapping her hands together. "You were her pick to win, and she wanted to snap you up as soon as she heard you were in the country."

"Plus, she owes me a favor, and this will give you massive exposure," Mark adds with a grin, as if it's all business as usual.

"Awesome." I smile nervously, feeling the anxious excitement bubble up inside me. Wow, *Rise and Shine America*—that's crazy! The realization hits me sharply; this isn't just another gig, it's an enormous opportunity, my first real test on a major U.S. stage. The thought of millions watching, judging, hoping—it's exhilarating yet daunting, and I feel the weight of expectation on my shoulders.

"Wait till you hear what's next," Mark teases, grinning wider than ever, clapping his hands together to snap me out of my dazed thoughts.

"*Starstruck America* wants you to perform your new single at their season two grand finale in October!" Mark beams, and I feel my breath catch in my throat, a whirlwind of excitement and fear tightening my chest. It's not just the prestige of the moment or the massive audience awaiting me. It's the realization that this could define the next chapter of my career, shaping the way the world sees me as an artist.

"HEY, did you want to grab a coffee?" Mark calls out from behind me as I'm heading out.

"Sure." I say, grateful for the moment to step away from the intensity. He smiles in return, and we head down the bustling street toward a nearby coffee shop.

As we walk, we chat casually—Mark talks me through ideas for my music video, his plans for a trip to the Bahamas in December, and about an 'amazing track' one of his other artists is producing for another huge international artist.

"You choose a seat. I'll pick up the coffee. What will you have?" Mark asks, holding the door open.

"An iced caramel latte, please."

He looks at me like I've grown two heads,

"You mean an iced macchiato, mate?" He laughs, feigning an Aussie accent.

I take a seat by the window, sinking into the comfort of the orange café armchairs on either side of a low brown coffee table. Outside, I spot a few boutique stores across the street, and my eyes land on a vintage shop tucked between a laundromat and an Italian restaurant. That looks *interesting*. I'll make a stop after coffee.

Mark walks over with two coffees and sits opposite me. Continuing from where we left off, he opens his tablet, revealing a mood board of golden beaches, sunsets, bonfires, and laid-back fashion.

"Yeah, so we're thinking San Diego for the shoot," he says, taking a sip of his brew.

"Why San Diego?"

"The beaches," he replies, grinning. "A bonfire beach party concept for the video. Your love interest? Your friend, the actor

Logan Fisher, is pretty popular at the moment. Great for generating buzz."

Oh, Logan. Riley's cousin. My mind flashes back to our awkward teenage kiss.

"What's Logan doing in San Diego?" I ask, sipping my drink, enjoying the sweet caramel.

"He's there for Geek-Fest, promoting his movie. Only time he's available," Mark explains.

"When do I fly out?"

"Next week," Mark replies casually.

Mark's phone buzzes. "Chloe," he answers, irritation flickering briefly.

"He did what?" He sighs. "Okay, five minutes." He shoots me an apologetic glance.

"Go ahead. I'll be fine," I reassure him.

"I'm really sorry." His eyes soften before he shoots to his feet. "You sure you're okay?"

"Yeah." I smile warmly. "Thanks for the coffee, Mark."

He rushes out, hails a cab, and waves goodbye through the window. I linger for a moment, anticipation already building for what's coming.

Crossing the street to the store, I notice its name, Odds and Endings, feels fitting. Like the kind of place where you could find everything and nothing at the same time. Maybe a place for me to find some *inspiration*. I toss my empty coffee cup into the trash outside and push open the glass door. It feels out of place against the vintage charm of the shop. The moment I step inside, I'm hit by the smell of aged leather and incense—warm and nostalgic, like a forgotten memory that never quite fades.

The store is overflowing with an eclectic mix of items: books stacked haphazardly, vintage rugs and furniture strewn about, random knick-knacks I'm sure I'll never need, but that somehow draw me in. There are old wooden tables, mirrors leaning against the walls, and countless light fixtures hanging from the ceiling, like they're waiting for someone to bring them back to life. It's a feast for the eyes.

A soft indie ballad croons quietly in the background, adding to the cozy, lived-in atmosphere. I spot a tall blond guy in a baseball cap talking with the shopkeeper. His crisp white shirt and designer jeans seem out of place amongst the mismatched treasures of the store.

I stop by a table covered in buttons—different shapes and sizes—and my fingers graze over the cool, smooth surface. Nearby, there's a wooden curtain rod where dozens of scarves hang, their fabrics catching the dim light. I run my hands through them, mesmerized by the textures.

At the back wall stands a large oak bookshelf, its wood dark and polished with age. I'm definitely coming back here with Philippa. I'd love that shelf for the new apartment.

I make my way toward the other bookshelves, stopping to glance at the variety of books on display. Something catches my eye—a signed Joan Jett T-shirt, hanging on a rack between two shelves. *Oh, score!* I grab it, noticing it's a little big, but I can make it work.

Next, I spot a big floppy hat, probably from the seventies, and pop it on my head, whistling to myself, getting lost in the small treasures surrounding me. The store is warm and earthy, full of history and character. I stand close to a shelf, immersed in its hidden gems, when a flash of red catches my eye.

A big red hardcover book with gold-leaf embossing, some of which has rubbed off. The cloth cover is worn and frayed at the corners, and on the spine, the title reads *Collection I of Creole and French Poetry*. Next to it is another book, bound in cream leatherette, titled *The Greatest Love Poems and Letters, Volume 1*. I pick them both up and tuck them under my arm. Maybe they'll provide some inspiration.

I turn on my heel, my mind already racing with ideas, when—*wham*! I collide with something hard. Wait, *that wasn't there before.* The large floppy hat falls over my face, blinding me for a second.

No, it's not a wall—I've run straight into someone. I lose my footing and topple over, my elbow grazing the bookshelf as I go down. In a rush, I try to reach out for something to steady myself, but it's too late. The books fall from under my arm, and before I can catch myself, my head makes contact with something, a sickening thud, followed by a crack.

Ouch.

"Sorry…shit," I hear a man hiss. Instinctively, I reach up to touch the back of my head. When I look at my fingers, they're covered in red. Blood. My blood.

And then, darkness.

Chapter 5

Collide

Beep...*beep...beep...beep...*
I crack my heavy eyelids slightly, peering through my lashes. Everything is white—too white. I squeeze them shut again. My head is pounding. I take a deep breath, the smell triggering a memory I can't quite recall in the haze, but it reminds me of despair.

"Nurse, nurse! I think she's waking up," a deep voice I don't recognize calls out, full of concern. Movement follows, and I hear a small *ding...beep...beep...*

"Ugh," I manage, dragging myself back to consciousness. I feel something move beside me—the surface dipping under their weight—and the clinical smell from earlier is gone, replaced by the scent of the ocean. It smells like home.

I open my eyes again, forcing them wide despite fluttering against the blinding brightness. Above me, a pair of stormy blue-gray eyes stare intently. I shift back slightly, even though my body and head are still heavy with fog.

Who the fuck are you? I want to say, but my throat tightens and my chest begins to hum with panic.

"Hi," he whispers, his voice low and close enough that his breath brushes softly against my skin. Recognition flickers through me—he's the voice from before, the one that smells like a sea breeze on a summer's day. Warm, comforting, and achingly familiar, even though he's a stranger.

I don't know why the scent relaxes me, but it does.

"Hi," I squeak back, my voice scratchy and weak as I shift beneath crisp, white sheets. What am I wearing? Anxiety blooms as my eyes dart around the room. It's sterile, impersonal, with cream curtains, a closed door off to one side, and a wide window revealing glimpses of the city beyond.

Where am I?

"You're in the hospital," he answers gently, reading my unspoken panic. "I brought you here."

My eyes flicker between him and the room, trying to process his words and take in my surroundings. The sheets feel like paper against my skin, my limbs heavy as lead. I hate hospitals. I spent enough time by my mother's bedside to last a lifetime.

He leans back from the bed, standing up, and I finally take in the sight of him. Tall—very tall—blond, wearing a white shirt and jeans. Wait.

He's the guy from the store!

"What happened?" I breathe, my voice barely audible. My head throbs, heavy and fogged with confusion.

He shakes his head, running a hand through his floppy hair. He looks almost embarrassed, opening his mouth to speak, but before he can say a word, a short, plump nurse with half-moon glasses bustles into the room, as if on cue.

"Hello, miss," she interjects briskly, her voice bright and practical. She swiftly grabs the buzzer from above my head, switching it off. "You're in the hospital. You've had a small accident. How are you feeling?"

"Fine…just groggy and sore," I manage, feeling like my body still hasn't fully caught up with my brain. "How long was I out?"

She tilts her head, giving me an odd look over the top of her glasses. "Groggy and sore? Miss, are you British?"

"No, Australian," I reply, rolling my eyes. At the mention of Australia, the guy beside me visibly perks up, his gaze sharpening, intent but unreadable. Something about the intensity in his eyes makes my chest tighten, uncomfortable under his scrutiny.

The nurse nods thoughtfully, jotting something down on her chart. "Full name, please?"

"Um, Eleanor Josephine Montgomery."

"Date of birth?"

I relay my birthday to her September 3rd, followed by the year I was born. I glance over at him and he frowns. I wonder what he's thinking.

"Parents?" says the nurse clearing her throat.

"Vida and Jack Harding—no, sorry," I say quickly, embarrassment heating my cheeks. I shake my head gently, trying to clear the lingering haze. "I mean Vida Harding and Mortimer Montgomery."

My eyes dart sideways toward the guy again, now seated on the couch under the window, catching him staring openly now. His stormy eyes widen briefly before he glances down at his hands, seemingly fascinated by his fingers.

"Alex here says he accidentally bumped into you," the nurse explains lightly, waving her pen in his direction. "You fell, hit your head, and he brought you in."

"Oh, shit." I gasp, my hand instinctively flying to the tender spot at the back of my skull. The dull ache blooms anew beneath my fingertips.

"You split your head open and needed stitches. You also have a minor gash on your elbow," the nurse says matter-of-factly, peering at me over her half-moon glasses before placing my chart at the foot of the bed.

My eyes widen as I glance toward Alex. He's still sitting quietly nearby, looking distinctly uncomfortable, as though he wishes the hospital floor might swallow him whole.

"Stitches?" I gasp, inspecting my arms more carefully. My left elbow is neatly bandaged. Despite the circumstances, I feel better than I probably should, and grateful that it isn't worse.

"The initial scans showed no brain bleeds, but because you passed out, you likely have a concussion and some swelling," the nurse continues gently. "We'll keep you overnight for observation and send you for another scan in the morning. Depending on those results, you'll likely be discharged tomorrow." She offers a quick, reassuring nod, then turns on her heel and strides briskly from the room.

I exhale heavily, frustration welling in my chest.

Seriously? Not even two weeks in New York and I've already landed myself in the hospital.

My eyes scan the unfamiliar room, landing on a neatly folded pile of my clothes and my purse, resting on a small table in the corner. I shift, swinging my legs toward the side of the bed, only to have Alex immediately appear by my side.

"Hey, you should stay in bed," he insists, his voice firm but gentle, one large hand resting lightly on my shoulder, steadying me. His touch sends an unexpected ripple of warmth down my spine.

"I'm sure I can manage," I say, irritation slipping into my voice, though I'm honestly too tired to argue. With a resigned sigh, I adjust myself, settling back into the bed.

"Alex, right?" I glance at him. "Could you grab my bag, please?" I gesture toward my purse, still resting on the chair.

Without a word, Alex crosses the room, gently lifting the purse, and hands it to me with both hands.

"Thanks," I murmur, appreciating his care, even if embarrassment still lingers.

"I think I owe you an apology," Alex begins quietly, sincerity etched plainly on his face. "You're in here because of me. Back at the store, you bumped into me, fell, and hit your head." Guilt shadows his expression, making him look momentarily vulnerable.

My cheeks go hot.

Of course, I think, cringing inwardly. Only I could knock myself out by bumping into someone.

"I guess it doesn't help that you're built like a wall," I joke weakly, trying to break the tension. "Not easy dealing with us hobbit folk."

"You like Lord of the Rings?" he asks, smirking as he shakes his head and runs a hand through his tousled blond hair. My heart stutters slightly—his jawline is sharp, his features strikingly handsome. Those eyes of his pierce right through me, leaving my face burning with a sudden rush of heat.

God, he might be the hottest man I've ever seen in my life.

"I do," I mumble, embarrassed at being caught staring. Quickly, I shove my hand into my purse, rummaging through it as a distraction, finally pulling out my phone.

Shit.

Five missed calls from Philippa, three from Riley, one from Mark, and a long, relentless chain of unread messages.

17:15–PIP

Do you have dinner plans? Andrew and I are going to SORA – you and Riley should join us for sushi. xo. P.

17:20–RILEY

Scored the interview! I'm so excited! Bye bartending hello art gallery! Drinks tonight let's celebrate!

18:45–RILEY

You screening calls? How's the studio, Pip wants to go to SORA! Sushi, sake then dancing?

18:59–MARK

See you at the studio on Thursday. Invite in calendar.

19:25–PIP

We're at SORA, table by the bar! Sushi time yum!

19:30–RILEY

Still at the studio? We're here! Should I order ahead?

20:00–PIP

I'm getting worried. Please answer!

20:40–RILEY

So you've either been eaten by a bear or you're with someone—CALL ME!

21:30–PIP

Where are you?

Oh, fuck, shit!

The clock on my phone says it's past midnight. If I reply now, it'll wake them. I'll wait to reach out in the morning. Dropping my phone to my side, I peek up to see Alex, still hovering by my bedside, his face washed with concern, guilt, and something else I can't quite pinpoint.

Oh, God. A face so handsome, too flawless—like it was carved for a world I'll never touch. The kind of beauty that leaves you stranded mid-sentence, forgetting how to breathe. Could I trust such a face?

"Don't you have somewhere else to be?" My voice comes out sharper than I intend. I don't want to seem ungrateful for his help, but I'm sure he's got better things to do than wait around on me.

"I guess." His lips quirk up into a smile, then he shrugs. "But

I'd like to make sure you're alright." He takes a seat in the empty visitor chair by my bedside.

His response catches me off guard. He wants to make sure I'm okay? Most likely out of obligation, avoiding a lawsuit if he can.

I cock my head to the side and it throbs. "You don't have a habit of assaulting random strangers, do you?" I say softer, making up for my earlier comment.

"I'm hurting, too. Internally bleeding, I suspect, from when you threw yourself into me." He chuckles, a deep laugh.

His joke is unexpected. And now I'm intrigued.

"Oh, would you like the bed, you poor thing? How selfish of me," I tease, lifting the covers slightly, the hospital gown shifting just enough to reveal the top of my thigh.

Alex's eyes widen, and I see him avert his gaze quickly, his cheeks tinged with red. "I should be used to girls throwing themselves at me by now," he scoffs in response, turning his head away.

Of course, he is. Look at him. He probably has a whole rotation of women at his beck and call. Women who don't trip over their own feet or stutter around hot strangers. He's not meant for someone like me. The thought comes forth, ugly and cruel.

I sigh, shaking my head, pulling the covers back over myself. I try to think of a clever comeback, but I'm interrupted by the opera that's happening in my stomach.

"What's good to eat around here?" I raise my hand, gesturing around the hospital room.

Alex turns back to me, his eyes mischievous. He looks like someone who could get away with murder and have his victim thank him for it.

"I could get the nurse to bring you some food," he offers, leaning back slightly.

I gape at him and stick my finger toward my mouth, pretending to gag.

"Seriously? Hospital food is so—" I gag again for effect, and Alex's eyes widen as he lets out a deep belly laugh.

"We can order in?" he grins, pulling his phone out of his pocket.

"Yes, please." I smile, a little too widely.

"I should check with the nurse first, see if you're okay to eat," he says, standing and adjusting himself. I can't help but gape—he's so tall.

Stop staring, Elena.

"Okay, well, here." I gulp, trying to recover, handing him my identification and health insurance card. "Would you mind passing that along to the nurse?"

He grabs the cards from my hand, his warm fingers brushing mine, and I feel a little electric shock run up my arm.

I gasp, aware of the way my body is reacting.

"Sorry," he murmurs. His jeans hug his body perfectly, and as he walks away, I catch a glimpse of how well they fit his ass. I lick my lips without meaning to.

God, I feel like a teenage girl with a crush. I'll sear that face into memory and cue it up for a solo DJ session the next time I'm alone with batteries and no shame.

What is going on? I don't even know this person.

Snap out of it.

Moments later, Alex returns. "All good," he says, walking toward the bed with a plastic wristband in hand. "Here."

He grabs my hand like he owns it and fastens the band around my wrist. I should pull away—the audacity of this man—but I don't, and time stands still. Goose bumps rise as his fingers graze my skin, and then his thumb drags slowly across the new band. My breath catches.

From this close, I can see his forearms—thick, veined, strong…and hot. My mouth goes dry.

New kink? Unlocked.

He takes a small step back, and I feel the air returning to my lungs.

"Thanks," I whisper, my voice hoarse and breathy. I manage a shaky laugh. "Are you…normally this handsy with strangers?"

"I carried you from the store, into a car, and the emergency room," he confesses with a smile. "You didn't complain then."

My eyes widen in shock.

He carried me. In his arms. *Those arms*. My heart thumps against my chest.

I assumed he would've called an ambulance, but he scooped me up like a sack of potatoes and went on his merry way.

Of course, I couldn't complain—I was unconscious. The shame.

"My hero." I cough, trying to clear my throat, and Alex chuckles, a smile spreading across his face. Oh, dear God, it's enough to make me lose any composure I have left.

"Food," he says, pulling his phone out of his pocket like he just remembered.

Stop staring at him like that.

I tell myself it's just the drugs. Yes, that's it—the drugs. That's why I'm acting like this. That's why I'm ogling him like *he's* the one good enough to eat.

While Alex orders, I watch him through my lashes, lips slightly parted, my heart skipping a beat.

He looks up and catches my gaze. I flush and quickly look away, focusing on my hands as they clutch the hospital wristbands.

"Food will be here soon," he announces, his voice smooth.

"Thank you," I mumble, barely able to meet his eyes.

"You're very welcome." That heart-stopping smile.

I gulp hard, trying to stay composed.

"So, how exactly did we…*collide*?" I ask, trying to change the subject.

"Ah, well, you were at the back section in the store," he starts, his voice smooth and casual. "I was looking for a book. I noticed you were standing there under your hat, and the book was above your head." He smiles slyly.

Okay, I get it, I'm short. Well, compared to him, I am.

"You turned and ran straight into me, and before I could grab you to stop you from falling, you lost your footing, stumbled back, and went down." He finishes with a nervous laugh. "You hit your head on a nearby table, and well, now you're here."

He recaps it like a news reporter. It's the most he's spoken since I woke up, and I notice the vague accent. I wonder from what magical dimension he comes from. He can't possibly be real.

"Yep, here." I sigh dramatically, trying to make light of it.

In this hospital. With him.

I don't know whether to die of embarrassment or thank the gods for this chance encounter.

"You should see the table," he adds, cocking his head to the side.

I giggle. He's handsome and funny—so unfair.

Before I can say anything else, a small man and a different nurse poke their heads through the door, knocking before entering. The man hands Alex a paper bag, and Alex gives him some cash.

The scent coming from the bag engulfs the room, and despite my hunger, Alex looks even more tempting. A thought that catches me off guard.

"How are you feeling?" the nurse asks, interrupting my train of thought.

"I'm okay. Just *hungry*," I admit, a little embarrassed at how crude that sounds in my head. I blush, hoping she doesn't notice.

Alex seems to catch on, and I notice a cheeky glint in his eyes.

Oh, God, I'm mortified.

The nurse nods, unfazed. "Take these after you've had some-thing to eat." She hands me a plastic cup with two white oval tablets in it, then places the chart back at the end of the bed before leaving the room.

"Hungry?" he asks.

"Starving." My voice is a little too hoarse.

His eyes darken with a thought, but he says nothing.

"That smells good," I comment, the smell of the food inter-rupting my inappropriate lusting over a complete stranger.

"I hope you don't mind Chinese food," Alex offers with a smile, casually rolling the hospital table over to my bed. "It's usually quick."

Shifting in the bed to sit up, my whole body feels like jelly.

Ugh, hospital beds are the worst.

"Chinese is fine right now. I could eat anything," I say, licking my lips.

Including you.

Oh my God, did I just…I quickly shake the thought from my head.

Alex starts unpacking the contents of the paper bag, a banquet fit for two. He grabs two of the boxes and heads back to his seat.

"You could sit on the other side of the table if you'd like," I suggest, feeling a little disappointed that he doesn't want to sit closer.

He looks at me for a moment, his head cocked to the side. His eyes are so intense, and I feel like I'm being analyzed. He prob-ably feels bad for me, and I'm reading too much into this situation.

"Okay." He grins, getting up from his seat.

That one word sends flutters to my stomach.

He waits for me to shift and cross my legs to give him more space. Placing his boxes back on the table, he sits on the bed, slip-ping off his shoes.

I watch him intently—he looks like a model.

Maybe he is.

We eat in silence for a moment. I'm too hungry to care, but then, with a mouthful of pork dumpling, he breaks the silence.

"So, what brings you to New York?" he asks, his voice soft and casual.

"Family and work," I reply between bites. My mouth is full, but I'm too ravenous to care.

"What do you do?"

He looks at me then, eyes narrowing slightly as though sizing me up. There's a glimmer of something in his gaze, but I'm probably imagining it.

Chewing quickly, I swallow before answering. "I'm a recording artist."

"Whoa," he replies, surprised. "What kind of music do you sing?"

"Mainly pop," I explain, my cheeks flushing. "And I dabble in a variety of different genres, depending on what strikes my mood."

He glances down at his food, his attention diverted. I feel a little self-conscious about my answer.

So stupid. I probably sound like I'm showing off.

"So, what about you?" I ask, trying to steer the focus off myself as I shovel more food into my mouth.

He pauses, eying me for a moment, then smirks. It's the kind of smirk that makes me wonder if he's laughing at an inside joke I'm not privy to.

"I'm self-employed," he states offhandedly, biting into his egg roll.

"Oh, cool." I nod, unsure of how to respond. His answer is vague, but I don't press.

"I'm Alexander Gustav Henrik Sigurdsson, by the way," he

adds, his smile widening. "But my friends call me Alex. It's nice to meet you, Eleanor Josephine Montgomery."

Wow, that's a hell of a name.

I roll my eyes at the use of our full legal names. But when it comes out of his mouth, it sounds almost…poetic.

"Alexander Gustav Henrik Sigurdsson," I repeat quietly. "Nice to meet you. And…please, call me Elena." I tuck a strand of hair behind my ear, not quite meeting his eyes.

"Elena," he purrs, drawing out each syllable like he's savoring it. "I like it…suits you better."

He leans in just slightly, eyes flicking to my lips. "And Elena, the pleasure's all mine."

My heart races, and I feel a little heady.

His voice…

God, why does that sound so good coming out of his mouth?

Is this what happens when you suppress every teenage impulse for years? One tall, model-built man with heartbreak eyes catches me mid-concussion, and suddenly I'm ready to throw away my entire belief system just to feel him hold me again, this time fully conscious.

We finish the rest of our dinner in silence, each of us lost in our own thoughts. Occasionally, I glance up at him to find him already watching me. Studying his features, his face is perfectly symmetrical, his lips are full, his eyes blue like the sky before a storm. With his name, I assume he's probably Scandinavian.

Eventually, the food coma takes hold, and I feel my eyelids grow heavy.

To my surprise and delight, Alex stays the entire night, helping me to the bathroom like I've shattered my spine, not knocked my head like a clumsy idiot.

It's mortifying. My pride's bruised worse than my skull. But he won't let me do anything alone. And every time his hands steady me, light and careful, I feel him peeling back walls I swore

were solid. Every touch whispers let me in, and worse, some traitorous part of me wants to roll out the red carpet, flip on the
welcome sign, and say okay.

I WAKE up to someone opening the blinds, the light spilling into
the room. Alex is awkwardly asleep on the guest couch, which is
far too small for his tall frame. I gently put my finger to my lips,
silently asking them to keep quiet so he doesn't wake Alex.

The orderly nods and helps me into a wheelchair, taking me
for a scan. On our way back to the room, I quickly send a text to
my sister, letting her know where I am. I turn my phone on silent,
ignoring its immediate buzzing.

She'll be worried, I think, but I want a few more moments
with Alex before I never see him again. The thought pains me.
Maybe we can be friends?

When we get back to my room, I freeze.

Alex is gone.

Of course, I didn't expect him to stay the whole night. Why
would he? I can't help the disappointment blooming in the pit of
my stomach. Suddenly, the bathroom door creaks open, and there
he is.

Our eyes lock, and a flutter dances beneath my skin.

"Good morning, Elena." He smiles, and relief washes
over me.

"Hi," I say, quietly, aware I probably look like I've been hit by
a bus and dragged halfway here.

He lifts me from the wheelchair and back into bed, brushing
off my half-hearted protests. I hate how easily I let him, but the
warmth of his hands on my skin makes it hard to think straight.

Before I can savor the moment, a nurse bursts in. I flinch at
Alex's lingering touch and shift my attention to her. She's petite,

with brunette hair, a cheerful smile, and dressed in standard scrubs.

"Miss Montgomery, how are you feeling this morning?" She smiles politely. "I'm Dr. Ryan."

Not a nurse, a doctor.

"Hi, I'm okay," I stutter, my voice still a little shaky from the unexpected attention I'm getting.

"Your scans look good. I'll need to check your vitals and take a look at your stitches before we can discharge you," Dr. Ryan says, grabbing the blood pressure cuff and wrapping it around my arm.

"Will your boyfriend be taking you home?" she asks, eyeing Alex.

Boyfriend?

Blood rushes to my face, and I glance up at Alex through my lashes. He doesn't flinch, merely nodding at the doctor as if he has every right to be here.

"Um, no, he's, um, my sister—he's not my boyfriend," I stammer, immediately regretting the way I clarify things.

I glance back at Dr. Ryan, then back to Alex. He winks at me.

What, why didn't correct her?

Dr. Ryan proceeds with the examination, shining a small flashlight into my eyes, then inspecting my head. I wince at the slight pain as she prods at the stitches. I feel a cool hand slip into mine, and I know it's Alex. My body calms momentarily, but heat surges up my arm, and I can't focus on anything else.

"Everything seems okay. We'll discuss aftercare and your follow-up appointment. Any dizziness or blurred vision, please come back to emergency immediately," Dr. Ryan states, pulling away.

She adjusts my head back gently. "You're not allowed to get it wet for the next twenty-four hours, and try not to use any products in your hair until the stitches dissolve in about a week."

Just then, a commotion outside catches my attention. The door opens, and a flustered nurse enters, followed by a *very* irritated Philippa. She storms into the room, immediately eyeing Alex, who hasn't released my hand.

He doesn't move it. I glance at him, confused, but he remains in position.

"Why didn't you call me?" Philippa seethes, eyeing Alex up and down.

I shrug, removing my hand from his, embarrassed at enjoying that moment a little too much.

"Would someone please explain?" She huffs, looking between the three of us.

"Miss…?" Dr. Ryan interrupts, and both Alex and I seem to exhale in relief.

"Miss Montgomery," snaps Philippa, prompting Dr. Ryan to proceed.

"If you would please step outside with me," Dr. Ryan continues, gently ushering her out into the hallway.

I risk a glance at Alex. He's looking at me with an intensity that makes my heart race, and I quickly avert my gaze.

"Sorry about my sister," I apologize, feeling bad for the way she barreled in here, though I don't blame her.

"It's okay." He smiles, brushing a strand of hair from my face with the gentleness of someone far too used to calming people down.

Philippa walks back in a moment later, her eyes glassy. She looks at Alex and then at me, her expression shifting from irritation to something softer, but also a little surprised.

"Oh, God! We thought something awful had happened." She gasps, her eyes filling with tears as she pulls me into a quick but tight embrace.

Oh, shit. Guilt hits me hard, fast, and without warning. "Sorry, Pip, it was an accident. I was out of it, and by the time I came to, it was almost midnight. Figured you'd be asleep."

"Well, you thought wrong. We've been sick with worry. The police wouldn't let us file a report because it hadn't been twenty-four hours yet. We assumed you'd run away—back to Australia or off with *some* guy," she exclaims, looking directly at Alex.

The thought warms something in me. My sister had been worried. I knew she cared in her own way. I didn't mean to make her panic. Still, it meant something.

"And you rescued her?" she directs at Alex, who looks at her with hardly any emotion on his face.

He nods. "Yes, I did."

"Thank you," she says. She tilts her head slightly like she's studying him. Then I see it—his mask slips.

"All good." He shrugs, shifting slightly, taking a step back. He coughs uncomfortably as he turns to the side.

Weird.

"The doctor tells me you're being discharged," she says, turning her attention back to me, pulling me out of my thoughts as she smooths her frazzled hair. I finally take a look at her and realize she's not dressed in her usual polished manner, but in navy sweats, her hair barely brushed, not a bit of makeup. She must have rushed here as soon as she received my message. The thought tugs at something inside me.

"I'm okay, but I need the bathroom." I smile at her, and she finally relaxes a little. I stand up, feeling a bit unsteady.

"I'll help you," Alex and Philippa say in unison.

She shoots him a glare, clearly annoyed, but Alex cocks his head to the side, unfazed.

"I can manage," I insist, grabbing my clothes and making my way to the ensuite.

When I come back, the room is tense. Alex is sitting on the guest lounge, and Philippa is leaning against the bed, holding discharge papers. Alex immediately stands and is by my side in two strides.

"Elena, I have somewhere I need to be." Alex hesitates. "Call me, okay?" He hands me a small piece of paper with his number on it, his hand lingering against mine once more, sending a shiver through me.

"Sure, I owe you for dinner last night." I nod, trying haphazardly to joke, my voice barely shaking, feeling shy under his intense gaze and gentle touch.

Philippa's eyes are practically burning into us.

"No, you don't," he whispers. Leaning down, he gently cups my face and plants a kiss on either side of my cheeks, leaving me blushing and breathless. He picks up his baseball cap and leaves the room. Finally, I take a long breath and try to calm myself.

"Was that an online date gone wrong?" she asks, her eyebrow arched, having watched the exchange unfold before her.

I burst out laughing, finally coming back down to Earth after the heady experience. When I catch my breath, I recall the entire absurd situation to her as best I can.

In the car, Philippa is on her phone talking to my father. "Yes, Dad, she's okay. A few stitches, nothing too serious. No, some guy. Yes, okay, I'll see you in the office later."

I nod absentmindedly, but my mind drifts back to Alex—his beautiful eyes, the calm presence that settled in the room when he was there. I've never met anyone like him before. How can you possibly have such a connection with someone you hardly know?

Is it chemical? I know no man has ever affected me the way he has—his intense gaze, the way his eyes pierced right through me, his hands that seemed to know exactly where to touch, and those lips…

"Elena…Elena!" Philippa calls out, her voice pulling me back to the present.

Oh, and that smile…

"Earth to Elena!" she yells, grabbing my arm and shaking me, snapping me out of my fantasy.

"Uh, yes?" I mumble, flustered, my mind hazy.

"Are you alright?" she asks, eyeing me like I've sprouted another head.

"Yes, sorry, just sleepy," I lie, forcing a small smile to cover up the real storm brewing in my head. I don't want to talk about Alex with her yet, not when I'm still so confused about the whole thing.

"What was that guy's name again? He looked so familiar," Philippa asks, but before I can answer, her phone beeps, and she's back to business, her attention fully diverted as she takes a call.

Alex, I think to myself. His name is *Alex*.

· · ·

I'M LYING in bed later that afternoon, back at Philippa's apartment, replaying every stolen moment with Alex like some love-sick teenager. Sure, I've had crushes in the past, but somehow, this feels different. Alex isn't a boy—he's all man.

His stormy eyes peered into my soul like he knew me. He touched me like he couldn't help it. And for once, I craved it. His closeness had felt natural, almost like he couldn't stay away, but maybe I'm reading too much into it.

The more I turn it over in my mind the more I wonder if the spark between us, could lead to something…*more?*

As thoughts of Alex swirl in my head, there's a shift—faint at first, like a tickle at the base of my skull. I barely recognize it. It has been so long. My fingers itch.

I leap out of bed and grab my guitar, my hands moving over the strings like they've been waiting. A melody surfaces, sprouting from the back of my mind, my heart finally finding the rhythm to say everything my words cannot.

Within half an hour, I've written a song. For the first time in years. It feels good. No, *great*.

Then, it dawns on me.

I've written a song.

About him. Alex.

For the first time, I'm inspired by something that happened to me.

And it feels euphoric.

This was the inspiration I've been searching for.

As I set the guitar down, my phone buzzes. It's Riley calling.

"Hey," I answer, fiddling with the piece of paper that holds the lyrics. My mind is still half lost in the song I just created.

"Babe, Pip was going crazy looking for you yesterday! Are you okay? Were you with someone?" she asks, playfully teasing. Under normal circumstances, I would laugh it off, but this time, things are different.

"Actually, yeah," I murmur, a grin creeping across my face as I remember the night with Alex.

The scream Riley lets out on the other end of the phone is so loud, I almost drop it. I quickly pull the phone away from my ear to avoid permanent hearing damage.

"Bitch! Tell me everything!" she shouts, still in shock.

I burst out laughing, unable to contain the giddy feeling bubbling inside me. "Okay, calm down."

I recount the incident to her slowly, almost as if savoring the memory. But as I speak, my excitement begins to dull, giving way to doubt. Without meaning to, I start downplaying everything that happened last night—and this morning.

Maybe it was just a kind stranger being polite after I had hurt myself.

But Riley isn't having any of it. "No way, Elena. I can hear it in your voice. If he wasn't interested, he wouldn't have given you his number!"

"Yeah." The memory of Alex handing me that piece of paper makes me feel hopeful.

"You're not imagining this. He's into you. I mean, come on, a guy doesn't act like that unless he's interested," Riley says, her voice firm. "I hoped that table would've knocked some sense into you. Babe, he made the first move. The ball's in your court now. If you don't go for it, I swear I'll come over there and go for round two on the head-knocking."

I laugh, the tension in my chest loosening just a little. "You really think so?"

"I know so. Trust me, Elena," she encourages me, her tone softening. "Go for it. What's the worst that can happen? If it doesn't work out, at least you'll know you tried. But I'm telling you—he's into you."

I pause, letting her words sink in. Riley's confidence in me gives me the boost I need.

"Okay, I'll do it," I agree, a little surer of myself.

"Hell, yeah, you will! Call me when you do." Riley cackles. "And don't forget, I'm rooting for you, so make me proud."

I chuckle, feeling a little more lighthearted.

I can do this.

After the call with Riley, I find myself sitting on the edge of my bed, phone in hand, staring at Alex's number. My heart beats faster the longer I look at it.

What am I doing?

I quickly glance at the lyrics to the song I wrote. I can't believe I'm about to send a text to a guy who made my heart race with a few touches and a smile. Something I've never done before.

I start typing, my fingers hovering above the screen for a moment as if I'm trying to summon the right words. It's so easy to overthink these things.

Hey Alex, it's Elena. I hope you got home okay.

I stare at the sentence for a second, then delete it.

Too formal, too distant.

Hey Alex, this is Elena from the hospital... No, scratch that. It sounds like I'm still stuck in ER mode.

After several failed attempts, I finally settle on something that feels right.

ELENA

> Hey, it's Elena. What a crazy way to meet someone new in the city! Anyway, thanks for your kindness last night.

I bite my lip, rereading it one last time.

It's simple and sincere.

I hit send before I can second-guess myself.

Sitting back, the weight of the decision starts to sink in.

Ding!

A message comes through. I freeze, staring at the screen.

ALEX

> Hey Elena, It was a pretty unique way to meet, a great story to tell our grandkids one day.

Grandkids?

My heart skips a beat.

Chapter 6

Edge of Desire

A dull pain in my head jolts me awake. I blink, disoriented. Where am I? I raise my hand in front of my dazed vision and realize I've pulled the duvet over my head like some sort of cocoon. Slowly, I sit up, and the room greets me with nothing but shadows, the soft glow of early morning sneaking through the blackout curtains.

I glance at my phone, still in my hand from last night, and see the time—nine thirty a.m. The buzzing excitement I've been trying to ignore stirs in my stomach.

Three unread messages?

I grin at the screen, replaying the playful, borderline flirty texts Alex and I had shared over the last couple of days, and well into last night. A welcome distraction from all the resting and recuperating I was supposed to be doing.

I wanted to rush to the studio, get the new song out of my head before it slipped away, but Mark had insisted I follow the doctor's orders. At least until San Diego next week.

Shifting out of bed, I walk over to the window and pull the curtains apart. Water droplets cling to the glass like crystal diamonds, making the outside world look almost magical. The sky is dull and gray, and the rain falls steadily, blanketing the city streets in a quiet, melancholy haze.

There's something about the way Alex texts—casual but enough to make my heart flurry.

I unlock my phone, already smiling, eager to read whatever he's sent this time.

A dull ache pulses in my head, dragging me from my thoughts. *Thanks, Alex*, I think with a half-sigh. A souvenir from our first meeting. But I can't help but smile as butterflies in my stomach dance at sight of his messages.

ALEX

Say yes to the date. Don't make me beg… unless you're into that.

You fell asleep on me, didn't you? Rude. Sweet dreams, Elena. Try not to dream about me too much. Or do.

Morning, little hobbit. Still in bed? Or already off-stealing hearts today?

Stealing hearts? Me? I scoff at myself. If only he knew.

I can't help but smile at the 'little hobbit' message. Maybe we'll watch *Lord of the Rings* together one day. The thought makes my chest flutter. He's got a way of making me feel like I'm the only person on his mind.

I bite my lip, unsure of how to respond. I decide on a casual text.

ELENA

Good morning, Alex. Staying in, doctor's orders! What about you?

After a refreshing shower, I slip into a soft pink lounge set and crawl back into bed. Laptop balanced on my knees, I check my phone—still no reply from Alex. I sigh, disappointment creeping in as I scroll through my messages.

Then, without thinking, I call Riley. I just need to hear her voice.

"Elena!" Riley sings into the phone, her voice bright and bubbly.

"Hey babe," I reply, trying to sound casual, but the excitement I'm feeling is hard to hide.

"How's it hanging?" she asks.

"A little to the left." I laugh, though my smile fades almost instantly. I hesitate, then say it out loud. "Alex asked me on a date."

Without missing a beat, Riley blurts out, "Say yes."

"But I barely know him," I protest, even though I know deep down, I'm already half-tempted.

"That's exactly what dates are for," she quips. "Getting to know someone." She laughs knowingly. "I mean, it's not like you've actually *dated* as an adult."

She's not wrong. I've never really had the chance to explore that side of things.

A movie date with a boy I *thought* liked me, only to get ditched. An awkward invite to a high school dance. It had been so long, *years*, since I'd even gone out with a guy.

None of it counted.

They weren't *dates*.

Not the way Alex meant it.

"Okay, maybe we could hang out as friends, or would that be weird?" I ask, fidgeting with my notebook.

"Um, no! Do whatever you're ready for," Riley exclaims. "You said he's handsome, right?" She's practically shouting now.

Handsome is too small a word for him. He has the kind of face that makes you burn with desire, and so tall, it's almost intimidating. Eyes as deep and stormy as the sea—dangerous, enticing, and far too easy to get lost in. Am I willing to surrender myself to it? I bite my lip, feeling that familiar ache in my chest.

"Listen, babe, I can't talk right now, but I'll text you at lunch. You have my permission to go have some fun, *as friends* or otherwise, though I hope for your sake, you pick the latter." She ends the call before I can protest.

With Riley's reassurance, I start typing a witty text to Alex—something cheeky, just flirty enough—when my phone buzzes.

My heart jumps.

No caller ID flashes across the screen.

"Riley?" I pick up.

"Elena."

It's him. The way my name rolls off his lips makes my skin tingle.

Damn.

"Yes, this is she," I respond smoothly, even though I'm practically melting inside.

What is wrong with me? I barely know him.

"Feeling better today?" Alex asks, his voice low and smooth, and I can practically hear the mischief in it. *What's he planning?*

"I'm alright. Resting like a good little girl," I say, rolling my eyes at myself for sounding so sarcastic.

"Well, I *like* good girls," he teases. I swear, the way he says it takes my breath away. "Can I come see you today?"

Oh. My. God.

I sit up straight, excitement flooding me. *Did he just ask to come over?*

"So you can flirt with me in person?" I push, a little breathless, not quite used to this version of myself.

"Absolutely." He chuckles, the sound making me smile like a giddy schoolgirl.

"Don't you have work or something?" I ask, biting my lip to hide my grin, hoping I'm not coming off too eager.

"Elena," he says with a playful sigh. "I work for myself. Plus, I'd like to come spend some time with you, as I'm out of town next week."

A nervous thrill fizzes under my ribs. I stand up to look around outside and make sure Philippa and Andrew are gone.

All clear.

"Really?" I quip. "I wouldn't want you to get in trouble with yourself."

"I'm sure myself wouldn't mind," he replies, his voice dripping with amusement.

"I'm sure he won't." I giggle, feeling bolder now.

"Text me your address," he says, and there's a clear note of anticipation in his voice.

"Okay." I start typing it out, but my fingers and nerves betray me.

This is happening. As friends or otherwise.

"See you soon."

"Bye," I murmur, already imagining what this might turn into.

Once I recover some sense, I quickly text him Phillipa's address. *Please don't be a serial killer*. A silent prayer as I send it off.

Next, I fire off a quick message to Riley, letting her know he's coming over. I don't know why I'm being so vague, but I don't want to give her the full play-by-play…yet.

Gingerly, I run a brush through my hair, avoiding the tender spot, and try to make myself look halfway presentable. He cannot see me in fluffy pink pajamas, no matter how comfortable they are.

Heart racing, I leap to the rack of clothes Rio left, frantically sifting through options.

Does anything here not scream club rat or desperate? With a sigh, I give up and cross to my dresser. A white camisole and black velour lounge shorts will have to do.

I dash to the bathroom, swiping on lip balm, blush, mascara—just enough to make me feel pretty.

Back in my room, I scramble to tidy up, tossing clothes into the hamper, straightening cushions, taking deep breaths between tasks. He's just coming over to hang out. It's fine.

But God, I'm nervous.

The penthouse phone rings, and I bolt to the living room to answer it.

"Miss Montgomery, there's a Mr. Sigurdsson here for you," says Issac, the doorman.

Shit.

I quickly exhale. "Let him up."

I try to catch my breath.

I've never been this jittery over a guy before. I sneak a last-minute check in the hallway mirror, running my fingers through my hair, my nerves dancing to the rhythm of my heart.

I hear the elevator ding, and take another deep breath.

There's a soft knock on the door. I count to ten before opening it.

And there he is—the blond god himself. He's towering in the doorway, looking impossibly striking in a black shirt, soft distressed jeans, and sneakers. His hair is slightly damp, and he's wearing that sexy grin I've come to expect. In one hand, he's got two paper bags, and in the other, a tray of drinks.

"Hi," I murmur, feeling the heat rising to my face.

"Hello, beautiful," he greets me, and before I can process it, he plants a soft peck on each of my cheeks. His scent—a mix of citrus and the ocean—wraps around me, making my heart race.

Beautiful.

He thinks *I'm* beautiful.

"Nice home," he says, closing the door behind him.

"Thanks," I mutter, trying not to sound too flustered. "It's, um, my sister's and her fiancé's. She's got great taste." My words stumble out a little.

Is it weird to feel this nervous? Then again, I've never actually done this before.

His eyes trail over me, then drop to my feet. They linger on my house slippers for a beat, then, without a word, he kicks off his shoes. That simple act—so casual, yet so deliberate—makes my heart race. I can't help but feel a little giddy, like he's playing along with some unspoken game between us.

His eyes briefly flick down to my lips and then my chest, lingering a moment longer than necessary before meeting mine again, a glint of something unreadable flashing in them. I feel... *exposed*.

I bite my lip, trying to ease the tension winding tight in my core. "Come this way." I usher him into the kitchen. He follows me in silence, like it's no big deal that he's here, standing in my space. He places the items he's brought on the kitchen counter.

"So," I say, flashing him a cheeky grin as I sit on the stool beside him, "to what do I owe this impromptu visit?"

"I was in the neighborhood, thought you could use some breakfast," he lies smoothly, his grin widening. He empties the contents of one paper bag, which has two wrapped bagel sandwiches, then picks up the other tumbler on the tray and hands it to me.

"I hope you like egg and cheese bagel sandwiches," he offers, handing one to me.

"Thank you, this is really thoughtful of you," I breathe, opening the wrapped sandwich.

Glancing at the red drink in my hand, I ask, "What is it?"

"Kiwi and strawberry," he answers, casually leaning up against the counter, sipping his own drink. He looks so at ease, like he owns the place.

I raise an eyebrow. "Oh, I'm deathly allergic to strawberries," I joke, my voice dripping with playful sarcasm.

His eyes widen in immediate panic, but before he can say anything, I take a sip and give him a wink.

Fruity.

I wonder if his lips would taste as sweet. I shake my head quickly, dismissing the thought before it lingers too long.

I'll save that image for later, when it's just me, my vibrator, and zero regrets.

He watches me carefully, his lips curved in amusement. "You're a cheeky little thing, aren't you?"

"Depends on who you ask," I quip back, enjoying the meal he brought for me.

His eyes glint with interest, and I feel a spark ignite in the air between us. "Is that so?" he says, his voice low and smooth, his gaze never leaving mine as he casually takes another sip. The warmth of his eyes makes my skin flush, my heart picking up its pace. I can feel the heat between us intensifying, even in the stillness of the room.

I shrug playfully.

"Hmm." His smile stretches wider as he finishes the rest of his drink, Alex's blue-gray eyes lingering on my lips, making the air feel thick with something unspoken.

I feel the nervous tension in my shoulders loosen, replaced by something more thrilling. The boldness that has been bubbling inside me rises to the surface.

"How's your head today?" he asks, his voice easing into something softer, his eyes tracing the line of my face as he shifts. His hand hovers near my head, and I feel the warmth of his touch, even from a distance.

"Still attached," I deadpan, taking another bite of the bagel. It's so good.

His expression changes, his playful smirk softening into something more thoughtful, then his brows furrow slightly.

"I almost forgot," he says, reaching for the other paper bag. Giving me a moment to finish my meal, he pulls out the contents—two books: *Collection I of Creole and French Poetry* and *The Greatest Love Poems and Letters, Volume 1*, as well as the Joan Jett T-shirt, and the ridiculous hat from the vintage store the other day.

My heart immediately stops, a warmth blooming in my chest as I take in the sight of the books and the familiar items. A mix of surprise and something else renders me speechless.

"Alex, you shouldn't have," I murmur, my fingers tracing over the book covers, a warm flush creeping up my neck. The thoughtfulness of his gift tugs at something deep within me, something unfamiliar yet undeniably sweet. "This is...really special."

"I didn't want you to lose the treasures you found the other day," he adds, his smile soft—shy, but laced with something undeniably sexy, proud even, like he's pleased I noticed the thought behind his gesture.

"Thank you," I whisper, the words catching slightly in my throat. A pause stretches between us, thick and humming. "Can I give you a hug?"

My voice is quieter than I mean it to be, uncertain, but the ache to be near him is *stronger*. My heart thuds against my ribs, loud enough that I'm sure he can hear it. I hesitate, fingers curling against my palms, torn between staying where I am or reaching for him.

"I mean, if that's okay?" I add quickly, trying to smooth the rush of emotion crackling under my skin. Pushing off the stool, I smooth my hands down my shorts, hyperaware of every inch separating us—and every inch I want to erase.

He opens his arms without hesitation, pulling me into him.

Solid and warm, he feels like comfort wrapped in temptation. My head slots perfectly against him, his height—easily over six feet—making me feel small, cocooned in a way that sends a strange feeling rushing through me. His body engulfs mine naturally, and for a moment, I let myself melt into the embrace.

The scent of him—like salt-kissed air and something darker, richer—wraps around me, making my head spin. His breath stirs the top of my hair, and neither of us moves, as though breaking the moment would mean admitting there's more here than either of us is ready to say.

"So…" I murmur, tilting my head enough to glance up at him, my hands still resting lightly on his chest. "How old are you?"

He lets out a low laugh, the kind that rumbles deep beneath my palms. "Thirty-six. Why? Are you starting to second-guess letting an old man get this close?"

My lips curve, but my heart doesn't get the joke—it's thumping wildly. "You're not old. Just…older." I hold his gaze, letting it stretch. "I'm twenty-two. Well, almost twenty-three."

"I *know*," Alex affirms, his voice dipping as he tilts his head, eyes locked on mine.

Something about that sends a slow, dangerous shiver down my spine.

I freeze for a second. *Of course* he knows. I told the nurse in the hospital. He remembered.

I search his face, but he's already one step ahead, lifting a brow like he's weighing the math, lips tugging into a slow grin he doesn't bother to hide this time. "Hmm. So I *am* robbing the cradle."

I swat his arm, heat blooming in my cheeks. "That makes me sound like a child."

"Not quite, you're only a *little* taller," he jokes, his voice laced with mirth, then his gaze drags over me in a way that makes my skin prickle. "Though you're the most tempting hobbit I've ever seen."

I open my mouth to fire back, but the front door creaks open, the sound cutting through the moment.

"Shit!" My heart kicks up. "I think my sister's home!"

His eyes widen slightly, amusement flickering there, until I grab his wrist and yank him toward my room.

"Come on!" I hiss, pulling him with more force than grace as we dart inside, shutting the door softly but quickly behind us. We press ourselves side by side against the wood, breathing hard.

For a second, we listen, frozen, as footsteps pad across the wooden floors. My heart thunders against my ribs. When I glance up at Alex, I realize just how close he is. Close enough that I can feel the heat rolling off his body. Close enough that if I turned my head, my mouth might brush his shoulder.

He grins down at me. "This feels very scandalous. Are we sneaking around now?"

I shush him, biting back a laugh. "Give it a minute. She might go straight to her room."

Seconds stretch, heavy and endless.

Finally, the sound of her footsteps fades down the hall.

I exhale, sagging against the door. "That was close."

Alex's smirk deepens. "I don't mind a little risk. Makes things exciting."

I eye him suspiciously. "Do you thrive on chaos, Alex?"

"Only when it involves a beautiful woman hiding me in her bedroom."

I shake my head, trying not to smile. "You're impossible."

I start to step away, but Alex moves first, pivoting so he's facing me fully. In one smooth motion, he presses his body into mine, trapping me gently against the door, his wrist still caught in my hand.

My breath catches.

He's so close, every line of him radiating heat, every breath threading into mine. I don't let go of his wrist, as if my fingers have forgotten how to move.

His gaze drops to my mouth, lingering there, before flicking back up to my eyes, a glance so quick I almost miss it. Almost.

The air between us crackles, humming with something wild and unspoken.

He lifts his free hand and cups my face, his thumb brushing lightly over my cheekbone. I think he might kiss me. I think I might let him.

My pulse jumps as I try to steady my breath.

"Do you plan on keeping me here all night, Elena?" he whispers, his mouth curving into a wicked, devious smile.

And nothing has ever sounded more tempting in my whole life.

Chapter 7

Crazy for You

Once the threat of Philippa discovering us had passed and we had the place all to ourselves again, Alex and I settled back into the living room, sitting on opposite ends of the sofa, gazing out at the green canopy of Central Park dulled by the gray sky and rain.

"It's quite the view from up here," he remarks.

"The perfect cage." I sigh, my eyes dropping to my lap.

"What makes you say that?" he asks, voice softer now, curious.

I shrug. "Long story."

"We've got time."

"Do we?" I quip back, arching my brow at him.

His expression shifts, sharpening slightly. "Well, no. I'm out of town next week, so I want to make the most of the short time we have."

My breath catches. "By going on a date?"

He leans in a fraction, the warmth of his voice curling between us. "Yes, Elena. No more texts. No more coy flirting. Just you and me. An actual date."

"But…I don't really know you," I blurt out, harsher than I mean to.

"You won't know if you don't ask." He shrugs, like it's the simplest thing in the world.

Fair point.

That's what dates are for, Riley's voice echoes in my mind, teasing.

"So," he adds, tilting his head, "what do you want to know about me?"

I think for a second. He waits, patient, expectant, like he already knows I'll give in.

"What's your family like?"

"Swedish. Big, loud, scattered," he admits, smiling. "My parents divorced when my sister and I were young. Then they both remarried, had more kids. Six of us in total, but we're all over the globe."

"You're not close with them?"

"My sister, yes. The rest…not really. We get together when we can, but it's rare." He chuckles under his breath. "My parents live two doors down from each other. They're the best of friends now. Weird, right?"

I glance away. "That's funny. My parents put an ocean between them."

His voice drops. "That must have been hard. It wasn't always easy for us either, but time…it softens things."

For a moment, I envy him. That time healed his family instead of shattering it. Bitter is all I know.

"My best friend, Riley, comes from a big family too," I say, trying to shake the heaviness off.

"That's interesting," he retorts, smiling a little. "But I'm not here to get to know your best friend, Elena. I'm here to get to know *you*."

"Oh." My gaze lingers, heat rising in my cheeks. "Okay."

"Why singing?" His brow arches.

No one's ever asked me that before.

When I told my mother, she smiled like she'd already known. She watched me sing into hairbrushes, scribble lyrics on napkins, and dance barefoot across the living room floor. But when I told my father, he barely looked up. He said it was a childish dream. A waste of time. Translation: *I was a waste of time.*

"I love music," I admit, twisting the edge of the pillow in my lap. "It was something my mom and I shared. She was Miss Universe, sang for the talent portion, but I was never into all the pageant stuff. I loved the singing part, though. I used to mimic her performances." I blush a little. "Music became ours."

I draw a slow breath. "And when I sing, people listen. I hope…they can hear what's in my heart."

He's staring at me like I've knocked the air out of him.

"Elena"—his voice is low—"that's really *special.*"

I shift uncomfortably, unsure of what to do with the way he's looking at me. "I wish everyone felt that way."

"Why wouldn't they?" Alex asks, eyes narrowing slightly.

My mouth goes dry. "My father doesn't…He's not supportive."

"You don't get along with him?" he presses gently.

"No. Not really."

"Why?" he asks, watching me carefully.

"Because…" I drop my gaze. "I'm a disappointment to him." I shake my head quickly, like I can erase the words. "Sorry, that's stupid, I shouldn't have said that. Sorry."

"Don't apologize. That's not stupid." He shifts closer, so close our knees brush, a spark leaping from the contact straight up my spine.

"*He's* stupid for making you feel that way."

Heat blooms low in my belly from where our bodies touch.

My skin prickles with awareness, like every nerve is reaching for him.

"And you grew up in Australia?" he asks.

"Yes. After the divorce, it was ugly," I say quietly. "My mom ran to the furthest place she could."

Alex's voice softens. "Where is she now?"

"She died a few years ago," I reply, the words catching. "Cancer."

I try not to let the ache bloom in my chest. I breathe, focusing on the here and now.

His expression softens. "I'm sorry, Elena. You've had quite the journey." He rests his hand on my leg.

The touch is cool, soothing.

"You could say that."

He leans back, hand still resting on my thigh, his eyes studying me. "Pardon me for being forward…"

I lift an eyebrow. "Alex, you invited yourself over. I think we're past worrying about being forward."

He laughs low in his throat. "Fair enough. You must know how beautiful you are, but your eyes. When you were lying in the hospital, I thought they'd be brown. Then you opened them, and damn"—he shakes his head, smiling almost to himself—"you took my breath away. They're…*beguiling*."

My throat tightens. My eyes have always felt like a curse, a mirror of my father's, a reminder of him even when he wasn't around. But to Alex, they're something that enamors him.

For a second, I want to let myself believe him.

"Bet you say that to all the girls," I murmur, trying to sound flippant.

"Only the ones I knock out." He smirks. He's so handsome, it's disarming.

A laugh bubbles out of me, slipping past the lump in my throat.

"What about you?" I ask, nudging his knee with mine. "What do you do?"

For a split second, something flashes across his face, a flicker of hesitation, before he raises a brow, a private thought passing behind his eyes. I catch the way his mouth tugs into a crooked smile, too quick, too easy.

"Talking about work is boring," he brushes off lightly, the corners of his mouth curving higher. "Unless, of course, it's your passion. Like singing is for you."

"It is." I nod. "Especially writing songs."

He's still such a mystery, giving me just enough to make me want more.

"Okay, tell me about your sister?" I question.

"She's a writer. Divorced, though who isn't these days?" He shrugs lightly. "I was actually buying her a book she wanted that day at the vintage store."

"Oh, I hope she got it," I tease, nudging him again.

"She did," he adds, voice softening. "It was for her birthday."

He shifts even closer, the side of his body brushing mine, his thigh warm where it presses against me.

The contact sends a flicker of heat straight through my chest.

"So," he murmurs, his voice dropping slightly, "what do you write about?"

I've only ever talked about that with my mom. The fact that he even asks warms something in me.

"My life, mostly. Love," I mutter, biting my lip. "Not that I really know anything about it. More about…wanting it."

"You've never been in love?" he asks, voice gentle.

"No. Have you?"

"You could say that. But I think there are different kinds of love. Different people, different ways."

I nod, my pulse quickening. "I'll take your word for it."

His smile curves, slow and sure. "Will you write about me?"

He doesn't know that I already have. The words are buried in notebooks. Melodies strummed into a song that he unknowingly inspired the second we collided.

"Maybe." My voice catches. "I'll think about it."

"I hope to hear it one day." He winks.

His fingers shift, drifting across the space between us, brushing against the inside of my thigh—light, tentative, electric.

Slowly, he starts to trace small circles on my leg, just above my knee, the barest pressure against my skin.

My breath catches, but I don't move.

I can't.

"So what's your passion?" My voice is thinner than I mean it to be, breathless from the way his fingers trace slow, dizzying circles.

He smiles—handsome, cocky, *knowing*—like he can feel exactly what he's doing to me.

"Photography. Travel. Good food." He shrugs, then pauses, his eyes never leaving mine. "And beautiful women," he adds, voice dropping lower.

My heart thrums like a trapped hummingbird against my ribs. And wetness pools at my center, just for him. *Fuck.*

The world outside the window blurs into green and gray, but all I can feel is the way his fingertips dance across my skin, like a secret written in a language only we understand.

We spend the rest of the afternoon lazing on the sofa, lost in easy conversation. He mentions that his birthday is coming up. August 3rd, exactly a month before mine.

The way he talks about past birthdays, the places he's traveled, the people he's met, makes me realize how much life he's lived compared to my sheltered existence.

There's a charm in the way he recounts stories, a quiet confidence that makes me want to listen forever. His goofy sense of humor only adds to his appeal, grounding him in a way that feels both playful and steady.

There's an irresistible pull between us, one I never expected to feel with a man his age. Maybe it's because of everything I've been through—my grief, the pressure, the growing pains.

Maybe that's why boys my age never resonated with me.

Alex reignites a flame I thought I'd snuffed out. He makes me feel like I can let go and fall into whatever this is.

Before he leaves, he lingers by the door, leaning up against it. His gaze locked onto mine with an intensity that makes my pulse quicken.

"You and me, tomorrow?" he asks, a knowing smirk tugging at his lips.

I arch a brow, playing along. "Yup, you and me—one date." My voice is teasing, but my heart pounds in anticipation. His eyes gleam with mischief, like he already knows how this is going to end.

"I'll have you begging for more," he murmurs, the confidence in his tone sending a direct jolt through me. It's a new feeling— one no one has ever made me experience before.

A slow smile spreads across my lips. "Is that so?" I bite my lip, testing him, inviting him to make his next move.

He steps closer, closing the space between us, his fingers grazing my chin. His thumb tugs at my bottom lip before gliding over it, slow and deliberate. My breath hitches, the air between us thick with unspoken desire. For a moment, time suspends, and I vibrate at the possibility of his lips on mine.

The penthouse elevator dings, and the doors slide open. Standing there, framed in the golden glow of the entryway, is my father.

His eyes widen as he takes in the sight before him—Alex and I, far too close, caught in a moment that I wish I could freeze or rewind.

If the ground could swallow me whole, I would gladly let it.

Alex straightens immediately, assuming the calm confidence he always carries himself with, tempered by something more measured, more calculated.

"Father." My voice is barely above a whisper. It's all I can manage.

Alex's gaze flicks to mine, his expression unreadable but careful. He gets it. He understands, after what I shared with him this afternoon. Without a word, he steps back, nodding once before saying, "I'll talk to you later."

And just like that, he strides past my father, stepping into the elevator as if nothing had happened. The doors close behind him with a quiet finality, leaving behind only thick, suffocating tension.

Mortimer doesn't move. He stands there, his expression unreadable, his sharp eyes assessing me, peeling back the layers of what he's witnessed. My pulse is hammering in my ears.

"Do you want to come inside?" I ask—my pathetic attempt to smooth over the awkwardness.

"Elena, who was that?" His tone is clipped and controlled.

I force myself to meet his gaze. "A friend."

He exhales sharply through his nose, stepping further inside. "Philippa told me about the accident." He raises his brow. "Is that him?"

I stiffen.

How much did she tell him?

"She said you met a man who stayed with you...Is that the friend?" he continues, eyeing me like I'm a puzzle he's yet to solve.

I exhale sharply, folding my arms. "Yes, and what of it?" My voice comes out firmer than I intend, but I don't back down.

"You're here barely two weeks and already getting into incidents with strange men. Men who don't even bother introducing themselves," he snaps. "Then I have to read about you on *Page Six*. I should sue the hell out of them for printing that garbage."

He drags a hand through his hair, frustration bleeding into something rawer. "If something happened to you—" His voice breaks.

At first, I think he's angry with me. But he's not. He's *worried.* The realization knocks some of my irritation down a notch.

This is new for him.

I went from a teenager to an adult in the time we've been apart, so it's not like I owe him an explanation about the comings and goings of my budding love life. "I'm fine. A knock on the head, some stitches, and a concussion, but I'm not dying." I try to make light of it. "And Kylie has the media handled. Don't give yourself a heart attack."

His eyes widen, but he recovers his composure quickly.

"Seeing my daughter in the arms of a rather imposing man was enough to give me a heart attack," he mutters, and I nearly choke. Mortimer Montgomery just made a joke?

What planet am I on right now?

I smirk. "You should've seen all the bikie gang members I used to entertain back at home."

He shakes his head, rolling his eyes at my humor. "This man seems a little old for you, no?" His voice is careful, like he's trying to avoid setting me off.

"Old? What, do you and he have adjoining beds booked at the Golden Oaks retirement home?" I scoff. "Father, it's fine. I'm an adult, he's an adult, and let's not forget that you and Mom had a significant age gap, too. So why should it matter?"

For the first time, his expression cracks slightly. A flicker of something crosses his face, something I can't quite name.

A long pause stretches between us. Then, finally, he sighs. "I came to check on you. Make sure you're recovering. That you're being *careful*."

My posture softens. "I'm fine, I promise."

His eyes search mine for any sign of doubt before he nods. "And you're settling in, okay? Not too homesick? Not making plans to run back home?"

I smile faintly. "I'm good. No running away. At least not yet."

He studies me for another beat before finally giving a small nod. "Good."

Then, after a brief hesitation, he adds, "And the album? It's coming along well?"

That catches me off guard. My father, asking about my music? I squint, unsure I heard right. "It's coming along."

"Good, good," he adds. "So, before Philippa's wedding, I hope you would consider talking to Carole."

The mention of her name makes me stiffen. The woman who destroyed my life. The mistress turned wife.

"Why?"

He sighs, unsure of how to approach this situation without it blowing up into a fight.

A flicker of realization hits me—his sudden interest in my music was nothing more than a thinly veiled attempt to butter me up for this request. A familiar disappointment claws up my spine. Was this the only way we could have a conversation?

Through strategic maneuvering and carefully placed pleasantries.

I realize he probably wants things to go smoothly for Philippa's wedding, and it's a hope we both share, given our tempers. It makes sense why he wants to 'manage' this situation—to mitigate the risk, so to speak.

"We're family, Elena. Like it or not, she's my wife. You've embraced Jack as your dad..." He hesitates on the last part, like referring to Jack as my dad causes him physical pain.

"She's not my mom," I snap, anger bubbling to the surface.

"No, she's not. And no one can ever replace Vida. She was a formidable force," he adds softly.

I cross my arms, shielding myself. I hate when he talks about her—he doesn't deserve to even speak her name.

"Please, if not for me, then for Philippa?" he pleads.

Philippa.

I don't want to put any more strain on her. She's been nothing but kind and accommodating since I came back. If this is one way I can repay her kindness, then so be it.

"Fine." I sigh, defeated.

His eyes glisten, and I let out a breath I didn't realize I'd been holding. For the first time in my life, we managed to talk without it turning into a battlefield. No raised voices. No slammed doors.

Maybe it's a step forward.

Maybe it's just a ceasefire in a war that never really ends.

Either way, I'll take it.

When I woke up this morning, I didn't expect to end the day with two guests under this roof, both unexpected, both pulling at different parts of me.

I close my eyes for a moment, letting it all sink in—the risk, the hope, the wild, aching possibility that maybe, everything is starting to change.

Chapter 8

Animal

The Drip is an eclectic little hole-in-the-wall café tucked away in a quiet part of Brooklyn. I'm grateful Alex texted me the directions last night. Otherwise, I'd be lost.

The distressed yellow door groans as I push it open, the scent of freshly ground coffee wrapping around me like a warm embrace.

The place is dimly lit, its back wall all exposed brick, and indie music hums softly in the background. The café is empty—mismatched chairs and tables scattered throughout, with lanterns casting a cozy glow against the dreary rain outside.

Behind the counter, a barista with tattooed arms and a sage-green beanie—an odd choice for July—barely lifts her eyes from her book as I enter.

Alex isn't here yet.

I choose a large wingback chair by the window, its striped fabric worn and faded, like it's survived a few lifetimes. The whole place has character—old records stacked haphazardly on shelves, suitcases spilling over with tiny potted plants, tattered coffee table books scattered across low tables. Outside, rain drizzles steadily. Pedestrians rush past with their umbrellas, lost in their own worlds.

And then, there he is. Alex.

Standing across the street, waiting to cross, looking as handsome as ever in a long-sleeved white shirt, casually rolled up to his elbows, revealing his strong forearms. The same arms that carried me, unconscious, into the hospital. The thought makes me cringe and swoon. His jeans cling just right, showcasing his athletic physique beneath.

He holds a hand—rather pathetically—over his head to shield himself from the light rain, his lips curling into a smirk as he spots me through the window.

I quickly look down, pretending to scroll through my phone, though my heart is already picking up speed.

The bell above the door chimes.

"Hi!" The barista's voice chirps from behind the counter, far more enthusiastically than when I walked in. I glance up to see her put her book down, her attention now firmly fixed on him.

I roll my eyes and shake my head.

Okay. So I'm not the only one who thinks he's good-looking.

Alex's gaze zeroes in on me. My eyes dart down, hoping he didn't catch me staring. Footsteps approach. I risk a peek.

Our eyes meet.

He smirks.

I melt.

Before I can second-guess myself, I rise to meet him. His arms wrap around me, the scent of rain and something fresh clinging to him. Before I can linger, he pulls back, planting a soft kiss on each cheek.

The European custom still feels strange to me, but endearing.

"Have you ordered?" he asks, voice smooth, his hand trailing lightly down my back, resting at the small of it.

I shake my head, offering a small, shy smile. "I was waiting for you."

Something shifts in his expression—*nerves?*

That's unexpected. Yesterday, he was full of confidence, so sure of himself.

Is it the pressure of today?

"Coffee?" His arm grazes my shoulder as we step toward the counter. "You drink coffee, right? Or we can go somewhere else." His words come out in a rush, a rare moment of uncertainty.

I place my hand over his, hoping to steady him. "Coffee's good."

The barista is still watching us, her eyes darting between us like we're the most interesting thing to happen to her all week.

"I'll have a caramel macchiato, please."

"Black coffee," Alex adds, still looking at me.

The barista smiles sweetly. "Can I tempt you with one of our organic, cruelty-free apricot bars?" She punches in the order before he even answers.

Alex turns to me, a playful question in his eyes.

I shrug.

"Yeah, we'll take two of those," he decides, handing over a fifty-dollar bill.

"Together or separate?" the barista asks.

He barely spares her a glance. "Together." A slow smile tugs at his mouth. "Keep the change."

I frown, reaching for my purse. "No, I can pay for myself."

He places his hand over mine before I can argue, his touch warm and firm. "It's a date, remember?" His eyes don't leave mine as he leads me back to the loveseat pressed against the exposed brick wall.

I expect him to take the seat across from me. Instead, he slides in right beside me. Our thighs touch.

He never lets go of my hand.

A blush creeps up my neck. Holding hands seems so…juvenile. But in this moment, it feels so intimate. Not that I have much to compare it to.

Our conversation picks up from where we left off yesterday, flowing between us so easily. His stormy eyes light up as we exchange stories about our cultures—Sweden, the Philippines, Australia. Between the two of us, we could start up our own little United Nations.

Our drinks arrive, but the conversation never ceases. He gently caresses my hand with his thumb, his long fingers and large hand engulfing mine.

While I talk, Alex leans forward slightly, his fingers curling around his mug, eyes fixed on me with an easy kind of interest. I'm not used to this feeling.

Is this what I've gone without all these years?

We bond over our shared experience as children of divorce. He jokes about his family traditions. Tells stories about backpacking through Europe with his friends, even the time he served in the Swedish military.

The nerves from earlier slowly fade away.

By the time our coffee cups are empty, I realize something. I like knowing things about him. And for the first time in a long time, I want someone to know about me, too.

"I had a wonderful time," I say as we stand, assuming the date is over.

"Done already?" He grins. "You agreed to a date. The day and our date aren't over yet." He leans down, his breath warm against my ear. "And maybe the night too."

The scent of coffee and apricots curls around me, making my head spin. Heat rushes to my cheeks.

Night?

I hope he isn't expecting anything. Panic rises in my throat.

"Um, that better be a PG-rated night date, because I am *not* that kind of girl." I barely manage to get the words out without tripping over them.

He winks, unfazed, and waves down a passing taxi.

I let out a nervous laugh as we pile into the backseat together.

He casually gives the taxi driver the address of our next destination and leans back, draping his arm around me.

For a moment, I stiffen—not from the closeness, but from *him*. There is something magnetic about him, pulling me in.

I exhale. Letting go, surrendering to the feeling.

"So, where are we headed?"

He smiles. "A surprise."

We ride the cab in silence, but not the uncomfortable kind. Instead, it crackles with unspoken tension, the kind that makes my pulse quicken.

To my disappointment, the ride ends too soon. The cab pulls up in front of a refurbished warehouse. Outside, the rain's softened to a mist, enough to walk through without getting soaked.

"What are we doing here?"

"Be a good girl and play along." He taps my nose, laughing under his breath.

The rational part of me is thrilled. But the irrational part panics.

He's probably an axe murderer who's brought me to my final resting place.

But Google came up with nothing!

Well, Google lied.

Philippa thinks I'm out shopping. I *should've* told her where I was.

Before I can think to text Riley, Alex takes my hand, calming my internal panic as he leads me toward the entrance.

"Surprise," he says, nodding toward the neon sign above the door, flashing that infuriatingly charming smile.

Indoor Extreme Sports.

My eyes widen.

Is he kidding?

"Oh!" I gasp, excitement bubbling up. "What are we doing?" I ask as we walk into what looks like an arcade.

He doesn't answer, walking straight up to the freckly teenager with braces behind the counter whose name tag says *Nick.*

"Two for laser tag, please," Alex says smoothly.

Laser tag!

I've never played before—this is so exciting!

I notice Nick's eyes widen slightly. His reaction to Alex feels…*off.* Like maybe he knows him. Or maybe he's surprised by how absurdly good-looking Alex is.

Same, Nick. Same.

"Fifteen minutes or half hour?" Nick asks.

Alex glances at me, waiting.

"Half hour, please," I exclaim, grinning up at him.

He lets out a low laugh, the sound curling heat through my stomach. "Bring it on," he teases, poking my side, his touch sending an electric current right through me.

Nick disappears into the back without a word.

"I've never played before," I admit, glancing around at the chaos—kids screaming, teenagers competing, exhausted parents barely keeping up.

Alex's eyes are on me, unwavering. "You're going to love it."

Something about the way he says it makes my breath hitch.

Nick returns with two flashing guns and vests with light panels and padding. Alex grabs one of the vests and gently pulls it over my head, his hands brushing my arms as he clips me in.

Nick holds the gun and explains how the contraption works. We listen intently; however, I'm distracted by the god-like man standing beside me.

"Too easy," Alex nods, clipping himself into his vest.

"Okay, so if you die, you can't shoot for five seconds. The

person with the most points wins." Nick sighs, explaining the rules, never once taking his eyes off Alex.

Strange. Maybe he's gay?

"You're going down," I tease, poking Alex's shoulder.

He feigns a dramatic wince, but his fingers tighten around his gun, muscles flexing beneath his shirt.

My eyes catch the movement—the sharp tension in his forearm, the way his bicep bunches enough to make my breath stutter.

A wicked hunger curls low inside, hot and unexpected.

I shove it down. Locking it away before it can take root.

Nick hands me my gun and gestures toward a dimly lit hallway lined with heavy doors.

"You guys are in Battle Zone Three," Nick adds, his tone flat with disinterest. "Once you're in, you have a few minutes to get into position before the timer starts."

"Thanks," Alex says, barely paying attention.

Nick musters a nod. "Good luck."

Alex rests his hand on the doorknob, turning it slowly. My pulse kicks up a notch as I start hatching a plan.

Before I can strategize further, Alex glances over, a knowing smirk tugging at his lips.

"If I win," he murmurs, "I want something from you."

The way he says it sends a prickle of heat down my spine.

"What is it?" I draw in a shaky breath.

He nudges me with his elbow, laughing. "You'll find out after the game. I wouldn't want you throwing it just to find out early."

His brows wag playfully, but my brain short-circuits, anyway.

Oh, my god.

What if he wants sex?

Surely not.

I mean, he wouldn't expect that on the first date. Would he?

Touching myself to him, fine. That's just thoughts.

But actual sex? Too fast.

Riley sleeps with guys all the time, like it's no big deal.

It is a big deal. I'd say no.

Obviously.

Unless I panic. Shit. What if he *assumes*?

What's the worst it could be?

"Relax," Alex adds finally, clearly reading every chaotic thought flashing across my face. His smile softens. "It's not sex. Unless you want it to be, of course." He winks, nudging me playfully.

I exhale, mortified.

Cool. Amazing. I am officially the most obvious person alive. I shake off the ridiculous panic, reminding myself to fucking chill out and have fun.

"Okay, I'm game. Hold this."

I let out a breath, handing Alex my gun as I gather my raven waves into a ponytail, tying it up and out of my face. Careful not to aggravate the small wound on my head.

When I glance back at him, his mouth is slightly parted, eyes locked on me like I was doing something scandalous.

His gaze lingers. Then…

"Hmm." It's more a sound than a word. Low. Appreciative.

Heat pulses between my thighs.

I arch a brow. "Eyes on the prize."

Alex's smirk deepens. "They are."

My stomach flutters traitorously.

Before I can overthink it, he hands me back my gun and opens the door, and we step inside.

The second the door clicks shut, we're swallowed by total darkness.

For a moment, there's only silence—the kind that prickles with anticipation, thick with the unknown.

Then I feel it.

A cool hand grazing down my back.

Slow. Deliberate.

A shiver courses through me. I freeze. Not in fear, but in the thrilling awareness of him.

His palm rests lightly against the small of my back. Not possessive. Not forceful. Just…there. Reassuring. A touch that shouldn't feel like a spark catching fire, but somehow, it does.

Instinctively, I reach out, my fingers brushing fabric—his shirt soft beneath my fingertips.

Then UV lights flood the room, neon streaks flaring to life along the walls.

I blink, taking in our surroundings—half-destroyed barricades and stacked bins, creating obstacles in the dimly lit maze.

Alex steps back, and that's when I see it.

His white shirt, glowing electric blue under the lamps.

A *painfully* easy target.

Our eyes meet. A single beat of silence, then we both burst into laughter.

Belly-aching, breathless laughter.

"I hate to break it to you," I manage between giggles, "but you're basically a human glow stick right now."

Alex tilts his head, amusement flickering across his face. "I could take it off?"

My mouth goes dry.

His smirk turns wicked. "All you have to do is ask."

There's something about the way he says it—not just teasing, but a dare.

My cheeks burn, hot and shameless. I realize I'm holding my breath, gripping onto my gun for dear life.

Alex chuckles, shaking his head. "If flirting is all it takes to disarm you, I'm afraid you're in for an ass-whooping."

I huff, shoving his arm playfully. "Game on."

An idea hatches in my mind: *Operation Distract and Destroy.* Two can play this game.

His stormy eyes flash dark, exhilarated.

And just like that, the war begins.

A familiar beat pulses through the air. 'Animal' by Neon Trees.

How apt.

The countdown flashes red on the wall.

10! 9! 8!

I grin, my pulse pounding in sync with the music. "Yes."

Before Alex can react, I lift the hem of his shirt with one hand, my fingers grazing over firm muscle. Warm. Taut. Just as I imagined.

"Maybe you *should* take it off," I whisper, emboldened, enacting step one of my plan.

His breath stops for a second. I've caught him off guard.

His gun hangs forgotten at his side, just as mine does. I press my other hand against his neck, tilting his face toward mine.

His pulse thrums beneath my fingertips.

His eyes darken, and he lets out a low sound of satisfaction.

Oh. That's nice. Really nice.

Focus, Elena.

7! 6! 5!

I rise on my toes, closing the space between us.

4! 3!

His gun clatters to the floor. His arms coil around my back, pulling me in, heat meeting heat.

BINGO.

2!

His breath fans over my lips. His eyes flicker closed.

Everything slows.

The neon lights. The pounding music. The countdown, now a distant hum.

He leans in—

So close.

So deliciously close.

1!

HONK!

The moment shatters.

Before he can react, I knock his gun away, seize my own, and bolt like my life depends on it.

Alex stumbles and curses, his balance thrown.

I cackle like a maniac, breathless and victorious, as I sprint into the dark maze.

"You're gonna get it!" his voice booms behind me, reverberating against the walls.

Adrenaline floods my veins.

Weaving through the dimly lit corridors, neon graffiti blurs past me, and the bass of the song pulses in my chest. *Operation Distract and Destroy* is off to a successful start.

"Come out, come out, wherever you are." His voice echoes through the maze, deep and taunting.

I bite my lip, cheeks flushing.

Damn him.

"Come and get me, big guy!" I shout back, my voice shaking with excitement.

I hover in place, torn between staying hidden and making a run for it. It's too dark. My eyes are still adjusting to the shifting neon glow. If he catches me here, I'll be cornered.

Not happening.

I risk a peek through the tall window, my pulse slamming against my ribs.

Clear.

I exhale sharply, forcing my legs to move. I push off the wall, slipping from cover, checking both sides before sprinting through the next opening.

The second I stop behind another barrier, I hear it.

"Elena."

His voice is closer now. *Too close.*

There's something thrilling about being chased—the way it sends pure, hot adrenaline surging through your veins.

Dropping into a low crouch, I press my back against a half wall. My breath is ragged with the danger of being caught, my fingers twitching around the trigger.

Then I spot him.

His damn white shirt, still glowing under the UV lights like a beacon, giving him away.

Rookie mistake.

He's behind a barrier, only the edge of his shoulder peeking out.

I grin, positioning my gun, lining up my shot.

And then, I fire.

Again. And again.

His vest lights up in flashing red, signaling a kill.

"Ha!" I laugh, a raw rush of victory bursting in my chest.

Alex lets out a low, sharp curse as his vest powers down.

Five seconds.

That's all I have before he's back in the game.

I scramble away, crawling behind a shattered corner, my hands shaking from the rush. Even though I won this round, I know one thing for sure.

Alex isn't done hunting me yet.

I manage to kill him twice, I think. But take a few hits of my own. My vest powers down, but I don't stop to check, narrowly escaping him on multiple occasions.

My heart slams against my ribs as I maneuver through the maze, weaving between barricades, trying to create distance.

I spot him.

Backed against a column a few meters away.

The space between us crackles, my palms slick with adrenaline, my breaths coming in short, excited bursts.

I line up my shot, aiming for his vest.

I fire.

Bullseye.

Alex sees me as soon as I pull the trigger, and in a split second, he moves.

Fast.

Too fast.

I try to stumble back, but I barely get a step in before—

Strong hands grab my waist.

A yelp rips from my throat as he lifts me clean off the ground, my body weightless.

"Gotcha," he growls.

I squeal, legs kicking in the air. My fingers dig into his shoulders, gripping onto him as he spins me around, pinning me against a solid wall.

I barely have time to react before he grabs my gun and tosses it aside.

I'm defenseless.

Breathless.

Pinned.

"You're in quite the predicament, Elena," he drawls, like he's relishing his time with the kill.

His chest presses against mine, and his arms cage me in. His scent wraps around me—citrusy, intoxicating.

I feel his breath against my cheek, slow and measured, like he's enjoying watching me squirm.

The tension tightens between us, my pulse skipping erratically, my skin alive where he touches me.

His fingers skim up my arm, slow, deliberate, his touch featherlight, but it scorches.

I inhale deeply, drowning in his scent. Fully aware that my body is betraying me completely.

The music thumping in the background fades into a low hum.

His arm tightens around my waist, pulling me impossibly close.

My hands grip his arms, my fingers sliding over the hard muscle, feeling the heat of his skin through his shirt.

I should push him away.

But instead—

I wrap my arms around his neck, my body melting into his like I belong there. Pulling him into me even closer.

His eyes darken, his gaze dropping to my mouth.

My heart free-falls, lost in the moment.

"Kiss me," I whisper, barely audible over the pounding against my rib cage.

Our breaths are ragged.

Alex doesn't hesitate.

His lips crash into mine. His hunger is palpable as he presses our bodies harder up against the wall, trapping us in a heat so dizzying, so *consuming*, I forget where we are.

A sound escapes me, something soft and wanting, as my fingers tangle into his sweaty hair.

When my nails scratch against his scalp, he moans into my mouth.

He tilts his head and deepens the kiss. Alex's tongue slides against mine, teasing and pulling me under his spell.

Strong hands tighten around me—one gripping my thigh, the other cupping my ass. A thumb brushes beneath the hem of my shorts, a barely-there touch that makes me shudder. Teeth graze my bottom lip, playful and teasing.

I melt, losing myself to him.

HONK!

The timer blares, the lights flicker back on, and the moment shatters like glass.

Alex lets out a low breath, his grip on me loosening.

My legs wobble, my body still thrumming with heat, but I

somehow manage to stay upright.

We stare at each other.

Breathless.

Caught.

Like we just did something we shouldn't have.

What. A. Kiss.

My mind is a mess of thoughts.

Alex runs a hand through his messy blond hair, exhaling a soft laugh, his gaze still heated.

"That was fun," he murmurs.

I take a second to find my voice. "Yeah."

I can still feel him—the heat of his lips, the way he stole my breath like it belonged to him.

I've been kissed before, but not like that.

It was electrifying and all-consuming.

We walk to the exit hand in hand, peeling off our vests and returning our guns.

Nick prints out a score sheet, handing it to me. I scan the numbers, my jaw dropping.

"No way." I protest.

Alex smirks. "What?"

I gape at the paper, shaking my head. "This must be wrong. I was sure I won!"

Alex laughs, his hair still in delicious disarray. "Doesn't look like it."

I cross my arms, pouting. "Alright, what do you want?"

He pretends to think, rubbing his jaw. "Hmm…Well, I have some demands."

I narrow my eyes. "Don't push it."

His eyes crinkle as he flashes a wicked grin, his voice dropping into that low, dangerous tone that makes my insides giddy.

"I win," he announces. "That means I get what I want."

I roll my eyes. "Oh, really? And what if I don't agree?"

Alex catches the hem of my shirt, pulling me into him smoothly, his lips brushing just against my hairline.

"I can be *very* persuasive," he whispers.

His breath skates down my neck, and my thighs clench without meaning to.

I swallow hard.

Suddenly, I feel like I lost a lot more than just a game.

Chapter 9

Crush

We stroll through the streets of Brooklyn, hand in hand, as the sun finally breaks through the clouds, casting a golden glow over the damp pavement. The humidity lingers, thick and sticky, curling around us like an embrace.

Then, I notice her.

A woman with a dog, staring directly at Alex. Not just a passing glance, but with recognition, her mouth agape.

Her phone is in her hand in an instant, and before I can process it, she snaps a picture.

What the fuck?

First Nick. Now her.

Before I can say anything to Alex, we round the corner. A mouthwatering scent floods my senses, and I lose my train of thought. The aroma of smoky meats, sizzling spices, and sweet pastries wraps around us, pulling me toward the nearby park. A convoy of food trucks is parked under a canopy of trees, their colorful signs advertising everything from Korean barbecue to gourmet tacos.

"Hungry?" Alex grins, his expression boyish and irresistibly charming.

"Always." I giggle, poking his side. Hard muscle meets my fingertips, the contours of his abs obvious even beneath his shirt.

We settle under the shade of a sprawling oak tree, claiming a weathered wooden picnic table. Our makeshift feast stretches between us—sticky, smoky ribs, grilled corn, soft tacos bursting with fresh salsa, cheesecake, and homemade pink lemonade.

I take a sip, letting the sweet citrus bite melt on my tongue.

"This is amazing," I exclaim, a smile tugging at the corners of my lips, not sure where to begin.

"I have to admit," Alex says, picking up a taco with ease, "the tacos in California are better. But these? Not bad."

I grin, licking a bit of salsa from my thumb. "Speaking of the West Coast, I'm actually headed to San Diego on Sunday to shoot the video for my debut single."

Alex pauses mid-bite, his eyes flickering with interest. "What a coincidence. I'll be in San Diego the day after tomorrow for the week."

I perk up, realizing we haven't really talked about his job. "Oh? Right, you mentioned that. What was it you do again?"

He takes a slow sip of his drink, his expression unreadable. "Hmm…A little bit of this and that."

I raise a brow. That was vague.

Before I can press, he smoothly redirects. "So, how long will you be on the West Coast?"

Evasive. Noted.

"I fly back the following Saturday." I shrug between mouthfuls of sticky, delicious ribs.

Alex's lips curve into a smirk. "Maybe we could meet up?"

His tone is casual, but there's something deliberate in the way he says it, like he's already planned it in his head.

I nod silently, pretending to focus on my food, but my mind is already spinning.

Why wouldn't he answer my question?

We finish our lunch, the conversation shifting easily, trading stories of memorable meals—my mom's home-cooked Filipino dishes, the time Alex accidentally set fire to a steak trying to impress someone.

He's charming, funny, and magnetic.

But that little piece of mystery clings to the back of my mind.

What exactly does Alex do for work, and why is he going to be in San Diego, of all places?

And why won't he tell me?

Before I can dwell, a cool droplet lands on my arm.

Glancing up, I notice the sky has darkened once more, and another drop hits my forehead.

"Shit," Alex hisses, right as the sky splits open.

The rain pours down in sheets, drenching us in seconds.

We scramble to toss our rubbish in a nearby trash can, laughing breathlessly as Alex tries in vain to shield me with his body.

It doesn't help.

The rain soaks through his white shirt, making it cling to him, outlining the solid lines of his chest, his broad shoulders, the ridges of his abs.

I wet my lips at the sight.

Before I can get lost in that thought, Alex hastily flags down a cab.

We jump in, shivering, breathless, soaked through, our laughter still hanging in the air between us as Alex leans forward, relaying the destination to the driver.

I glance over at him.

"Looks like the open-air cinema is off the table." He sighs, shaking his head.

His hair is damp, messy, and his shirt? Completely ruined.

And yet, somehow, he's never looked better.

Arriving in NoHo, we take refuge from the downpour within the sleek confines of Alex's modern, masculine penthouse.

Penthouse. So he's clearly successful at…whatever it is he does.

And yet, he's so damn evasive about it.

Maybe he's in the CIA. Or an assassin.

Is there such a thing as a Swedish mafia?

The rain drums steadily against the windows, as do my nervous thoughts, a rhythmic hum filling the space as I step inside, shaking the chill from my bones.

It dawns on me—I'm in *his* home.

Soaking wet.

We're alone.

"Welcome," he says. "I'll be right back." He flashes me a charming smile before disappearing down the hallway.

His home is tidy, modern, with an open-plan kitchen and living space. In the corner, there's a study nook filled with books, various vintage cameras, and a desk with his laptop. Black and white photos match the monochromatic scheme of the home.

Alex returns moments later with a fluffy white towel and hands it to me, my clothes clinging to my skin. I wrap it around myself, self-conscious about how my damp clothes expose every curve of my body. I'm a walking wet t-shirt contest.

"Nice place," I murmur, shifting under his gaze.

"Thanks," he says, then disappears—only to come back shirtless, wearing nothing but gray sweats and a towel around his neck, holding out a fresh change of clothes like it's no big deal.

I freeze.

Time seems to stop as I take him in—his sculpted physique, broad shoulders, and defined abs impossible to ignore. He's in incredible shape and moves with an effortless confidence, completely unaware of the effect he has on me.

I gulp. Speechless.

"You can change in my room if you'd like," he suggests, like he hasn't short-circuited my brain.

My mouth goes dry, and I nod. Clutching the clothes like a lifeline, I escape before I make a fool of myself.

Inside his bedroom, my gaze drifts across his space. A sleek king-size bed with charcoal gray sheets. Minimal decor, but undeniably manly. It's exactly what I would have pictured for him.

Trying not to let my thoughts wander, I peel off my wet clothes, slipping into the warmth of the fresh set he gave me. The softest gray shirt and shorts, which feel like butter on my skin. As I towel my hair dry, something catches my eye: a dresser lined with carefully arranged personal items.

A few framed photographs.

One in particular holds my attention. A snapshot of Alex on a beach with two friends, his blond hair ruffled, his smile wide and unguarded.

It's a version of him I haven't seen yet.

Young, carefree.

I linger a moment longer before I join him in the living space. He's in the kitchen, boiling water.

"Tea?" he asks, glancing over his shoulder.

"Please," I murmur, stepping closer. "And…thanks for the clothes."

Watching him move, every flex of muscle pulls at something low in me. I long to feel his touch—the hug from yesterday, the kiss we shared earlier, the way his hands held me like he couldn't help it. My heart flutters against my ribs. Before I can stop myself, I slip behind him, arms circling his waist. I press my cheek to the heat of his bare back. His skin hums undermine. The ache quiets.

His body tenses slightly before relaxing into my touch.

I breathe him in as a deep hum vibrates through him. His large hand finds my wrist, his thumb tracing a slow, lazy circle over my skin.

"Shame about the rain," he muses.

"I figured you planned it, getting me here, wet and undressed."

His chest shakes with laughter. Then, in one swift motion, he turns and lifts me onto the counter with ease.

A surprised squeal escapes me, my hands flying to his shoulders. He steps between my legs, filling every inch of space between us, his palms resting firm against my thighs.

Our eyes lock.

His stormy gray gaze mirrors the downpour outside—wild, intense, brewing with something seductive.

A silent understanding passes between us.

His fingers brush a loose strand of hair behind my ear before he nuzzles into my neck, his breath warm against my skin.

"That's exactly right." His voice is low, rough, dripping with intent.

A sharp thrill rushes through me, heat unfurling in my stomach.

Kiss me.

Then—

The kettle sings.

Ugh. I squirm in frustration.

Alex exhales a quiet laugh, stepping back to pour the water into two mugs, the moment between us briefly severed.

There's something incredibly sexy about watching him make us tea.

Shirtless.

My eyes catch on his strong forearms, the veins along them, those large hands. I gulp, wondering how they might feel all over me. I take my time, tracing every inch of him, tucking it away for later.

"You know," he starts, glancing over at me, "I think now is the perfect time to cash in on my prize."

That again. I was hoping he'd forgotten.

"What prize?" I tease, swinging my legs lightly from the counter.

He gives me a look. That slow, wicked smile. "The one I won fair and square."

I roll my eyes. "You cheated."

He chuckles, leaning against the counter, his gaze dark with mischief. "I played to win."

I exhale, shaking my head. "Alright, fine. What do you want?"

His smirk deepens, but when he speaks, his voice turns sincere, quieter.

"I want you to sing for me."

What?

Out of all the things I expected, this wasn't one of them. It catches me completely off guard.

"Just for me," he adds, his expression unreadable.

My insides somersault.

I hesitate, fidgeting slightly. "You want me to serenade you?"

He nods. "If that's what you want to call it."

His voice is steady, but there's something else beneath it. Something that makes my breath shallow and my pulse uneven.

This is more tender than a kiss.

More exposing than touch.

I glance at him.

Alex watches me, his expression unreadable as I take a steadying breath.

Singing for an audience doesn't faze me, but this? Singing for one person—for him—feels precariously intimate.

His lips twitch as if sensing my hesitation. "Come on, let's get comfortable." He grabs our mugs of tea, nodding toward the lounge area.

I slide off the counter, following him toward the plush couch in the dimly lit living space. The rain continues its rhythmic tapping against the window.

Alex settles onto the sofa first, setting our mugs down on the coffee table, before grabbing the shirt sitting on the armrest and putting it on. He leans back, stretching one arm across the top of the cushions, his gaze lazy but attentive.

I hover for a second, nerves buzzing beneath my skin.

Then he pats the space beside him.

"Don't tell me you're shy, Älskling?" he teases.

"Älskling?"

"It's darling. In Swedish." He winks.

I blush.

The endearing nickname catches me off guard—the way it rolls off his tongue so smoothly, it melts straight through the cracks in walls I've spent years holding up.

I let out a nervous breath and settle in beside him, close enough that my thigh brushes against his.

Alex shifts slightly, turning his body toward me, waiting.

I clear my throat, pressing my palms against my knees for grounding. "I rarely do private concerts."

A smug grin tugs at his mouth. "I guess I'm special, then."

I shake my head, but a smile curls at my lips.

Closing my eyes briefly, I take a deep breath and let the melody settle before letting it spill out into the quiet space between us.

The words come softly at first, a breath above a whisper, before finding their strength.

I don't hold back.

I sing with all of it—the ache, the longing, the love I've never quite known but have always dreamed of.

The moment is weightless.

By the time I finish, the room is silent except for the faint hum of rain against the window.

I open my eyes.

Alex is staring at me.

Not just watching—he's completely lost in me.

His usual cocky smirk is gone, replaced by something almost dazed.

"Elena," he breathes, his voice hoarse, reverent.

His fingers twitch, like he wants to touch me, but isn't sure if he should.

Then he does.

A gentle brush of his fingertips against my jaw, his thumb tracing my cheek.

"That was…" He stops himself, shaking his head slightly, as if struggling for words.

Before I can respond, before I can overthink it—

He pulls me into his lap and kisses me—deep, consuming. I straddle him, arms locked around his shoulders, sinking into the heat of him.

I lean into the kiss, savoring the taste of him.

Then I feel it.

His hard bulge. Pressing against me.

A rush of panic crashes into the desire. My breath hitches. His hands slide over me, slow, certain, as if he knows exactly what he's doing to me.

Our lips part as his mouth moves lower, dragging along my chin, my throat. He licks, sucks, bites just enough to make me moan. My head tilts back. My hips grind into him, and I feel the wetness pooling.

And then—air.

My eyes flutter open.

The *want* is real. So is the fear.

Heart racing, a hit of panic tinges my emotions as I think about where this might lead, down a path completely unknown to me.

Virgin territory.

"Alex," I whisper, in between gasps. "Alex?" I'm drowning in a mixture of desire and vulnerability.

"Mmm." His lips massage kisses against my neck.

I exhale shakily, my fingers gripping the fabric of his shirt.

"There's something I need to tell you." My voice is barely above a whisper.

He leans back, his wild gaze locked on mine, silently urging me to go on. It nearly disarms me.

"I…" I hesitate, my throat tightening. "I'm a virgin."

I brace for shock, awkwardness—something.

Instead, his expression doesn't change.

No flinch. No judgment.

Then a low chuckle escapes him.

"I must confess, Elena," he deadpans, "I am not."

I let out a surprised laugh, tension snapping like a rubber band.

Alex's grin widens, his eyes bright with mirth, warmth—and something deeper.

"It's no big deal," he murmurs, brushing a loose strand of hair from my face. "We'll take things at your pace."

Relief floods me.

Then, his lips curl into that damn smirk.

"Though I should warn you." His voice drops to a low, intense growl, his hand trailing slowly down my spine. "I'm *very* good in bed."

My mind races with a million dirty thoughts, and I swat his chest.

"Alex!" The thought both excites and terrifies me as heat creeps into my cheeks. I hide my face in his neck, breathing in the scent of him.

"Elena"—he traces his fingers down my back, making me shiver—"you don't have to be ashamed. It's impressive, actually," he says softly.

"*Impressive?*"

"That a beautiful woman like you hasn't been ravished like she should. It's a crime, really. Is there something wrong with the men of Australia?" he asks, his voice filled with mock disbelief.

We both laugh, the sound cutting through the tension and easing my nerves.

And for the first time, I realize—

I don't feel afraid. I sigh, my fingers absentmindedly tracing the fabric of the borrowed shirt.

"Alex, there's something you should know about me," I say, my voice quieter now. "I don't trust easily."

I feel his gaze on me—calm and unwavering.

"I've been hurt before," I continue, exhaling softly. "For a long time, I thought it was easier to keep people at arm's length and focus on other things—school, my career—rather than get caught up in something that could hurt me,"

I don't elaborate. I don't want to ruin the moment.

Alex doesn't push, and for that, I'm grateful.

His fingers brush against the back of my hand, the warmth of his touch grounding me. "And now?"

"Now…" My lips twitch slightly, barely a smile. "I don't know. I feel like throwing caution to the wind. I'm starting to see things differently. Wanting things I've never experienced, searching for something *more*."

Alex's gaze darkens, his fingers stilling against my skin.

"And what do you want?"

I swallow, my pulse thrumming like a live wire.

"You."

The word slips out in a whisper, weighty and raw, carrying years of suppressed longing.

I've wanted him since the moment I saw him in that hospital —the connection, the pull, the danger of it all.

His breath hitches, his lips parting slightly like my confession has knocked the air right out of him.

Then a grin spreads across his face, and for a moment, he looks just like the photo in his bedroom, and I like that I made him feel that way.

For once, I don't overthink. Curiosity and desire drowning out the fear and anxiety.

"Can…I touch you?" The words spill out before I can second-guess them, bold and breathless. My fingers twitch, aching to explore his body—if he'll let me.

Alex exhales slowly.

"Anywhere you want." He nods once, voice hoarse.

I reach for the hem of his shirt and tug it over his head in one swift motion. I want to see and feel every inch of his body.

His eyes are hooded.

I lick my lips, taking in the shape of him—his chest, the lean definition of muscle and skin. My fingers skim across his torso, slow and light. Warmth radiates off him, alive under my touch. I press my palm to his chest, right over the steady thrum of his heart. I move slowly, deliberately, mapping every ridge and plane like it's mine to remember.

His eyes burn, breaths becoming heavier with every passing second.

I find his hands and guide them to my thighs, pushing them beneath the fabric of my loose shorts. His fingers meet my skin, and his grip tightens.

Slowly, I pull his hands back out and slip them under my shirt.

Alex's eyes widen.

The moment his fingers touch my stomach, his body tenses. Between my thighs, his bulge throbs against me.

His hungry gaze flickers to mine, realization dawning when he feels my breasts. No barriers. It pulses again, radiating heat through me, my body throbbing in response. I grind myself against him. Desperate to soothe that ache.

A deep, guttural sound rumbles from him before his teeth sink into his bottom lip, his restraint hanging by a thread.

"Elena," he murmurs, voice thick with need.

Alex leans in, his nose brushing along the column of my neck. Breathing me in, his warm breath sends tingles down my spine. His hands cup my breast, his fingers kneading softly, testing my reaction.

A gasp escapes my throat, my back arching slightly as he brushes his thumbs over my nipples. A dark chuckle vibrates against my throat.

"So sensitive." His voice is soft, barely a whisper.

Then Alex's lips are on mine, swallowing my moan in a kiss that's deep, slow, and utterly consuming.

His tongue sliding against mine, savoring every second.

I barely notice when he shifts, pressing me against his perfect body. The heat of him. The solidity. The sheer intensity of the moment.

When he pulls away, I'm breathless, and my world tilts off its axis.

Alex's thumb drags along my lower lip, his gaze never leaving mine.

"Can I touch you? I want to watch you come for me."

The words pulse between us, spoken with quiet, devastating confidence.

I've never had an orgasm with someone else before, and a wave of anticipation and nervous excitement crashes over me.

I nod, shyly at first, but there's no hesitation. I want this. I want to know what it feels like with someone else.

With him.

Alex exhales sharply, his restraint snapping like a frayed wire.

He grabs me by the waist, shifting me easily off his lap and laying me down beneath him.

The weight of him is new, comforting.

Alex traces his lips over my skin, leaving a trail of fire in their wake.

I barely have time to catch my breath before he positions himself beside me, his leg grappling mine, holding me open, his hand gliding lower—his touch as measured as it is unrelenting.

Alex moves with an unbearable confidence, like he has all the time in the world to unravel me piece by piece.

I suck in a breath as his fingers skim the elastic waistband of my shorts, the bare skin of my hip, teasing, exploring, learning me.

"You're trembling."

Alex's lips ghost over my jaw, his voice laced with something dark—almost reverent.

I hadn't even realized.

"It's not—I mean, I'm not scared," I manage to whisper, swallowing past the lump in my throat.

I feel his slow, satisfied grin against my neck. "No," he says, his hand slipping between my thighs, fingers tracing the edge of something forbidden. "You're not scared at all."

I shake my head, breath ragged, body wired tight.

His lips graze my pulse point. "Tell me if you want me to stop."

I exhale shakily, gripping his bicep. "No, please, I want it," I beg, hungry for him, starved for years. "*Touch me.*"

His breath catches for a second. Then, without another word, his hand brushes my panties to the side as he slides lower, pressing against me.

A sharp, helpless gasp escapes my lips as his fingers spread me.

Oh.

My body reacts instantly, heat pooling, nerves short-circuiting, as he strokes my clit with slow, devastating precision.

Alex's mouth curves against my skin. "So wet." His voice is pure sin, his fingers exploring, testing. "Is that all for me, Darling?"

"Yes," I pant.

"Good girl," he growls.

My entire body betrays me—hips jerking as his fingers circle right where I need him most.

I let out a soft whimper, my fingers clawing at his bicep. "Alex—"

He hums in satisfaction, his teeth scraping lightly along my throat, nipping just enough to make me shudder.

"Relax," he murmurs, his free hand slides beneath my shirt, lifting it and placing his lips on my bare nipple.

My back arches, the sensation threatening to overwhelm every fiber of my being.

His fingers glide with maddening precision, stoking the heat building inside me. Each pass is a spark, a wave—jolting me back to life.

Alex's mouth finds my breasts, his tongue tracing my nipples, lips worshipping them into stiff peaks.

A new kind of pressure builds, something foreign, something I can't quite chase on my own.

I squirm, my breathing fractured and uneven.

Alex knows.

He can feel it.

"Give it to me," he whispers against my skin—his voice low, coaxing, drenched in dark promise.

His fingers press a little deeper, moving in perfect rhythm, tuned into my every reaction, every shaky breath, every desperate whimper.

I feel like I'm going to break apart.

My body is winding tighter, hotter, sharper, something tantalizingly close, but just out of reach.

Alex senses it immediately, his pace shifting slightly—his fingers relentless and determined, mouth devouring my breasts with greedy focus.

"Elena," he groans, almost like he's the one unravelling.

And then—

The pressure snaps.

A shattered, breathless cry spills from my lips as pleasure slams into me, hot and all-consuming, spreading through me like wildfire.

My back arches, fingers digging into his shoulders, waves of pure ecstasy crashing over me as he coaxes me through every last tremor and aftershock of my orgasm.

It takes a moment for my breathing to slow, my body still pulsing from the intensity of it all. Alex pulls away, his breath just as ragged.

I look up at him through my lashes, dazed, lips parted, chest rising and falling in uneven breaths.

His eyes are dark and hungry, watching me like he witnessed something holy.

His thumb drags lazily across my thigh.

"Fuck, that was…" I pant, my tongue unable to find the words.

A slow, satisfied grin tugs at his lips.

"You're incredible," he murmurs, pressing a lingering kiss to my shoulder, his voice still thick with need. "And so, so beautiful."

My skin burns under his touch, but before I can say anything, he leans in, kissing me deeply, stealing whatever breath I might have had left.

Alex pulls away, withdrawing his fingers from my pussy and slipping them into his mouth.

My eyes widen, and my heart almost goes into cardiac arrest.

Did he…after a mind-altering orgasm—he does *that?*

"You taste so fucking sweet," he groans, licking his lips.

My lungs seize with want. Luckily, my mind manages to recover.

"You can't have dessert before dinner," I tease, surprising myself.

He smirks, laying his head on my chest as we watch the rain outside.

I don't know where this night will end, but for the first time…

I don't care.

Chapter 10

Your Song

New York in early July is brutal. The sun stings my skin, the concrete simmers underfoot, and Riley has dragged me to the fourth apartment of the day, sweat beading on both our brows. She initially moved into a cramped studio in Queens, sharing the space with two other women, both aspiring models. But now that she'd landed a job at an art gallery, she'd finally had enough of living with two skinny bitches who were way too in love with nose candy—and had definitely stolen her Doc Martens.

Not that I blamed her. Between their manic energy and shared sleeping arrangements, I didn't know how Riley lasted as long as she did. And considering the way her patience had worn razor-thin by the second apartment viewing today, I doubted she'd survive another night. I glanced at her sideways, noting the tightness around her eyes and the relentless tapping of her fingernails against her thigh.

God, please let this place not suck.

"So, what does the ad say for this place?" I ask, falling into step beside Riley as we head toward the next apartment.

"Two-bedroom, some tech guy, but at least I'll have my own room." She shrugs, tucking the tattered newspaper under her arm.

"I wish you'd let me help you, babe."

I've had a sizeable trust fund sitting untouched since my twenty-first birthday, something I always resisted using. The prize money from winning *Starstruck* and royalties from my first album —modest but enough—meant I never had to. With me staying with Philippa and my father gifting me an apartment, offering Riley support feels only right. She'd been there when I needed someone most. The least I can do is return her kindness and loyalty.

"Elena, I can't do that, you know I can't," Riley chides, her lips pressing into a thin, stubborn line.

"Why not? It's just money. Might as well go to someone I love—someone who needs it," I insist, nudging her shoulder gently.

She smirks, side-eyeing me playfully. "Okay, rich bitch, you gonna be my sugar mama now?"

"Yes, absolutely. Especially if it means you can stay in New York without working three jobs just to stay afloat."

"I did think stripping might be a lucrative gig to get into." She cackles, tossing her hair back like she's already picturing herself under neon lights.

"Or maybe high-end escorts," I tease, nudging her elbow. "You'd be raking it in quick with your special talents."

"I'll be fine, babe. The job's good enough—stable, at least. My boss might be uptight, but the money's decent. And if I find the right roommate, I can swing a small art studio space to rent."

"Can I buy, like, a thousand lap dances to cover your rent?" I grin.

"Tempting. I mean, for you, I'd do it for free, but it wouldn't be right," she says flatly, though her eyes flicker with amusement.

"Ugh, fine, but the offer stands, okay?" I shrug, dropping the bravado.

"I appreciate that. Really." She sighs.

We fall into step again, the sidewalk buzz picking up around us as the city rushes by in all its usual chaos.

"So, how's the painting going? Does New York inspire?" I ask, glancing over.

"I haven't had much of a chance lately. Not enough room in Polly Pocket's Dream House." She shrugs. Her tone's light, but I can see the tightness in her jaw, the way she presses her lips together. She's trying to make it sound like a joke, but it's not. Her creativity is suffocating in a too-small apartment she doesn't love.

"I feel terrible," I blurt out.

"Why?"

"Because New York was *my* dream. The music thing. And I feel like I dragged you into this—and now you're miserable."

"Babe," she says, pausing long enough to make sure I hear her. "I'm not miserable. And New York was *our* dream. You and me taking over the city. Making it our bitch. Like Carrie and Samantha."

"You're clearly Samantha."

"Yeah, obviously. You already found your Mr. Big," Riley says with a smirk.

"Oh my God." I gasp. "Do you think Alex is *my* Big?"

She shrugs. "I mean…he could be."

"That whole situation was fucked though," I mutter. "So I hope not. Give me an Aiden, any day."

"He makes furniture *and* he's hot—yes, please." She laughs, but it doesn't quite reach all the way. I can tell she's stressed. It's in her shoulders, in the way she's holding herself tighter than usual.

"Okay, if you won't let me help you financially," I coax, looping my arm through hers, "at least let me shout you lunch."

"That I can do." She nods.

We approach a large red-brick complex on the corner, its windows glinting in the sunlight. Riley glances at the scrap of newspaper again.

"I think this is it."

She buzzes the apartment number and we wait, shifting restlessly on our feet. The heat slicks on our skin. I pat the sweat off my brow, and Riley fans herself with the newspaper.

"Come up," a voice crackles through the speaker.

We climb three flights of stairs and buzz again at the door marked '3B.' It swings open, revealing a lanky guy wearing thick glasses, his greasy hair hanging limp around his face, with a ferret perched comfortably on his shoulder.

"Hi, I'm Ben. You must be Riley. Come on in," he mutters, his eyes darting everywhere but directly at us. He pauses awkwardly, scratching his head. "I thought you were a guy."

The apartment is tidy enough, but the smell—it hits me instantly, sharp and unmistakable. Ferrets. Interesting. The furry creature scuttles from Ben's shoulder, bouncing off the couch onto a pile of scattered toys in the living room.

"Sorry to disappoint," Riley murmurs, her voice tight, the corners of her mouth dropping as her nose wrinkles slightly. She smells it too—the pungent scent of an animal with absolute free rein over the place.

Ben ushers us inside, guiding us toward a tiny, empty room barely large enough to fit a queen bed. Riley nods politely, though I catch the subtle flicker of doubt in her eyes.

"Are you okay living with a girl?" Riley asks cautiously.

"As long as you're good living with Dax and Kira," Ben replies, entirely serious.

Riley and I exchange confused glances.

Who the fuck are Dax and Kira?

Suddenly, a second ferret bounds up Ben's arm, nestling affectionately against his neck. "Isn't that right, Miss Kira?" he coos, gently petting the small creature.

Realization washes over Riley's face. "Yeah…they seem *awesome*," she replies uncertainly.

"They are," Ben agrees, kissing Kira lightly on the head.

This is getting weirder by the second.

"So, how soon can I move in?" Riley asks abruptly.

Riley, no! I silently plead. But it's too late—she's already talking logistics with Ben, who looks completely indifferent to the entire conversation.

We say our goodbyes and quickly make our escape. My nostrils thank me the moment we hit fresh air.

We head back into Manhattan for lunch and some well-earned drinks.

"So, you're really going to move in with Ben and his ladies?" I ask, sipping my iced tea and trying not to laugh.

Riley takes a sip of her pink lemonade. "My own room is a luxury I can't pass up."

I scoff. "But the smell—"

"I'll learn to live with it." She shrugs. "Maybe get some delicious candles. He seems harmless enough."

She takes another sip, then shifts her gaze to me, eyes sparkling with curiosity. "Oh, speaking of things that smell…delicious, how did it go with Alex?"

Heat floods my cheeks instantly, betraying me.

"That good, huh?" she pushes, a slow, knowing grin spreading across her lips.

"He's just…he's *so* hot." I sigh, unable to keep the stupid smile off my face. "Tall, sexy, and intense. I don't know, Riley. He's nothing like the boys back home. He feels like a man."

"At thirty-six, he better be," she teases, nudging me gently.

I hesitate, biting my lip. "I told him I'm a virgin."

Her eyebrows shoot up. "And? How'd he take it?"

"He was…remarkably cool about it." I shrug, warmth rising again as I recall exactly how *cool* he'd been—and exactly how he'd made me come apart beneath him.

Riley narrows her eyes suspiciously, leaning in close. "Okay, what aren't you telling me?"

"Nothing." I giggle, ducking her stare. "Eat your damn sushi."

"Did he eat *your* sushi?" she asks.

"Oh my God, Riley—no!"

You taste so fucking sweet.

His voice echoes in my ears, low and sinful. I hide my face in my hands, my cheeks burning brighter.

"Look at you." Riley laughs, delighted. "I've never seen you so giddy over someone before."

"I know," I admit softly, lowering my hands. "He just… unravels me."

"Good." She winks, lifting her drink to me. "You could use some unraveling."

We finish up our drinks, the afternoon sun dipping lower as we settle the bill and leave the restaurant. Riley loops her arm through mine, still teasing mercilessly about Alex as we head back to Philippa's penthouse.

I'm still smiling like a fool as we reach the front entrance, when Isaac, the friendly older doorman, steps forward to meet us.

"Miss Montgomery," he says warmly, tipping his hat. "Some flowers arrived for you this afternoon. I had them sent up."

Riley's eyes widen, her lips curling into a mischievous grin. "Flowers, huh? Someone's pulling out all the stops."

My heart dances.

I'd never received flowers before.

"Thank you, Isaac," I add, quickly dragging Riley toward the elevator before she can pry any further. But I can already feel her eyes on me, sharp and curious, as we step inside the elevator, anticipation swirling through me like champagne bubbles.

As soon as we step into the apartment, the scent of them hits me like a freight train.

There they are, in all their marvelous glory—rich, velvety red roses, arranged artfully in a glass vase.

They sit proudly atop Philippa's pristine kitchen island, their bold crimson striking sharply against the tasteful creams and muted neutrals of her carefully decorated home.

"Oh, babe," Riley gushes, bounding toward the extravagant display. She snatches up the small, cream-colored card, fanning herself dramatically before handing it over to me with a flourish. "Someone's smitten."

My pulse flutters like hummingbird wings, nerves tumbling wildly as I reach out, fingers grazing the heavy cardstock. My eyes catch on the embossed letters: *A.W.*

Hmm. Probably the florist?

Curiosity burning, I open the card, revealing the short, elegant handwriting inside:

"Älskling, you are beguiling. Thank you for the private concert. See you again? Yours, Alex."

Every inch of my skin tingling as I reread his words. A rush of giddiness dances its way through me.

"What does it say?" Riley demands eagerly, bouncing impatiently at my side.

I hesitate, biting my lip, my voice barely above a whisper. I read it.

Riley's scream pierces the quiet of Philippa's penthouse, her delight echoing off the high ceilings as she shakes my shoulders, practically dancing around me.

My heart pounds wildly, overwhelmed by Alex's words and Riley's exuberance, both hitting me like a wave.

"Call him!" Riley demands with urgency. "Say yes!"

"Riley, he's in San Diego," I say with a shrug, trying to play it off.

"Weird. You're headed there too, right?" she asks, raising a brow.

"Yeah. Coincidence, for sure. But…yeah, he said we should meet up," I admit, fiddling with the edge of the card.

"Then call him, text him, make it happen—the ball's clearly in your court," she says, matter-of-fact.

"I don't know…" I mumble.

"You like him, right?" Riley presses, eyes on me.

"Yeah," I admit, the word slipping out quieter than I expected.

Until Alex, boys had come and gone like unfinished songs— light verses, no chorus, barely leaving a mark. But he crashed into my life like the sudden beat drop in a song. Inevitable, bursting with quiet anticipation before rising into a crescendo.

Riley watches me for a beat longer, reading the shift in my face, then she softens. "Okay. I'll give you some privacy. I've got to pack anyway. Call your hunk-a-spunk." She grins, pulling me into a warm hug before stealing one last dramatic inhale of the roses, the scent now wrapping itself around me like a spell.

"Love you," I call after her.

"Love you most," she calls back, already halfway down the hall—and then she's gone.

I can't call him. Not yet. Not while my fingers itch to capture this ache, this dizzy, spinning feeling still blooming in my chest.

It's all for him—every beat, every line already humming in my blood.

I slip into my room, barely breathing, grabbing my notepad

and guitar from where they wait near the window. I drop to the floor, legs crossed, the weight of the roses still lingering in the air like perfume.

The words spill before I can stop them. The melody follows, simple and slow at first, then rising, lifting like the breath after a kiss.

'Cause it's your touch, your hands, your name in my mouth.
First time I let someone in, didn't shut them out.'
Lost in the melody, my mind drifts.

"So, did you tell Logan that you like him?" my mother asked, her face full of hope, voice light, like we were talking about shoes, not boys.

"I don't know, Mom." I sighed, watching her as she chopped vegetables with rhythmic precision. "I feel like guys only want one thing. They call me frigid...and the girls, they make fun of me for being quiet."

She didn't pause in her slicing, just gave a small hum of disapproval. "I'm glad you're being cautious and not letting boys use you. But don't shut people out, Anak. Give them a chance to know you. You might be surprised."

"Jason invited me to the movies and basically asked me to suck his—" I cut myself off, lowering my voice, "—you know what before the movie even started."

She gasped, knife pausing mid-air, looking like

she was ready to castrate him. "That boy is a pig. Next time, slap him in the balls."

"Sure you don't want to cut them off?" I said.

She barked out a laugh, and I joined in, a high, warm sound that filled the kitchen.

"That's exactly what I mean! Is it so bad to want the kind of person the singers write about in songs? The one who makes your heartbeat fast like it might burst?"

She smiled at that, slicing the last of the carrots. "My special girl, that's a lot to ask of one date."

"Hey, it worked for Romeo." I shrugged.

"Yeah, and then they died," she deadpanned.

We giggled like schoolgirls.

There was a pause, soft and fleeting, like the moment before a sigh.

"I'm probably not the best person to take advice from, I suppose. Look how your father and I ended up."

"Yeah, but he cheated on you," I said, rolling my eyes.

She turned back to the stove, her shoulders squared, the back of her neck rigid. She shrugged—casual, light—but I caught it. That flicker of regret. The quiet collapse behind her ribs. Pride, cracked years ago. She hid it well, but when she spoke about him, it was always there. Like a scar she could never scrub clean.

———— ··· ————

THE MEMORIES of my mother crack open something deep in me. Her voice echoes faintly—full of wisdom and comfort, flooding back in waves that leave me hollow and full all at once.

I wish she were here. I need her advice, her calm certainty.

Because the truth is, I'm scared. Scared of jumping into something with Alex, scared of what it would mean if I let myself fall too fast. But the feeling of being wanted by someone like him—someone so confident, so magnetic—is intoxicating. It wraps around the oldest part of me, the wound I've carried since childhood, the one that whispers that I wasn't enough. He quiets that voice.

Making me feel like maybe I am enough.

Now I have written two songs about him. He is the first person I've ever written about before I even knew it.

I used to write about what it would be like to find love, to want love, to need love, without ever having experienced it. I locked myself away to protect myself, too scared to get hurt, too scared to try.

Now, this unshakable feeling is consuming me. He's the one who sparks a lyric before I even hear the chord. He is the drop, the pulse, the melody my heart has been searching for.

My phone sits beside me. I reach for it, thumb hovering over his name.

Alex.

I send him a message—simple, easy, something that won't give too much away.

ELENA

They're beautiful. Thank you.

I hit send before I can second-guess it.

I don't even notice I'm humming the song.

His song. The one I couldn't get out of my head.

My phone buzzes almost instantly. I hit answer.

"Hello." His voice hums through the line, smooth and amused. "You got my surprise."

"I did." I smile, curling into the throw blanket wrapped around my legs. "They're wonderful. Thank you again."

He chuckles, low and pleased, like he already knows the effect he has on me and enjoys it.

"How was the flight?" I ask, trying to sound casual, like I haven't been waiting for this call all day.

"Not too bad. A little turbulence over Colorado, but nothing I couldn't handle." He pauses. "When do you fly out?"

"End of the week. Will you still be there?"

"Yes," he says easily. "So…do you have an answer for me?"

My fingers tighten around the phone. My heartbeat stutters. "About what?" I tease, stretching it out, even though I already know exactly what he means.

"A second date."

My lips curve before I can stop them. "Okay."

Silence. But I hear it—that quiet breath, the subtle shift of someone smiling to himself. That smug little sound he makes when things go his way.

"Good." His voice dips slightly. "Maybe we can meet up while you're here."

"Okay," I murmur, already picturing it. Sunlight. Heat. His hands. All of it.

"Do you know where you're staying?"

148

"I'll text you the details," I add, shifting onto my side, the phone warm against my cheek.

"I can't wait. Do you like animals?"

"Yeah," I grin. "So long as it's not ferrets."

He laughs, and it spills through the speaker like warm honey.

I close my eyes and let it wash over me. God, I'm in trouble.

A grin tugs at my lips as I bite down gently, my chest aching in that warm, dizzying way I thought I'd forgotten.

And just like that, I'm already counting the days until I can see him again.

Chapter 11

Rather Be

After days holed up in the studio, recording the songs I had written about Alex as last-minute additions to the album, the day had finally arrived. Philippa said she'd meet me after work, and I'd already sent Riley a quick text to come over.

I can hardly wait. Although hesitant at first to accept the apartment from my father, as the weeks went on, the need for my own space won out. Living with Philippa and Andrew was fine, but stifling.

Eventually, the idea of freedom—of distance—made the unwanted gift easier to swallow.

Now, excitement hums low and restless beneath my skin. After such an electric session, sitting still feels impossible.

When the key turns in the lock, a thrill sparks sharp and sweet through me.

My apartment.

Stepping inside, I kick off my shoes and take in the perfection of it all. Philippa has outdone herself. Every piece of furniture has been selected with a level of taste I wasn't sure I deserved, but damn, do I love it.

The apartment is a beautiful blend of minimal vintage eclectic —modern simplicity with old-world charm. The living room has a warm, neutral palette, with a velvet sofa in forest green, my favorite color. Vintage brass floor lamps cast a soft glow, and a mid-century coffee table with delicate carvings sits in the center. A large, built-in bookshelf stretches across one wall, already stocked with some of my favorite novels and a few I know Philippa picked out. The bookshelf from the vintage store where I met Alex makes me smile.

I trail my fingers over the velvet cushions, marveling at how it all feels so...*me.*

The open-plan kitchen is sleek but has touches of character— marble countertops, antique gold fixtures, and open wooden shelving lined with ceramics and delicate glassware. My father has clearly spared no expense. That thought alone both annoys and warms something in me. For all his faults, this was his way of showing he cares.

I move down the hall, peeking into the second bedroom—now a cozy music room, complete with an upright piano, a record player, and an impressive vinyl collection. My guitar rests on a stand beside the window, its polished wood gleaming in the golden light. The third bedroom, a spacious spare room, is deco- rated simply at the moment, but a thought comes to mind.

Stepping into my bedroom, my jaw drops. The centerpiece is an ornate, four-poster bed with billowing linen drapes, a perfect contrast to the minimalist nightstands and the soft, neutral-toned bedding. The walls hold framed artwork—some classic, some modern, all carefully chosen. A reading nook sits by the window, complete with a tufted armchair and a side table stacked with books.

It's beautiful. Thoughtful. A mix of Philippa's impeccable style and my father's resources, but somehow, it still feels like mine.

This is it. My first home.

I drop my bag onto the kitchen island and pull out my phone to text my father, who is in Chicago for work.

Got the keys. Moved in. Thank you.

It feels too formal, too short. I sigh and delete it. Then try again.

ELENA

> Hey, just got into the apartment. It's amazing. Thank you for this—really. Hope your trip is going well.

That's better. I hit send, turning my attention to the champagne chilling in the fridge, courtesy of Philippa.

As if on cue, the front door bursts open.

"Let's get this party started!" Riley sings, twirling in with a bottle of tequila raised above her head.

"There goes the neighborhood," I laugh.

Philippa follows, much more composed, but holding a small bag from the trendy new Filipino bakery nearby.

"I assume you haven't eaten," she says, setting it down.

"Not since breakfast," I admit, popping the cork off the champagne.

Three glasses clink together.

"To new beginnings," Philippa toasts. "And no longer crashing at my place."

"To independence!" Riley adds, taking a big gulp.

"To...*everything*," I smile as the bubbles tingle against my lips.

I turn to Philippa, feeling a swell of emotion rise in my chest.

"Pip," I utter, and she raises an eyebrow at the unexpected sentimentality in my tone.

"Thank you. For all of this." I gesture around the apartment. "For making me feel welcome here in New York, for looking out for me when I probably didn't deserve it, and for putting so much effort into making this place perfect."

Philippa's expression softens, and for a moment, I see the warmth beneath her usually polished exterior.

"You're my sister, Elena. Of course, I was going to make sure you had everything you needed." She smirks. "And besides, you deserve your own space. Plus, a fully stocked fridge—I've seen you take down an entire charcuterie board solo. Can't let you get hangry."

I laugh, shaking my head, but the lump in my throat remains. "Still, it means a lot. More than I can probably explain."

Philippa smiles, squeezing my hand briefly before letting go. "Then that's all that matters."

"Aww, you guys," Riley sings, watching the exchange between us. "I love this." She gestures between the two of us.

We all laugh.

"Group hug!" Riley bellows, pulling my sister and me into an embrace.

One drink turns into two. Then three. Then, a very questionable shot of tequila that Riley convinces us to take.

Philippa, ever the responsible one, cuts herself off early.

"I should go before you two get messy," she announces, swiping her purse off the armchair. "Elena, try not to let her burn the place down. I'll see you tomorrow," she adds, reminding me of the brunch we have scheduled.

"No promises," Riley says with a grin as Philippa rolls her eyes and makes her exit.

The second she's gone, Riley turns to me, her eyes sparkling with mischief.

"Now, how many drinks will it take to get you to spill about your first date with Alex?"

I feign innocence.

"A lady never tells."

"You? A lady?" she exclaims. "Come on, I've been dying to know, and you held out on me the other day! So don't skimp on the juicy details."

My face goes warm all at once, but I can't stop the smile that takes over my face.

"Fine…It was…" I sigh, searching for the right words. "Insanely good. He planned this epic day: coffee, laser tag, food trucks, and, um…" My voice trails off, remembering the mind-blowing orgasm he gave me, blushing at the thought.

Riley gasps, cutting me off.

"Wait. Did you—?" She wiggles her eyebrows suggestively.

A nervous laugh spills out of me, and I shake my head.

"No, not *that*. But let's just say, um…I didn't leave unsatisfied."

Riley screeches, grabbing my arm.

"Elena Montgomery! Are you telling me you had your first non-solo orgasm?"

I bury my face in my hands, but the laughter bubbling out of me gives me away.

"Maybe."

She flops back against the couch dramatically.

"This is a monumental occasion. My best friend finally had a 'real' orgasm with an insanely hot Swedish hunk? I could cry."

I snort.

"Please don't."

"This calls for another shot." She grabs the tequila, pouring two more.

"To Alex, orgasm-giver, and for finally rocking your world. Cheers!"

We clink our glasses and down the shots, both of us dissolving into a fit of giggles.

As the laughter dies down, I sigh. There is still so much I want to know about Alex. I'm greedy for any little bit he'll give me. A part of me is also wary because it feels as though he's holding back in some ways.

Riley notices and tilts her head at me. "So, what's the catch?"

I hesitate.

"He's great, really open about his family and himself, yet— he's super evasive about his job."

Riley waves a dismissive hand.

"Maybe he's trying to be mysterious. You're probably over-thinking it. I wouldn't worry too much."

"Maybe," I admit, though the nagging feeling remains.

"We'll see."

"Well, when do you see him next?"

I chew my lip, thinking.

"We're both in San Diego next week for work. So I think he wants to take me to the zoo for our second date."

"Perfect. That means more orgasms," she teases, sinking deeper into the sofa.

"I hope."

Riley grins.

"Oh, I almost forgot, I'm seeing Logan. He's starring in my music video," I add, starting to feel the effects of the alcohol.

"Logan? Cousin Logan?" she slurs, confused.

"Yeah, he'll be at Geek-Fest. Mark got me tickets."

"GEEK-FEST! I'm coming!" she screams.

"Don't you have work?"

"I'll say I'm scoping out an artist, visiting galleries. Or I'll quit and come anyway," she rambles tipsily.

Our celebrations carry well into the night. Riley's blitzing margaritas in the kitchen, head thrown back, singing off-key to whatever playlist she's hijacked. The blender whirs violently, drowning her out, but I don't care.

Watching her dance barefoot through my shiny, way-too-perfect kitchen—carefree, wild—makes something in my shoulders loosen.

It feels…right.

Like maybe this place could be ours. The beginning of the dream we once dared to hope for.

Our New York.

The blender groans to a stop. Riley glances at me, one brow lifting as she reads me like a damn book.

"You okay?" she asks, still holding the lid, like she's ready to launch into full therapy mode if I so much as blink too long.

"Yeah." I smile, cheeks warm—partly from the tequila, partly from the idea forming in my head. Solidifying faster than the frozen margaritas she's about to pour.

She doesn't move. Watches me closely now, lips twitching like she already knows.

"Elena," she says slowly, tilting her head. "You're looking at me like you want to make out with me or something."

I let out a breath, laughing into it. "I know I complain about all of this," I start, words bubbling up before I can stop them.

She snorts. "You? Complain? Never."

I roll my eyes.

"Seriously, babe." My throat tightens. "I wouldn't have gotten through any of it—the shit with my family, with my mom—without you. I don't think you realize how much I need you."

Her face softens. For a second, I think she's going to crack a joke. But she doesn't.

"Of course I know," she admits gently. "But you don't have to say that."

"I *want* to say it." My heart's pounding—too fast, too loud, like it already knows what I'm about to do. "And I want to ask you something."

She raises an eyebrow, as she tries to read me. "Okay…are we getting married? Because the answer is yes."

I scoff, shaking my head. God, she makes it easier to breathe.

I push off the counter and step closer.

"Move in with me."

The words land between us, heavier than I expect.

Riley's eyes widen. Her mouth parting slightly. "Wait… *what?*"

"Move in. Here. With me."

She glances around the apartment, brows furrowed. "Elena, you can't be serious. I can't afford this place. I mean—look at it. This is like, millionaire level shit. You'd be subsidizing my whole life."

I shrug, trying to act like my heart isn't about to break free from my chest. "So? I'm not asking for your rent, Riley. I'm asking for *you.* To be here. You need a place, right? That apartment in Queens fell through again. I don't want you living with weird roommates and someone's emotional support lizard."

She huffs out a laugh, shaking her head, but there's something glassy in her eyes. "They were ferrets, actually. And unfortunately, they did unionize. They weren't keen on sharing the space with another lady."

"Even worse."

She holds my gaze for a long moment. The humor fades. She realizes I'm serious.

"Babe…" she says softly. "I don't want to take advantage of you."

I reach for the blender before she can finish pouring, grabbing it gently from her hands, and start filling the glasses she set out.

"You wouldn't be." My voice comes out quieter now, but steady. "You've been my rock, Riley." My heart swells. "You're the one person who's been through everything with me. You're more than just my best friend—you're my beloved, my *family.* I don't want to do this alone. I *can't* do this alone."

Her face crumples just a little—that look she gets when she's fighting back tears.

"You'd really want me here? Like…every day?" she whispers, like she doesn't quite trust the words. "I mean, I sing in the shower. *Badly.*"

I smile, something in me lifting as I watch the resolve fade from her face.

"You think I don't already know that? Please."

She laughs, wiping quickly at her eyes, and I nudge her shoulder.

"Please say yes." I look at her, willing her to see how much this means to me. "It'll make this feel less like…a gilded cage my father threw me into."

Riley lets out a long breath and leans back against the counter, staring down at the margaritas like they might have the answer.

"Okay," she says finally, nodding. "Yeah. Let's do it. Roomies."

Relief hits so hard, I feel dizzy, though it's also likely from the booze.

"Roomies," I breathe, grinning like an idiot as I lift my glass in a toast.

Riley raises hers, her smile wide now, eyes shining.

"To margaritas and questionable life choices," she announces, voice thick but teasing.

I clink my glass against hers. "To making this place feel like home."

She gasps—and then, without warning, pulls me into one of those crushing hugs that squeeze the air right out of my lungs.

"I love you, babe," she whispers into my hair.

"I love you most."

And for the first time since my father handed me those keys, I feel something I haven't let myself hope for.

Home.

Later that night, I flop onto my bed, the fabric cool against my skin, my head pleasantly spinning. My limbs buzz with warmth. I let out a breath, stare up at the ceiling, then roll onto my side, already reaching for my phone. I don't even think—I tap his name.

It rings. My heart aches with want.

"This is a pleasant surprise." Alex's voice slides through the line, low and amused, rough with sleep.

My lips curve without meaning to. "That's me, full of surprises," I murmur, curling my fingers into the sheets. "Did I wake you?"

There's a pause, then a soft, lazy chuckle. "No. But I wouldn't have minded if you did."

I exhale slowly, letting the sound of his voice wrap around me. "I was thinking about you."

"Oh?" His tone dips, silk laced with heat. "And what exactly were you thinking about?"

I hesitate, only to drag it out. I want to hear the shift in his breath when I say it.

"About how good your hands felt on me."

A sharp inhale cracks through the line. That sound—tight, caught—hits me right between the ribs.

"Elena…" He says it like a warning. Or maybe a plea.

I wriggle under the covers, my skin too hot. My fingers trail over my ribs.

"I can still feel you," I whisper. "The way you touched me. The way you pressed your hand right—"

I feign a moan before biting my lip to stifle a giggle.

"Tell me," he cuts in, rougher now. "What are you doing right now?"

I shift. "Lying in bed."

"Are you wearing anything?" His voice drops, low and menacing.

"A tank top…No panties."

He makes a sound—half curse, half groan. "You're making this distance hard, aren't you?"

I smile, my heart thudding against my ribs. "Do I make *you* hard, Alex?"

"Yes." His voice is tense, like he's saying it through gritted teeth.

"What would you do to me?" I tease, my voice sweet.

"What do you think I'd do?"

"I think you'd take your time." I press my thighs together. "I think you'd make me beg for it."

Another groan, longer this time. "Do you want me to make you beg for it?"

"Yes," I whisper.

"And what do you want?" His voice is low and breathy. I hear him shift, and wonder if he's touching himself. The thought makes me ache.

My hand slips lower. My breath catches as my finger brushes along my entrance.

"I want your mouth." I gasp as my finger grazes over my clit. "I want to feel you everywhere. I want you to ruin me."

"Jesus Christ," he mutters. His voice shifts—darker now, hungrier. "Touch yourself, Darling. Imagine it's me."

"I already am." I press harder, spreading my wetness in slow, gentle strokes.

"Fuck, Elena," he groans. "That virgin pussy will feel so tight around my cock."

I nearly come from just his words, his breath ragged as we pleasure ourselves—matching each other, word for word, moan for moan—until the night blurs, the room spins, and we finally let go.

Sleep finds me with his name still on my lips.

THE ROOM IS TOO BRIGHT—BLINDINGLY so. My head pounds like a relentless drumbeat, every throb a cruel reminder of last night's indulgence. My mouth is dry, my limbs heavy.

Where am I?

Oh. *My* apartment.

I groan, throwing an arm over my eyes, but the damage is already done. Sunlight streams through the half-drawn curtains, stabbing at my retinas without mercy.

My body aches—not from exertion, but from the telltale signs of too many drinks.

What time is it?

I squint at my phone, lifting it with sluggish fingers.

Nine thirty a.m.

"Fuck." My voice is hoarse, raspy, like I slept with my mouth wide open all night.

Brunch is at ten thirty.

Which means I have exactly thirty minutes to go from *this* to something passably presentable, and be back at Philippa's.

Panic jolts through me like a shot of espresso. The thought of coffee makes me ache. I *need* it bad.

I throw off the covers and instantly regret it. The room spins.

Too fast.

I suck in a breath. One foot on the floor. Then the other. *Okay. I can do this.*

Catching a glimpse of myself in the mirror confirms my worst fear: I look like hell. Champagne, two bottles of tequila, and an entire pitcher of frozen margaritas swirl in my stomach like a warning.

Thanks, Riley.

Great. Just great.

My insides lurch. Focus. *Don't throw up.* You don't have time.

I stagger to the bathroom, twist the faucet, and splash cold water on my face. It helps—barely. Another glance in the mirror. My hair's a wreck, last night's mascara is smudged halfway down my cheek, and one camisole strap is clinging to my shoulder for dear life.

There's no time to dwell. I need a miracle.

I take the fastest shower of my life—washed and dried in under five minutes—and march straight into the closet and start rifling through hangers like a woman on the brink.

My fingers land on a white T-shirt. I yank it on and pair it with my favorite jeans—the ones that hug just right and give me the illusion of longer legs.

Shoes: sneakers. No contest. Especially if we're running wedding errands.

Accessories? No time to overthink it. Gold chain necklace. Stack it. A few rings. Tiny gold hoops. Just enough to fake effort.

I sling my crossbody bag over my shoulder and take a breath.

Hair: *disaster*. I spritz in some texturizing spray, rake my fingers through it, and let it fall into some kind of beachy chaos.

Good enough.

Tinted moisturizer. Bronzer. Mascara. A swipe of berry balm. Done.

I check my phone. Nine fifty-five a.m.

Shit.

Chapter 12

I Like Me Better

The harsh lobby lights in Philippa and Andrew's building have me questioning every life choice that led to this moment.

Head pounding.

Hungover.

Hungry.

And, of course, uncaffeinated—because I couldn't figure out the stupid, overpriced coffee machine Philippa installed in my new apartment.

A dangerous combination.

Maid of honor reporting for duty—and for the promise of coffee, waffles, and maybe something for this fucking headache.

I couldn't care less about this brunch. Even less about weddings.

All that effort, only to unravel slowly, silently. To grow distant. To choose silence over apology before self-imploding.

Maybe I'm too young to be this cynical.

Perhaps I'm exactly old enough to remember how my parents' marriage shattered so hard they put continents between them.

Or maybe I've never loved anyone enough to believe forever is anything more than a vow made with fingers crossed behind your back.

"Be kind to your sister," my mother's voice echoes in my pounding head.

Ugh. Fine. I'll play nice.

I cling to the hope that brunch will deliver something worth chewing—something greasy, sweet, or both.

While I'm looking somewhat forward to the promise of brunch, I'm less than thrilled for what will follow after—shopping for a honeymoon wardrobe with Philippa.

What kind of self-indulgent bullshit is that?

Even I cringe at my sour mood.

But I'm not nice when I'm hungry.

Or hungover.

And right now, I'm both.

But it's for Philippa. She put together the apartment of my dreams; it's the least I can do for her. I sigh, releasing my annoyance.

I catch my reflection in the glossy lobby doors—jeans, T-shirt, sneakers.

Casual and comfortable.

We couldn't be more different.

Chalk and Cheese. Night and Day.

If I were to take a guess on what Philippa was going to wear today, my money's on tweed. Pearls for sure. If Riley were here, we'd be placing bets—or at least a few shots—on it.

Shots. I shudder at the thought.

I press the elevator button as another hand collides with mine, sending a jolt up my arm.

"Whoa, my bad," a deep, amused voice rumbles beside me.

I look up—*way* up—into a pair of striking green eyes framed by thick, dark lashes.

Green.

My favorite.

A mischievous and dazzling smile spreads across his face, dimples on his cheeks, revealing perfectly straight teeth, and I immediately regret every life choice that led to me standing here, mildly hungover, in front of this: an Adonis sent by the gods to mock me.

My jaw drops.

I never lose my thoughts. But for a second, I do.

I take a step back, looking away as I try to scrape my dignity off the floor, then tilt my head—just enough to steal another glance.

Devastating.

Tall, so tall. Taller than Alex, even. Hair, the color of rich, dark chocolate, and long enough to be tousled. With the kind of subtle scruff that makes a man look both rugged and refined. He's broad-shouldered, built like an absolute unit, the sign of a man who doesn't just spend time in the gym but enjoys it.

His black button-down hugs his frame. Tight, sleeves rolled to the forearms, veins pulsing across his skin—*those forearms*. The kind that look like they've done things.

Built things.

Broken things.

Pinned someone.

Don't.

His fitted jeans, leather belt, and black sneakers are casual yet completely unfair. Like he woke up and looked this good without even trying.

I drink him in without meaning to. I'm mid-appraisal when I realize—*he's* watching me.

Watch him.

Busted.

The smirk on his lips deepens and so do those damn dimples,

but before he can call me out, the elevator dings, announcing its arrival.

Saved by the bell.

I slip inside, reaching to press 'PH3', only for our hands to brush again.

Another jolt.

Another glance.

Slower this time.

What the fuck. Is New York full of tall hot fucking men? Or am I just repressed and horny?

Probably both.

This man is a walking problem.

"Beautiful day, isn't it?" His voice fills the elevator, velvety and low, deep and completely inappropriate for this enclosed space.

"Yup," I say, too high. Too quick.

God, get it together.

I drop my gaze to my sneakers like they hold all the secrets of the universe.

"I'm Broderick, by the way." His voice is as smooth as his jawline. Of course that's his name—tough, manly, sounds like it chops wood and breaks hearts.

I nod like my brain isn't short-circuiting.

"El—um." I clear my throat. "Elena."

His smile widens, and now it's smug.

The way he looks at me should be illegal—and he knows it.

"Elena," he repeats, trying it on like a tailored suit. "Pretty name."

Butterflies dance in my stomach, or maybe that's just because I'm hungover. I'm going with the latter.

My heart thumps in my chest, and I swallow, trying to ignore it.

It's not just his face, it's the confidence. The calm way he takes up space like he's never had to fight for a room to notice him.

I force a breath, trying not to let it hitch.

Who is this guy? I need—no, *want*—to know more.

"So," I utter, desperate to reassert some kind of control, "do you…live in the building, or enjoy loitering in lobbies and touching strangers' hands?"

He chuckles, slow and low, shaking his head, eyes fixing right on mine. "No, *Elena*. I don't live in the building."

The way he says my name—like it's a secret. My heart skips a beat.

And just like that, I'm fucked.

He tilts his head, studying me like he's trying to place something.

"You must be Phil's little sister?"

Oh. He knows Philippa?

"Yes," I drawl, wary now.

"You look like her. Kind of. Except those eyes…" He pauses, just long enough. "They're enchanting."

Normally, I hate when people say that. My eyes are not a personality. But when *he* says it, I practically melt.

No. Focus.

I raise my brow. "How do you know Pip?"

"Through Andrew." He shrugs.

And there it is.

Ugh. Fantasy ruined.

He must be one of *them*. A trust-fund bro wrapped in pure sex appeal. Andrew Sinclair's friend, all legacy and old money. Ivy-educated, trust-enshrined.

Annoyance flickers, snuffing out the earlier buzz. *Great.*

He extends a hand. The Rolex flashes, and it's practically a punchline.

I shake it anyway, ignoring the way it engulfs mine.

Ignoring how warm his palm is.

How *good* it feels.

I pull back quickly. Nod. Controlled.

"*The* maid of honor," he teases, eyes glinting. So he knows who I am.

A jolt shoots straight between my thighs.

Oh, for fuck's sake.

My hormones are traitorous. Where's Alex when you need him?

I scowl at him.

His grin falters—just a hair. Then something shifts. His eyes darken. The charm sharpens.

A challenge.

I refuse to blink first.

Instead, I pull out my phone, effectively ending whatever *that* moment was.

ALEX

Good Morning Älskling.

A smile tugs at my lips.

I quickly type back.

ELENA

Morning, thinking of you.

Which isn't entirely true, because right now, I'm practically eye-fucking this guy. I roll my eyes.

The elevator is silent except for the soft whoosh as we ascend. But I feel it—the weight of Broderick's gaze, the awareness humming between us.

I force myself to focus on my screen as Alex's response comes through.

ALEX

Better now that I know you woke up thinking about me.

A mixture of guilt, annoyance, and amusement fills me, and I bite my lip to hide my smile, thinking of the predicament I'm currently in.

Broderick shifts, leaning in slightly, and damn it, he smells good. Like warm amber, cedarwood, and trouble. My body betrays me with the smallest shiver. *Annoying.*

"You're a friendly one, aren't you?" Broderick's voice breaks the silence as the doors slide open.

I glance up to find him watching me with that same lazy amusement.

"Charming," I reply, flat and disinterested.

He huffs a quiet laugh but says nothing as he strides ahead, ringing the doorbell with an ease that tells me he's done this before.

The door swings open immediately.

"Brody! Come in." Philippa beams, stepping aside to let the ridiculously attractive annoyance into her home.

"Shoes off, please," she chirps, already padding back inside.

I toe off my sneakers and slip on house slippers from the nearby basket. Broderick, meanwhile, takes his sweet time untying his shoes, fingers deft and meticulous.

I glare at him just for existing. He chuckles, eyes flicking down.

Pink unicorn socks.

Fuck.

Of all the mornings to throw on the first pair I grabbed without looking, it had to be this one. I resist the urge to curl my toes under, but Broderick's slow smirk tells me he's already clocked them. *Fantastic.*

Philippa, blissfully unaware of the tension brewing, leads us inside. She's wearing a yellow tweed dress. *Called it*. The sight of her in house slippers makes me snort.

"When did you get back from Germany?" she asks Broderick, I assume.

"Last night."

Germany? Consider me intrigued. I'd never been anywhere except Australia, New York, and LA.

"You must be exhausted," she coos, showing genuine concern for him. It's maddening. Who is he to her?

"I'm fine. Nothing a cup of coffee can't fix." Then he grins.

Goddamn it. That smile and those dimples should be illegal.

I don't know if I'm annoyed or horny.

Annoyed. Obviously…Right? I find myself staring again.

He notices. His lips curve in amusement.

Pretentious bastard.

I look away.

Annoyed, definitely annoyed.

"Ready to go, Pip? I could murder a cream cheese bagel and a mountain of bacon," I say, redirecting my attention to my sister, who glances at her watch.

"How much did you and Riley end up drinking last night?" she asks, all sugar and smug.

"Ugh, too much."

She chuckles.

"That might explain the attitude," Broderick mutters.

I shoot him a look sharp enough to slice. He's really pissing me off.

"We're waiting for Andrew," Philippa says sweetly.

"Andrew…I thought it was just *us*?" I frown.

She claps her hands like she's hosting a damn talk show. "Oh, didn't you check the calendar invite? This is the *maid of honor meets the best man* brunch!"

I freeze.

No.

No, no.

"Wait." I turn to Broderick. "*You're* the best man?"

He flashes a megawatt smile, his dimples on full display, smug and sparkling. "Surprise, sweetheart."

Fuck.

I close my eyes as they roll to the back of my head. I won't give him the satisfaction.

I press my fingers to my temples. If I concentrate hard enough, maybe I can will my body into another dimension.

Well. Shit.

Andrew's voice booms from the hallway.

"Broderick Schwartz, my *man!*"

They meet in a back-slapping, chest-thumping embrace—two perfectly sculpted Ken dolls, reunited.

Schwartz.

I wonder, absentmindedly, if he's from *that* Schwartz family —the diamond dealers. The backbone of New York jewelry. Loaded to the gills. Old money. Montgomery-level old.

Doesn't matter.

What matters is he's sticking around.

Which means I have to keep my cool.

And rein in my thoughts.

Hard.

— ·· —

IF I HAD KNOWN my morning would come to this, I would have prepared accordingly. And by *prepared*, I mean feigned illness, overslept, or mysteriously disappeared to Paris.

Instead, now I'm here, seated at a nauseatingly chic café, sipping an aggressively overpriced mimosa while Philippa glows as she retells the story of how she and Andrew met.

"You know," she says quietly, leaning in, "after that…situation in the meeting room, Andrew wouldn't shut up about me. He was obsessed. Wanted to know everything."

"So, you stalked her?" I deadpan to Andrew, who looks positively wistful, like he's reliving a Renaissance painting.

"Can you blame me? She's stunning." He shrugs, utterly unbothered.

"Smooth," I mutter, shoving an entire strip of bacon into my mouth. *No regrets. Bacon fixes everything.*

"So what happened next?" I ask, mouth full.

"Well, Andrew wasn't sure how to ask the company owner's daughter out, or if he even should, so…he roped Broderick into helping," Philippa says with a shrug. "They came up with this whole plan to get me to that Columbia alumni mixer. Broderick had his assistant contact my office about a potential property we might be interested in."

"How romantic. Nothing gets you going like the threat of a property acquisition, huh, Pip? A love story for the ages."

She grins, totally unashamed. "So, imagine my surprise when I get to the mixer, and Andrew's there. We started talking, I asked him out and…well, the rest is history."

"Broderick was the bait. Best wingman ever. You totally fell for it," Andrew exclaims.

"I thought you all went to school together?" I say, shrugging, spearing a piece of egg.

Philippa shakes her head. "Oh, no, Andrew and Broderick did —they're both well past their prime." She winks.

Andrew clutches his chest. "Wow. Harsh."

Broderick shakes his head, laughing. "Damn, Phil. I'm thirty-two. I'm not set for pasture just yet."

"We all graduated from Columbia," Philippa adds. "But they finished long before I even started freshman year."

I nod, like I care, working through another bite, pretending to be somewhat interested.

Broderick leans back in his chair, eyes still on me over the rim of his coffee cup.

"What gets *you* going, Elena? If not property deals…bacon and eggs?" His tone's casual, but there's something loaded beneath it, like he's already imagining the answer.

The tingle that slides down my spine is completely unfair.

"If I told you," I snap, raising an eyebrow, "I'd have to kill you."

I swallow the last bite of bacon.

Andrew coughs through his mimosa. "Damn, bro, you've lost your edge."

They chuckle at one another, and I know it's at my expense.

Dickheads.

I zone out as Philippa launches into floral arrangements and monogrammed stationery. *Yawn.*

Waffles vanish off my plate as I pray—*pray*—this headache, both the one in my skull and the one sitting across from me, disappears.

Broderick Schwartz—international man of mystery, owner of those dimples, that smile, those forearms, best man—leans back like he owns the air around him, all long legs and lazy confidence, swirling his coffee like he invented caffeine.

And those eyes.

He catches me staring—shit.

A smug grin spreads across his face. "Tell me something, maid of honor—"

I roll my eyes. "It's Elena."

He smirks. "Elena." My name glides off his tongue like he's savoring it.

Rude.

He chuckles. "You don't like me?"

"What gave it away?" I reply, all mock sweetness.

"The glaring. The sighing. The way you stabbed your waffle with the precision of a trained assassin." He chuckles, cocking his head.

I glance down.

Oh. Yeah, okay. Maybe I'm being *slightly* dramatic.

Andrew and Philippa are watching us like we're some kind of brunch-floor comedy act.

Before I can respond, my phone buzzes.

ALEX

Survived brunch yet? Or do I need to send a rescue team?

I beam at my phone and reply.

ELENA

Wedding talk is a bore, but the bacon makes up for it. Will signal if extraction is needed.

Broderick playfully peeks at my screen. I tilt it away, shooting him a glare, but his grin only deepens. He's enjoying this far too much.

"Oh…she does smile," he teases, his confidence irritating.

I glare at him in response. The less I give, the more he will get the message.

His brow arches, his perfectly dazzling green eyes sparkle— they actually *fucking* sparkle. "Boyfriend?" he asks.

"Boyfriend? What boyfriend?" Philippa chirps, her eyes wide, looking between the two of us as she takes a sip of her mimosa.

"It's no one," I lie, too quickly. Is it? Alex is…it's all too new to say. But this isn't the time to unpack that.

Philippa leans in, her eyes narrowing. "Hold on…are you seeing someone?"

Broderick chuckles under his breath, adding, "Her boyfriend is *very* eager this morning."

Oh, fuck's sake, can you not?

I shoot him another look.

Philippa gasps, eyes wide. "Wait. Is it Alex? The guy who landed you in the hospital?"

"Hospital? A little rough for foreplay, isn't it?" Andrew interjects.

My face flames. Philippa snickers.

Broderick lets out a bark of laughter, loud enough to draw a glance from the next table. If the ground could swallow me whole, I'd send it a thank-you card.

"Thanks, Andrew," I say through gritted teeth, my eyes shooting him daggers.

He and Broderick exchange a glance—quick, too pleased with themselves, like a silent high-five.

Philippa raises a brow. "So, you *are* seeing him?"

"No comment." I scowl at Broderick, pissed that he's getting under my skin so badly. Then he has the audacity to wink at me with those devilish green eyes.

She gives me a look as if to say *we'll talk about this later*.

Andrew, grinning, chimes in, "Pay no mind to Broderick, he only teases pretty girls."

"Only the prettiest," Broderick adds smoothly, flashing a panty-dropping smile, dimples on full display, sending shivers right to my core. I'm *fucked*.

"So, Best Man, how long have you known Andrew?" I push, trying to redirect the conversation away from my *very* new love life situation.

"Oh, Andrew and I go *way* back," Broderick says with his whole chest.

"He's practically family," adds Philippa, with sweet indignation.

While they reminisce about the golden days of college, I am free to finish my food in peace without any further interruption from 'Mr. Tall, Dark, and *Impossibly* Annoying.'

"So, there's a reason we asked you two out to brunch today." Andrew looks over at Philippa, the shared look between them full of quiet conspiracy.

"We've planned most of the major events, the rehearsal dinner, bridal shower, but we'd love it if you could work together to do a combined bachelor and bachelorette party," Philippa gushes, her eyes full of excitement.

I choke on my mimosa.

Broderick grins like it's Christmas morning.

"Elena, I know you're busy with your upcoming album release, but Broderick is here and you can work together on it," she adds.

"Yeah, Elena, lean on me," Broderick taunts, holding his hand to his chest, broad and muscular under that black shirt.

My jaw tightens.

If it were for anyone else, I would tell them to fuck off, but it's for Philippa, and if I can repay her kindness in any way, it would be to swallow my pride and plan *the* best fucking bachelorette party for her.

"Pip, of course," I say, through gritted teeth and a forced smile.

"Fantastic," he adds smoothly. "Teamwork makes the dream work."

I scowl at Broderick, who looks like he's won the lottery. He's enjoying this way too much, and that smug grin makes me want to throw my mimosa at him.

I can't wait to get out of here. The thought of shopping for Philippa's honeymoon wardrobe doesn't seem so bad after all.

THE BOUTIQUE IS FILLED with soft music and the scent of overpriced perfume, the kind of place where even looking at a price tag might cause spontaneous financial ruin. Philippa is in her element, meticulously sifting through racks of silk, lace, and impossibly tiny swimwear, while I trail behind her, holding an iced coffee like it's my lifeline.

Meanwhile, I'm fighting the urge to take a nap on the floor, post-food coma.

"Elena, honestly, if you ever *do* go on a proper romantic vacation, at least have something like this packed," Philippa muses, holding up a delicate white lace nightgown.

"Sex advice from my sister. Pack sexy outfits for man to tear off, check."

She laughs. "It's half the fun of it, you know."

I scoff. "Pip, I barely have time to sleep, let alone jet-set on some romantic vacation. That's if I even had someone to take me in the first place."

Though if I'm being honest, the idea doesn't sound too bad. A getaway, somewhere exotic, maybe, just me and Alex—no stress, no expectations. *Just us*. That's something I could see myself doing.

She rolls her eyes, placing two onto her growing pile. "One for you and one for me," she winks. "Speaking of non-existent love lives—Alex?"

I nearly choke on my coffee. "What about him?"

Philippa gives me the look. The one that says she sees right through my nonsense. "Don't play dumb. Are you seeing him?"

"I don't want to talk about it."

"Oh, come on, we're supposed to be bonding," she sings.

I exhale, running a hand through my hair. "It's…new. Like really new. I don't even know what it is yet."

"So you *do* like him." Her voice turns soft.

"Yeah, I think so," I admit, hesitating a little.

She pauses for a moment, then tilts her head, studying me. "Okay, but what about Broderick?"

I shrug. "What about him?"

"Oh, come on, Elena. You two were practically sparring with each other all through brunch. I swear, if sexual tension could be bottled up, we'd have enough to start our own perfume line." She folds her arms. "Be honest. What do you think of him?"

I take a long sip of my iced coffee, stalling. "I think…he's annoying. And smug. And entirely too full of himself."

Philippa raises an eyebrow. "And attractive?"

I groan. "Fine. Objectively, yes, he's attractive. But so is a fire, and you don't stick your hand in the flames just because it's pretty."

She scoffs, shaking her head. "I'm just saying you seemed… aware of him."

"I was aware of how irritating he is," I correct. "Trust me, there's nothing to talk about there." I lie, because admitting the truth—even to myself—isn't something I'm ready to entertain.

"I've never even had a relationship, so I genuinely have no idea what this all is. I'm just going with the flow," I add, hoping for some sisterly wisdom.

"Never?" she asks.

I nod, staring at my hands. Relationships had always felt like something other people figured out—like an inside joke I wasn't in on.

"Look, I get it. Relationships can be terrifying. You're putting yourself out there, and that's not easy. But if you spend all your time overthinking, you'll miss out on something amazing."

I frown, running my hand through the nearby rack. "What if I don't even know what I want?"

She squeezes my arm. "Then let yourself figure it out. No rush. No pressure."

I glance at Philippa, full of confidence and so sure of herself. Poised, like she was born under better lighting.

"You know," I say, nudging her, "for all the times you annoy me, I do appreciate you."

She gasps loudly, clutching her chest.

"Elena Montgomery, was that a moment of genuine sisterly affection?"

I scoff, immediately regretting it.

She closes her eyes, tilts her face to the ceiling.

"Hold on. Let me *savor* it."

I roll my eyes, but I'm smiling.

Just a little.

Chapter 13

How Will I Know

The few days leading up to our trip to San Diego blur past in a whirlwind.

Riley moves into my apartment the day after brunch—a relief for both of us. I don't have to worry about her safety anymore, and she doesn't have to worry about her art supplies becoming ferret casualties.

We pack together, our suitcases filled with swimsuits, sundresses, and too many shoes, the excitement humming between us.

Our flight is the final cherry on top. First class.

Our first time ever, together, which makes it even sweeter.

Courtesy of the label, of course.

We practically dissolve into giggles exploring the suites, pressing every button like wide-eyed tourists, feeling for the first time like we're *really* living our dream.

When we land in San Diego, Mark is waiting for us with a grin.

We settle into our hotel suite—two bedrooms, huge windows,

a view that looks like it belongs on a postcard. The ocean sparkles just beyond the glass, endless and bright.

I've always loved the beach.

Something about the way the horizon blurs into forever makes it easy to lose yourself. In dreams, in memories, in all the things that still might be.

Mark scrolls through his tablet while I pick at my lunch.

"Okay, so today's a free day, just to get settled and rest," he says.

I nod between mouthfuls. "Nice."

"Tomorrow, you've got promo photoshoots for social media content and the single cover."

He taps the screen a few more times, skimming the schedule.

"Then interviews. Evening is free, then three full days of shooting, Geek-Fest, a free Friday, and you fly out Saturday morning."

"Oh. That's…not a lot of free time."

Alex and I had agreed on a date, but we hadn't pinned down a time or place yet. With the way things were sounding, it wasn't looking promising.

Mark glances up at me, almost apologetic.

"It's a tight schedule. And there'll be a few night shoots too."

"That's what we're here for, right?" I sigh, pushing my half-eaten plate away before taking a sip of my drink.

Mark nods.

"Exactly. Is there anything I can do for you? Any touristy things you'd like me to arrange?"

I want to call Alex first, to see what his plans are before making any decisions.

"Let me get back to you on that," I say.

"Sounds good. I'm on the floor below if you need anything. Rio and Inga are flying in this afternoon for the week," he adds, getting up and walking toward the door.

"Enjoy your day," I call after him.

Then, Riley steps out of her room, flashing Mark a devilish grin.

"You're leaving already?"

"Plenty of work to keep me busy," he shrugs, a slight flush creeping up his neck.

"Boo, Mark, you're no fun."

"That's what my ex-wife would say," he throws over his shoulder before opening the door.

Well, that was awkward.

"See ya," I wave, trying not to laugh.

Riley blows him a kiss, and Mark shakes his head, smiling as the door clicks shut behind him.

"You're a menace." I laugh at Riley.

"Only for a silver fox." She snickers.

I shake my head while pulling out my phone and shoot Alex a quick text.

ELENA

Hey, we're officially West Coast!

I wait for a moment, but he doesn't text back right away.

He's probably busy with *whatever* it is he does.

The mystery still lingers between us.

With the rest of the day free, Riley and I head down to the beach, eager to make the most of the glorious weather. We frolic in the water, chasing seagulls, cackling until our sides hurt.

After some much-needed hydrotherapy, we head up to a beachside restaurant for refreshments.

Leaning my chin on my hands, I ask, "What'll you have?"

Riley peruses the menu, her face kissed pink from the sun.

"Watermelon margaritas sound good. Maybe tacos?"

I smile.

"I didn't see those on the menu, but I probably should lay off the alcohol. Don't want to be puffy tomorrow."

She laughs.

"I'm fine being the puffy chaperone."

"Alright. Watermelon margaritas and tacos. Be right back," I chirp, hopping off the stool and heading toward the bar.

I relay our order to the bartender before wandering back to our table overlooking the beach. The sun hangs low in the sky, painting everything in gold. It's later in the afternoon, and the world feels softer, slower. I've never seen the sun set from this side of the world before. In Jervis Bay, it always sank behind the mountains, rising over the water instead. But here, in San Diego, the sun melts into the ocean.

My phone buzzes, interrupting the easy silence. It's Alex.

"Hey, Riley, it's Alex. Do you mind?" I ask, pointing to my phone.

Her eyes dance with amusement. "Babe, of course not! Answer."

I hit the button.

"Hi." My voice is soft, aware of Riley watching me like a hawk.

"Älskling," Alex says, his voice warm but worn around the edges.

"I'm sorry I'm only getting back to you now. Today's been… busy."

"That's okay," I murmur.

"What days are you free this week? We should go on that second date."

My heart flutters.

We go over our schedules and quickly realize there are really only two days we can make it work.

We settle on an evening date, the night before I have to shoot the music video for 'Sparks.'

The call is brief.

He sounds distracted, preoccupied.

Riley watches me the whole time, her chin resting on her hand, grinning like she's witnessing the best reality TV show of her life.

When the food arrives, she immediately shovels tacos into her mouth, still grinning.

"You seem different around him," she says between bites.

"Different how?" I ask, dipping a chip into some salsa and popping it into my mouth.

"I don't know…your back's a little straighter, more proper. Maybe even a little stiff."

I groan. "He's kind of intimidating. I don't know how to explain it."

"I get it." Riley waves her margarita. "You *like* him. You're worried you'll say the wrong thing."

Before I can argue, two guys saunter over to our table, all sun-bleached hair, board shorts, and easy surfer grins. Very typical of the guys back home.

"Sorry to interrupt, ladies," one of them interjects, pointing to himself. "I'm Connor, this here's Jake. We were wondering if we could buy you two drinks?"

Riley flicks her eyes to me, her face screaming *hell yes*.

I look back at her, sending a silent *no thank you* shrug.

She looks back with a silent *please*.

I would never want to twat-swat my best friend. So I take a deep breath and nod.

Her face lights up with glee. "Why, of course you can! Pull up a chair."

"Woah, did you hear her accent, man?" Jake says to Connor, bumping his shoulder. "Fucking hot, dude."

I roll my eyes.

Charming.

"Where are you guys from?" Connor asks, sliding into the seat beside Riley.

She giggles, flipping her hair over her shoulder like she's in a shampoo commercial.

Jake pulls up a chair beside me, and if I was stiff before, I am absolutely stone now.

I've seen Riley flirt her way through plenty of men. These two will be no exception.

"Australia," she coos sweetly. "Are you two locals?"

They chuckle, nudging each other like overexcited puppies.

"Yeah, yeah."

"I'm Riley, by the way," she says, pointing to herself. "And this is my best friend, Elena."

The guys nod.

"Nice to meet you two," Connor says flashing a smile.

"You're very quiet," Jake adds, looking at me.

"Am I?" I reply, raising an eyebrow.

He scoffs.

"Yeah. But you're a straight-up smoke show, so it's cool."

"She is hot, isn't she?" Riley jumps in, trying to defuse the awkwardness with a bright laugh.

They buy us a round of drinks, and while Jake keeps trying to flirt with me, I barely give him an inch. One-word answers, polite smiles.

I'm not interested in either of these guys. They remind me too much of the douchebags back home and I can't even pretend otherwise.

Meanwhile, Riley works her magic, flirting easily, first with Connor, then with Jake when he joins in.

By the time the sun dips below the horizon, she's exchanged numbers with Connor and even arranged to meet up with him on one of the days I'll be tied up with work.

Jake leans over toward me, a hopeful grin on his face.

"Elena, think I can get your number?"

Before I can respond, Connor chuckles and throws an arm around his friend.

"Dude, she's not interested. Leave the girl alone."

"Sorry, Jake," I say, polite but firm. "Connor's right."

Connor whoops, teasing, "Damn, man, she's cold."

Cold.

It isn't the first time I've been called that by boys like them.

Frigid. Ice queen.

Words thrown at me by guys who didn't like being told no, who didn't like that I wouldn't put out. But I'm not about to lead Jake on, not when my heart is already tangled up with someone else.

I like Alex. I *want* Alex.

And while Jake is pleasant enough to look at, he doesn't make my pulse race or my chest tighten the way Alex does. Not even close.

Once they leave, Riley turns to me, her eyes wide.

"What was that?"

I shrug, taking a sip of my drink.

"Babe, he was hot *and* interested." Riley nudges me.

"Alex is hotter," I tease.

"I'll believe it when I see it," Riley quips back.

"Plus, it feels kind of *wrong*, like I'm cheating. And you know how I feel about that."

"I'm sorry, did I miss the part where Alex asked you to be his girlfriend?" she questions, shaking her head in mock disbelief.

"What do you mean?"

"Babe," she exclaims, leaning in like she's about to deliver a masterclass. "It's not cheating until you put a label on it."

"It still feels wrong."

"Elena, no. It's about keeping your options open." She sighs, shaking her head like I'm a lost cause.

Options…like Broderick?

That thought comes out of nowhere and slaps me in the face.

What the fuck, brain.

I shake the thought off.

"Until you and Alex slap a label on it—or agree you're exclusively dating—you're still a free agent."

"Okay, Master Fisher," I shoot back, raising my glass. "I'll take your word for it."

"You should. I hook 'em in, line and sinker, have my fun, and toss them back. Swim, little fishy, swim away." She grins wickedly. Like the heartbreaker that she is.

We laugh, clinking our glasses together.

"I don't doubt it." I chuckle.

Riley's smile fades slightly, her gaze sharpening.

"Do you know if Alex is seeing anyone else?"

The question slams into me harder than I expect.

Something twists inside, tight and sour.

Jealousy.

A new, unfamiliar shade of it. I've only really ever felt envy toward my sister, and even then, it always felt petty, childish. But this is different. This feels *palpable.*

"I hope not," I say, a little too quickly.

THE NEXT DAY, after the shoot, Riley and I spend the afternoon shopping and taking in the sights.

She's arranged a date with Connor later that evening, the same night Alex and I have *our* second date.

To say I'm tingling with excitement is an understatement.

I called Alex earlier, and he told me to dress casually. Thank God Rio is easily accessible—he helps me put together an outfit that fits the brief, but is still sexy: fitted jeans, a black off-the-shoulder top that clings to my body, tucked neatly into the waistband, paired with strappy heels.

Rio suggests wearing my hair up to accentuate my neck. I don't even hesitate. I loved the way Alex kissed me there, and I hope tonight he will again.

I head down to the lobby to wait for him.

My phone buzzes in my hand, and I answer.

"Hey, where are you?"

"I'm in the parking garage. Come downstairs."

"Okay, on my way." My voice comes out shrill as I'm already moving toward the elevator, pressing the down button. "I'll see you soon."

"I'll be here," he says before ending the call.

My stomach flutters in anticipation.

The elevator arrives, and I step inside, tapping my foot impatiently as it descends. When the doors slide open, there he is, dressed in a navy polo, jeans, and sneakers, leaning casually against a sleek silver sports car, looking like something out of a dream.

"Well, damn." He smirks. "You're the best thing I've seen all week."

I bite my lip, heat rushing to my cheeks, as I walk toward him.

"Come here," he growls, grabbing me by the waist and pulling me flush against him.

His hand cups my jaw, tilting my face up before he presses a soft kiss to my lips—warm and full of promise.

He holds me there, firm and possessive, his body solid against mine.

My arms instinctively wrap around his neck. With heels on, I don't have to stand on tiptoes. We're almost perfectly aligned, like it was meant to be.

He takes my hand, his fingers threading easily through mine, and leads me to the car.

Opening the door, he lowers me gently into the seat. It's low, and in heels, I'm grateful I manage it gracefully enough.

He rounds the car, sliding into the driver's side with a casual ease that only makes him more dangerous to my already fragile composure.

"Nice car."

"Had to do something to impress you," he teases, throwing me a sideways glance.

"You're already pretty impressive," I blurt out, surprising myself with the honesty.

He chuckles low in his throat, shaking his head, a slow, knowing smile curving his mouth. "I could say the same about you. You look…" His eyes skim over me, setting my skin on fire. *"Fucking sexy."*

He kicks the engine over, the deep rumble roaring to life and vibrating through the seat, through me, pooling heat in my belly. I press my knees together, clenching my thighs without meaning to.

And it's like he knows. His hand slides casually onto my knee —claiming me.

Our eyes meet, and the air between us thickens, charged and electric.

"I'm excited for tonight," he murmurs.

"Where are we going?" I ask, breathless.

He laughs under his breath. "The aquarium."

I stare at him in disbelief. "I've never been to an aquarium before!"

"Really?" He flashes me a grin, puffing out his chest as if he's proud he's giving me yet another first.

"Never." I shake my head, clapping my hands with glee.

His smile grows, boyish and heart-stopping as he pulls out of the garage, humming along to the radio.

His hand stays on my knee the entire ride, tapping lightly to the beat, a silent anchor between us.

When we pull up at the aquarium, the lights are dim, the entrance deserted.

"It looks closed." I pout, glancing over at him.

He grins, that secret, devastating grin, and takes my hand again. We approach the doors, and a security guard appears, unlocking them as we step closer.

"Sir," the guard greets, nodding.

"Everything all set up?" Alex asks.

"Exactly as you said," the guard replies.

My heart pounds. We're here…alone?

Alex turns to me. "Let's go."

His fingers graze my chin, just enough to make my breath catch. That gaze, steady and sure, burns straight through me, melting away every last shred of hesitation.

When he looks at me like that? I'd follow him anywhere. No questions. No logic. Just *yes*.

I place my hand in his, and he leads me inside, through a dimly lit lobby roped off for crowds. Now empty.

He lifts the rope with a grin, and we sneak underneath, laughing quietly like we're kids about to cause trouble.

The exhibits are lit up in soft neon hues, casting the world in dreamy blues, greens, and purples. We wander between glowing tanks of fish, marveling at the strange, colorful creatures. The jellyfish are my favorite—translucent, pulsing softly, hypnotic.

I stand mesmerized, lost in the dance of the jellyfish, when I feel Alex move behind me, his arms wrapping around my waist, his chest solid and warm against my back.

I nestle into him, breathing him in, my heart stuttering against my ribs.

"You're so beautiful, Elena," he whispers, his breath brushing the shell of my ear. "I can't stop thinking about you." He holds me tighter, like he's trying to memorize the moment, the feeling of me in his arms.

"You should probably get help for that," I tease, turning in his embrace to face him.

He smiles, and before I can say anything else, he leans in and plants a soft kiss on my lips, a kiss so tender it makes my knees weak.

"I should," he murmurs against my mouth, "but I won't. I'm too far gone."

"What is it that you like about me?" I ask, brushing a soft kiss to his mouth. "Aside from my beauty," I add, rolling my eyes.

"I don't know," he murmurs. "I feel like we're both searching for the same thing."

"What's that?"

"Someone who understands us."

The words land hard—simple, honest. He sees me. Not just the surface, but the part I keep tucked away. My heart thuds hard against my ribs.

"Do you think I understand you?" I whisper.

"I hope you do," he says, brushing a loose tendril of hair behind my ear. "Or at least will…with time."

After a short while, he leads me deeper into the aquarium, down a hallway lit only by electric candles lining the walls, soft golden light flickering in the dark.

At the end, the space opens up into a breathtaking room where the exhibit stretches from the floor to the ceiling, towering at least nine feet high, columns of kelp swaying in the water. Alien-like creatures floating around.

The whole room glows an ethereal turquoise. It's magical.

In the center, an indoor picnic is set up—cushions and padded blankets scattered across the floor, surrounded by candles of all different sizes, flickering like tiny stars.

I gasp, covering my mouth with trembling fingers. "Alex… you really did this for me?"

He shrugs, almost sheepish. "I had some help."

"Oh my God," I breathe, my voice catching. "This is incredible."

I walk toward the picnic, moving slowly, taking everything in.

He stands back and waits, watching me with his hands tucked into his pockets.

I press my hand over my open mouth, completely awestruck. The tempo of my heart feels like it's grown wings and taken flight, soaring out of my chest.

I close the distance between us, launching myself into his arms.

He catches me easily, his hands cupping my ass as I wrap my legs around him, holding on like he's the only solid thing left in the world.

"What are you doing to me?" I whisper, my voice trembling.

"Is it working?" He grins, smug but impossibly soft at the edges, like even he can't believe this is real.

My breath stumbles out of me as I confess, "No one's ever done *anything* like this for me."

He leans his forehead against mine, voice rough with emotion. "I want to give you the world, Älskling."

"Alex," I whisper, my hands framing his face. "I don't want the world. I just want *you*."

I kiss him, pouring every dizzy, overwhelmed feeling into it. His lips part for me instantly, his tongue sliding against mine with a tenderness that makes me moan into him. My fingers tangle in his no-longer-neat hair, pulling him closer, needing more.

I feel him lower us onto the cushions, his body pressing down against mine, fitting perfectly. Alex breaks the kiss just long enough to look at me—*really look at me*—seeing me in a way no one else ever has, his eyes touching every part of me that's been waiting to be found.

I trace the line of his jaw with my fingertips, feeling him tremble under my touch.

"Where have you been my whole life?" I whisper.

His only answer is a kiss. Slow, deep and endless.

His fingers glide along the curve of my jaw, a touch so light it makes me shiver.

"Beautiful," he whispers, leaning up and off me. "I could kiss you all night…" he murmurs, voice low, lips brushing mine, "but I thought you *might* enjoy dinner first."

"You thought right," I manage, voice barely above a breath. "What's on the menu?"

I push up onto my elbows and sit upright.

He grins, rubbing his hands together. "You might not know this, but San Diego has a pretty legit Filipino food scene."

My brows rise in disbelief. *He didn't.*

He unzips a black cooler bag beside us, and I'm instantly hit with the rich, familiar scent of garlic and soy, something smoky and sweet blooming in the air.

"I got Filipino barbecue skewers, rice wrapped in banana leaves…The lady at the store threw in a bunch of stuff."

"Alex…" My voice falters, thick with emotion. My heart soars, full and fragile all at once.

We eat cross-legged on the rug, trading bites and stories, laughter curling between us like steam. He's obsessed with the adobo—rightfully so—and tells me facts about the Weedy Seadragons in the tank in front of us, how they're native to Australia, and perform intricate courtship dances. I smile at the thought.

Even seadragons date.

"I wanted to bring you a little bit of everything," he says with tenderness. "Australia. Philippines. Here. With me."

"You're so thoughtful." My voice is sincere. "Thank you."

"I wish we had more time." He sighs.

"Work's crazy." I shrug, hoping he'll offer something more. "You're here for work too, right?"

He hesitates. "You could say that."

Still holding back.

"Can I ask you something?" I venture.

He nods once.

"Are you embarrassed by your job or something? I mean…it just feels like a normal thing people talk about."

He opens his mouth, then closes it. "Elena, I…"

But whatever he's trying to say, it stays lodged somewhere behind his eyes.

I shift closer, nestling into him. Letting it go. For now.

The silence stretches between us, not uncomfortable, just full. The light from the tank glows against the walls, the kelp swaying in slow motion. It feels like we're underwater too, suspended in something soft and private.

"I hope one day you can trust me enough to tell me," I whisper.

"I think we'll get there," he murmurs, brushing his lips against my temple. "I just want you to know me for me."

"Okay."

He pulls me down with him, and we lie there together, surrounded by glowing water and the flicker of electric candles. I tuck myself into him. He turns to kiss me, slow and certain, one hand on the small of my back.

He shifts slightly, hovering over me now. The kiss deepens, his tongue caressing mine in slow circular motions. My fingers thread into his hair, pulling him closer. I lose myself in the warmth of his mouth, in the weight of him above me.

Then he breaks the kiss, breath grazing my cheek.

"Can I make you feel good?" he asks, voice ragged, eyes locked on mine.

"You want to touch me again?"

"Please."

I tilt my head, teasing. "Why haven't you asked me to have sex with you?"

He lets out a low laugh, as if I've knocked the wind out of him. "Do you want me to?"

"Not tonight," I say, biting my lip. "But eventually…maybe."

He smiles, that slow, disarming smile that always seems to reach his eyes. "When you're ready, Elena."

His mouth finds mine again, softer this time.

"There are *so* many things we can do before then," he murmurs against my lips.

"Is there?"

"Oh, yeah." He kisses the corner of my mouth, the line of my jaw. "I want to take my time with you."

His hand trails down my neck, across my collarbone, and lower still, until he's cupping me through my top, his palm warm and claiming. A soft moan escapes me, unbidden.

"I want to savor every minute of your innocence."

He drifts lower, fingertips brushing down my stomach, swirling his warmth, seeping through the fabric. My breath catches. Every inch of me is alive, humming in anticipation.

"You're a rare beauty," he murmurs.

His hand slides to the button of my jeans, popping it open with ease.

Oh, there it goes.

Then comes the slow drag of my zipper—a hushed, metallic note that plays straight down my spine.

"I want to own all your pleasure." His voice is low, the kind of promise that makes my thighs clench involuntarily.

Then he pauses, gaze flicking to mine, waiting.

"Do you like touching yourself?" he asks.

My cheeks flush. I nod. "Yes."

And I do. Often. Especially lately. Especially when I think about him.

His eyes darken. "How about inside?"

I shake my head.

He shifts above me, the softness in his expression grounding me.

"I am going to *savor* every quiver as I feel you unravel around my knuckles," he growls into my ear, his breath a teasing brush of warmth against my skin, igniting sparks that race down my spine.

"Will it hurt?" I gasp, nerves twisting sweetly into desire, my voice barely a whisper caught between caution and craving.

"No, Darling, not the way I'll do it," he murmurs, brushing a kiss across my lips.

He hooks his fingers into the waistband of my jeans and panties, easing them down just to my knees. The cool air hits my skin, and I shiver.

His lips find my neck again, kissing the spot just below my ear.

"I love having easy access to your neck," he says against my skin, and I melt.

His mouth travels along my collarbone, soft kisses trailing fire. "Prop yourself up, Darling," he murmurs.

I push up onto my elbows, my breath shallow. He reaches behind me, expertly unhooking my strapless bra. It slips free, and he tosses it into the shadows without a glance. I laugh, biting my lip.

Bye, I guess.

He gently pushes me back down onto the cushions, tugging my top down until my breasts spill free. His hands slide over them, warm and sure, followed by his mouth.

The second his lips close around my nipple, I gasp.

Oh my God.

He licks at each peak, flicking with his tongue, then blowing cool air over the sensitive tips until I shudder. His hand trails lower, fingers ghosting down my body, over my hips, until he reaches the place I ache the most. His touch is featherlight at first, a teasing slide through the lips of my pussy. I gasp at the contact.

"You're so wet," he murmurs, pressing kisses between his words.

He parts me gently, finding the sweet spot I always go to first when I'm alone. He circles it slowly, then dips to collect more slick and spreads it back up over my clit, rubbing in lazy, perfect circles. My body arches toward him.

"Alex," I whimper, grasping at his bicep, trying to stay grounded.

Touching myself is one thing—*this* is something else. This is surrender.

His fingers drift lower. My legs falling open on instinct.

He presses one finger into me, slow and patient, stretching me in a way that makes my mouth fall open.

"How does that feel?"

"So good," I breathe.

"Think you can take another?"

I nod, breathless. "Yes."

"Good girl." His grin turns wicked as he bends again, mouth finding my breast while he slides the second finger in beside the first.

I feel it—the fullness, the pressure. I tighten around him, and he groans against my skin.

"So fucking tight."

He presses his thumb to my center and begins to move in a rhythm that feels divinely orchestrated, precise, and devastating. His fingers curl inside me, and I cry out.

One of my hands claws his bicep, the other the blanket below.

His lips never stop. He kisses, sucks, and grazes my breasts with his teeth, keeping me spiraling under the weight of every perfectly placed touch.

It's overwhelming.

It's everywhere.

It's *him.*

The pressure builds. My thighs tense, my legs begin to tingle and stiffen.

"Alex," I gasp, eyes rolling to the back of my head, body trembling. "I—oh, fuck, I—"

My climax hits in a slow-burning wave that turns molten at the center, detonating outward. I scream his name as I squirm and fall apart under him, hips jerking, toes curling, body vibrating from the inside out.

"Fuck—oh, fuck, fuck—Alex!"

I'm wrecked. Shattered and trembling.

He holds me through it, not stopping until I gasp for breath, chest heaving, limbs limp and loose.

He finally eases his fingers out, slow and careful, and rolls to his side to face me.

"How was that?" he asks, brushing hair from my damp forehead.

"I'm speechless," I pant, laughing softly.

A wicked smile tugs at the corner of his mouth. "You know you just squirted, right?"

I did what?

He grins and holds up his glistening fingers. "Look how wet you were, your pussy shot all over me," he says, like it's something to be proud of. Then he brings them to his mouth and licks them clean, his gaze firmly fixed on mine.

I catch my breath. I don't know whether to be mortified or turned on. I settle on the latter, basking in the afterglow.

"Hmm…like fucking honey," he groans, voice dripping with hunger. "I can't wait to bury my face between your thighs and devour every last drop."

I giggle, flushed and floating.

God, neither can I.

Chapter 14

Do I Wanna Know?

The waves lap along the shore, stars twinkling in the sky.

Sitting by the bonfire, I glance at Logan, then down at the red cup cradled in my hands.

"Cut!" calls the director.

"You did great," Mark says softly, draping a blanket over my shoulders.

It's almost three a.m., and exhaustion has begun to creep into my bones on the third and final day of filming my music video at La Jolla Cove.

The director approaches Logan and me, his expression encouraging but focused.

"Elena, that was perfect. For this next shot, we'll reset here by the fire. You're looking into your drink, reflecting. You glance toward Logan, shake your head gently like you're chasing away a memory. Then you stand, toss the drink aside, and walk briskly to Logan. Logan, you pick her up, embrace her tightly, and then lean in close, almost kissing. End scene."

"Sounds good," Logan says, his eyes bright, his long blond hair dancing in the breeze.

I smile, giving Logan a playful thumbs-up as we head back to our marks.

"Places!" the director calls.

I hand the blanket back to Mark and take my spot by the fire again. Inga bustles over, dabbing a powder puff against my face and fussing with my hair before stepping aside.

"Action!" the director yells.

My song begins playing, and I silently mouth the lyrics, slipping into character. As I move toward Logan, he easily lifts me into his arms. My heart jolts, instantly transported back to Alex carrying me during laser tag, butterflies flaring in my stomach.

But when I look up and realize it's Logan, not Alex, holding me, a giggle bubbles out before I can stop it, completely shattering the romantic tension.

Shit.

"Sorry, sorry." Laughter still clings to my voice as I stumble through the apology. The director shakes his head like he's used to this.

It takes another four takes before we finally nail the shot and another two hours before I'm in my bed. I close my eyes and suddenly, it's morning, and the bright sunlight feels blinding. I groan, forcing myself up to start the day.

Riley and I spend the morning ordering room service and getting ready. She's chirpy, clearly having had a full night's sleep. I'm on my second cup of coffee, my eyelids barely hanging on.

Logan and Mark arrange our entry into Geek-Fest, and we're quickly greeted by a perky girl with bright turquoise hair, vibrant red lips, oversized glasses, and a Geek-Fest shirt.

"Hi! You must be with Logan," she says brightly, her grin way too chipper for how much my head is pounding. She leads us backstage to the green room, chatting the whole way.

Inside, Logan is slouched in a gray chair, looking every bit as tired as I feel.

"Hey, Hollywood, nice to see you again!" Riley calls out, her curls bouncing as she heads straight for him.

Logan lifts his head and gives her a tired smile, pulling her into a quick bear hug before plopping himself back in the chair.

"Hey, cuz." He shoots me a glance, mouth tipping into a crooked grin. "You look how I feel."

I groan. My eyes feel like they have gravel in them.

"How'd you pull up?" he adds, studying me.

I drop into the chair opposite him, rubbing my face. "Barely functioning," I mutter, my voice hoarse.

He lets out a low chuckle, shaking his head. "Yeah, same. I don't think I've had less sleep in my life."

I huff. "I think my body's still on that beach, freezing, dancing like it's two a.m."

Logan groans. "Don't remind me. Whoever thought cold nights on a beach was a good idea deserves a slap."

Riley raises a brow, glancing between us. "So that's why you guys look like the undead."

Logan grins tiredly. "I'm pretty sure we hit dawn before they called the last take."

I mutter, slouching deeper into the chair. "I'm running on fumes and bad coffee."

Logan nods in solidarity. "I think I'm still wearing yesterday's deodorant."

Riley snorts, amused.

"So, I'm guessing you're *not* up for the VIP party tonight?" Logan asks, raising a brow.

A party? I can barely keep my eyes open.

"We'll be there!" Riley chimes in before I can even open my mouth, her grin wide and determined.

Just then, a staffer pokes her head in. "Mr. Fisher? They're ready for you."

Logan stands with a sigh, stretching like it takes all his effort. "Showtime." He flashes a small grin before following her out.

The door shuts behind him, and Riley wastes no time grabbing a chocolate-covered strawberry from the table, turning to me with a glint in her eye.

"Wanna check out the exhibits?" she asks, taking a bite like she already knows I'll say yes.

I sigh, feeling like I've been steamrolled, but Riley's excitement is hard to resist.

"Sure." I offer a tired but real smile.

As we walk around the convention center, it's wall to wall with attendees, some dressed in incredibly elaborate costumes. There's so much to see and take in.

A few fans recognize me, stopping briefly to snap photos and ask for autographs.

Despite the buzz and excitement all around us, something else soon grabs my attention, and my heart drops straight to the floor.

Riley and I pause near a towering promotional poster, and my breath catches in my throat.

There, looming above us, with piercing eyes and a fierce, battle-hardened expression…*It's him.*

Alex.

My cheeks burn as I stare up at his face, larger than life, like the universe is playing some cruel joke on me.

"What the actual hell is this?" I snap, my voice sharper than I intend, but I can't stop the anger rising in my chest.

Riley turns to me, confused. "What do you mean? It's a promo poster for *The Almighty Nordic Gods*," she says casually, as if that explains anything. Like I'm supposed to know.

I whirl around to face her, eyes wide, heart racing. "*This*." Gesturing manically at the poster, my hand trembles slightly. "This is *him*!"

Her brows knit together. "Him?" she echoes, clueless.

"*Alex!*" I hiss, glaring at her like she should already understand.

Riley blinks at me, her mouth opening and closing like she's trying to catch up. "Wait…*your* Alex?"

I let out a shaky breath, my anger simmering below the surface. "Yes, *my* Alex. Or…not *my* Alex, apparently."

She stares at me, and then her eyes start to widen as the pieces finally click into place.

"Hold on." She points between me and the poster, connecting invisible dots, her voice stretching with disbelief. "Are you telling me your Alex—handsome stranger Alex—is *that* Alex? Alexander fucking Westerberg? The blond god from *The Almighty Nordic Gods*?!"

I cross my arms, glaring up at the poster. "Apparently," I mutter, my voice thick with sarcasm.

Riley scoffs, almost like a squeal. "Oh. My. God. Elena, you've been hooking up with *him*? He's, like, an actual celebrity!" She's grinning now, practically bouncing on her toes, clearly way too entertained by this.

I shoot her a withering look, air thick in my lungs. "Yeah, trust me, I *just* found out too."

Riley's eyes stay glued to the poster, her mouth still agape, while I press a hand to my forehead, trying to steady my breathing.

"I mean…wow, okay." Riley shakes her head, clearly stunned. "This is kind of insane."

I let out a bitter laugh, still staring up at his stupid, beautiful face. "Yeah. You think?"

Riley nudges me gently, still trying to process. "Elena…are you okay?"

I shake my head, doubt clawing at my throat. "No. No, I'm not. Because the guy I thought I was falling for? He's been lying to me this whole time."

"Wait, you didn't know?" she asks.

"No," I hiss through gritted teeth.

She falls silent, finally realizing how deep this cuts. And as I stand there, my heart shattering piece by piece, I wonder if I ever really knew him at all.

My pulse roars in my ears as I try to process what I'm seeing. The crowd around me fades, voices blending into a distant hum like I'm underwater.

Riley must notice because her hand closes firmly around my wrist, grounding me. But it's too late—the anger is already burning hot and fast through my veins, and before I can stop myself, I'm moving.

I stride toward the panel doors, every step fueled by betrayal and disbelief.

My gaze sweeps the stage, my eyes darting between the actors seated in a neat row. One of them—an actor I vaguely recognize—is wearing some kind of ridiculous horned helmet. Beside him is a stunning blonde with legs for days and a smirk like she owns the world.

And there, in the center—like this is all perfectly normal—sits Alex.

"Excuse me," I blurt out to a staff member standing in the aisle, my voice tight with urgency. "The guy speaking now—who is he?"

The staffer arches a brow, caught off guard, but answers right away. "That's Alexander Westerberg. He plays Thor—Thor Odinson, on *The Almighty Norse Gods*. He's—"

His words blur into nothing as I stare at Alex—*Alexander Westerberg*—sitting there like he belongs to this world of flashing cameras and screaming fans, grinning that magnetic smile that made *me* weak in the knees.

A whirlwind of anger and confusion churns inside me as he

laughs at something the moderator says, his eyes scanning the audience, oblivious to me.

"Does anyone have any questions?" the MC calls out, smiling wide.

Without thinking, I raise my hand high—sharper, faster than anyone else—and practically snatch the microphone the moment it's offered.

"*Me.*" My voice is strong and unwavering.

Alex's gaze lands on me, and instantly, his smile falters, and his entire body stiffens.

"Hi. I'm Elena Montgomery."

The name hits him like a punch. His face drains of color as whispers ripple through the room.

Beside him, the blonde glances between us, her smirk growing even more pleased, as if she knows something I don't.

I tilt my chin up, refusing to let my voice shake. "I'm curious…What draws you to your character?"

It's a stupid question. I don't care about Thor or his character arc. I care about the man sitting on that stage—the man who lied to me.

Alex leans forward, his fingers tightening around the mic, recognition—and something like guilt—flashing in his eyes. The confident, charming mask he wears so well slips for a moment, long enough for me to see the truth.

He clears his throat and starts to answer, but I'm not even listening. Some carefully polished nonsense falls from his lips, but it's all static to me now.

I don't even wait for him to finish. Chest tight, I turn sharply toward Riley, who's hovering close by, wide-eyed.

"Let's go," I whisper, voice cold.

She nods quickly; her usual spark dulled as she scrambles to follow. "Yeah. Sure," she breathes, falling into step beside me as we push our way out, leaving Alex—and everything I thought I knew—behind.

Back in the safety of the green room, I am seething, pacing back and forth, trying to make sense of what happened.

Why would he lie to me? Was it a game to him? I feel like such a fool. I fucking hate liars. What else has he lied about?

My mind is a flurry of fury and insecurities.

"Are you okay?" Riley asks, her voice barely a squeak.

I shake my head, unable to even articulate the rush of emotions swirling inside me at this moment.

Riley gently hands me a bottle of water, and I gulp it down, hoping it can douse the boiling rage simmering beneath my skin.

"Hey." Her voice is soft, cautious, almost hesitant. "I don't want to add fuel to the fire, but…"

My heart sinks further. "Go on," I mumble, dreading whatever bombshell she's about to drop.

"It's about Alex," she begins carefully, biting her lip. "There are rumors that he's seeing someone—Madison, the actress from the panel. His co-star."

That explains the smug look on her face.

I shake my head slowly, disbelief choking me. My throat tightens painfully, anger and embarrassment knotting inside me. Grabbing a pillow, I press it against my face, screaming silently into its soft fabric. How could I have been so stupid? This is exactly why I avoid relationships. I'm such a fucking idiot.

A gentle knock interrupts my self-loathing. I remain hidden behind the pillow as Riley moves to answer it.

"Ms. Montgomery," one of the staff calls tentatively from the doorway.

I don't move, face buried, silently begging for an asteroid to end my misery.

Riley answers quietly, "Yes?"

"Mr. Westerberg is here," she announces hesitantly. "He's...
insisting," she emphasizes softly, uncertainty coloring her voice.

"I don't care," I mutter stubbornly, my voice muffled by the
pillow.

Even as I tell her I don't care, my body does. My hands
tremble slightly, my breath uneven. I press my palms against my
thighs, forcing myself to stay in control. I won't let him see me
like this. I won't let him know how much this hurts.

She quietly withdraws, but moments later, the knocking
returns, more urgent now.

Riley sighs and swings the door open again, arms crossed.

"You've got a lot of nerve showing your perfectly sculpted
face around here, mate," she snaps, though even angry, his looks
are enough to disarm anyone into submission.

I hear his voice before I see him—deep, frantic, but still trying
to hold it together.

"Elena—" he breathes, desperation lacing every syllable.

"Just say the word, babe," Riley murmurs, leaning close to
me, "and I'll make like Steve Irwin and crocodile-wrestle him
outta here."

Despite the fury raging inside me, a small laugh escapes,
breaking through the heaviness like sunlight through clouds.

Thank God for Riley.

"Let him in." My voice is low, defeated but resolute. "I need
answers."

Riley shoots me a worried glance but nods. She lingers in the
doorway a moment longer before pressing my phone gently into
my hand.

"Text me if you need me, okay?" she whispers, her eyes
flicking to Alex with a look that's both pissed and starstruck.

I nod silently, grateful, watching as she slips out and closes
the door behind her.

The room feels like it shrinks when he steps in, but he doesn't come too close. His usual calm, collected mask has cracked, replaced with something raw and vulnerable.

His eyes, darker than I've ever seen them, search my face like he's looking for a lifeline.

"Elena," he pleads again, softer this time. "Please. Let me explain."

I lift a hand, stopping him, trying to hold myself together. My breath shakes as I draw it in.

"Explain *what* exactly?" I ask, my voice cold but trembling. "Explain how you *conveniently* forgot to mention that you're some famous actor? Is that why you were so evasive about what you did for work? Because—news flash, Alex—*omitting* the truth is still *lying*."

He doesn't interrupt, doesn't even try, as I barrel on.

"Or maybe you'd rather explain how you're *dating* your co-star while doing—whatever *this* is—with me? Where would you like to start?"

My throat burns, and I hate that my voice cracks on that last word.

He runs a hand through his hair, exhaling sharply. "When you didn't recognize me, it was a *relief*. For once, someone saw me as *me*. Just *Alex*. Not *Alexander Westerberg, the actor*."

There's real sadness in his eyes now, but I push it away, forcing myself to stay strong.

"I didn't plan for this," he goes on quietly. "At first, yeah, I was attracted to you—how could I not be? You're beautiful, Elena. But then, there was more. A chance for something *real*— and I didn't want to ruin it by telling you everything too soon. I wanted to feel normal with you."

Compliments will get him nowhere. I cross my arms tightly, though I feel my resolve falter slightly.

He steps closer, eyes searching mine. "You can't tell me you don't feel it, too. The *chemistry*, the pull. You make me want to show you the world. Ruin you. Make you mine." His voice drops, eyes darkening, filled with something deeper than lust—something almost like longing.

But I won't let him sweep me away with those words.

"And Madison?" I say sharply, holding his gaze.

He swallows. "We were…*something*, I guess. But we were never exclusive. And the key word is *were*. I ended things before I met you."

A small part of me exhales in relief, knowing I hadn't unknowingly stepped into someone else's relationship.

"And the name *Sigurdsson*?" I ask, my voice softer, curious despite myself.

His lips slump into a sad smile. "My mother's maiden name. I use it for privacy—hotels, restaurants. It's an alias."

It makes sense. But still.

He takes a step closer, and I don't move.

"You have to know, Elena. I never meant to deceive you." His voice breaks slightly. "I…I wanted to protect what we had. What we could have had. Dating in this industry—it's brutal. You rarely meet people who see past the fame. People who don't want you, only what you can give them. And with you…" His words trail off as his eyes search mine, pleading.

For the first time, I see *him*—not the man on a poster, not the charming guy who swept me off my feet—but the man who, despite everything, is standing here, vulnerable and alone.

And my heart aches.

Because *God*, I care for him.

I think about that first date, the way he looked at me like I was the only person in the room, the way he held me like I was something precious.

But that trust feels fractured now.

I take a shaky breath. "Alex…thank you for explaining. I can't begin to understand your world, and honestly? I don't know if I ever could. I'm new to all of this—*dating*, letting someone in—and I was starting to trust you."

His face brightens slightly with hope.

Which makes what I say next feel like a punch in the gut.

"But you lied. And I can't pretend that it doesn't hurt that you couldn't trust me with this," I whisper. "I don't think we should see each other anymore."

The words hang heavy in the air between us.

His face drops, pain flashing across his features. "Elena, *please*," he pleads, stepping closer.

Afraid that if he touches me, I'll cave, I take a step back and turn away, my eyes stinging.

And he gets it.

I hear the door open and close softly behind him, leaving me alone in the silence.

The tears I've been holding back slip down my cheeks.

My chest aches, hollow and empty. Like he's taken something with him when he left.

The thought of never seeing that soft look in his eyes again, never feeling his electric touch, his warm arms around me…

It's almost unbearable.

But I stay standing, even as my heart breaks.

After an emotionally exhausting afternoon, I decide to skip the rest of Geek-Fest and the VIP party, leaving Riley to enjoy it without me. I head back to the hotel early, desperate for some much-needed sleep—and honestly, to wallow in my swirling thoughts of Alex.

As I sink into the bed, my phone dings.

For a split second, my heart lurches—*Alex?*

But no.

Ugh. Broderick.

Just seeing his name makes my eye twitch, the memory of our

brunch exchange still fresh, and yet, annoyingly, I realize I'm already grinning like a fool. Damn it.

BRODERICK

Hey Elena, it's Broderick. Got your number off Phil. We need to talk ideas for this joint Bach party?

ELENA

Karaoke & cocktails!

His reply comes almost instantly, and soon, we're ping-ponging snarky texts like it's a competitive sport.

BRODERICK

So, your idea for the bachelor weekend is karaoke and cocktails? Cute. Did your grandma help plan it?

ELENA

Better than your suggestion of beer pong and hot wings. What are we, frat bros, reliving our glory days?

BRODERICK

At least frat guys know how to have fun. Your idea sounds like a PTA fundraiser.

His smugness makes me grit my teeth.

ELENA

Excuse you. Karaoke is a time-honored Filipino tradition that brings people together.

BRODERICK

If by 'brings people together' you mean 'destroys friendships and eardrums with off-key singing,' then sure.

ELENA

If you lack talent, just say so.

BRODERICK

My talents lie elsewhere.

ELENA

In a ditch?

BRODERICK

Damn, killer, why you gotta be so mean?

ELENA

Consider it payback for your horrific behavior at brunch.

BRODERICK

You secretly loved every minute of it.

His last text stops me cold, fingers hovering over the keyboard.

Did I...*love* it?

No. Definitely not.

But my traitorous brain replays his smirk, those infuriatingly green eyes, the way he looked at me like he *enjoyed* getting under my skin. And worse, how some part of me enjoyed it too.

My breath catches on a smile. Nope. Not happening. He's just a pretty face, like overpriced wall art. Something you admire from a distance.

Before I can reply, another text pings.

BRODERICK

I'm calling. I need to hear you struggle to resist me in real-time.

What the actual fuck.

Incoming Call.

I stare at the screen, debating if I should throw my phone across the room. But my thumb, apparently lacking all sense, hovers over *accept*.

"Hello? Who's this?" I answer, feigning disinterest, though a smile creeps onto my lips.

Damn it.

"Ouch, my ego. How will I ever recover?" Broderick teases, his deep voice playful. I can practically *hear* the grin in his tone, and somehow, it makes me giddy.

I shift on the bed, aware of how ridiculous I must look, smiling like an idiot.

Get it together.

"Tell me you loved it," he coaxes, voice low, like he already knows the answer.

"You wish," I shoot back, gripping the phone a little tighter.

He chuckles softly, the sound warm and rich. "Oh, I don't need to wish. *I know.*"

I roll my eyes, even though he can't see me. "What makes you so sure?"

There's a pause, and when he speaks again, his voice dips, teasing but smooth. "Because you answered the call."

My breath catches before I can stop it.

Fuck.

He laughs—a real, full laugh that cuts through the tension. "And karaoke, really, El?"

El? What is this—some frat boy shortcut? It sounds weird.

"It's Elena," I mutter, but I bet he's already smirking like he knows I won't correct him again.

"You afraid of embarrassing yourself in front of me, *Brody*?" I say lightly, deliberately using his nickname, though my voice holds a hint of caution, Alex's betrayal still too raw to fully lean into this game.

"I don't embarrass easily. But I couldn't carry a tune in a bucket. Unlike you, Songbird." His voice dips softer, more sincere.

I freeze. *Songbird.*

"Stalking is illegal, you know?" I bite back.

"Hey, looking you up online is perfectly legal. I checked." He chuckles. "You've got serious talent, El. You'll put us all to shame. Please have pity on us."

He says it again—*El*—low and sure, testing whether he can get away with it. Color rushes to my cheeks. I'm flattered, but wary.

"Okay, Mr. Internet Detective." I shoot back with a grin. "Any other bright ideas for the weekend?"

"How about the Hamptons? The Montgomery Estate's big enough for everyone, right?"

I sit up—it's a *good* suggestion.

"That's actually…perfect, Brody."

He laughs, deep and smooth. "Aww, look at you calling me Brody. Are we gonna braid each other's hair and be besties forever?"

A giggle bursts out before I can stop it, and for the first time all day, I feel lighter.

"I needed that," I confess, softer than I intend, vulnerability slipping through the cracks.

His tone shifts instantly, more serious. "Everything okay? The boyfriend giving you trouble?"

I freeze. "He's not my boyfriend," I say quickly, shutting that down.

Broderick is quiet for a moment, then his voice softens. "Trouble in paradise?"

"Next topic," I deadpan.

He chuckles.

"Don't let him get to you, gorgeous." His voice is deep, sincere.

Gorgeous?

I smile to myself, warmth blooming in my chest, though I push it down, not ready for this.

"Thanks, Brody," I murmur, genuinely.

We drift into safer ground, tossing around ideas and assigning tasks for Andrew and Philippa's weekend.

Before I know it, it's midnight. We've been on the phone for hours, laughing, teasing, and somewhere in the middle of all the banter, that heavy ache over Alex starts to ease.

Still, when I finally hang up, I stare at the ceiling, knowing one thing for sure—Broderick Schwartz is devastatingly good at getting under my skin.

And I'm not sure if I want him to stop.

I'M jolted awake by my phone vibrating loudly on the bedside table. Squinting at the screen, dread fills me when I see multiple missed calls and texts from Alex. It's two a.m. I sit up, anxiety gripping me tightly as I read through his incoherent messages. He's downstairs, drunk and barely able to string sentences together.

Throwing on my sweater, I rush down to the lobby, where I find him slumped in a plush chair, his head resting heavily against his palm. As I approach, he looks up, his eyes glazed and unfocused, and he smiles—a goofy, playful grin.

He stinks of liquor, not his usual fresh, ocean scent. The sharp tang of whiskey mixed with something else—regret?—lingers around him, a stark contrast to the clean, crisp presence I'm used to.

"Elena," he slurs softly, reaching clumsily toward me. "I'm so sorry."

My heart aches seeing him like this. I should turn around. I should let someone else deal with him. But as he lifts his head, looking at me like I'm the only thing steady in his world, I can't walk away.

I gently wrap an arm around him, supporting his weight. "Come on, Alex. Let's get you upstairs."

Back in my room, I guide him to sit on the edge of the bed. His weight is heavier than I expect, his body sagging against mine as I help him up. The scent of whiskey clings to his clothes, layered beneath the remnants of his cologne, now dulled by the night's excess.

Kneeling in front of him, I carefully remove his shoes and jacket, my fingers trembling slightly.

"Now we're talking," he slurs as he sways back and forth. I steady him with both my hands, his skin warm beneath my touch, a reminder of just how close we were.

"You shouldn't be doing this," he whispers, his voice thick with regret. "I messed up everything."

"It's okay," I say softly, trying to reassure him—and myself— as I gently wipe his face with a cool, damp cloth, erasing the traces of his night.

As I stand, he pulls me in, resting his head on my chest. He breathes in the scent of me and lets out a low moan, and instinctively, I run my hands through his hair, earning me yet another moan. "I'm sorry I hurt you," he mumbles into my chest in earnest.

I press my eyes shut, fighting back tears. My throat tightens as I hold him in this embrace. He feels small like this in my arms, a vulnerability I'm not used to seeing with him.

"Sleep it off, Alex. We'll talk in the morning."

He nods slowly, eyes flickering shut as I help him lie down. I should be angry. I should walk away and let him figure this out on his own. But as he grips my hand, his fingers trembling slightly, something inside me can't let go.

He looks so lost, so unlike the confident, untouchable man I first met. Maybe that's why I stay, because I know what it's like to feel alone

I lay beside him, unsure if I can even get back to sleep, watching this beautiful man as his chest rises and falls. Occasionally, he murmurs 'sorry' in his sleep or speaks in Swedish, his words slurred but full of emotion. I clench my jaw against the feelings clawing their way to the surface. I should be angry. I should feel nothing. But emotions don't work that way, and Alex —drunk and vulnerable—feels like something too fragile to break apart right now.

Staring up at the ceiling, I reflect on the events of the past few weeks—how he cared for me in the hospital after I hit my head, his small, thoughtful gestures, the perfect dates he planned. These don't seem like the actions of a man who was intentionally trying to deceive me.

Maybe he was telling the truth. Maybe he really did want me to get to know him as him, without all the trappings that come along with his fame. What if the shoe had been on the other foot? I haven't reached the level of success he has, so I couldn't possibly understand how isolating that life can be. But in some ways, I could. I know what it means to be lonely, to self-isolate to protect yourself. I did it when my mother got sick. I did it when she died.

Loneliness does strange things to people. It makes them desperate. It makes them weak. Maybe that's why, even after everything, I don't pull away. My eyes grow heavy, my body sinking into the mattress beside him.

Two lonely hearts, finding solace in each other.

Sleep takes me, not because I'm tired, but because for the first time today, I stop fighting myself.

Chapter 15

Iris

The first thing I register is warmth. The second is weight—his head on my chest and his arm draped lazily across my waist, the slow rise and fall of steady breathing inches from my face. My brain, still sluggish from sleep, takes a second to catch up. Then it slams into me all at once.

Alex.

In my bed.

My eyes snap open. My breath catches. Technically, our first sleepover. The realization makes my stomach flip.

Memories of last night flash back, him drunk, sad and defeated.

This is fine. This means nothing. It was one night, and me being a decent human being. And yet, my heart doesn't quite get the memo as it hammers against my ribs.

The weight of him and this whole situation presses heavily into my body, making me squirm.

He stirs and groans.

"Alex?" I rouse him gently.

His head turns to meet mine, his eyes open, and realization

creeps over his face, but I see it—the slow unfurling of recognition as his mind catches up. His lips part like he's about to say something, then close again. A beat of silence stretches between us.

Then, his arm tightens, slightly, like a reflex before he seems to realize where he is, where we are.

"Elena," he murmurs, his voice rough from sleep, my name rolling off his tongue like a secret. His brows pull together, and I brace myself for the questions. But they never come.

Instead, he exhales a slow breath and shifts, his body brushing against mine in a way that makes my pulse trip over itself.

His voice is softer when he speaks again. "Did I…" His brows knit deeper as he struggles through the fog of memory.

"You didn't do anything," I say, my voice firmer than I expected. "You were drunk. I…" My throat bobs as I swallow. "I didn't want you to be *alone*."

His lips press together, his jaw ticking slightly like he's trying to figure out how to respond to that. Then, his eyes flicker over me, slow and searching.

I should move. Get up. Create space. But I don't.

Because his face is inches from mine, and in this hazy, morning-lit moment, it doesn't feel reckless. It doesn't feel like a mistake.

It just feels…inevitable.

His fingers pulse against my waist, and for a second, I think he's going to pull away. But then his thumb brushes the fabric of my shirt, a whisper of a touch that causes my breath to falter.

Even though I'm furious at him, I'm more annoyed at my body's reaction toward his touch, his presence enough to undo me.

"Elena." He whispers it, reverent. Heavy with all the things he wants to say, the explanation for what happened between us.

"Hungry?" I ask, trying to break the tension.

His eyes darken, and he nods.

As I order room service, Alex takes a much-needed shower. He emerges minutes later, clad in a plush robe, his damp hair curling at the ends. His movements are slower, his usual effortless confidence dulled by exhaustion and too much alcohol from the night before.

"I'm sorry about last night," he murmurs, hanging his head as he sinks onto the edge of the bed, no doubt nursing a hangover.

I don't respond right away. Instead, I take him in—the way his shoulders slope forward, the hint of regret in his posture. He looks different, smaller somehow—the weight of his choices pressing down on him.

My heart softens.

"What happened last night?"

"Searching for answers at the bottom of a whiskey bottle, it would seem," he says with a sigh, offering a weak, self-deprecating smile.

A flicker of doubt creeps in. Does he regret coming here last night? Insecurity claws at my chest. Was this a mistake? I was the one who ended things, the one who pushed him away. Surely, he wouldn't want anything to do with me now.

Then, as if sensing my uncertainty, he shifts slightly, his tired eyes locking onto mine.

"Though," he says, voice laced with teasing, "I don't regret the actions that landed me in bed with you this morning."

The playful remark is weak, diluted by his hungover state, but my heart still betrays me, lurching forward, foolish and delusional.

Does he still want me?

Do I still want him?

The thought both excites and frustrates me. But no matter how badly I want to believe him, the shadow of his lies still looms over us.

"We should talk about what happened."

He nods, his expression tightening.

I inhale, steadying myself. "What would possess you to lie about your identity? Help me understand." My voice is softer than I intend, a quiet plea.

He exhales slowly, straightening his shoulders, as though bracing himself.

"Do you know what it's like to meet people who only want a piece of you? Who don't care about you, just what you can give them? An autograph, a photo, an introduction to a director, a meeting with my agent." His voice is raw, carrying the weight of something long unspoken. "The world thinks they know me because they know *about* me. But no one understands what it's like in this world of shallow, fake people."

My pulse skitters.

"Then, after the vintage store, when we were in the hospital, something about you felt familiar. I couldn't place it at first." He shifts, his eyes flicking to mine. "But when you woke up, I remembered. The bar. You were dancing."

My brow lifts. *The bar?*

His eyes sharpen. "You were magnetic. And when I saw you again…it felt like *kismet*."

The memory slams into me. The blond man at the bar that night. The swarm of flashing cameras.

It was him.

The room tilts slightly. My fingers tighten around the edge of the couch.

Was this fate? Or another coincidence I'm desperate to sculpt into meaning?

Part of me wants to believe it.

It's almost poetic—two strangers orbiting the same city, lost in our own gravity, until the moment we collided.

I feel it now—a melody forming at the base of my spine,

blooming behind my ribs. Another song, already pushing to be born. My fingers ache to find a piano. To capture this feeling.

But I say nothing.

I let him keep going.

"When you looked at me..." His voice catches. "It wasn't like everyone else."

He steps closer. The air sharpens.

"You didn't flinch. You didn't perform. You just saw me."

He shakes his head, jaw tight. "And I hadn't had that in a long time."

His voice drops, almost a whisper. "It felt like a clean slate. And I was selfish. I didn't want to lose it."

My breath stutters.

"Your innocence..." He exhales like he's afraid to finish the thought. "It captivated me. You make me look at the world completely new. Everything is sharper, rawer, when I'm with you."

A muscle jumps in his cheek. His hand lifts, hovers near mine, but he holds himself back.

"I want to show you everything," he murmurs, voice low and aching. "Corrupt you. Keep you. Make you mine until there's no part of you untouched by me."

He draws a shaky breath, his eyes burning into mine.

"I tried to stay away. I told myself you were too young, that it was wrong, but the moment you looked at me with those beguiling eyes, Elena..." His voice fractures, raw. "I was yours."

My eyes widen. I'm at a loss for words.

"No matter how hard I tried, I couldn't fight it. I don't think I can give you up. I've never wanted anything, anyone, more desperately in my life than I want *you*."

He. Wants. Me.

For a moment, my heart stops. He wants *me*.

Something unravels in his face—tightness loosening, the

strain of holding something in too long. His mask drops, and for the first time since I learned the truth, I *see* him.

Not the actor.

Not the handsome, confident man who shook my world and inspired lyrics to bloom in my heart.

Just him.

The way his shoulders tilt forward like he's bracing for rejection. The flicker of shame in his eyes when he looks at me, then away. The hunger beneath it all. Not for fame, not for control— for *connection*.

Like me, he's been lonely, searching for something real.

My fingers curl at my sides. My ribs ache from holding it all in.

The walls around my heart crack, just enough.

Enough to let him in.

He sighs, running a hand through his damp hair. "I'm sorry for lying—or omitting the truth. But I'm not sorry for the circumstances that led me to you. Everything else was real, Elena. The moments we shared, the conversations we had—those were all me. I just wanted you to know who I am."

His eyes are wide, the passion raging behind them.

"Darling, *please*. I don't want this to end. I'm not ready for this to end. I'm begging you—just give me another chance."

My breath hitches.

For the first time in my life, I feel like I am standing on the edge of something unknown—something terrifying and exhilarating all at once. And against all logic, I want to fall into it.

So, I do.

I close the distance between us, lifting his face with my hands, my fingers brushing against the stubble along his jaw. His eyes darken as he takes me in, but he doesn't pull away.

Neither do I.

I kiss him. Softly, tentatively, like I'm testing the weight of something fragile.

His breath stutters, and then he's pulling me into his lap, his hands gripping my waist as if anchoring himself to me. My fingers slide into his damp hair, and for one stolen moment, everything else fades.

It's him and me. And the undeniable pull between us.

With a sudden surge of emotion, I push him down onto the bed, breaking the kiss. His back meets the mattress, his gaze locked onto mine, startled but intrigued.

"Don't ever lie to me again, Alex." My voice is firm, steady, leaving no room for misinterpretation.

His chest heaves, his lips slightly parted, but he doesn't argue. He doesn't try to explain.

Because we both know the truth—I can't unfeel what I felt. I can't rewrite the moments that made me believe in him, that made me care. And that might be the worst part of all.

No more lies. No more chances.

I repeat the words, letting them settle between us like a final warning.

Something flickers in his expression—understanding, maybe even relief. Then, a slow, genuine smile tugs at his lips, breaking through the weight of everything unspoken.

And when I lean back down, pressing my lips to his again, he meets me there, without hesitation, without pretense.

I'm thankful that when the food arrives, Riley is still asleep in her room. Alex and I wheel the trolley into mine and close the door behind us.

While we eat, he talks about his show, Alex finds it amusing that I've somehow managed to avoid watching it. And judging Riley's reaction, she's clearly a fan. I've never been much of a TV person, though I used to enjoy movie nights with my mom and Jack, especially adaptations of books I'd read.

I learn he's been acting for most of his life, starting out as a child actor in Sweden before breaking into the U.S. market, initially as a model, which makes sense, because he's impossibly handsome. But then, his big break and success in other roles followed.

The remnants of breakfast lie scattered across the room service tray, the rich aroma of coffee still lingering in the air.

But I barely register any of it. Because Alex is watching me, his eyes fixed on mine as we lie in bed together side by side.

His gaze is heavy, filled with something that coils low in my stomach, sending a ripple of anticipation through me.

"You're staring." I try to sound unaffected.

"You're beautiful," he counters, his voice smooth and certain.

Heat creeps up my neck, a blush burning beneath my skin. I roll my eyes, but he doesn't let me look away. Instead, Alex leans forward, brushing a lingering kiss along my jaw, trailing slowly down the sensitive slope of my throat. A soft sigh escapes me before I can stop it, betraying my anticipation.

He eases me onto my back, his weight pressing deliciously into me, warm and solid. His fingertips skate along my thigh, featherlight, teasing, sending electric shivers dancing through my limbs.

"So soft," he breathes.

I tense beneath him, nerves and curiosity mixing into something potent, irresistible.

"Alex…" My voice hitches, breathless and uncertain.

"Mmm, I'm still hungry," he growls wickedly, as though he didn't just demolish a towering stack of pancakes and enough sausages to feed an army.

His lips descend again, mapping a path downward, slow and deliberate, tracing the dip of my collarbone, the swell of my chest, the soft curve of my body. His hands are already slipping cheekily beneath the fabric of my robe, the material whispering against my skin.

A rush of nerves floods through me, tangled up in excitement, anticipation, a thousand feelings I can't name. Alex pauses, his fingertips pressing slightly harder into my skin, reassuring and possessive.

"Let me taste that sweet pussy," he murmurs against my skin, the words warm along my hip, sending another wave of heat crashing through my veins.

I bite my lip, staring into his darkened eyes.

"I want to feel your thighs quaking on my shoulders, until you're dripping down my chin and begging me for mercy," he murmurs roughly, his mouth trailing fire over my skin. "Tell me you want it, Elena."

My pulse thuds unevenly in my ears as I nod, a little breathless. "I want you…*Please*, Alex."

His smile curves against my skin, wicked and full of promise. "Good girl, so polite. Let me take care of you."

A trembling sigh slips past my lips as his strong hands gently guide my thighs apart, exposing me slowly, reverently. He dots tender, maddeningly delicate kisses along the inside of my thigh, each one lingering longer, pressing deeper into my skin. My breathing turns ragged, eyes fluttering shut as his mouth travels upward, teasing closer with exquisite patience, torturously slow.

"Spread those pretty legs Darling."

His breath ghosts across the tender spot between my thighs, making me shiver and ache. When his tongue parts me, grazing my clit with aching softness, a gasp tears from my throat. The sensation is sharp and bright, exploding like fireworks behind my eyes.

Holy shit.

I pull at the sheets beneath me.

Fingers are great, but fuck, this is ecstasy. I would happily have him live between my thighs, all day, every day.

"Oh, God—Alex," I whisper, fingers twisting urgently into his hair, anchoring myself to reality, terrified that the dizzying sensations will sweep me away entirely.

He chuckles against my center, which only makes me squirm. He steadies my hips with his hands.

His tongue moves with devastating skill, slow circles giving way to deeper, hungrier strokes, then he sucks with his lips, soft and tender, exploring every sensitive nerve, coaxing every trembling reaction from my body. Pleasure coils tighter inside me, building relentlessly until it borders on pain. My hips instinctively rise to meet him, chasing every electrifying touch. I tug on his hair, holding on as his mouth claims the tenderest part of me.

"Just like honey," he mumbles, buried between my thighs, moaning with satisfaction as he devours me—stroke after languid stroke of his tongue—until stars burst, blurring my vision. My eyes roll back as I unravel beneath him, gasping, shaking, coming undone in waves of white-hot sensation.

I bite my lip, stifling my moans, knowing we're not alone in the hotel suite.

My body arches sharply, trembling uncontrollably as he continues his sweet assault, drawing every last ripple of orgasm from me.

I grab a pillow and smother my face, crying out in ecstasy, screaming his name until my throat is ragged.

My chest heaves, my heart hammering wildly, thighs quivering around him as he slowly eases me back down, pressing gentle, lingering kisses to my sensitive flesh, softening the intensity with tender care.

Alex remains between my thighs, kissing my skin delicately. I'm still floating somewhere above the bed, limbs boneless, heart racing, when—

The door swings open.

"Hey, I was thinking we—Oh my God!"

Riley's voice cuts through the haze, sharp and horrified.

I scream—an honest-to-God, mortified scream—as I yank the covers over me.

Alex, to his credit, has the nerve to look amused. He sits up slightly, wiping his glistening mouth with the back of his hand before looking over his shoulder at a very pale, very shocked Riley.

"Jesus Christ, Riley!" I curse, scrambling to sit up.

Her eyes are wide as she takes in the sight of us, me flat on my back, Alex between my legs, then she slaps a hand over them. "I didn't know you were having a religious experience in here!"

"Oh my God, *get out*!"

"I'm trying!" she shouts, eyes closed, arms flailing as she stumbles backward. "I can't see where I'm going!"

Alex chuckles, completely unbothered, like he isn't partially to blame for my current state of exposure and embarrassment.

I shove his shoulder as I scramble to sit up and recover what's left of my dignity. "Stop laughing, this isn't funny!"

"Oh, it's a little funny," he says, eyes dancing with amusement.

I glare at him. Then back at Riley, who is still standing there, shielding her eyes like she's been permanently scarred.

"Why are you still here?!" I shriek.

She turns blindly toward the door, arms extended like a tragic, stumbling zombie. "I'm leaving, I'm leaving!"

And with that, she slams the door behind her.

A heavy silence lingers in her absence.

I collapse onto the bed, groaning. "Fuuuck."

Alex grins, leaning over me, his lips tracing the shell of my ear. "Well…now that the moment's ruined," he murmurs, completely unfazed, "want to see if we can get it back?" I shove him, laughing despite my lingering mortification.

After the events of the morning, Alex and I dress, and I see him out.

"I'll see you back in New York." His eyes search mine, as if making sure we're still on the same page.

"Yeah, we fly back tomorrow."

He lingers in the doorway, his hesitation warming something inside me. Then, without a word, he leans down and presses a soft kiss to my lips—gentle, unhurried, like a silent promise.

And then he's gone.

I close the door, exhaling deeply, my body still buzzing with the weight of the last twenty-four hours. It all feels so raw. So new.

From the other side of the hotel suite, Riley's muffled voice rings out. "I'm coming out now!"

"It's safe, he's gone," I call back, rolling my eyes.

Her door swings open, and she practically skips into the room, her expression a mix of pride, amusement, and sheer entertainment.

"Girl."

I groan, already blushing as I run a hand over my face.

She collapses onto the couch, grinning like she's won a prize. "You two *clearly* made up. There is so much to unpack here," she announces, folding her legs beneath her like she's gearing up for the premiere of a new movie.

I hesitate, shifting my weight from one foot to the other. "Riley..."

Her eyes widen. "Oh my God, are you about to tell me that was your first time—"

"No!" I cut in quickly, heat creeping up my neck. "I mean, that was a first. That has never happened before."

Her jaw drops. "And with Alexander freaking Westerberg, of all people?!"

I blush beet red.

"How does it feel having a literal A-list actor on his knees for you?"

It felt amazing, for all the reasons. But it also made me feel desired. It's thrilling to feel this way.

I chuckle, taking a seat beside her. "Why do I tell you anything?"

"Because you refuse to go to therapy, because I'm your best friend, and because you love me." She yanks the pillow away and leans forward, eyes sparkling. "And also because I live for this kind of gossip. Don't hold out on me now. I've been waiting years for you to finally get some *real* action. Let a girl be happy for her bestie."

They're all valid points.

I shake my head, but my lips betray me, curling into a small smile.

"Fine. On our date at the aquarium the other night, he, you know..." Taking my two middle fingers, I insert them into a loose fist, mimicking what Alex did to me. "And...you obviously saw what he did this morning."

"Okay, it's good you're taking things slow." Riley's eyes are wide, and she nods.

I bite my lip. "Yeah, he said he wants to savor it and own all my pleasure."

She swoons, dramatically collapsing on the couch and fanning herself.

I laugh at her. For years, I always listened and gasped at recounts of her sexual exploits, cheering her on, scraping my jaw off the floor at some of her more daring pursuits, and now, I'm the one sharing. Even if it's tamer in comparison, it feels good to have *something* to share. For so long, my life played in monotone, then Alex burst in like a symphony, and now I feel music in my bones again.

"Babe, you're telling me not only did he give you an *under-the-sea* production of *Puppetry of the Pussy*, but now that six-foot-something Viking dreamboat is going full hotel buffet on you before noon?" She laughs, giving me a slow, dramatic golf clap. "You're living the dream."

"He is hot, isn't he?" I say, a little giddy.

"Yes! Now tell me—was it Oscar-worthy, or are we talking high school theatre production?"

I bite my lip, hesitating, but then—what's the point in pretending? I blush, covering my face with my hands. "It was…incredible. I mean, I didn't know my body could even do that."

"Do what?" she asks, brow raised, amused and intrigued.

"You know, *squirt.*" I whisper the last word, feeling the heat creep up to my ears.

"He made you *what*?! Oh, God bless that beautiful man!" Riley squeals, her hair dancing around as she throws her hands in the air like she's having a spiritual awakening. "He's a fucking stud and he knows what he's doing…How does it feel to be God's favorite?"

I giggle, shaking my head. "You're ridiculous."

"I'm just saying, this is big. And I don't mean his schlong." She sits up straighter. "Elena, you're dating Alexander Westerberg. A-list actor. Supermodel. International heartthrob. You're, like, the envy of half the world's female population right now."

The weight of her words settles over me, and I chew on my lip. *Dating.* It feels too soon to call it that, doesn't it? And yet, what else is this?

Sensing my hesitation, Riley nudges my knee with her foot. "Look, I know this is all new for you, but babe, you're hot, he's hot. Just enjoy it."

I frown slightly. "Enjoy it?"

"Yes." She nods firmly. "Try not to overthink things like I know you do. Have fun and collect those orgasms like Pokémon cards."

I inhale, letting her words sink in.

"Okay, I'll try."

"Good…But," she adds, leveling me with a look, "also take care of yourself."

I nod slowly. "I know."

"Do you?" She tilts her head. "I don't just mean rubbers and birth control. I mean look out for yourself. You've never done this before. And I don't think you're the type to do casual. Just check in with him, figure out what this is and where you stand."

I shift uncomfortably. "I don't know what this is yet, Riley. I just—" I hesitate. "I like him. And I want to see where this goes."

She studies me for a moment before breaking into a smile. "Then that's all you have to know right now."

A warmth settles in my chest. She's right. For once in my life, I don't have to have everything figured out. I just have to *feel.*

Riley grins again. "Now, I have one last question…"

I arch a brow. "What?"

She smirks. "Have you seen his dick yet?"

I hurl a pillow at her face.

Riley is still cackling as she dodges it, but before she can fire back, my phone buzzes loudly on the coffee table, the screen lighting up with *Kylie.*

I frown.

"Oof." Riley winces. "That can't be good."

I sigh, swiping to answer and putting her on speaker as I lean back against the couch. "Hey, Kylie, what's up?"

"What's up?" Her voice is exasperated, her signature no-nonsense tone kicking in immediately. "Oh, nothing much, just the entire internet losing its mind over you and Alexander Westerberg!"

"What?"

"I'm sending you the link now, but long story short, there's a piece about you and him from Geek-Fest, and it's making waves. And to make things even more interesting…" She pauses, like she's bracing herself. "A new photo of the two of you on a date in Brooklyn just surfaced."

Riley and I exchange a wide-eyed look.

"Wait, what photo?" I ask quickly.

"You know better than to ask me that," Kylie huffs. "The internet sees all. You're in Brooklyn, at some little hole-in-the-wall place, sitting next to Alex, and it looks…" She hesitates.

"It looks like what?" I press.

"Like a date. A real one. Not some staged, publicity stunt date, an actual date."

Fuck, that was us at The Drip on our first date! Such an invasion of our privacy.

Kylie continues, undeterred, "It's already picking up traction. The tabloids are running headlines like *'Alexander Westerberg's New Mystery Woman'* and *'Could This Be His Next Big Love Story?'* So far, it's speculative, but Elena…" Her voice softens slightly. "This is going to blow up. We need to be strategic."

I exhale sharply, pressing my fingers to my temple. "So, what do we do?"

"Well, first, do I need to prepare a statement?" Kylie asks. "Are we confirming? Denying? Staying silent?"

Riley wiggles her eyebrows at me, silently mouthing *confirm it* like an absolute menace.

I shoot her another glare before focusing back on the phone. "I-I don't know." I hesitate, my pulse thrumming. "Alex and I haven't even talked about this."

"Well, you better talk to him soon, because if you don't control the narrative, someone else will."

My voice sticks in my throat. This is all happening so fast.

"Kylie, I don't want to be known for who I'm dating. I don't want this to overshadow my album launch. What should we do?" My voice is edged with concern because this is all new to me. I never expected to get involved with someone whose fame was of this magnitude.

Kylie exhales, the sound clipped with the kind of exhaustion only PR teams experience when dealing with celebrities who hate being celebrities.

"First, we take a firm stand: no comments on your personal life. Let everyone speculate all they want, but we do not feed into it."

I nod, even though she can't see me. "Okay. That makes sense."

"Second, public appearances need to be planned from now on. No more spontaneous dates that can be misinterpreted or used against you. If you're seen together, it needs to be intentional. We get ahead of the story, not behind it. Alex's people have already been in contact with me."

I shift uncomfortably, the weight of her words pressing in. "That sounds…controlled."

"It's PR. Controlled is the whole game." Kylie's voice isn't unkind. Then she hesitates, like she's about to drop the real bomb. "You also need to talk to Alex about whether you're planning to take this relationship red-carpet."

I falter, eyes wide. "What does that mean?"

"It means," Kylie sighs, her voice calm but direct, "do you want to be photographed together at events? That's essentially a hard launch of you as a couple. You don't confirm anything, but you also don't deny it. You show up together. Let people specu-late. If asked, you give neutral responses: 'He's great,' 'I'm proud of his work.' Simple. Elegant. Non-committal."

"Okay," is all I can manage because my mind is spiraling.

"But if you take that approach and you break up"—Kylie doesn't hesitate—"there will be fallout to manage."

Silence.

I press my fingers to my temple. This is exactly what I didn't want.

"Look," Kylie adds, softening slightly. "I know you're not used to this, but this is the reality of dating someone like Alexander. You and your budding career come first. I am here to protect *your* image. I couldn't care less about him, but you need to decide what you're comfortable with. Because the second you step onto a red carpet with him, it's game over. The world will start seeing you as part of his story, whether you like it or not."

The thought chills me.

I don't want to be someone's story. I want to be known for mine.

Riley, who's been listening with wide eyes, finally speaks. "Damn," she mutters. "It's like you're negotiating a peace treaty."

I throw a glare in her direction.

"Got it, Kylie, thanks."

Kylie exhales, relieved. "Good. Talk to Alexander and let me know what you decide. Now, go enjoy your last day in San Diego and please, for the love of all things holy, if you're with him, stay inside."

The call ends, leaving a heavy silence.

I stare at the phone, feeling like the ground has shifted under me.

TINA'S HOT TAKE

Alexander Westerberg's New Flame? Spotted at Geek-Fest with Mystery Singer!

Move over, Madison Walsh! Hollywood heartthrob Alexander Westerberg might have a new leading lady. Just weeks after being spotted with on-again, off-again flame, Madison, Westerberg was seen getting awfully close with rising musician, Elena Montgomery in Brooklyn only a week ago. But who is she?

Montgomery isn't just any up-and-coming artist. Her father, Mortimer Montgomery, helms one of New York City's oldest and most powerful dynasties, with stakes in everything from skyscrapers to senate fundraisers. With a last name like that, it's no wonder she's caught the attention of Hollywood royalty. Montgomery has largely avoided the spotlight, having spent the last few years in Australia where she won Starstruck Australia, a prestigious singing competition. With her debut U.S. album on the horizon, she's making a name for herself—but could this newfound romance overshadow her rising career?

Tension at Geek-Fest?

Things took an interesting turn during a panel interview at the event, where Montgomery and Westerberg exchanged a few pointed glances and clipped responses. Fans quickly picked up on the tension, speculating whether their history runs deeper than they're letting on.

But the real kicker? Westerberg was later spotted in the lobby of Montgomery's hotel. Coincidence? Fans aren't so sure. With both stars headed back to New York, this story is far from over.

Stay tuned.

Chapter 16

Complicated

The city bustles outside my window, the steady pulse of New York moving without me. I should be out there—working, networking, preparing for my album launch. Instead, I've spent the last few days laying low, dodging the media frenzy that followed Geek-Fest and the ridiculous speculation about Alex and me.

We agreed—no red carpet, no public confirmations, no feeding into the gossip. For now, at least.

Well…I agreed. Alex didn't care either way. In the end, I think his PR team convinced him it was smarter to keep things quiet.

It was the smart decision. The right one.

But it hadn't stopped the headlines. Or the photos. Me at the grocery store. Me on a walk. Me heading into the studio.

I felt like I was always being watched.

And it hadn't stopped the unease curling in my stomach.

And now, my father wants to talk.

That alone is enough to spike my anxiety.

Montgomery family 'talks' are never casual.

The black town car he sent to collect me pulls through the gated driveway of my father's private limestone townhouse, the kind of Upper East Side estate that screams old money and quiet power. The home is pristine—marble steps, a wrought-iron balcony, ivy creeping up the façade. I stayed here a few times when I visited, but it never felt like home to me.

Because it never was.

I step out, tugging my jacket tighter around me, already bracing for whatever this conversation is about. My father doesn't summon me to chat. If he wants to see me, there's a reason, and I have a feeling it's not just about my album.

The butler lets me in without a word, leading me toward the grand sitting room, where I find my father exactly as expected—seated in his favorite leather armchair, a whiskey glass in one hand, skimming through the Financial Times like nothing in the world ever touches him.

And then I see her.

Carole.

Sitting elegantly on the opposite chair, a porcelain teacup in hand, dressed in muted beige cashmere and understated diamonds. She doesn't belong in this house—or at least, she never should have. But she does now.

My insides tighten. Of course *she's here.*

"Elena," my father greets me, barely glancing up from his paper. "Good of you to come."

I force a polite nod. "You said it was important."

Carole sets her teacup down delicately, offering me a warm smile. The kind that's always been too soft for me to fully trust. "It's been a while. How are you, dear?"

I hold back the sharp retort burning on my tongue. The woman who broke my mother's heart—who stood in the wreckage of our family like it was hers to claim—doesn't get to call me 'dear.'

But I didn't come here to fight.

"I'm fine." The words are clipped, my gaze snapping back to my father. "You wanted to talk?"

He finally sets the paper aside, leveling me with that cool, assessing stare that makes my skin prickle.

Mortimer exhales, tapping the edge of his glass. "Your name is in the press too often and for the wrong reasons."

I roll my eyes. There it is.

"If you mean the rumors about Alex, then yes, I'm aware."

Carole tucks a strand of hair behind her ear, her voice gentle and concerned. "It's…a lot of attention all at once. We wanted to check in on how you're handling it."

I blink at her, caught slightly off guard.

My father, of course, has no such softness. "You need to get ahead of this before it spirals."

I exhale sharply. "It's already under control. That's what PR people are for."

Mortimer gives a slight nod of approval, like I've finally said something that makes sense to him. "Good. But you need to be intentional about how you're handling this. Right now, the media is dictating the narrative. If you want to be known for your music, you need to shift the focus."

Since when did he start caring about my career?

The thought catches me by surprise, stunning me into momentary silence.

"And how do you suggest I do that?" I ask.

He leans back slightly, already prepared. "How about attending and performing at The Montgomery Annual Charity Gala?"

I stiffen. "What?" The words hit me like a stone dropping into my stomach. The Montgomery Charity Annual Gala. The last time I attended, I spent the entire night being introduced to executives my father wanted me to impress, like I was some well-groomed show pony, not a person. Now, he wants to use me again, but this time to clean up a PR mess I never even made.

"Controlled. Professional. Something that highlights your philanthropy and career—*not* your personal life. The moment you take ownership of the narrative and your career, the media will follow."

My fingers clench in my lap, his sincerity catching me by surprise. He wants to help? I know he's not wrong. But the idea of dressing up and performing for the sake of my 'image' feels manufactured. Like I'm playing a part I never asked to play.

Carole watches me thoughtfully before speaking, her tone softer. "Elena, we're only suggesting this because we want what's best for you. Your album deserves the spotlight. It would be a shame if people forgot that in favor of gossip."

Her voice is so genuine that I almost feel guilty for assuming the worst when I walked in.

Almost.

Still, something about all of this makes me uneasy.

I inhale, forcing my voice to stay even. "I'll think about it."

Mortimer nods, satisfied. "Good."

The butler arrives with refreshments, and for a while, the conversation shifts—Philippa's wedding, my album, the new apartment.

For a moment, it almost feels normal.

Then, as I stand to leave, Carole reaches out, gently touching my arm.

"And Elena?"

I pause, glancing back at her.

She smiles softly. "Just…be careful. The press loves a love story, but they love a scandal more."

The words stick with me long after I walk out the door.

The moment I step out of my father's townhouse, I feel like I can breathe again.

But the tension doesn't ease, her words tightening around me like a vice.

I shouldn't be surprised—typical Mortimer. Calculated. Strategic. Turning a conversation about my career into a chess move for optics.

And Carole…she was kind. She always is. But that last comment?

"The press loves a love story, but they love a scandal more."

The way she said it, like she knew something I didn't—it hasn't stopped replaying in my head.

By the time I get back to my apartment, I'm already gripping my phone, texting Riley.

ELENA

Home. Bring wine. It's a crisis.

RILEY

Be there in 10. Do I need to grab ice cream too?

ELENA

Probably.

RILEY

I knew it.

Fifteen minutes later, Riley bursts in like she's making a life-saving rescue, a bottle of rosé in one hand and a pint of chocolate chip cookie dough ice-cream in the other.

She takes one look at my face and sighs. "Yikes. You've got the I've been *Monty'd* look."

I groan, flopping onto the couch. "You have no idea."

She uncorks the wine with frank efficiency, pouring two very full glasses before plopping down next to me.

"Okay, spill. What did Daddy Dearest say this time?"

I take a deep sip before answering. "He wants me to perform at the Montgomery Annual Charity Gala."

Riley's brows shoot up. "Wait, seriously?"

I nod.

She whistles, leaning back. "Huh. Okay, I gotta admit—that's not the worst idea. You're launching an album. It puts the focus on your music and not your…*extracurriculars*."

I give her a look. "Did you call my dating life 'extracurriculars'?"

She shrugs. "I'm trying to be classy about it."

Before I can answer, my phone buzzes.

Kylie.

I sigh. "Perfect timing."

Riley leans in. "Put her on speaker."

I do.

"Kylie, let me guess—you're calling about the gala?"

Her sigh is sharp. "Oh, good. You already know. That saves me time."

I pinch the bridge of my nose. "Let me guess, you think it's a good idea, too?"

"Of course I do," she says, like it's the most obvious thing in the world. "It's the perfect opportunity to shift the narrative away from Alexander. It lets the press focus on your music while also making you look like the poised, philanthropic artist you are. Win-win."

I groan, rubbing my temples. "God, not you too."

Riley smirks. "That's two votes in favor, babe. I think you're outnumbered."

"Okay, I'll coordinate your diary with Mark. The Montgomery PR team will already have selected media presence there, so that's covered, Kylie out," and the call ends.

I stare at the ceiling, feeling utterly betrayed, like I've somehow lost all autonomy over my own life.

Riley shifts beside me, her tone uncharacteristically measured. "Babe, you knew this would come with the territory. Even if you weren't dating Alex, with your insane talent, your career was always going to put you under a spotlight. This speeds things up."

I exhale sharply, rubbing my temples. "It's not just that. It's him using it to 'control the narrative.' It's the idea of playing a part for the press instead of letting my career speak for itself."

Riley tilts her head, eyes filled with equal parts amusement and brutal honesty. "Elena, I love you, but you knew this was part of the deal. The moment you got serious about music—the second you started dating a literal walking Calvin Klein ad—your life became public domain."

I groan. "Don't remind me."

I hesitate.

Because I'd been avoiding him since the story broke.

Riley watches me carefully, the teasing edge in her expression softening into something more thoughtful, steady.

"Stop hiding," she says gently. "You should talk to him."

Her voice is maddeningly matter-of-fact, as though this isn't something I've been agonizing over for days.

Oh, Riley. I could never survive this insane, unpredictable life without her.

I exhale, pushing away my pride, my nerves, and pick up my phone. My fingers hover for a moment before I type out the message.

ELENA

Hey, settled back in NYC. Come over for dinner and a movie?

The second I hit send, anxiety coils in my stomach. I don't have to wait long for a response. My phone vibrates almost instantly.

ALEX

Älskling, sounds good. Can I bring anything?

I stare at the screen, my heartbeat skipping at the familiar Swedish endearment.

Riley, ever the nosy menace, peeks over my shoulder. "Aww, he cares."

I roll my eyes, trying to ignore the small flutter in my chest. "Mind your business."

She grins, plucking her wine glass off the coffee table. "Oh, babe, you are my business."

An hour later, a knock sounds at my door.

Before I can move, Riley beats me to it, flinging it open with all the theatrics of someone who was waiting for this moment.

Alex stands there, unfairly sexy, dressed in a black shirt and jeans, his hair still slightly wind-ruffled. He holds a bag of takeout in one hand, a second smaller bag tucked beneath his arm.

Riley eyes the takeout before she even acknowledges him.

"You're late," she announces, snatching the bag from his hands. "But you brought food, so I'll allow it."

Alex chuckles, stepping inside. "Nice to see you, too, Riley, under different circumstances."

My face heats up, fuck, that's right—the oral interruption.

"Riley, Alex, Alex, Riley, but you both already knew that," I say by way of introduction in between sips of wine.

She inspects the containers. "Sushi? Fancy."

"Figured I'd keep it safe." He follows her toward the dining table. "Didn't want to show up with burgers if Elena was in a salad mood."

Riley snorts, dropping into her chair. "Trust me, she only eats salads when forced."

I groan, sitting down across from her. "Are you two seriously discussing my eating habits right now?"

Alex grins, setting the smaller paper bag beside me.

I glance at it, raising a brow. "What's that?"

He shrugs, the corner of his mouth tugging up in that lazy,

infuriatingly charming way. "Dessert. Thought I'd make up for *everything.*"

The word lands. Perhaps he understands how the intense media attention is affecting me.

Riley claps her hands together. "Oh, he's *good.*"

Alex smirks. "I try."

I shake my head, fighting back a smile as we dig in.

The conversation is easy, familiar. Riley launches into her latest dating disaster, complete with exaggerated hand gestures and a very dramatic reenactment of a man attempting to 'neg' her at work. Alex laughs, shaking his head, and I watch the way his shoulders relax, the way his eyes crinkle at the edges.

And every so often, I feel his gaze flick toward me.

An hour later, Riley stretches her arms dramatically, glancing at the time.

"Welp." She claps her hands. "Sorry to love and leave you guys, I got myself a hot date." She winks.

"Wait—what?" I gape at her. "Riley."

She grins, backing toward the door. "You kids behave."

Alex, the absolute menace, smirks. "No promises."

Riley waggles her brows at me. Then she's gone.

The second the door clicks shut, a different kind of silence settles.

The kind that hums with possibility.

I turn toward Alex, exhaling a soft scoff. "That was subtle."

He laughs. "Extremely."

A pause.

The air between us shifts as the weight of unspoken words settles in.

He leans back in his chair, but there's nothing relaxed about the way he's watching me. The way his fingers drum lightly against the table, like he's holding back from reaching for me. Like he's waiting for me to stop running.

Then, he speaks.

"Any reason why you've been avoiding me lately?" His lips curve into a smirk, but there's an edge beneath it. A quiet tension.

I exhale, my fingers tracing the rim of my wine glass. There's no dodging it now.

"If I'm being honest," I start, choosing my words carefully, "it's all been…overwhelming."

Alex's smirk fades, his expression shifting into something softer, more attentive. He doesn't interrupt.

I exhale sharply, pushing my hair behind my ear. "I didn't expect this. When this all started, I had no idea it would turn into this. I get it now, why you kept your identity a secret. In some ways, I wish we could go back in time."

His face drops.

"Not before I knew you," I clarify. "I wasn't prepared for this. All this attention." I sigh. "It's a lot. *You're* a lot."

His brows lift slightly, amused. "I'm a lot?"

I shoot him a look. "Alex. Be serious."

He chuckles, but it's quiet, almost self-deprecating. "I am serious. You think I don't know that? That I don't realize what being with me means, why I tried to shield you from it, even for a short time?"

I stare at him, feeling the weight of his words. Because of course he knows. This is his life. The cameras, the tabloids, the constant scrutiny—it's not new to him. But it's new to me.

"I don't know how to navigate it," I admit. "How to handle the fact that my name—my work—is now being linked to yours in ways I can't control." I look down at my hands, my frustration creeping in. "It's like we're puppets on a string, letting PR teams decide what we can and can't do. Who we can be seen with, where we can go, what we say."

Alex sighs, running a hand through his hair. "I know. It's frustrating as hell." He leans forward, resting his elbows on the table, his gaze locking onto mine. "But, Elena, you're not in this alone. We'll figure it out. *Together.*"

I chew on my lip, my emotions tangled between relief and hesitation. "And if it gets worse? If it starts affecting my career?"

His jaw tightens. "Then we deal with it."

I scoff. "It's not that simple."

"It's not," he agrees. "But I've done this long enough to know that the only way through it is to decide what we want and stand by it." His voice dips lower. "So what do you want, Elena?"

I swallow the lump in my throat. Because despite the whirl-wind, the overwhelming media storm, the pressure—the answer has always been the same.

I want him.

I meet his eyes, my voice quieter now. "I don't want to lose myself or my hard work in all of this."

His expression softens, his fingers reaching across the table to brush against mine. "Then don't. I'm not asking you to change or to let them define you. I want to be in this with you."

I let out a slow breath, my fingers curling slightly around his. "Okay."

"Then get over here, I miss you in my arms."

I hesitate for only a second.

Then I move.

My chair scrapes against the floor as I stand, the space between us shrinking as I round the table. Alex doesn't move, doesn't push, he just watches. His eyes are piercing, dark, patient, filled with something steady and sure that makes my heart trip over itself.

When I reach him, he pulls me in instantly, his hands gripping my hips as he tugs me onto his lap like I belong there.

And maybe I do.

I let out a breathy laugh as I settle against him, my hands pressing against his chest, his warmth seeping into my skin.

Alex exhales like he's finally right where he's meant to be. His arms wrap around me, one hand splaying wide across my lower back, the other sliding up my spine, fingers threading through my hair.

"Better," he murmurs, his voice low and rough, his lips brushing against my jaw.

I shiver, my breath catching. "You're very demanding."

He grins, nosing along my cheek. "Only when I know what I want."

And right now, I know exactly what he wants.

The tension that has been building all evening tightens between us, threading through my veins like a live wire. His fingers flex against my hips, holding me there, anchoring me, but it's not enough.

I tilt my head, brushing my nose against his, teasing. His breath stirs against my lips, his grip tightening slightly.

"Elena," he murmurs, his voice a hushed warning, as if he's barely holding himself back.

I don't want him to.

I close the distance, pressing my lips to his—slow at first, tender and playful.

Then Alex makes a sound—low, deep, almost pained—and whatever restraint he had left shatters.

The kiss turns hungry, his hands gripping me tighter as he pulls me closer, pressing me against him like he needs me to breathe. I feel the heat of him everywhere, the firm press of his chest against mine, the way his fingers slide up beneath my shirt, skimming my skin, tracing fire in their wake.

I tilt my head, deepening the kiss, swallowing the groan that rumbles in his throat. His hands slide lower, gripping my thighs, shifting me against him. I throb with desire.

My fingers tangle in his hair, tugging slightly, and he groans, his teeth nipping at my lower lip.

I gasp against his mouth. "Alex—"

He doesn't stop.

Doesn't slow.

And God help me, I don't want him to.

I grip his shoulders, pressing into him, needing more, feeling his hands slide beneath my shirt, his fingers digging into my bare skin.

He lifts me and lays me out on the dining table, taking in the sight of me, sprawled out, wild, and wanting.

"Take your shirt off," I beg breathlessly, longing to feel his skin. He takes it off in one smooth move, and his lips are back on mine, starving and desperate.

His mouth trails down my throat, slow and teasing, the scrape of his stubble leaving sparks in its wake. I tilt my head, giving him more access, and his grip on my hips tightens in response. His breath is warm, unsteady, a sharp contrast to the cool air against my flushed skin.

He begins taking my shirt off.

Then—

A loud knock at the door.

We both freeze.

Breathing hard.

Alex's lips hover over mine, his breath warm against my mouth.

"You have got to be kidding me," he groans, his voice thick with frustration, his forehead resting against mine.

The knock comes again. Louder.

"Elena? It's Riley. I forgot my purse. Which also has my key!"

I let out a mortified laugh, burying my face in Alex's shoulder.

He groans again, dropping his head against my neck, muttering something in Swedish that I'm pretty sure is a curse.

He pulls back, breathless, still dazed from the heat of the moment, from the way my body still thrums with desire.

Alex looks at me, his pupils blown wide, chest rising and falling unevenly.

"This isn't over," he murmurs, his fingers tightening against my jaw.

I pulse in anticipation.

No. It's definitely not.

Chapter 17

Before You

Adjusting the diamond-studded clasp on the red satin gown Rio chose for me, I exhale slowly, steadying myself. The grand ballroom of the Astoria Hotel glitters under the warm glow of chandeliers, the air thick with the hum of conversation and the clinking of crystal glasses.

Tonight matters.

The Annual Montgomery Charity Gala—raising funds for a dozen causes, all carefully curated and tax-deductible. But beyond the polished smiles and champagne, it's something else entirely.

It's the first time my entire family will be under one roof.

And that alone makes me nervous.

"Elena!"

Riley's voice cuts through the crowd, and moments later, she's at my side, her amethyst gown making her cascading red curls shine. Her eyes are alight with mischief.

"Sorry I'm late, work was shit…Damn girl, you look like a whole damn movie star."

I laugh. "I have Rio to thank for that," I say, twirling for her. "Sorry work was shit. You look hot, though," I add.

"Bosses. But God bless Rio, that stylish, sassy gay man doing the Lord's work." Riley gives me a once-over before linking her arm through mine. "Now, let's get you a drink before you have to flash that perfect little rich-girl smile at all these people."

Before we can move toward the bar, a voice—low, smooth, unmistakable—interrupts.

"Elena."

My breath hitches slightly before I turn, already knowing who I'll find.

Broderick.

He is striking in a tailored black tuxedo, the crisp lines emphasizing the breadth of his shoulders, the way it fits like a second skin. His eyes lock onto mine with an intensity that sends heat curling through me.

For a moment, we stand there, caught in something unspoken.

Our conversation on the phone softened something in me. Sure, he's a rich douche, but he was kind enough to make me smile when I needed it.

Riley's eyes widen as she takes him in for the first time. She's stunned into silence—no flirty remark, no smug little smirk. Even his looks have her thrown.

"Do I know you?" I joke, my lips curving into a smile, trying to downplay the way my pulse kicks up a notch.

"Oh, my bad." Mischief flickers in his gaze. "Here I thought you were Phil's maid of dishonor—I mean, honor."

I roll my eyes but can't suppress the laugh that slips out.

"You clean up well." The words slip out before I can stop them. Understatement of the century. The man is beyond gorgeous. I feel guilty even noticing, but I'm a woman with eyes —and he's definitely easy on them.

I feel Riley's eyes boring into us, glancing back and forth like it's a verbal tennis match.

Broderick smirks, slow and deliberate. "I could say the same about you, but that would be downplaying it."

His eyes drag down the length of me, raking over the gown clinging to my curves, the bare skin at my shoulders, the dip at my back. The way he's looking at me sends heat rushing to my cheeks.

I feel exposed.

Too exposed.

Riley nudges me, snapping me out of it. I catch her knowing smirk.

Before I can respond, Philippa and Andrew appear, breaking the tension like a splash of cold water.

Andrew and Broderick pat each other's backs before he gives Philippa a friendly hug.

"There's my stunning little sister," Philippa coos, pressing a kiss to my cheek. "You're going to steal the show tonight."

She's dressed in a glittering champagne-colored gown, elegant as always. Andrew greets me with a warm smile, but Philippa's sharp gaze flicks between me and Broderick, catching everything.

"Elena, that drink?" Riley asks, her voice deceptively casual, but I know better.

"I can grab you ladies something," Broderick offers, flashing that damn megawatt smile—the kind that makes my stomach flutter in a way I refuse to acknowledge.

"We'll be right, mate," Riley cuts in smoothly before I can answer.

Philippa's lips quirk slightly at the exchange, her eyes narrowing as she looks at me. "I could also use a drink," she says, her smile slow and calculating.

Shit.

As the three of us walk toward the bar, Riley yanks me into a quiet corner, Philippa hot on our heels.

"Elena," Riley starts, her voice laced with accusation. "What the fuck was that?"

"What?" I feign innocence.

"Don't be coy. You and *Bradley* eye-fucking each other, and why didn't you tell me about him?"

Guilt knots in my chest. I have no excuse, but I still feel like I need one. Like I'm betraying Alex somehow, even though he's not here.

"I didn't tell you about him because there's nothing to say, and it's Broderick," I correct her, trying to keep my voice steady.

"And you're defending him," Riley shoots back, eyeing me like I've grown two heads.

"You should've seen them at brunch," Philippa adds, clearly enjoying this way too much. "If looks could strip someone naked, Broderick would've been down to his boxers."

"Oh my God," I groan, covering my face. "It's nothing."

Riley snorts. "Babe, that was *not* nothing. That was *I want to climb you like a tree* energy."

I glare at her, but Philippa nods in agreement, raising a brow. "So you *are* interested?"

I hesitate. My mind screams at me to say no, to dismiss it, to make some half-hearted excuse. But the heat still lingering in my body from Broderick's stare tells a different story.

"It's…complicated," I admit finally.

Riley gives me a pointed look. "Because of Alex?"

A sharp pang runs through my chest at his name. Thinking of him makes my heart ache. He hasn't asked me to be his girlfriend yet, so by Riley's standards, I'm still a 'free agent,' but why do I feel guilty? There's history there—emotions and feelings tangled.

But Broderick is different. He's something else entirely. A pull I don't understand. A tension that's partly annoying, kind of funny, but also magnetic.

"We're…around each other, because of Philippa's wedding," I deflect, shooting my sister a weak glare.

Philippa smirks. "Didn't realize seducing the best man was part of your maid of honor duties."

"Pip!" I shriek.

"What'll it be, ladies?" the bartender asks.

Philippa leans in. "Something hydrating. My sister's a little *thirsty.*"

The bartender chuckles.

Riley throws her head back, laughing. "Babe. You are so fucked—metaphorically speaking."

And for the first time tonight, I think she might be right.

Across the room, my father and Carole are watching. My father, ever the businessman, is deep in conversation with a senator, while Carole offers me a small, polite nod. It's odd seeing her here, playing the polished socialite wife. It still isn't easy, but I'm trying.

We head back to our table and take our seats. Broderick's gaze is smug as he watches me from across it. I keep my expression neutral, refusing to give him the satisfaction—or Riley and Philippa any ammunition. He arches a brow, as if I've just raised the stakes—and he's more than happy to play.

While the speaker talks about the charities, silent auctions, and donations coming in, she calls Broderick up to the stage.

He winks at me as he stands, his large hands buttoning his suit jacket as he makes his way to the podium. I sip my drink, desperate to mask the smirk cracking on my face.

I will not show any emotion. Riley nudges me knowingly.

"Good evening, everyone," he says, his voice smooth and confident.

"It's an honor to be here tonight, surrounded by people who understand the power of generosity. We've just been told that we've raised seven million so far—enough to build hundreds of homes in various third-world countries. That's not just a number; that's real families who will have a roof over their heads because of you."

What?

My mind tries to reconcile the man standing at the podium with the one I thought I knew. I pegged Broderick as a corporate finance guy, the type who closed million-dollar deals over whiskey and handshakes—practical, sharp, maybe a little ruthless.

But this? This is unexpected.

"Goodman Enterprises is known for building cities, infrastructure, but initiatives like this are what really matter. A house isn't just walls and a roof; it's safety, dignity, a future, and not everyone is that fortunate. And if we have the power to change that, how can we not?" he continues, his beautiful eyes sparkling with passion.

He speaks with a quiet conviction, no arrogance, no bravado —just a certainty that what he's doing *matters*. And the way the room hangs on his every word, I realize I'm not the only one seeing him in a new light.

"So tonight, I'm personally pledging five hundred thousand dollars to this initiative, not as an investment, but as a promise. I'm hoping there are some generous pockets here tonight who will match or even surpass my donation. And together, we can make sure more people get to claim that right."

I swallow; my pulse steady, but my thoughts racing. Maybe I underestimated him. Maybe there's a side of Broderick I never thought to look for. Sure, he's rich, but maybe he's got a genuine heart under all that money and privilege.

And now, I can't stop looking. Even though I should.

"Thank you," he says finally, his eyes glancing out at the crowd before catching mine. I drop my gaze immediately as my heart starts to rush in my chest.

"Wow," Riley whispers in my ear, and I know I'm in trouble.

As the formalities conclude, the time comes for me to take the stage and officially open the dance floor. The lights soften, casting a golden glow over the ballroom as I settle onto the piano bench, my fingers grazing the cool ivory keys. A hush falls over the crowd, anticipation humming in the air.

With a deep breath, I begin to play, my voice threading through the space in a soft, aching ballad—something slow, something meant to be felt.

As I sing, my gaze drifts across the dance floor. My father holds Carole close, the two of them swaying intimately, their smiles warm and genuine. It's strange, seeing him this way—content, at ease. It isn't the version of him I grew up knowing, but it's one I'm slowly coming to understand. Philippa and Andrew dance nearby, their movements graceful and easy, the kind that comes with knowing and loving someone for years.

And then there's Broderick.

He stands off to the side with Riley, their heads bent close, deep in conversation. The flickering candlelight plays against the sharp lines of his jaw, the way he nods, the glances he steals in my direction. Riley says something, smirking, and his gaze lingers on me a beat longer than expected.

Are they're talking about me?

I can see it in the way Riley's eyes twinkle with mischief, in the way Broderick's expression shifts—curious, thoughtful, unreadable. I try to focus on the song, on the delicate notes beneath my fingertips, but I can't shake the feeling that, in this moment, I'm being seen in a way I'm not sure I'm ready for.

And yet, I keep singing.

As the evening wears on, I find myself caught in more fleeting glances with Broderick. I try to look away, pretend I don't feel it, but the pull is undeniable. There is something different in the way he looks at me tonight—something unreadable, something waiting. It's nothing. Probably the lighting. Or the wine.

Eventually, he crosses the room, closing the distance with casual ease.

"You planning to ignore me all night?" he asks.

I glance up at him through my lashes, heart thudding like a baseline I can't control . "I'm not ignoring you."

He leans in, his breath brushing warm against my neck. "Prove it."

Every muscle in my body tightens. My thighs clench.

Fuck.

I clear my throat and take a slow sip of champagne as he straightens again, far too composed.

"Dance with me?" he asks, extending a hand like it's already settled.

I pause, eyes drifting from his hand to that maddeningly smug face. Broderick's eyes sparkle beneath the twinkling lights, dimples deepening with that grin he knows damn well is dangerous.

I shouldn't.

He tilts his head, all charm and challenge—and just like that, my willpower wavers. Who the hell says no to *that* face?

"One dance," I say softly, then slide my hand into his. His grip is warm. Steady—*too steady*. My pulse jumps in response, and I try to ignore it. It doesn't mean anything. Just…proof. That I'm not ignoring him.

The band plays a rendition of "I Finally Found Someone" by Barbra Streisand, all strings and delicate piano chords.

Around us, couples begin to sway, drawn to the pull of it. Broderick steps in, his hand finding the small of my back as if he's done it a hundred times before. My other hand rests lightly against his chest, the heat of him seeping through the fabric of his tux.

The lyrics drift through the air around us, echoing a feeling I desperately want to ignore—one that seems to unfold, note by note.

"I have to say," he murmurs, voice low enough for only me to hear. "I didn't know you had that in you."

I tilt my head up at him, one brow raised. "Had what in me?"

He smirks, the corner of his mouth twitching like he's trying not to grin. "Watching you online versus seeing you tonight—*it's different*. You had the room in the palm of your hand."

I smile, teasing. "I'll be sure to send you a signed copy of my album—one for my newest number one fan."

"Include a poster," he says, eyes glinting. "I'll hang it on my wall."

A flush creeps up the back of my neck, but I laugh it off. "And coming from the man who pledged half a million dollars to build homes for people in need? I think *you* win tonight's 'most impressive' award."

He chuckles, the sound deep and warm, reverberating against my palm. "It's not a competition, but I'll take the compliment."

"Don't get used to it," I say, though my voice is softer than I mean it to be.

His thumb brushes across the bare skin at the back of my dress—barely there, just a lazy circle. My spine straightens, every nerve locking into place. He keeps dancing like he hasn't done anything.

"You were incredible, El. Really."

I look up, meeting his gaze again. And then I can't look away. The ballroom, the music, the hum of voices—it all fades away. It's his eyes. Unflinching. Like he's seeing something I'm not ready to admit exists.

"You're not so bad yourself," I say, trying to keep it breezy, though the warmth in my chest betrays me. "I was so wrong about you."

His mouth curves. Not a smirk. Just soft. Honest. "So you *do* think I'm impressive."

I roll my eyes, trying to keep the heat crawling up my throat at bay. "I think you're tolerable."

Broderick's hand tightens at my waist, not enough to be obvious, just enough to pull me closer. I feel the change in my breathing before I notice I've moved in. His breath hits the side of my neck.

"I'll take it," he whispers.

I freeze. Just for a second. My whole body lights up with tension, seeping into my bones, and suddenly, I don't know what to do with my hands. Or my face. Or my feelings.

Fuck.

We keep dancing—slow, quiet. The world blurs at the edges, tuxedos and ballgowns fading into nothing. As if there's nowhere else to be.

His hand stays exactly where it is. I can feel his heartbeat under my fingers. I don't dare look up again.

I stop thinking. For once. I follow his lead, moving with him in a rhythm that feels instinctive—as if our bodies have always known each other.

And then the song ends. We both linger for half a second too long.

I step back, breathless, chest rising and falling like I've run a sprint. I can't read his face. I don't want to.

Across the room, Riley raises an eyebrow so high it nearly reaches her hairline.

I mutter something about the bathroom and make a break for it.

The gala is for a noble cause, sure. But as I accept a flute of champagne from a passing waiter, the real event of the night isn't my performance, the speeches, or the silent auction. It's in the quiet exchanges, the invisible lines being crossed. And the unrelenting pull of a man who refuses—no matter how hard I try—to fade into the background.

———··———

AFTER A FEW TOO MANY DRINKS, Riley, Philippa, and I decide to have an all-girls sleepover at my apartment. Sitting in our extravagant ballgowns barefoot, half unzipped, makeup disheveled, we share a bottle of wine between us with "Sway" by Bic Runga crooning in the background.

I sink deeper into the plush couch, a glass of wine dangling from my fingertips.

"You know what's crazy?" Riley breaks the comfortable silence, her voice full of humor.

"Hmm?" Philippa and I echo at the same time.

"You went from no guys to two guys in a matter of weeks," Riley drawls from her end of the couch, one knee tucked up as she scrolls through her phone. "You been making milkshakes in private?"

"What?" I blurt out, chuckling under my breath.

Philippa, sitting elegantly in an armchair—because, of course, she can't lounge like a normal person—sips her wine, watching us over the rim of her glass like a cat ready to pounce.

"Don't 'what' me, babe." Riley grins, eyes glinting with mischief. "You're in quite the pickle."

"There really isn't anything to talk about," I mutter quickly, heat rushing to my cheeks. "Broderick and I are..." I falter, unsure how to finish that sentence. Friends? Acquaintances forced into the same wedding party? Something more?

"Yes, please," Philippa purrs, her gaze sharp. "Enlighten us, Elena. What exactly are you?"

I throw my head back against the couch, groaning. "Friends, I guess."

Riley snorts. "Yeah, you sound real convinced."

"Sounds like you're working overtime to assure yourself of that," Philippa adds, her eyes glimmering.

"It doesn't matter," I shoot back. "I'm *with* Alex."

Riley arches a brow. "Oh? So you've defined the relationship?"

"Well, not exactly," I say, swirling my wine glass.

"So, you're still a free agent." Riley smirks knowingly.

I roll my eyes. "No. I mean, I want Alex. He's the one I want." I say it firmly, like speaking it out loud might make it true.

Philippa exchanges a look with Riley. "If you say so."

"I do."

"Okay," Riley says slowly, a wicked grin spreading. "But let's say—hypothetically—there was *something* with Broderick. What would that be?"

I exhale sharply. "I don't know. I don't even know how I ended up in this mess."

Riley scoffs. "Oh, no, poor you. Two hot, successful men chasing after you. What a nightmare."

Philippa, ever composed, doesn't take the bait. "You sound surprised."

"Of course I'm surprised," I groan, leaning forward. "I have nothing to compare this to! I wasn't some serial dater before, Pip. I didn't—" I hesitate, swirling my wine. "I never thought I'd be here. Torn between two completely different men, trying to figure out how this even happened."

Riley rolls her eyes. "Well, I know what I want. Alex. No contest."

Philippa lets out a slow breath. "Of course you'd say that."

"Obviously! He's hot, exciting, makes her feel *something*. Admit it, babe, when you're with him, it's thrilling."

I chew my lip but don't argue. She's not wrong.

Philippa isn't impressed. "He's complicated. You know that, Elena."

"Oh, here we go," I mutter.

"You need someone steady. Someone grounded, especially with your career." Her eyes soften. "Broderick's caring, steady, and accomplished."

Riley scoffs. "Steady? *Boring*. No matter how stunning the packaging."

Philippa's gaze sharpens. "Because he doesn't bring chaos? Broderick is real, Riley. Not a fantasy."

"God forbid Elena has some fun for once," Riley snaps. "Just because you like the safe option doesn't mean she should."

Philippa narrows her eyes. "And just because you run through men like it's a sprint, doesn't mean she should."

The room goes still.

Riley's eyes are wide, hurt flashing across her face. "Wow. Okay. That was low, even for you."

"Both of you, stop," I say, rubbing my temples. "This isn't some reality show, and I'm not a prize."

Riley crosses her arms. "On this season of *The Bachelorette*, Elena's search for love continues."

Philippa and Riley laugh. I shoot them a glare.

She sighs. "Fine. But it's a big deal—this has *never* happened before. And come on, you have to admit the contestants are delicious. But seriously, babe, you need to figure out what *you* want. Not what *we* want for you."

Philippa, voice softer now, adds, "On that, I agree. Just don't lose yourself in the excitement. Think about what kind of love lasts."

I exhale, staring at the deep red liquid in my glass. And then, before I can stop myself, the words spill out.

"I don't know what I want, Pip. How could I?" I gesture vaguely with my glass. "I'm twenty-two years old. I was practically raised in a bubble. Before I met Alex, I'd been kissed, felt up, and left high and dry. That's about it. And now? Now I have two men making me question everything, and I don't even know what the hell I'm doing."

There's a beat of silence.

Philippa's expression softens, but Riley—Riley nearly chokes on her wine.

"Wait, *what?* Are you telling me—hold on, hold on." She sets her glass down like she needs both hands to process this. "Are you telling me you're *still* a virgin?"

My face flames. "Jesus, Riley, shout it louder. I don't think the people across the street heard you."

Her eyes are huge. "But you and Alex—I thought you—"

"Riley, please, I don't really want to hear about my sister's *sexcapades*." Philippa raises her hand.

"We haven't," I admit, gripping my glass tighter. "And it's not like I planned it this way, okay? I've spent so much of my life not thinking about romance, not really dating, and now I'm here, and it's…" I sigh. "It's a lot."

Philippa reaches out, squeezing my hand. "Elena, there's nothing wrong with that."

Riley, still wide-eyed, lets out a low whistle. "Damn, you have Alexander Fucking Westerberg, Heartthrob King of Sin and Orgasm-Giver, and Broderick, CEO of I Would Climb That Like a Tree, Heal The World Hot Hottie, *both* lusting for you."

I groan. "When you say it like that…"

"You want my honest opinion?" Riley asks, teasing.

"Do I have a choice?"

She smirks. "Nope. Screw 'em both."

I nearly spit out my wine, and Philippa chokes on hers beside me.

"Separately. But together would be fun." Riley winks.

Philippa, trying to regain composure, tsks. "Or, you know,

pick the one you connect with. Broderick is kind. But whatever you decide, don't hurt him. He doesn't deserve that."

"And he's hot enough to make nuns rethink their vows," Riley adds.

I laugh helplessly. "God, I hate you both."

Philippa smiles, softer now. "No, you don't. But you *do* need to figure out what you want. It's not fair to string them both along."

She's right. I think.

"Also," Philippa adds quietly. "I'm sorry, Riley. That was a low blow earlier."

Riley exhales. "Yeah, well…I didn't have to bite your head off either. I'm sorry too."

Philippa gives her a small smile, and Riley raises her glass toward her in a silent toast.

I watch them, warmth blooming in my chest despite everything.

"I love you guys," I murmur, even as I rub my temples. "You're impossible, but I love you."

Riley smirks. "We love you, too. Even if you are a hot mess."

Philippa squeezes my hand. "Especially then."

And yet, as I lean back against the couch, wine glass trembling slightly in my hand, one thing clings to me like a bruise that won't fade. That loneliness that aches deep inside.

The part of me that Alex seems to understand, because he's felt that loneliness too. He was drawn to it and perhaps I was drawn to his, two lonely ships, passing in the night. I know one thing for sure, we're definitely lovers, definitely not nothing.

But then there is Broderick, who makes that loneliness disappear altogether, makes it so it isn't even a thought in my mind. His warmth is like the sun—endless, a safe harbor to sail into. Someone like him could never understand that loneliness. Yet, would he even want me if he knew how unlovable I am? How the first man who was supposed to love me, want me, was willing to toss me aside. We're definitely friends, but definitely not nothing either.

Alex *is* the safe choice. And he's still here, even after I shared it all with him. I have let him in when I've turned others away. And maybe that's it—I opened up to him and that allowed Broderick to pass through, too easy, too quickly.

He wouldn't choose me. Not if he knew. He likes what he sees like most boys do. Broderick is too good for someone like me. He would never get it.

He could never understand. Would he?

Chapter 18

Under My Skin

It's hard to believe it's been almost a month since I arrived in New York. Between days spent in the studio, radio interviews, and quiet movie nights in with Alex—nights that inevitably turn into heated make-out sessions, leaving movies unfinished—I've barely had time to prepare for Philippa and Andrew's joint weekend celebration. With time running short, I invite Broderick over after work.

He told me he usually didn't finish until nine—sometimes later—but when I said I'd probably be in bed by then, we settled on a more reasonable five o'clock.

I don't know why seeing him again after the gala makes me nervous, but I've changed my outfit four times—finally settling on a fitted black T-shirt and jeans. Classic. Casual.

I lay out my laptop, snacks, and notepads across the dining table. Tidy the apartment. Run a cloth over the counter I've already cleaned twice. I'm doodling absentmindedly on the edge of a notepad when the buzzer goes off.

I cross to the wall and press the button. "Hey."

"Hey, El." His voice comes through the buzzer.

"Come on up."

I smooth my hand down my jeans. My insides flutter, restless and electric.

Why am I so nervous?

Pacing the entryway, I try not to overthink until I hear the knock.

Deep breath. I open the door.

There he is. Suited up, gorgeous as ever, bag slung over one shoulder. Flowers in his hand.

Flowers?

"Hot date?" I ask, nodding at the bouquet.

"Kinda." He chuckles. "They're for you. To congratulate you on the new place—and my mother would smack me over the head if I showed up empty-handed."

He hands them to me. Pink tulips.

Oh. He brought *me* flowers.

"That's…unexpected."

"That's me—unexpected. So, are we gonna stand out here and work, or are you gonna invite me in?" He smirks.

"If you insist," I say, rolling my eyes.

I place the tulips in a vase on the dining table as we take our seats. He pulls out his tablet, scrolling through the guest list, pointing out who has and hasn't RSVP'd. Broderick assigns himself the task of following up with the stragglers—he knows the entire list personally, which makes sense.

As he talks, I can't help but stare. He's so confident, so smug and cocky, that I'm completely distracted. His words drift into background noise, my focus shifting instead to the quiet intensity in his eyes, the easy way he moves. Halfway through our conversation, he shrugs his jacket off, and my attention snaps to how taut his shirt stretches over his chest, how the buttons strain slightly, hinting at the toned muscle beneath.

My mouth goes dry. Heat rushes to my cheeks.

There is lust here for sure. While Alex is billboard handsome, Broderick is rugged and manly, drop-dead gorgeous. Both hot, both good-looking. Maybe Riley is on to something.

"One less thing to chase." He speaks absently, eyes still on his tablet.

I barely hear him. God, what is wrong with me?

"Did you talk to your father about Montgomery Estate?" he asks, pulling me sharply from my thoughts.

I blink rapidly, heart stumbling. "I thought you were going to do that." I shake my head, trying to clear it.

He lifts a brow, amused disbelief coloring his expression. "We assigned that task to you."

Shit.

"We did?" I cough, voice embarrassingly hoarse.

Focus. Stop ogling him.

"He's *your* dad," he says, shrugging. "Makes sense."

His words hit like ice water—sharp, bracing, all lingering warmth instantly doused. I recoil internally, any desire quickly extinguished. Right, *my father*.

"Fuck. Shit. Sorry," I hiss softly, embarrassment pooling hot in my chest.

"Call him now," he says calmly, as if it's nothing at all.

"That usually requires a little more emotional preparation," I groan, shoulders slumping.

"Well, I'm here for emotional support."

If only he knew. I roll my eyes at him, unlocking my phone, and scroll to *Father* in my contacts, tapping it once.

Why does even that word fill me with dread?

I stare at the screen like it might bite me, thumb hovering a beat too long before pressing call. It rings. Broderick watches from next to me, one brow lifted, the corner of his mouth tilting enough to make me smirk despite myself.

The line clicks.

"Eleanor," my father answers.

My smile drops.

"Elena, please," I correct him.

"Sorry, sorry. Bad habit. I must change it on my phone. I'll have to ask Colin how to do that."

My jaw tenses. "All good." The sugar in my voice clashes with the metallic tang at the back of my throat.

"To what do I owe the pleasure?"

I brace myself for his disappointment, hoping he doesn't think I'm irresponsible for leaving this to the last minute to organize.

"I'm so sorry to spring this on you so late, but we need to use Montgomery Estate for Philippa and Andrew's bachelorette weekend."

"Of course, Elena, you're welcome to use it anytime," he says.

The relief comes fast, hot and full-bodied, like a valve released behind my ribs.

"When is it?" he asks.

"Two weeks from tomorrow," I say through clenched teeth, hoping he doesn't blow up at the last minute of it all.

"That's…tight, but it should be okay. Do you need it fully staffed?"

I glance at Broderick. He gives a small shrug, then nods.

"Yes. Yes, please," I say quickly, trying not to sound too eager.

"Alright, I'll let Colin know," my father replies, his tone calm and matter-of-fact.

"Thank you."

"My pleasure," he says. "Enjoy yourself. You haven't been to the Hamptons since you were twelve."

"I know," I say softly. "And thank you again."

"Yes, thank you, Mr. Montgomery," Broderick calls, voice calm, unbothered.

I narrow my eyes at him.

"Broderick, is that you?" my father asks.

"Yes, sir." His voice is polite and professional.

I look at him like he's grown two heads…*sir.*

"You're with Elena?" he adds, a note of curiosity curling at the edge of his words. Maybe even amusement.

"We're planning the event." There's a hint of a smile. "You know, as best man and maid of honor."

"Oh, that's delightful. Well, you two have fun. Carole and I are headed to dinner with some friends."

Did Mortimer Montgomery just tell me to have fun with Broderick?

What the fuck.

"Of course, Father. Thank you again."

I hang up before he can say anything else, thumb hovering over the screen until it fades to black in my hand. My palm is damp. I wipe it against my thigh, pretending it's not from nerves.

"Eleanor, eh?" Broderick's eyes light with humor, lips already curled like he's been holding that in the whole call.

"Don't start. It's my grandmother's name." I huff, popping a gummy bear into my mouth and chewing harder than necessary.

"Makes sense why you wanted to do all the geriatric activities for the weekend. In bed by nine. Secretly an old granny, are you? *Eleanor?*"

I throw a gummy bear at him without even aiming. He catches it easily and pops it into his mouth.

"Call me that again and you'll be leaving here in a body bag."

He barks out a laugh—sharp, open-mouthed, the kind that fills the room.

"You could try," he says, leaning back in his chair, all smug and confident. "But you're a *little* disadvantaged." He pinches his fingers together.

"A little lethal," I mutter, scowling at him. "I have easy access from down here, a slice to your Achilles tendon, and you'd go down like a bag of bricks."

His grin deepens, dimples flashing.

Dimples. I could swoon, but coupled with his arrogance, it only mocks me.

"Anyway, my mom always taught me that good sleep means good skin," I add, fingertips brushing along my cheekbone.

Mom.

The word lands wrong. My smile fades before I can catch it.

Broderick's eyes flick over to me, softer now. Less teasing.

"You do have good skin," he adds quietly.

"Yeah. Thanks," I whisper, looking down.

He doesn't move, just watches me. His voice drops.

"Hey. You okay?"

I nod, then shake my head. "Yeah, it's…" I breathe out. "It's been a while since I've talked about her. It's like…she's slipping away from memory the more I live my life."

He nods slowly, lips pressed together.

"I get it. Happens to me too," he says. "I don't even remember what my dad looks like anymore. Not unless I'm staring at a picture. He's been gone so long, it's like…pieces get foggy."

I bite the inside of my cheek. My throat tightens. There's nothing useful in my head—no comforting line, no tidy sentiment.

So I nod again.

I realize how little I actually know about Broderick. Other than that he's Philippa and Andrew's friend, a guy who is drop dead gorgeous with a cocky attitude to match. I didn't know his father had passed. I didn't know his grief sat under his skin like mine does.

"I'm sorry about your dad," I murmur.

I study him. The kindness in his eyes. The way the light clings to the sun-warmed gold of his skin. I wonder if he likes being outdoors. I wonder what he looks like when he's completely unguarded.

He smiles, but it's not full. Sitting somewhere behind his eyes, quiet and thoughtful.

We stare at each other, neither of us moving. Holding the silence between us like it might crack if we breathed too loud.

"Do…you want to talk about it?" he asks, voice low and steady as his hand finds mine.

It's warm. Solid. Not searching—just there. Soothing in the way that sneaks up on you, like background music you didn't realize was calming you down until it's gone.

I shake my head.

"We've got a lot more to cover," I say, trying to keep my voice even as I straighten up, bones shifting into place like armor.

I can't let him in. I shouldn't.

I don't pull my hand away, even though I should. Even though it lingers too long, saying more than I want to hear right now.

"Okay." He lifts his hand, fingers brushing lightly as they leave mine, and turns back to the tablet.

The absence is instant. Cold rushes into the space where he was.

We settle back into a quiet rhythm, crossing items off the list one by one. Room assignments, scheduled activities, catering services, logistics, welcome bags—the works. Each tick of the checklist loosens the weight between us.

"We work pretty well together." He slips his tablet back into his bag.

"That we do. I hope Andrew and Pip have a great time." I sigh, stretching my arms overhead.

The movement pulls my shirt tight across my chest. I notice, but more than that, I notice *him* noticing.

His gaze lingers.

Brief. Sharp.

Then his eyes flicker, jaw tensing slightly, and he shakes his head once. Like he's brushing something off. Like he's reminding himself *don't.*

So he's not completely immune.

The thought flares and fades just as fast.

"So, Broderick." I stretch his name out, shifting in my seat. "Can I ask you something?"

He leans back, one arm draped casually over my chair. "Sure. What do you want to know?"

"When did you and *Mr. Montgomery* get so…*cozy?*"

He doesn't flinch. "He's a business acquaintance. We've worked on a few projects and initiatives together. I've worked with Phil, too."

He shrugs like it's nothing. Like it's normal.

"So you work for The Montgomery Group?"

"Not exactly." He shifts slightly. "I've got my own company —Goodman Enterprises."

"Wait, *you* own Goodman Enterprises?" My jaw falls to the floor. He's in his early thirties and owns a billion-dollar company.

He shrugs like it's nothing. "But some of the work I do aligns with The Montgomery Group. It's good business."

He pauses, then adds, "Your father's been somewhat of a mentor. He sits on our board."

My brain scrambles to catch up. Broderick owns Goodman Enterprises. My father mentoring Broderick. Sitting on his board? It doesn't compute. Or maybe it computes *too* well.

And I don't like it.

"Mentoring you?" It feels dirty leaving my mouth.

Broderick doesn't flinch. "Your father's a shrewd business-man. El, I get that you don't like him, but there's no one better to learn from."

Oh, he picked up on my dislike for Mortimer. If Mortimer was shrewd, so was he.

"Aww, do you guys golf together and wear matching polos?" I shoot back, leaning into the bite.

"Yeah," he says, deadpan. "I think we have a matching plaid set."

We both laugh.

Fine. Mortimer Montgomery runs a billion-dollar empire. Anyone in business would probably claw their own face off to be mentored by him. I can't blame Broderick for the hustle, even if he *is* from money. That's how rich people stay rich: brush shoulders with the rich, or richer, and keep climbing.

I tilt my head, eyes narrowing.

"So…what exactly *is* good business?" I ask, softer now. The question feels like it matters more than I want it to.

From the gala, I gathered they build stuff around the world. But his venture—it has me curious. I want to know what makes Broderick tick.

"Major redevelopment projects around the world. Ethical housing. Urban renewal, especially in third-world countries. Major infrastructure. Stocks. I also fund a few successful tech start-ups—mostly proprietary tech for property management."

He says it like he's rattling off lunch options. No ego, no showmanship. Just facts.

I study him.

There's something disarming about the way he speaks. How open he is. No pretense. No careful calculations or smoke screens.

When I asked Alex the same question, he'd dodged it—eyes flashing, lips curving around half-truths. Sure, he was trying to keep his identity hidden. But still. The comparison doesn't go unnoticed.

"What?" I exclaim. "That's kind of a big deal."

"Not really." He shrugs, casual as ever. Like owning entire city blocks and rebuilding countries is no more impressive than remembering to water his plants.

I narrow my eyes.

Liar.

I pull out my phone and quickly type his name into the search engine.

My eyes widen instantly.

Article after article floods my screen.

On him.

On his work.

"The billionaire builder with a heart of gold," I read aloud, my lips curling into a teasing grin.

"El—" he protests, looking almost embarrassed, reaching for my phone. I stand, walking away, laughing.

"Oh, look at you, hot stuff, 'Forbes Under Thirty-Five,'" I announce with mock excitement, waving the phone *just* out of his reach.

He lunges forward, and I lean back further, nearly tripping.

He could easily grab it if he wanted to, overpower me, but he's being respectful. The challenge of pushing him to the edge excites me.

"Social Entrepreneurship Award, two years running!" I continue dramatically, still scrolling. He wraps an arm around my waist, tugging me toward him as I squirm playfully.

"Viral TED Talk on Housing Dignity—wow, Broderick, so humble," I tease breathlessly, giggling even as his fingers brush my ribs, tickling softly.

"Enough," he growls, voice low. His eyes dance with humor, but I dodge again, eyes glued to the screen.

"Oh my God," I gasp theatrically. "Graduated summa cum laude from Columbia with a double degree in Business Management and Engineering?" I raise a brow at him, impressed despite my playful tone. "Wow, you're actually a nerd."

"Okay, seriously, stop." He chuckles, tightening his grip. I twist away, but he's quicker, pinning me gently against the edge of the table, reaching again for the phone.

"Wait, wait—there's more!" My heart races, cheeks flushed. "Leader in sustainable housing initiatives, investor in renewable energy startups, founder of numerous global crisis relief projects…" I trail off, breathing heavily as he finally manages to pry the phone from my hand.

But he doesn't step back.

He holds my gaze, close enough that the warmth of his body melts through my clothes. Our laughter fades slowly, replaced by ragged breaths and something charged. My pulse thrums, echoing in my ears, as his eyes trace my features. His gaze dips to my lips, lingering.

I brush my tongue over my lips. I don't move away. Neither does he.

Time pauses, suspended in that fragile sliver of silence between us. His fingers brush a loose tendril from my cheek, lingering softly, warm against my skin. The rough pad of his thumb grazes along my jawline, sending tiny sparks tumbling through me.

My heart slams violently against my ribs, so loud I'm certain he hears it.

Kiss me.

The thought comes swiftly, unbidden, terrifyingly honest.

What? No, I shouldn't—but I can't think clearly. Not with him standing *this* close, the air thick, pulsing with something dangerous and inevitable.

His eyes lock onto mine, deep green, endless. Slowly, he lowers his face toward me, close enough that the heat of his breath whispers against my lips. My eyes flutter shut, pulse roaring, every muscle in my body singing as I wait, breathless, for his lips to *finally* touch mine—

My phone rings sharply in his hand—loud, intrusive, and unapologetic.

My eyes fly open as reality crashes back. *Fuck.* I squirm from under him, pressed against the table, breath ragged, skin burning. He takes a reluctant step back.

I can't believe *that* almost happened.

It was the edge I was toying with, but hadn't expected.

He glances down at the phone ringing angrily in his palm, his expression a tortured mix of longing and pent-up frustration. Then he flips the phone over, glances at the screen, and something shifts, his face dropping sharply. Disappointment flickers, raw and undisguised.

Wordlessly, he hands me the phone, stepping back and dragging his fingers roughly through his hair.

I look down, heart sinking into my stomach.

Alex.

Broderick clears his throat, breaking the silence. My phone feels hot and heavy in my hand. I turn away slightly, tapping the button.

"Hi," I answer, my voice higher, breathier than I want.

"Hello, Älskling," Alex replies, voice smooth and soothing, sliding easily over my nerves. "The photos of you from the gala look incredible. I *like* you in red."

My heart hums erratically in my chest, dancing between the lingering heat from Broderick and Alex's easy compliment.

Which is it? I honestly don't know.

A lump of guilt forms in my throat. "Do you?"

He chuckles softly, rich and knowing, a sound that pulls a reluctant smile onto my lips.

"Are you busy tonight?" he asks gently. "Can I come see you?"

My gaze darts instinctively toward Broderick. He's still

standing there, seemingly unbothered, scrolling aimlessly through his phone.

No. Not now. Definitely not now.

I step quickly into the kitchen, craving distance, privacy, space to think and breathe.

"Actually, I'm just wrapping up a meeting. I can come to you instead?" I offer quietly.

"That sounds good," he replies, his voice gentle. "Have you eaten? We can make dinner if you'd like."

"If gummy bears count as food," I joke weakly.

He laughs again, softly amused. "Ah, no. Let me take care of you Darling."

His offer sounds so tender and sincere. He wants to take care of me, while my skin is still scorched from Broderick's touch.

"Okay," is all I can manage through the shame.

"See you in an hour?"

"See you then," I say, ending the call quickly.

Smoothing my shirt down, I straighten my spine and flip my hair back over my shoulder. I try to scramble my composure before walking back into the dining room, forcing my breath to steady.

"Hey, sorry about that." I wave it off, casually.

"All good." Broderick's eyes flick up from his phone, his voice guarded now. "The boyfriend?"

"No, not exactly," I snap, sharper than intended. Alex and I haven't exactly defined things. I'm not even sure how it works. Does he formally ask me? Is there some kind of ceremony? Do we wear matching name tags? The whole thought makes me uncomfortable.

One thing I *am* sure of, though—whatever happened now between Broderick and me can't happen again.

"About before," I start awkwardly.

"Yeah, sorry—that was—" he interrupts, equally awkward.

"Yeah."

We stumble over our words, sentences half-formed, broken, neither of us able to fully acknowledge what nearly happened. My teeth sink into my lower lip. We almost kissed.

Almost.

Did I want it? I'm not sure. What if Alex hadn't called?

"It's cool, El," Broderick says, shrugging easily, his smile faint but forced. "We're cool. Sorry about all that."

"I've got to head out," I announce quickly.

"Hot date?" Broderick asks, voice carefully casual, eyes searching mine for an answer he doesn't really want.

"Something like that," I reply softly, forcing a playful shrug.

I try to ignore how his smile falters, how disappointment flickers briefly at its edges before he manages to conceal it.

"We good?" I ask, my voice gentle now, a little uncertain.

"Yeah, we're good," he echoes quietly.

But the look in his eyes—the subtle strain beneath the surface—doesn't quite convince me. I open the door, ushering him out, my stomach twisting as he brushes past me.

We're anything but good.

The thought of being alone with Broderick at the Hamptons feels loaded with temptation.

Maybe Alex could come along. I think it's his birthday that weekend, anyway. We could spend time together. I could get Broderick off my mind.

What's the worst that could happen?

Chapter 19

Radio

As soon as Broderick is gone, I dash to my bedroom, already pulling my T-shirt over my head as I go. My clothes hit the floor without ceremony. I stand there, unsure of what to wear.

I like you in red.

I can't wear the gown I wore to the gala, obviously, but I do pick out another dress hanging in the back of my closet, compliments to Rio, saved for an occasion such as this—tight bodice, cinched waist, and flaring out and cutting above the knee, the perfect balance of cute and sexy.

I smooth the fabric over my hips, glancing at myself in the mirror.

I hope he likes this.

I busy myself, desperate to shake off the remnants of what *almost* happened with Broderick, even as the echo of it lingers. I focus instead on what *might* happen tonight.

The last time I was alone at Alex's place, he touched me like no one ever had before. Like I was something rare.

I'd be lying if I said I wasn't hoping for more tonight.

The memory flashes—his lips on my skin, *there*—and the way my name sounded in his mouth.

I blush, warmth blooming across my cheeks.

At the vanity, I apply a touch of makeup—not too much. Enough to make me look and feel like I haven't been pacing emotionally between two men all night.

I run a brush through my hair, tossing it back off my shoulders. Lip balm. Perfume. Wallet. Keys.

Then I pause.

My eyes drift toward the drawer beside my bed. I open it slowly.

Condoms.

I stare at them. *Maybe.* I hesitate, then grab one and slip it discreetly into my purse.

I should probably look into going on the pill, I think absent-mindedly, zipping my bag.

Just in case.

I settle into the cab heading toward Noho, to Alex's place. Before I can invite him to the Hamptons, I should ask Philippa first.

Pulling out my phone, I settle on a text.

ELENA

Hey Pip, can I invite Alex to the Hamptons?

I hit send, then lean back, watching the city flash by—alive and pulsing as we move through the night traffic. Windows blur with neon and taillights. My phone dings.

PHILIPPA

Alex? Your Alex?

He's not my Alex.

Not really. Not yet.

I type back quickly.

ELENA

Yes, please. It's his birthday that weekend too.

I stare at the screen, the message hovering in my lap like it might change everything.

Another ding.

PHILIPPA

OKAY.

A smile tugs at the corner of my mouth. I'm giddy. A little breathless. She agreed. Now all that's left is Alex.

By the time I reach his building, my pulse is already ticking faster. I ride the elevator in silence, the mirrored walls catching the red of my dress, the flushed pink in my cheeks.

The butterflies are already fluttering, wildly. Heat gathers low and slow beneath my skin.

The elevator hums toward the top floor.

I press the buzzer. The door opens a moment later, and there he is.

White T-shirt. Loose gray sweats. His hair damp from a shower, curling slightly at the ends. He smells clean, fresh. His skin glows, flushed from the heat.

He looks *so* good. So sexy.

"Hi," I squeak.

His eyes widen as they take me in, sweeping from my heels to the hem of my dress, then climbing slowly, deliberately, up my body. They stop at my chest. He lingers.

He likes what he sees.

"You dressed up for me?" he asks, voice low, rough. His gaze darkens.

I nod, lips parting, but I don't get the chance to speak.

He yanks me by the waist and lifts me clean off the ground. I gasp, arms looping around his neck as my legs wrap easily around him. My purse slips from my shoulder, landing somewhere on the floor.

He kisses me. Hard.

Urgent. Hungry. Like he's been waiting all day.

His fingers grasp the nape of my neck.

I melt into him, breath stolen, every nerve lit, and don't care that we haven't talked. That things are undefined. That this might not be a good idea.

All I know is his mouth, his hands, the heat spiraling fast and unstoppable between us.

Then my stomach growls.

Loud. Immediate. So obnoxiously human, it breaks the moment clean in half.

He pulls back, eyebrows lifting as he stares at me. Then he grins.

"Hungry?"

"I guess so." I giggle, embarrassed, cheeks flushed as I cling to him.

He sets me down gently, his hands lingering at my waist. "Let's get you fed then."

I reach for my purse, scooping it off the floor as we head inside. The lights are low and warm, "I Only Have Eyes for You" by the Flamingos playing softly on his record player. The kitchen is already alive—pots bubbling gently on the stove, fresh ingredients neatly lined up.

"Can I help with anything?" I ask, hovering near the island.

"No, Älskling," he says, turning toward me, that lazy grin back on his lips. "Let me cook for you."

He moves in close, hands slipping around my waist as he lifts me onto the counter with effortless ease.

"Sit here on display like the sexy little thing you are," he murmurs, planting soft, lingering kisses along my neck. Each one makes me gasp, my breath catching as goose bumps rise across my skin.

"Wine?" he asks, pulling back to meet my eyes.

"Yes, please," I whisper, still a little breathless.

He opens a bottle of rosé with practiced ease, the cork popping gently before he pours the blush-pink liquid into a glass. He hands it to me, fingers brushing mine.

"Thank you." I take a sip. It's cold, sweet, and crisp—the perfect distraction.

"Good?"

I nod. "It's perfect. How was your day?"

He turns back to the stove, sprinkling sea salt over thick cuts of salmon. "Busy. We got our scripts for the next season of filming."

"Oh, that's exciting." I swirl the wine in my glass, letting the words hang lightly.

"Yeah." He nods, focused on the stove. "They're also doing final rounds of edits on *The Kingmaker*. Should be out in theatres soon."

His voice dips for half a second, like there's something else he wants to say. But he doesn't. Instead, he pivots.

"How's your album coming along?" he asks, placing the salmon in the hot pan. The sizzle fills the room as his body angles slightly toward me.

"Great," I reply. "I recorded two more tracks last week—they're thinking a September release."

"That's good." He glances at me over his shoulder. "What are the new songs about?"

I take a long sip of wine. My throat tightens as I force it down.

"You," I admit, biting my lip. Heat climbs up my neck, flushed and spreading—embarrassment or wine, I'm not sure which.

His brows lift, eyes dark with something unreadable.

"An honor," he says softly, then turns back to the pan, flipping the salmon with steady, deliberate calm.

My heart thumps against my ribs, stupidly loud in my chest.

"Speaking of honor." I rush the words before I lose my nerve. "Would you honor me with your presence at the Hamptons? It's the weekend of your birthday—my sister's joint bachelorette party with her fiancé. At my family's house. I mean, if you don't want to, that's fine. You probably have plans. It's your birthday… of course you'd have plans—"

I stop myself before I spiral.

He closes the space between us without a word, hands sliding over my thighs, parting them gently as he steps between.

I look up at him, breath caught in my chest.

"The Hamptons with you?" he murmurs, cupping my face, his thumbs brushing along my jaw. "Sounds good to me."

Then he kisses me.

It's slow—like he's sealing a promise, RSVPing with his tongue.

Before I can chase the warmth of it, he pulls away.

Ugh. Come back.

But he's already turned, back at the stove like nothing happened. The air around me still buzzes, every nerve jolting for more. I take another sip of wine, the rosé slipping down too easily on an empty stomach. I'm lightheaded. Warm. A little floaty.

He plates the food—salmon, roasted potatoes, crisp green vegetables, a simple salad—and sets it down on the dining table with quiet confidence. It smells incredible.

We sit. He tugs my legs into his lap, his hand settling on my bare knee like it belongs there. I settle into the feeling, the moment. It's domestic, almost tender, but charged underneath.

"I can't wait for you to hear them," I say between mouthfuls, trying not to sound too giddy. *This is so good.*

"Your album?"

"Yes. Maybe after the Hamptons. Or"—I glance at him, hopeful—"you could come to the studio while we're recording?"

He chews thoughtfully, then nods. "Let me get back to you on that. I've got a few things lined up, but I'm sure I can make the time."

"Okay."

He's quiet for a second, then glances up at me.

"Actually…would you be interested in being my date to the red carpet premiere for *The Kingmaker*?" he asks, drawing lazy patterns across my skin

My fork pauses mid-air.

Red carpet.

Paparazzi.

With him.

That sounds…official.

Is this it? Is this the talk?

"Is that a good idea? When is it? That seems official, like *really* official, and the media, oh."

He chuckles, deep and easy. "It's not for a while. Just floating it on your radar."

"Okay." The word comes out slowly as I try to process. Not quite the talk I was hoping for. "I mean, I'll think about it. I'll talk to Kylie."

Now that the media buzz around us has died down, Kylie's been gently steering me toward low-key, off-grid dates. Private dinners. Hotel lobbies with back entrances. Nothing too flashy, nothing too public. She doesn't trust the press—or the fans who treat Alex like a public commodity.

He takes a long sip of wine, watching me over the rim of his glass. "You know, a few calculated public appearances might actually drum up more interest for your new album. Your older stuff's been getting some airtime again, hasn't it?"

He's not wrong.

His fans—fierce, loyal, intense—flooded toward my music, giving my old album new life. So much so that the tracks are charting again. The attention is flattering, sure, but part of me bristles.

I want my work to stand on its own.

"Alex…I wouldn't want to use you like that." The words come gently. "It's not right."

He looks at me, and for a second, something shifts. His eyes widen—not in shock, but in something softer. Gratitude. Relief.

"That's so refreshing to hear," he whispers. Quiet, almost like a confession. He's told me before how people have used him, twisted their proximity into opportunity. Madison included.

He always looks so composed, so glossy and unbothered, but with me, he lets the polish slip. Shows the boy underneath the fame. And I like that version of him. I *want* that version of him.

"Do you want to stay over tonight?" he asks, his hand squeezing my thigh, gentle and warm.

I blink. "I didn't bring anything—no toothbrush, no clothes."

"You could sleep naked." He winks. "Like I usually do."

My breath catches.

The condom in my purse suddenly weighs a hundred pounds.

I shouldn't have packed it. Am I ready for that? For him? For what it would mean?

Fuck.

"Elena," he says softly, like he sees the storm crossing my face. "Relax. We don't have to have sex. Stay over. Spend the night. We can talk. I've got a spare toothbrush. You can borrow something of mine."

There's no pressure in his voice.

"Okay," I whisper.

We finish the rest of dinner, rosé included. Conversation flows easily now, a soft blur of shared stories and low laughter. We talk more about the Hamptons—I leave out the part about a certain best man—and drift into music playing low in the background. He tells me about his sister, Ingrid, the writer who lives in England. The way his voice warms when he mentions her makes me smile.

The hours slip by unnoticed. By the time we finally head to his bedroom, it's well past midnight.

He pulls out a pajama set for me—soft cotton in a deep maroon—and hands it over with a gentle smile.

"Help yourself to any skincare. There's heaps. I get sent a lot of stuff," he says, gesturing toward the ensuite. "I'll give you some privacy."

He slides the door shut behind me.

He wasn't kidding. The counter is adorned neatly with rows of expensive skincare, high-end labels, and tiny frosted jars. Lotions, serums, and potions in glass droppers. I undress slowly, folding my clothes into a tidy pile on the bench.

I twist my hair into a messy bun, shower, brush my teeth, remove my makeup. Wash my face with something that smells like cucumber and money.

The routine feels quiet. Mundane.

Is this what it would be like? Sharing a space with him. Doing ordinary things beside someone extraordinary. I can't help the thought.

And I can't help how much I like it.

When I step back into the bedroom, the lights are low, casting everything in soft amber. Alex is already in bed, propped against the pillows in nothing but briefs. My breath hitches.

His body is lean, golden, chiseled to perfection. He looks over at me and grins.

"Come here," he pats the space beside him.

I bite my lip as I walk to the edge of the bed, fingers hooking the waistband of his shorts. They're far too big, already slipping down my hips. I let them fall and step out, climbing in beside him.

His gaze catches on the bare stretch of my thighs—and lingers. Hunger flashes across his face, raw and unguarded.

He wants me.

The thought hits like a rush. Like a drug. That someone like *him* would want someone like *me*.

I settle under the sheets, keeping to my side, heart racing.

"You're so far away," he murmurs before pulling me into his arms.

I squeal, giggling as he tickles my sides, then gasp when he steals my laughter with his mouth. His lips are warm, minty.

When did he brush his teeth? I don't care. I melt into the kiss, my body arching instinctively into his.

His hands roam over my—waist, hips, breasts—fingertips skimming like he's trying to memorize every curve. I groan softly into his mouth.

"Alex," I whisper, breathless.

He pulls back just enough to look at me. Smirks as he brushes my hair from my face.

"Temptress," he murmurs. "You keep this up, and I'll forget every last ounce of control I have."

I let out a shaky laugh. "Wait—when did you brush your teeth?"

He sighs. Then laughs, low and warm, his chest shaking. "Elena, I'm trying to seduce you, and you're asking about my dental routine?"

"Sorry."

"The other bathroom." He turns off the bedside lamp, and we're engulfed in darkness, save for the light from the city below, shining through the windows.

I giggle again, nuzzling into him. The tension breaks, but not completely. Not with the way he's holding me.

He kisses me again, this time soft. A peck. He pulls me onto his chest, his hand tracing my back, slow and soothing. My cheek rests against him, rising and falling with each breath.

His fingertips keep moving. Gentle, rhythmic strokes against my spine. A quiet spark. My skin tingles beneath his touch, like his fingers are dipped in heat.

"Can I ask you something?" I murmur.

"Of course." His breath is warm on my forehead.

"What's sex like? For a guy, I mean."

He's quiet for a moment. Then his voice drops lower.

"Well, for me…I feel lightheaded. All the blood rushes down there. It's primal. All you want to do is bury yourself inside a warm pussy."

The word slides through the air like silk and fire. My nipples harden instantly beneath the soft fabric of his shirt. My breath slows. Deepens.

"The moment you slide in," he continues, dragging his fingertips in patient, winding motions along my back, "it's like you're home. You fit like a puzzle piece. The heat. The wetness. Every stroke pulls you in deeper, like your whole body's being swallowed."

I clench and throb with each word. My skin prickles with heat.

"Then everything builds," he murmurs. "Faster. Hotter. Until you tip over the edge. Honestly, it doesn't take much. Not for a man. Women—" his voice softens again "—you're more… *nuanced.*"

My throat tightens. I'm so aware of every inch of my body. The slick heat between my thighs. The ache curling low in my belly.

I shift against him, heart pounding, unsure what to say.

He keeps rubbing my back. Slow. Steady. Like he knows exactly what he's doing.

"Can I ask *you* something?" he ventures after a moment, voice soft against the dark.

"Sure," I murmur, curling a little closer.

"I know you haven't had sex…" He pauses, searching for the words. "But have you done anything else…before me?"

I hesitate. My fingers twitch slightly against his chest. The question is fair. But the answer? It's mortifying.

"There was one guy," I admit.

His hand stills for a moment on my back, then starts moving again, encouraging me to go on.

"I was maybe seventeen. I don't even know if it *counts* as anything. He had no idea what he was doing. Said he wanted to finger me, but…"

I bite the inside of my cheek, heat rising to my face.

"He kept rubbing the side of my groin—like, nowhere near where he should've been." I snicker softly. "I don't even think he knew *where* to put his hands. I started chafing with how hard he was going."

I close my eyes at the memory. The second-hand cringe still lingers.

"I wanted to say something," I add, voice quieter now, "but I didn't know how to correct him without making it worse. So I kind of let it happen."

Alex doesn't speak right away.

Then he chuckles softly. "No, I don't think that counts." His voice is warm with amusement. "Then what happened?"

"He asked me to give him head," I admit, burying my face slightly into his shoulder.

"And what did you say?"

"I told him I couldn't…because of my braces. Then I bolted."

Alex's laughter is instant, full-bodied. His chest shakes under my cheek as he throws his head back. I feel the sound before I hear it. I laugh too, mortified and delighted.

We settle again into the silence. A breath shared.

"It doesn't exactly inspire lust," I murmur.

His hand stills on my skin. "So what does inspire you, Elena?"

The word lives in my throat, blooming warm and bold. I throb just thinking it.

"You," I whisper.

His breath catches.

"When you look at me," I add, voice thick. "When you touch me."

He shifts beside me, the heat between us rising as his hand trails up my thigh. Fingers light but deliberate.

"Like this?" he asks, his voice raspy, soaked in hunger.

"Yes," I breathe, biting my lip. "Like that."

"What else?" he asks, fingers gliding higher, teasing.

"I like that thing you did. With your…" I trail off, shy again.

"Tell me, *Älskling*," he murmurs, mouth grazing my ear. "Don't be shy—not with me. Not about this."

"Your mouth," I squeak, laughing softly into his chest. Heat floods my face.

"Oh, dirty girl." He laughs low, wicked and velvety. It rolls through me like thunder.

"You're a young, beautiful woman, Elena. You're allowed to want it," he says, brushing a kiss against my neck. "To crave it." His mouth moves lower, every press gentle, every shift precise— each one a tremor down my spine.

"To desire it."

His fingers slip under the edge of my panties, slow and sure, and he drags them down my thighs. My legs lift instinctively, welcoming him, aching for him.

Wetness gathers between my thighs—thick, heavy, undeniable.

"Are you giving me permission to be horny?" I ask, my voice ragged, shaky with anticipation.

"Absolutely," he murmurs, his voice dark and delicious. "Consider it sage advice."

He parts my thighs and nestles himself between them, his breath ghosting over my skin. Then I feel the wicked stroke of his tongue along the inside of my thigh.

My hips jerk. I gasp.

"You should always listen to your elders," I manage between moans, the world tilting slightly around me.

Then his mouth is on me.

Soft, reverent, maddeningly slow.

His tongue moves with purpose, circling, teasing, tasting. He finds the exact spot and stays there, building pressure, rhythm, heat. My back arches off the bed, a broken sound leaving my lips.

He groans against me, tongue dragging deeper.

Then, without warning, he slips a finger inside me.

I cry out—sharp and breathy—as my body clenches tight around him.

He doesn't stop. His mouth keeps working me, lips and tongue in sync with the slow thrust of his finger. Then two.

I gasp, my body stretching around the fullness, the ache building fast and desperate.

"You're so tight," he growls into me. "Your pussy's begging to be filled."

The words punch straight through me. My thighs tremble.

But then he slows. Still buried in me, his voice softer now, curling like smoke.

"But not tonight, Elena," he murmurs, pressing a final kiss to the inside of my thigh. "I want to savor every moment. Take my time with you before I lose myself inside you."

My body turns to flame.

His tongue returns to my clit, its rhythm, steady and focused, every stroke coaxing me higher. His hands grip my thighs gently, holding me open, holding me together as I squirm under him. I can't think, can't breathe. All I know is *him*—his mouth, his warmth, the delicious tension tightening with every flick of his tongue.

He growls, and it vibrates through me.

My hands clutch the sheets, my mouth slack as moans rip out of me.

And then it crashes through me—wave after relentless wave. I shudder around his mouth, thighs locking tight, a broken cry escaping as I come, sharp and overwhelming. Every nerve alive, electric.

"Alex…Fuck!" I scream and squeal in equal measure.

He holds me through it. His tongue and lips keep moving as if he's determined to catch every last quiver.

I twitch with every brush of his tongue, too sensitive, too raw, but he doesn't stop until I'm gasping, breath catching in my throat, chest heaving with the aftershocks.

And in that moment, everything and everyone else disappears.

When he finally rises, his breath ragged, I pull him into me, needing to taste him. I kiss him hard still trembling.

But I don't taste him, I taste me, slick and salty. He did this. To me.

That's when I feel it—his hardness pressing against my thigh.

"Can I…" I hesitate, nerves fluttering before boldness takes over. "Is there anything I can do to make you feel good, too?"

His lungs seize for a second, stunned.

"I'm hard for you, Elena." His lips drag up my neck. "Do you want to feel what you do to me?" he asks.

"Yes, please."

"Since you asked so nicely," he teases, before taking my hand, slow and careful, and guiding it between us.

I wrap my fingers around him. He's hot. Hard in my palm.

His breath catches as I start to move my hand, his hand never leaving mine. He groans into my mouth, his hips stuttering forward once, then again. As he fucks my hand. I pump him, squeezing and twisting in a rhythmic motion, my fingers barely touch.

His other hand cups the back of my head as we kiss deeper, slower. He swells in my grasp, his muscles tight, breath growing heavier, each moan making me wet all over again.

The rhythm builds between us, and I feel myself clench. Then he groans, moaning my name into my mouth as he finds his climax.

It's the first time I've ever made someone come—and damn, it feels good. Power mixed with pride, curling low in my belly.

Now I want more. I want to know everything.

Every button to push, every sound he makes when it's *my* hands, *my* mouth, *my* body driving him wild.

Next time, I'm not lying there gasping his name, I'm taking notes, I'm showing off.

God help him, I'm googling.

He's not the only one who gets to be good at this.

Chapter 20

Treat You Better

The Montgomery estate in the Hamptons looks like it belongs on the cover of an architecture magazine—which, to be fair, it has on more than one occasion. White-pillared elegance perched on sprawling green lawns, with a private stretch of beach glistening in the distance.

It's grand, pristine, and perfectly curated—ironic, considering the people gathering under its roof this weekend are anything but.

The joint bachelor and bachelorette party for Philippa and Andrew is already underway. We drove up together last night, but while Philippa, Andrew, and Riley are settling in, I'm out running last-minute errands for Philippa's bachelorette festivities.

As I step out of the car, bags in hand, the faint scent of salt from the private beach drifts through the air. But something else hangs heavier in the atmosphere.

This is the weekend Alex and Broderick will be in the same place for the first time, and I have no idea how I'm going to survive it.

That almost kiss, still lives rent free in my mind.

I barely have time to process the thought before Riley bursts through the grand doors like a human firecracker.

"Finally!" she groans, throwing her arms around me in a dramatic hug. "If I have to listen to Andrew talk about his latest investment strategy for one more second, I'm going to drown myself in the pool."

I laugh, adjusting the grocery bags in my arms. "He's really in business mode, huh?"

"He practically confiscated my snacks. Crumbs are apparently a threat to humanity."

Before I can respond, a low, familiar voice cuts through the air —smooth, deep, and laced with something undeniable.

"If I'd known this weekend was an open invitation, I would've reconsidered."

A prickle of awareness slides down my spine before I even turn around.

Broderick.

He stands casually at the top of the steps, the afternoon sunlight catching the sharp angles of his face. His green eyes lock onto mine, steady, unreadable—but something in his gaze lingers, sharp enough to make my stomach clench.

Dressed perfectly in linen trousers and a fitted navy shirt, sleeves rolled up to reveal strong forearms, he looks composed, completely at ease. But I know him well enough to recognize that underneath, he isn't.

Riley lets out a low whistle beside me. "Careful, *Bradley*. You almost sound jealous."

Broderick's lips twitch, but his voice stays smooth, unbothered. "I don't get jealous."

"Plus, you're the co-host," I tease, shifting the weight of the bags. "You can't back out now, chicken."

He exhales a small, almost amused breath before stepping forward to take the bags from my hands.

Our fingers brush.

A fleeting touch.

But it's enough.

A sudden warmth curls up my arm, betraying me completely as heat creeps up my neck. And before I can even process the reaction—

The unmistakable sound of a sleek convertible engine hums into the driveway.

I don't have to turn around to know who it is.

Alex.

He swings open the car door before the vehicle even fully stops, stepping onto the gravel like he's meant to arrive late, like the party only really starts when he shows up.

He tugs off his sunglasses, eyes scanning the estate before landing on me. A slow, knowing smirk curling at his lips.

"Hey, *Älskling*," he coos, striding toward me with an effortless confidence that always makes my pulse skip.

Before I can react, he scoops me up in an embrace, spinning me slightly as if we have all the time in the world.

I let out a startled laugh, hands gripping his shoulders.

"Hi," I murmur shyly, lost in the moment. "Happy birthday."

I lean in, pressing a soft kiss to his lips.

Alex hums approvingly against my mouth before pulling back enough to murmur, "This place is incredible." His gaze flicks toward the house, excitement gleaming in his expression.

But then, his attention shifts.

And everything in the air changes.

I feel it before I even turn to look.

The moment Alex's eyes land on Broderick, the atmosphere sharpens.

It isn't obvious—not outright—but I know them both well enough to recognize the subtle shift.

The way Broderick's posture stiffens, his jaw ticking slightly.

The way Alex's smirk deepens, his gaze flicking over Broderick in a way that isn't just curious.

It's assessing.

Sizing him up.

Broderick doesn't move, doesn't react, but his grip tightens ever so slightly around the grocery bags.

Oh, no.

I barely have time to consider how bad this could get before Alex turns back to me, mischief dancing behind his gaze.

"Aren't you going to introduce me to your…friend?"

There it is. That slight, intentional pause before *friend*, like he already suspects something more.

Broderick speaks before I can.

"Broderick Schwartz. The *best* man."

His voice is calm, controlled, but the way he stresses *best*? Deliberate.

Alex's gaze flickers with amusement as he takes Broderick's outstretched hand, gripping it firmly.

"Alex Westerberg."

Neither of them lets go immediately.

I swear, I feel a low current of tension crackling between them, like the air just before a storm. Riley's eyes are filled with amusement as her gaze bounces between the two.

Finally, Alex pulls his hand away. Leaning closer, he slips it into mine, interlacing our fingers.

He tilts his head slightly. "So, how do you two know each other?"

Broderick doesn't hesitate. "We work together."

A chill skates down my spine.

"What?" Alex raises an eyebrow. "Work together?"

"She's the maid of honor." His tone stays smooth, unreadable. "And I'm the *best* man."

Best. Again.

I exhale sharply.

What in the pissing contest is this? Riley bites her lip, trying to stifle a smile.

Alex, of course, sees right through it.

His smirk widens, his grip tightening. "Ah." His eyes slide back to me, twinkling with amusement. "The best man, but not *her* man," Alex quips, not bothering to hide the sting.

What the fuck, Alex?

Broderick's jaw locks.

Riley's hand flies over her mouth.

"I don't have time for whatever *this* is," I mutter, letting go of Alex's hand and spinning on my heel and striding into the house.

Inside, the estate is a flurry of quiet luxury—the soft clinking of glassware, the faint hum of activity from the staff prepping for the day's events.

Across the kitchen, Philippa perches on a barstool in designer swimwear, sipping champagne.

"Here," I say, reaching into my bag and handing her sunscreen.

She lights up. "Yay! Thanks, little sis! Can't have tan lines before the wedding."

Behind me, I hear footsteps as Alex, Broderick, and Riley finally make their way inside.

Riley gives me a look, but I ignore it, turning to Alex. "I'll show you where you can put your things."

Before Broderick—or anyone—can speak, I grab Alex's hand and pull him toward the grand staircase.

My bedroom is warm, bathed in golden afternoon light filtering through sheer curtains.

Alex leans against the doorframe, watching me with a slow, knowing smirk. "So," he murmurs, "am I finally getting my birthday present?"

I glance at the blue box sitting on the bed. But I have a feeling he means something else entirely.

"Only if you're a good boy." I press my lips to his gently, before pulling away and grabbing the box. I hand it to him, my heart thudding. "I hope you like it."

He opens the lid, brow arching with curiosity. Inside, a card: *For all the moments we'll have together—Happy Birthday.* Beneath it, a vintage Leica M6 camera.

His breath catches. "You found one," he whispers, eyes wide.

"Do you like it?"

"Elena…I love it. Thank you."

Setting the box down, he lifts the camera and turns it over in his hands, opening it to see that it's already been loaded with film. He smiles again. Then snaps a picture of me.

I laugh. "Alex!"

He grins, setting the camera aside and pushing me gently onto the bed, tickling me as I squeal. Hovering over me, he presses a soft kiss to my lips.

"There's one more gift," I murmur, nerves coiling tight in my stomach.

His brow arches, but a smirk tugs at the corner of his lips. "Oh, yeah?"

The air between us thickens. I breathe him in, sliding my hands down his chest before gently pulling him up and off the bed. He follows as I guide him toward the oversized armchair by the window.

I push him and he drops into it with a lazy sprawl, legs spread wide, arms resting on the armrests like he owns the world.

"Bossy today, huh?" he teases, though his eyes have darkened, heat simmering in them.

"You could say that." I smile faintly and lean in, pressing a soft kiss to his lips before sinking to my knees between his legs.

His gaze sharpens, watching me with a hunger that makes my pulse race.

Running my hands slowly up his thighs, I feel the muscles flex under my touch, relishing the way his breath catches.

I want to see him fall apart.

But then—

I hesitate.

Because the truth is, I'm not exactly sure what I'm doing. I know the general concept, thoughts of late-night research making me blush, but I've never actually—

Alex leans forward slightly, brushing my hair back.

"You've never done this before?" he murmurs, his voice softer now, searching my eyes.

I shake my head.

He exhales slowly, his thumb dragging over my bottom lip, eyes locked on mine. "So innocent," he teases.

"Teach me how to please you," I whisper, breathless.

His eyes darken further, something primal flashing through them. "Unbutton my pants," he instructs, voice rough.

I obey, my fingers working to open the button, then the zipper, revealing the black fabric of his briefs beneath.

"Take them off," he says, watching me like a predator fixed on his prey.

My lips part, hands trembling slightly as I slide both his pants and underwear down, he lifts his hips as I pull them off completely.

Oh.

I freeze.

I knew what to expect, but last time I touched him, it had been in the dark. Seeing it in real life, in the light—hard, thick, veiny, standing against his body—is...

Intimidating.

Alex lets out a low laugh, clearly amused. "That's cute," he murmurs, brushing my hair back so he can see my face. "You like what you see?"

I blink. Still staring. Too stunned to pretend otherwise.

"Yeah," I say, too fast. "Bigger than I expected."

His grin spreads, cocky and slow. "Oh, yeah?"

I roll my eyes, heat rushing to my cheeks. "Don't let it go to your head."

He raises an eyebrow.

"Well, your *other* head."

My pulse still races, but curiosity wins. I reach out, slowly, wrapping my fingers around him.

He twitches in my hand, and the sound he makes—half-groan, half-growl—sends a fresh rush through me.

"Now stroke it," he instructs, voice deeper, rougher. "Like this."

His hand covers mine, just like last time, guiding my movements—slow, firm strokes up and down his length.

I follow his lead, watching his face as his jaw tenses, his chest rising and falling with every exhale.

"That's it," he murmurs, his fingers sinking into my hair.

I lean forward, my breath ghosting over him.

"Lick the tip, like a popsicle," he instructs.

I follow his instructions, running my tongue over the soft, sensitive skin, tasting the saltiness of him.

Alex lets out a low, shaky groan.

I flick my tongue over him again, this time taking my time with each stroke.

"Good girl," he breathes, tightening his grip around the nape of my neck, guiding me.

Encouraged, I flick my tongue over him again, wetting the head of his cock, watching his abs clench as he struggles to stay still.

I kiss the tip softly, then run my tongue along his length, pressing wet kisses down the vein along the underside.

His hand flexes in my hair.

"Now…" He says panting. "Open wide and take me in."

I lick my lips, nerves spiking, but do as he asks. I part my lips and slide down and around his shaft.

The guttural moan that tears from his throat is worth everything.

"Fuck, Elena," he hisses, hips jerking slightly. "Just like that. Take your time."

I work him deeper, feeling the stretch of my cheeks, the heat, my jaw adjusting as I find my rhythm.

"That's so good, Darling," he groans. "So good for me."

His fingers tighten in my hair as I bob my head, licking and sucking him, learning what makes him curse and grip me harder.

"God, you feel amazing," he growls, his hips starting to thrust up into my mouth, controlled but desperate.

I look up through my lashes, seeing his head tipping back against the chair, his fingers clawing against my scalp, his mouth parting slightly as he lets himself go.

I'm doing this to him.

Me.

I feel powerful.

I'm drunk on it.

My core throbs with need, but I focus on him, letting the sound of his broken moans guide me.

"Fuck—I'm gonna come," he groans. "Take it. Be a good girl and swallow it all."

I nod, moaning around him, making him shudder.

I move faster, lips sliding, sucking harder. His body tenses beneath me—every muscle pulled tight—until he lets go with a raw cry of my name, fingers gripping my hair like he's holding on for life.

He comes hot and thick against my tongue, spilling deep, and I swallow, just like he wants. The taste, the sound of him, the way he shudders, makes my whole body pulse.

When he's done, he gently eases me off, brushing his thumb over my wet, swollen lips.

"Holy fuck," he whispers, looking down at me like I'm the only thing in the world.

I study his face, breathless, heart pounding.

"That was a first," he murmurs, a lazy smile spread across his face.

"A first?"

"No one's ever let me guide them like that," he says, voice rough, still catching his breath. "No one's ever trusted me like you did."

I wipe my mouth with the back of my hand, still kneeling between his legs, flushed and smug.

"Well," I smirk, looking up at him, "I'm clearly a fast learner."

He stares like he wants to drag me onto his lap and have his way with me, like I've just become his new favorite sin.

"Plus, you make it easy," I say, grinning up at him. "You're a very convincing teacher."

Heat curls in my chest—there's something heady about knowing I gave *him* a first.

He lets out a strangled laugh, fingers sliding into my hair again, thumb brushing the corner of my mouth. "Convincing?"

"Sexy," I correct, lifting my chin. "Unreasonably sexy. Like, unfair-to-the-public levels of sexy."

His eyes darken, mouth curving with something wicked. "Then consider this your A-plus."

I bite down a smile. "Do I get a gold star?"

"Maybe." He leans in, lips at my ear. "If you're a naughty girl."

Heat sparks low. I clench, just to feel it—the afterglow, the ache, his breath skating down my spine.

"I think…" I whisper. "I'd like that."

And for the first time, I almost can't wait either.

He makes me feel wanted—*craved*—like every breath I take is something he needs to touch.

THE SOUND OF SPLASHING WATER, music, and carefree laughter drifts through the air as Alex and I step outside onto the sunlit patio to rejoin the festivities. The pool shimmers under the afternoon glow, surrounded by white-cushioned loungers, cabanas, and clusters of guests clad in chic designer swimwear.

Philippa's bachelorette entourage is gathered near the private bar, all sun-kissed skin and champagne flutes, looking like something out of a high-fashion editorial. Andrew's crowd—a mix of business moguls and trust-fund heirs—stands near the outdoor lounge, trading stories over cocktails.

Everything looks perfect.

Except for the fact that as soon as we step outside, I feel it.

Broderick's stare.

His eyes sweep over me once, slowly, lingering just a second too long. And Alex notices.

His fingers tighten slightly around mine, his jaw tensing, but he says nothing. The air between them is thick, unreadable, but I feel it settling in my chest—a silent, territorial tension.

I force a smile, pretending not to notice.

"Let's get some food," I say quickly, tugging Alex toward the buffet, desperate to redirect the energy before something happens.

Alex lets me lead him away, but I can feel the silent challenge still hanging between them.

Riley, sprawled poolside with a margarita, has clearly clocked the whole thing. The second we pass, she slinks over, looping her arms around me like we're about to share something scandalous.

"Oh, babe," she murmurs, eyes glinting. "Your life is officially the world's hottest territorial pissing match."

I shoot her a warning look. "Stop it."

"What?" she grins. "I mean, I love a good brooding, possessive stare-down, but at some point, you do realize they're gonna have to fight it out in some high-stakes, shirtless duel, right?"

Alex arches an eyebrow. "You think I'd lose?"

Riley releases me, lifting her drink like this is all some sport. "You weren't supposed to hear that." She scrunches her nose, feigning innocence.

Alex's chuckle is low, but the edge beneath doesn't go unnoticed. His fingers tighten around mine in a subtle, unmistakable claim. He leans in, lips brushing my ear, voice a silk-draped threat.

"I don't have to fight for you," he murmurs. "You're already mine, *Älskling*."

Riley takes a long, slow sip, eyes flicking from Alex to Broderick, then back again.

"Honestly? I'd pay to watch."

I groan. "Not helping."

She winks, tapping her glass against mine.

Alex smirks, but I feel the tension humming off him as he squeezes my hand again.

Before the conversation can spiral further, we get intercepted by none other than Philippa's friends. A group of perfectly polished socialites, all boobs, sleek blowouts, and designer bikinis. And the second they see Alex, their conversation dies mid-sentence.

"Oh my God," one of them gasps, gripping another girl's arm. "Is that Alexander Westerberg?"

"It is," another whispers, eyes going wide. "Philippa, you did *not* tell us he was coming!"

Philippa, who's now beside us, takes a leisurely sip of her champagne and gives a pointedly amused glance my way. "Elena's plus-one." The way she says it is neutral, but there's an unspoken meaning beneath it. Philippa's friends, however, are not neutral.

"Oh my God, Alexander, I *loved* your last campaign," one of them purrs, touching his bare forearm. "The Paris spread? Absolute art."

"Didn't you date Madison Walsh?" Another giggles, twirling a piece of her hair.

"Wait, weren't you just in Milan? What was it like?"

The fawning only gets worse. Philippa's friends lean in closer, lilting laughter, fingers brushing Alex's arm like they can't help themselves. He eats it up.

That signature smirk slides into place—smooth, magnetic, lethal. The kind that makes women lose their footing and their dignity in the same breath.

He's in his element. Untouchable.

I haven't seen this version of him since the Geek-Fest panel. This isn't *Alex*, this is *Alexander*. The public persona. Polished and charming. He slips into it like it's a second skin.

And I *should* be fine with it.

But something twists low in my chest, sharp and tight. Not jealousy. Not exactly.

Just the sickening awareness that I have to share him. That even with his arm around me, the world doesn't see *us*. They see *him*.

Unattainable, desirable, and still up for grabs.

The worst part?

I don't even need to look. I *feel* Broderick watching. Across the patio, his presence clings to me like smoke. His stare—sharp, quiet, accusing—lands between my ribs.

What are you doing with him?

Alex must sense it.

His hand slides lower on my waist, fingers pressing in just enough to make a point. His stance shifts subtly, cocky and deliberate. Like he's staking territory. Like he wants Broderick to see.

And I can't tell if it's pride or panic that fills my lungs. Desperate to move past the moment, I turn to Philippa. "Everything looks perfect," I say, forcing a bright, easy smile. "I just want to make sure you have everything you need."

Philippa gives me a knowing look but doesn't press. "Everything's great," she assures me, swirling the champagne in her glass. "Though I *do* think some of Andrew's friends are a little… surprised by the guest list." She flicks her eyes meaningfully toward Alex.

I don't miss the way a few of Andrew's friends are casting sideways glances, murmuring amongst themselves, probably wondering why a celebrity is suddenly in their midst.

And Broderick? Broderick still hasn't looked away.

I take a slow breath. I told myself I was going to focus on Alex. I chose this. So I press closer to Alex, burying the discomfort, and pretend I haven't seen the slight tick in Broderick's jaw —the one that makes my insides knot.

There's only so much I can take before going full feral on those perfectly toned, over-perfumed bitches. Their fawning has long since crossed into open flirting.

So I leave Alex with his fan club, flashing a tight smile that probably looks more like a snarl, and slip inside under the guise of checking on things.

Really, I just need air.

I move through the house on autopilot, heels clicking sharply against the marble, offering empty nods and polite smiles until I reach the front porch.

Finally, quiet.

The door clicks shut behind me. I press my palms to the railing, breathe. And then I feel him before I see him.

Broderick.

"Hey, co-host," Broderick calls out, smooth and teasing. Full of humor.

No. I do *not* need this.

I don't even glance back. I just turn on my heel and storm down the stairs to the driveway, needing air, needing space, needing…*not them.*

The sun hits my skin. I inhale deep, trying to exhale the frustration boiling beneath my ribs.

But then I hear them.

Footsteps. Two sets.

I don't have to turn to know.

Oh, for fuck's sake.

"Elena," Alex calls, his voice tight.

"Elena," Broderick echoes, just as firm, just more concerned.

I spin, heat flooding my chest. "You have *got* to be kidding me."

They both freeze. Neither of them looks guilty.

That only pisses me off more.

"Seriously?" I snap. "What is this? Duel at dawn? Fight to the death? What's next, a literal dick-measuring contest?"

Alex drags a hand through his hair, jaw flexing. "No one's fighting, Elena."

Broderick lets out a breath—sharp, skeptical.

"Oh, don't do that," I groan. "Don't stand there like you're both innocent. You were acting like goddamn *cavemen.*"

I turn on Broderick first, fury rolling off me. "You don't think

I notice you glaring at me like you've got something to say but won't?"

Then to Alex, venom rising in my throat. "And *you*—standing there while Avery practically dry-humps your arm, like she was two seconds away from dropping to her knees right there."

Broderick's eyes snap to mine. For a second, something raw cracks through—frustration, yes, but also something else. Something deeper. Something I don't want to name.

Alex doesn't move. Arms crossed. Lips pressed tight. Not backing down. "Elena, you don't get it," he says, his voice low. "This isn't, she wasn't—"

SPLASH.

I shriek, freezing as icy water drenches all three of us.

Alex curses loudly. Broderick lets out a sharp, shocked inhale. He looks like he's about to throw fists.

I turn slowly, dripping wet, only to find Riley standing ten feet away, grinning like an absolute devil.

With a garden hose.

"I had to do it," she says, shrugging innocently, adjusting the hose like she's holding a firearm. "You guys were getting a little too heated."

Alex drags a hand over his soaked hair, glaring. "Are you insane?"

Broderick just stands there, rubbing his eyes, completely drenched and visibly unimpressed.

I wipe water from my face, stunned.

Riley grins wider. "That was getting *painful* to watch. You should be thanking me."

I sputter. "You hosed us down?!"

She doesn't even flinch.

"Well, I *thought* about dumping a bucket over your heads, but this was more efficient."

Alex lets out a disbelieving laugh. "You are *so* lucky you're her best friend."

Broderick exhales hard, muttering something under his breath as he runs a hand through his now-wet hair.

Riley tilts her head. "Oh, *trust* me. You guys needed that. Plus, you're welcome for the free wet T-shirt contest. Very entertaining."

Alex looks like he's actively debating his life choices. Broderick looks like he wants to fire her into the sun.

And me?

I burst out giggling.

Because honestly? This is exactly what they deserve.

———— • ————

THE POOL PARTY WINDS DOWN, the sun dipping lower in the sky, casting a golden glow over the private beach. Most of the guests have either gone to their rooms to rest before the evening or are drunkenly wandering the estate, basking in the lingering afterglow of a day spent under the sun.

Alex leaves earlier for a birthday dinner with his friends—something I'm invited to, but as co-host of the weekend, it doesn't feel right to leave.

Or at least, that's what I tell myself.

Really, I just want a quiet moment with my thoughts.

I sit alone at the edge of the private beach, my toes buried in the cool sand as the waves lap rhythmically against the shore. I've done this so many times before at home. The air is thick with salt and warmth, the sound of the ocean soothing, but my mind is anything but quiet.

Then, there's a soft crunch of footsteps in the sand behind me.

I don't have to turn to know who it is.

Broderick.

He settles next to me, close enough that I feel the heat radiating from his body, even as the cool breeze from the ocean brushes my skin.

"Hey, co-host," he murmurs, his voice low, familiar, with that hint of teasing that always makes my heart flutter in ways I can't explain.

He silently offers the second beer in his hand, and I take it, shaking my head with a soft huff of amusement. "Are we just sticking with that now?"

He smirks, staring out at the waves. "Well, it's easier than calling you the woman who's slowly driving me insane."

Driving him insane?

The almost kiss.

I roll my eyes, but a smile tugs at my lips anyway, and I take a slow sip of the drink, hoping it'll calm the nervous fluttering in my chest.

For a while, we sit there in silence—comfortable and tense all at once—listening to the waves crash against the shore.

Then, after a long moment, he breaks the stillness.

"I'm sorry about earlier."

I turn toward him, brows furrowing. "What was that about, Broderick?"

He exhales, running a hand through his damp hair, gaze fixed on the darkening ocean like it might give him the answers he's searching for.

His jaw tenses. His voice is rough when he finally says, "You want the truth?"

My fingers tighten around my glass. "Yeah."

He doesn't look at me—can't, I realize—his eyes locked on the horizon.

"I like you, Elena. And that night at your apartment...I haven't been able to get it off my mind."

The confession hits me like a wave, knocking the air from my lungs.

He likes me?

But he's not done.

"And, yeah, I know you're with him." His voice drops lower, like it hurts to say it aloud. And when he finally turns to me, I see it—he's jealous.

He shifts beside me. "I just need to know…are things serious?"

"I…don't know. This is new to me." I fidget with the beer in my hand.

"And if it wasn't new? Could I be an option?" he asks, his eyes searching.

"Broderick, I don't know." I fight the lump in my throat, guilt clawing its way up.

The words hang between us, heavy, impossible to ignore, tangled in the salty air and the crashing waves.

Because I'm hurting him.

Without meaning to.

Trying to deflect, I force a laugh—light, almost teasing. It tastes wrong in my mouth.

"Broderick, you're gorgeous, kind, mega successful. I'm sure there's a queue of women waiting to fall at your feet."

My breath catches, and something mean coils in my chest.

Jealousy. It flashes sharp across my ribs at the thought of him with anyone else.

Don't.

I shove the thought down, take a sip just to have something to hold. The glass clinks against my teeth. My hand won't stop trembling. I shouldn't even feel this way. I have Alex. I want Alex. I don't deserve to feel jealous, not over Broderick.

He huffs out something that resembles a laugh, but it's hollow, thin. A sound stretched too tight.

"Yeah? Maybe." His eyes stay fixed ahead. "But they're not you."

My heart stops. For a moment. I stare at him, wide-eyed. His face is soft and searching.

I clear my throat, barely keeping my voice steady. "But why? We hardly know each other."

His shoulders lift in a shrug, slow, resigned. "I don't know, El. Why does the sun rise? Why does the moon pull the tide?" He turns to me now. "Sometimes someone just…gets under your skin. And stays there. Doesn't matter how long you've known them."

I freeze. The words land somewhere raw.

The silence between us folds inward, heavy with everything we haven't dared to say.

I wish the waves could drown out the symphony in my chest.

Broderick's words linger in the air like suspended notes— warm, honest, and painfully beautiful.

I'm caught between two songs, unsure which one my heart has already begun to sing.

Broderick leans back, bracing on his hands. The distance between us feels both infinite and razor-thin.

His voice is quiet now, almost broken. "You don't know how much I wish you met me first."

The breath I've been holding rushes out in a single exhale. I stare at him, trying to keep it together.

There it is.

The thing I haven't let myself name.

The thing that might ruin me if I let it grow.

What if I'd met Broderick first? Would we be here, stuck on this impossible merry-go-round, spinning in circles with no end?

But the darker thought, the one I can't let myself say out loud? If I'd met Alex *after* Broderick…would I still be feeling this way?

Would it be *Alex* sitting beside me now, telling me I'd gotten under his skin? Would we have almost kissed?

Caught in a war inside my chest, I don't know who I'm fighting anymore—him, Alex, or myself.

I force out a soft laugh to hide the panic rising inside. "But I didn't," I say quietly, the words heavier than I intend. "We can't play that game."

Broderick turns fully to face me, his green eyes dark, intense.

"And if we could?" he asks softly.

I look away, heart pounding, because I don't have an answer. Because if I admit I've thought about it too—even for a second— there would be no turning back.

Silence stretches between us, thick and charged. Just like that moment that lingered between us at my apartment.

Broderick studies me for a long moment before letting out a quiet scoff.

"You know," he murmurs, taking a sip of his drink, "for someone who always speaks her mind, you sure have a hard time being honest about this."

I stiffen, glancing away. "I am being honest."

Am I?

No. Not really.

He shakes his head, smirking, but it's softer now—sad, even. "No, you're not. You're saying what makes it easier. What makes sense."

I bristle. "Broderick—"

"Relax," he adds gently, cutting me off. "I'm not asking for anything. I just needed you to hear me say it."

I let out a breath I hadn't realized I was holding.

The silence that follows isn't comfortable this time. It's thick with all the things neither of us dare admit.

After a moment, I finally whisper, "I don't want to hurt you."

Broderick laughs quietly, shaking his head. "Too late, El."

The sound of the nickname he'd given me on his lips—like it means something more—makes my heart clench.

Before I can speak, he nudges my foot gently with his, the corners of his mouth twitching into something resembling a smile.

"Besides, I'm a big boy. I'll live."

I giggle, relieved that at least he's trying to lighten the mood.

"Yeah, you really need to lay off the steroids," I quip back.

Broderick barks a laugh so hard, it breaks the tension with ease. The dimples returning to his face.

His grin turns playful. "That said, I fully expect you to buy me a drink tonight to make up for all this emotional trauma."

I smile, shaking my head. "Fine. One drink."

"Two," he counters, smirking.

I narrow my eyes, playing along. "One and a shot."

Broderick chuckles, and this time, it's real, warm and deep. "Deal."

For a moment, things feel lighter.

But deep down, I know this isn't over.

Because no matter how much I try to pretend otherwise, his words cling to me.

And no matter how hard I try to shut it out...

I keep wondering about the what-ifs.

What if I had let him kiss me that night?

What if I had met him first?

Will it be easier after this weekend, after the wedding? When we're no longer circling each other out of obligation?

Surely then, it'll go away.

Won't it?

Chapter 21

Firestarter

The mirror fogs with heat and hairspray. Someone's got a Prince remix pulsing through the speaker, and the bathroom is alive with girl energy—heels kicked off, dresses half-zipped, lipstick tubes rolling across the counter like dice.

I press the tip of my eyeliner to my waterline and drag it, slow and steady. It gives my hands something to do.

"He's so hot," Sienna groans, elbow-deep in the steamer as she waves it over her satin dress. "That jawline? How are you not banging him twenty-four-seven, Elena?"

Avery snorts from where she's perched cross-legged on the sink. "I saw a photo of him on a red carpet recently. He looked like sex in a tuxedo."

"Honestly," Philippa utters, ironing out her hair in long, impatient strokes, "he's attractive, sure. But also completely full of himself. He seems intensely aware that he's good-looking. I don't know how you do it, Elena."

I shrug, a little smug.

Riley flops backward on the bed in the adjoining room, voice floating through the open door. "Yeah, but when you look like that, why wouldn't you be? I'd be insufferable."

They all laugh.

I force a laugh, but it lands flat. They haven't stopped talking about Alex, and honestly, I'd probably join in on objectifying him if my mind wasn't still stuck on that conversation at the beach. Alex is out with friends for his birthday dinner. We'll see each other later at the club. It'll be fine. Whatever's lingering between Broderick and me, it will pass.

I hope.

I dip my brush into a palette, keeping my eyes low, blending eyeshadow into the corners.

At least they're not talking about Broderick. Which is good.

What if you met me first? His words haunt me.

"Hey Philippa," Natalie calls from behind her curling iron, twisting a strand with practiced ease, "is Broderick seeing anyone?"

Fuck, I spoke too soon. I stare at her through the mirror. Natalie is beautiful, toned, tanned, with long brown hair.

Philippa catches her own eye in the mirror, one brow arching with a look that says *please*. Then she smirks.

"Yes—his job. You know him. Gym, work, charity, repeat. I don't even know how he manages to squeeze in time to see his mother."

"Tragic," Natalie sighs dreamily. "I could fix that."

Her words hit me, my chest tightens. I shouldn't feel like this. Natalie is perfect. They would work well. They run in the same circle. It makes sense.

"I'd love to see you try." Philippa flips her hair off her shoulder. "The last girl didn't even last a month. He was in Dubai. Or Singapore. One of those. She dumped him before he even got off the plane."

"Cold," Riley mutters from the bed.

"Yeah." Philippa pouts, completely unserious. "It's sad, honestly. He's a great guy. Loyal to a fault. Married to the mission. But I think…for the right person?" She glances down, smoothing gloss onto her lips. "He'd move mountains."

The words land heavy in my chest.

I trace my lip liner in slow, controlled strokes, eyes locked on my reflection. My throat tightens, too fast, too sudden. I breathe and refocus on the task.

For the right person.

A flash of him in my apartment. The look in his eyes when he leaned in. That pause, half a breath before a kiss that never came. My fingers had curled in his shirt. My pulse had stuttered.

He would've kissed me. He *wanted* to.

If it weren't for Alex's call.

Now here I was, pretending I didn't care while they all sat around laughing, planning Broderick's hypothetical girlfriend and thirsting over Alex like we weren't all tangled in the same messy web.

The lipstick in my hand shakes slightly as I reapply.

Broderick deserves someone who won't hesitate.

And I'm not sure if that could ever be me.

I have Alex. I shouldn't even be thinking about him. But what if…

"Hey, you're quieter than usual?" Riley asks, placing a warm hand on my shoulder.

"Just tired," I lie.

Riley narrows her eyes at me. "Okay."

She waits in silence, the kind that says, *I'm here when you're ready.*

The room cracks up again, pulling me out of my thoughts.

I stare at my reflection. Cheeks flushed. Lashes curled. Eyes too tired for someone about to step into a night of champagne and dancing.

But I love dancing.

I straighten my spine, smooth out my ponytail, and take a deep breath. My dress is red.

Alex will like it.

It clings in all the right places—tight, short. My heels are higher than I'm used to, courtesy of Rio's additions to my wardrobe. Confidence stitched into every seam.

I look the part. I press my lips together and smile. No one would think the wiser.

"All right, ladies, enough boy talk, I'm cutting you all off," I announce, voice light, laced with that same feigned confidence I wear on stage. The mask.

The version of me I wish I could be all the time.

They giggle and shriek in response, heels clacking, perfume clouding the air as we spill downstairs.

The guys are already waiting in the entrance, dressed in understated designer goods. Some in suits, others in polos, hair styled perfectly, expensive watches catching the light.

Andrew's eyes widen when he sees Philippa gliding down the stairs—his bride-to-be in a white bodycon dress, tighter than anything she usually wears. The push-up bra was worth the investment, judging by the look on his face. Her hair is dead straight, makeup a little heavier than usual, her skin shimmering with glitter.

Andrew's cousins, James and Cole Sinclair, the other grooms-men, and a few of his friends let out wolf whistles as we descend the steps.

"There they are."

"Looking good, ladies."

"Damn, Sienna."

"Looking good, Avery."

Standing next to them and looking completely unfair is Broderick, taller than the rest, in a black shirt, tight and tucked into black pants. He wears a leather jacket and boots.

"Fuck, he's hot," Natalie hisses under her breath, stealing the words right out of my mouth.

He looks up just as Natalie and I are the last to join the group. His eyes flick to her—then past her—right at me.

He winks.

I blush.

Natalie turns her head over her shoulder and shoots me a look.

I roll my eyes and shake my head like it means nothing. We're friends. I'm trying—desperately—to convince myself of that.

"He's all yours," I say to Natalie, voice a little too high, a little too forced. She beams a huge smile at me and wags her brows.

Outside, I hang off to the side as everyone gathers by the limousine.

"Damn, El, you really know how to twist the knife," he whispers over my shoulder.

"This old thing…" I giggle.

"You owe me that drink," he says, holding the door open.

He offers me his hand. A spark shoots through me at the contact, sharp and sudden, as I climb inside.

"If I'm not mistaken, I think I owe you a shot as well."

Broderick slides in beside me, our bodies pressed close in the tight space. Riley gives me a look.

That look.

She knows something's up. I must not be hiding it well.

I take a breath, try to rearrange myself, and my face.

The ride is short, loud, wild. One of the guys pops a bottle of champagne, spraying a few of the girls, who squeal and groan. Thankfully, I'm not in the firing line. This time.

THE VANGUARD IS the place to be in the Hamptons—VIP lounges, sets spun by celebrity DJs, velvet cigar rooms thick with smoke and secrets. Bottle service flowing. Everything drips with sin and indulgence.

Broderick and I had a roped-off corner reserved near the bar, prime real estate with a clear view of the main floor.

Sienna and Avery are already grinding on each other, soaking up the attention from Andrew's friends like it was their job. Andrew and Philippa are up against a booth wall, looking like they're about to make me an aunt. Somewhere in the crowd, Riley is spinning circles around Cole, her curls bouncing as he tries to keep up.

Broderick is lingering off to the side, half-shadowed by a strobe light, his face lit from his phone screen.

I saunter over, heels sinking into the plush carpet. One glance.

Emails.

I roll my eyes. The guy is working.

"Let's get you that drink, best man!" I yell over the pounding bass, grabbing Broderick's arm.

His eyes widen in amusement, then he flashes that full, maddening smile, dimples cutting deep.

"Lead the way, gorgeous," he says, leaning closer, voice brushing my ear.

Gorgeous…my heart skips a beat.

We push through the crowd. Bodies crush around us, hands brushing skin, heat thick in the air. Each step shoves us closer, his chest at my back, his breath at my neck, until we break through the tide.

His arms wrap around my waist, steering me, his taller frame guiding as he sees the gaps better. We reach the bar.

It feels good, though I know I shouldn't be feeling this way.

"What'll it be, Mr. Schwartz?" I ask, tilting my head up.

"I'll have an old fashioned. Michter's, please."

I nod just as the bartender turns. "What can I get started for you guys?"

"Two old fashioneds with Michter's bourbon. And two shots of tequila."

Broderick exhales through his nose, huffing. "Damn. Want to add a side of regret with that?"

"You'll drink it and be grateful." I smile.

He laughs, rich and unfiltered.

The bartender gets to work.

"Hand it over," I say, palm out.

"What?"

"Your phone. I caught you emailing. We're here to have fun, not run Goodman Enterprises. So hand. It. Over."

He grins, slow and wicked. "Make me."

Oh.

I press him back against the bar's edge where the crowd thins, and I dig into his pocket like I own it. He doesn't fight back.

"What the fuck—El!" he yelps, half-laughing, half-squirming. His eyes widen—surprise and hunger flashing.

"No more work tonight. Or else." I shove the phone into my purse.

"Yes, ma'am."

"Ew. None of that," I mutter, scrunching my nose.

"Hey, we're American. We have manners, especially around ladies. Though that"—he nods at my purse—"was not exactly ladylike."

He chuckles. The bartender slides the drinks across the counter.

I slap down cash before Broderick can reach for his wallet and nudge him toward the quieter end of the bar.

"Shots first. Unless you're chicken?"

He raises a brow. "Alright."

We lick, clink, and throw the tequila back in unison.

The burn hits hard, coarse and clean.

I suck the lime and drop it in the empty glass.

"Fuck, tequila is cruel," he coughs.

I giggle, the buzz hitting. "Weak."

He coughs again, and I can't help but laugh. For someone his size to be taken down by a little tequila—it's almost comical.

I pat him on the back. "Need me to call an ambulance, big guy?"

He chuckles, and so do I.

"Hey, you've got some—" he says, brushing his thumb along my lip. His hand lingers, cupping my jaw. "Salt."

Everything stills.

The bass throbs in my chest. His thumb lingers. My lips part. His touch is warm—gentle. I can't help but lean into it, every part of him drawing me closer.

"Elena?"

That voice.

It slices through the haze like cold steel.

My stomach sinks.

I jolt back. Broderick's hand drops.

I turn my head and spot Alex just a few feet away, half-lit by the strobe lights—bravado wrapped in disarming calm. A navy blazer, shirt unbuttoned just enough to catch the light. He doesn't need to try. The room rearranges itself around him anyway.

Fuck.

"There you are, *Darling*." The sweetness in his voice doesn't match the edge in his eyes as they move from me to Broderick and back again. Steady. Measuring. A grin playing at his mouth like he's already won. Broderick straightens, jaw tight, but doesn't move. Doesn't flinch.

I silently pray they've put their measuring tapes away for the night.

My fingers twitch around my glass. My purse digs into my ribs.

I can't do this again. Not another one of their silent wars. It was already two too many.

"Yeah, here," I mutter. "Let's head back."

I grab my drink, clutching the strap of my purse like a lifeline. I nudge Alex to follow as I pass, shoulders stiff, eyes forward, slicing through the crowd back to the roped-off comfort of our section.

If you look up *awkward* in the dictionary, my face would be the definition. Probably next to *self-inflicted.*

The three of us rejoin the group without a word. Broderick drifts back to the wall, same spot as before, nursing his drink and studying anything that isn't me.

Alex and I sink into a low loveseat.

"What was that about?" he asks, light on the surface, but there's an edge threaded through it.

"I owed Broderick a drink," I say, brushing it off. I sip the old fashioned—smooth, warm, a little too much like Broderick—and set it on the table.

"How was your birthday dinner?" I ask, trying to divert the topic from Broderick.

"Good. Would've been better if you were there." His eyes are full of sincerity, and it makes my heart melt.

I feel terrible for missing his birthday dinner.

"Well, I'm here. How can I make it up to you?" I lean in, batting my lashes at him, my shoulder brushing his.

He chuckles. It's low and dark like he knows I can't make good on that right now. Sliding his hand along my leg and lifting it into his lap, his fingers trail from my heel to the hem of my dress.

"You look…breathtaking tonight."

I tilt my head, narrowing my eyes. "Bet you say that to all the girls."

"Only the sexy ones." He winks.

His hand catches my jaw. He pulls me in and kisses me—deep and hungry like he's staking a claim.

Fuck.

I break the kiss. "Alex," I whisper sharply. "People might see—"

I glance around. Sure enough, there are whispers. A few phones angled too deliberately.

"Let them," he says, and pulls me back in. This time, he doesn't stop at a kiss—he lifts me fully into his lap.

I surrender. His lips feel like heaven, and he massages my tongue with his until I'm putty in his hands.

I feel him—hard and growing—pressing into my thigh. The heat of him, thick through his pants, pulses against my skin. His fingers trail up my leg like he's memorizing every inch, dragging until they find the hem of my panties. He doesn't move further. Just toys with it. Flicks the elastic, letting it snap back, biting into my skin.

I gasp into his mouth, a low moan caught in the back of my throat as my hips shift, yearning for more. I'm wet, tequila and lust searing through me.

I want him to touch me, my body begging for release. He could brush my clit right now and I'd probably orgasm from it.

He grabs my ponytail and tugs it. My head tips back, exposing my neck, and his mouth is at my ear, hot breath curling down my spine.

"Ahh." A groan escapes my mouth.

"Imagine me holding this while I fuck you from behind."

My thighs clench. Breath stutters. The image hits like a lightning strike—me bent over, him deep inside, that fist in my hair, his voice in my ear.

God.

I get wet at the thought. My chest rises fast. Skin flushed. I'm seconds away from dragging him into some corner—

"Babe! Come dance with us!" Riley's voice breaks through, slicing the moment clean in two.

It takes me a second to catch up.

"Please," Philippa adds, wobbling slightly in her heels, her lip gloss smeared, eyes glassy.

Alex's grip tightens around my waist. He's not ready to let go. Neither am I.

I turn to him, heart still sprinting. "Duty calls," I say, breathless, kissing the tip of his nose like it'll steady me.

"Put on a show for me," he murmurs, then squeezes my ass from under my dress, firm like he's staking a claim.

I yelp, half-laughing, half-flustered as Riley tugs me toward the dance floor. I glance back once.

He's watching.

Jaw set. Eyes dark.

And I'm still throbbing.

Riley twirls me and we start to move, hips swaying, arms loose, the beat sinking into my bones. The electricity of Alex's touch still clings to my skin, a ghost of heat I can't shake.

Riley slides behind me, her hand curling around my neck. I turn, my back pressed to her front, grinding as the bass throbs between us.

"Babe, you're in trouble," she purrs into my ear, her breath sticky-sweet with tequila. The lights strobe across her face. Philippa dances somewhere in front of us, lost in her own rhythm, hair stuck to her lip gloss.

"Why?" I shout over the music, spinning to face her again.

Riley just smirks.

The rhythm builds. It feels good to dance—mindless, messy, sweat gathering at the base of my spine. Riley grabs my hips, turning me slowly, deliberately, until I'm facing the VIP section again.

And there they are.

Alex, legs spread, one arm slung over the back of the couch, watching me like he wants to drag me back into his lap and finish what he started.

Broderick, standing. Stiff. Glass in hand. He's looking anywhere but at me.

Our eyes catch. Just for a moment.

Then he looks away. Takes a long sip of his drink. Says something to Andrew, who doesn't even glance up.

The music keeps pulsing, but I don't feel it anymore.

"We almost kissed," I whisper into Riley's ear, holding her close, swaying.

"Who?" she asks, arms flung out like it's just part of the choreography.

"Broderick."

"What the *fuck*," she hisses, stumbling a little. "Oh my *God*."

"Guys, this is the *best* night," Philippa slurs somewhere beside us, spinning in place like a kid at a birthday party.

Of course.

Trust Philippa to choose *this* exact moment to let go completely. Then again, if there's ever a time to lose it, it's your bachelorette party, right?

"You're so cute," I say, placing my hands on either side of her cheeks and pressing them. Philippa scrunches her nose playfully.

"I love you, you're the best," she stammers her words as she throws an arm around me.

"I love him so much," she adds, pointing straight at Andrew, glass in hand like it's a wand.

Then Philippa pretends to cast out a fishing line and reels it in, her tongue between her teeth, concentration fierce like she's actually trying to catch a marlin.

We turn just in time to see Andrew take the bait, grinning as he steps onto the dance floor.

With Broderick in tow.

Fuck.

Oh, *fuck.*

Riley grabs my wrist. Her eyes find mine—wide, wild, *do not panic.*

But it's already happening.

Andrew sweeps in, wraps his arms around Philippa, and they start to dance, her squeal echoing over the music, limbs loose, drunk on love and liquor.

Then Broderick.

Steps beside me. Resting his hand on my shoulder, warm, steady, sending a pulse straight through me.

"Elena," he says, leaning down and brushing his lips against my ear, voice low against the beat, the warmth sends a shiver down my spine.

I freeze for a half-second. Maybe it's the alcohol. Maybe it's the way he smells—woodsy and delicious.

"I'd like my phone back, please." His voice is low, but his request cuts through my lust.

What? No! All he'll do is stay on it for the night and sulk in the corner. Not on my watch.

"No phone, Brody! Have some fun." I grab his arms like strings on a puppet, flinging them around as I sway my hips into the beat. Riley whoops behind me, our own personal hype girl, hair flying, face flushed.

Broderick laughs—low, real, unguarded—his head tipping back just enough to make my chest tighten.

"Let loose, dance with me," I yell, gripping his arms and shaking them harder. "Woooooo!"

His smile deepens. Dimples cut through. Eyes catch the neon and glitter, bright and open—so *him*, it hurts.

Then Riley stiffens beside me.

I barely register it before a cool hand wraps around my arm and tugs.

I turn and let go. Dropping Broderick's arms.

Alex.

Fuck, I totally forgot all about him. I'm such an asshole.

He doesn't say a word, just steps in, palms my face, and kisses me.

He's sending Broderick and me a clear message. His lips press like he's stamping his name into mine. I lose myself in him—for a breath, for a heartbeat—before pulling back and spinning around, grinding into him. His hands find my hips, firm, pulling me into the rhythm as he moves to the beat of the song.

Beside us, I catch it.

Broderick taps Andrew's shoulder. They exchange a few words, then Philippa slips her hand into Andrew's, and the three of them disappear off the dance floor.

Gone.

A tall stranger slides up beside Riley, and just like that, she's in motion again—arms around his neck, laughing, hair whipping in time to the beat.

"He wants you," Alex whispers, voice dark and smug against my ear as he nips the tip with his teeth, it sends a jolt right between my thighs.

"Who?" I ask, not bothering to turn.

"The best man," he chuckles, smug and close.

"Does he now?"

I know that.

Broderick told me himself. That almost kiss. The pause between us, heavy with things unsaid, the question of *what ifs* still clinging to my skin like sweat.

I turn, facing Alex fully, my arms sliding around his neck, my body flush against his.

"And what are you going to do about it?" I challenge.

He smiles, slow and sure, fingers tightening on my hips. "I don't even have to try." His lips brush my jaw, his voice oozing confidence. "And Elena...I don't share."

Everything in me stills.

It wasn't my intention to make Alex jealous, and to be truthful, I hadn't expected it, but something about the way he says it strokes something inside me. The need to be wanted, to be chosen. To be *enough*.

He's making it so clear. He wants me.

This sexy, magnetic man—watched, chased, desired by so many—*wants me*.

Doesn't he deserve to be chosen, too?

Chapter 22

Dangerous Woman

Strobe lights carve the club into shards of color and smoke. Alex bonds with some of Andrew's friends over a few sloppy lines of cocaine, clapping him on the shoulder, shouting something I can't hear over the bass hammering through the floor. Who knew men were so simple?

We move like a current, tangled and messy—lips, hips, my knees buckling between the shots Philippa, Riley, and I slam back. It's wild to see my sister like this, loose and laughing in a way I've never seen before, head tipped back, hair clinging to the sweat on her neck.

Somewhere in the haze, I feel him. Broderick.

Leaning in the shadows with a drink, jaw set tight, watching. Brooding.

I want to go to him. My body leans that way without thinking. But the pull of Alex is too magnetic, too intoxicating, dragging me back under the crush of bodies and bass.

The night unravels fast, slipping through my fingers in a blur of heat and sound, until someone yells for the limo and we spill into the street—a mess of limbs, laughter, lipstick smudged and shoes forgotten—bringing a whirlwind of chaos back to the pristine, proper gates of Montgomery Estate.

The debauchery of the rich and uninhibited.

We clamor through the front doors, the sound of cackling echoing off marble floors, kicking off heels, jackets dropping like breadcrumbs behind us.

Alex tugs my hand, pulling me up the stairs two at a time, his mouth finding the crook of my shoulder, careless and breathless. We tumble into my room, the door slamming shut behind us.

I lock it. Learning from past mistakes.

He presses me back against the wall, hands skating under the hem of my dress, mouth teasing mine with that crooked smile he knows makes me stupid.

"Do you want to fuck?" he murmurs, voice low and rough against my jaw.

It's the first time he's asked for it.

I let my head fall back, eyes fluttering shut. For a second, the word *yes* burns the tip of my tongue. Not like this, not while Broderick still lingers in the quiet place of my mind, not while we're both sloppy drunk and him high on cocaine.

"Not tonight," I whisper, threading my fingers into his hair, tugging gently. "But…maybe we can do other things."

His grin is slow, wolfish. "Other things," he repeats, savoring it.

I nudge him back with a laugh, stumbling toward the bathroom, my dress sticking to my skin. "But first, I need to get cleaned up."

Alex leans in the doorway, lazy and seductive. "Maybe we get cleaned up together," he suggests.

The bathroom is all marble, lit by the soft spill of gold from the bedroom. I twist the taps, watching steam swell thick in the air, clinging to the mirrors, curling around the edges of the room.

Behind me, I hear Alex, the soft tug of his shirt slipping free. When I glance back, he's standing bare, unapologetic.

My throat tightens.

I'd seen pieces of him before—him shirtless, his cock in my mouth earlier—but this…Seeing him completely is something else entirely.

He's a marvel.

Alex steps closer, voice low and careful. "Can I undress you?"

I nod, my body already trembling before he even touches me.

"Elena," he murmurs, a faint smile at the corner of his mouth, "you're stunning. Don't hide from me."

He turns me by the hips until I'm facing the mirror. I catch sight of myself, a wild mess. My hair is no longer sleek, my pony-tail looser. Eyes burning. Lips swollen from too many stolen kisses. I should feel embarrassed. Instead, I feel *alive*.

Slowly, agonizingly, he drags the zipper of my dress down, the sound of it splitting the air, thread by trembling thread.

His fingers brush the straps, grazing my skin, sending a violent shudder through me as he peels the tight fabric away from my shoulders. The dress puddles at my waist, the bra unclasped with a flick of his hand, falling away.

Cool air kisses my flushed skin, the contrast biting, making me arch back into him without thinking. He pulls the dress down further until I'm left standing there in nothing but a scrap of lace, breathing hard, every inch of me bare to him.

Alex presses his mouth to the curve of my shoulder, his breath warm, the scrape of his stubble rough and electric. "You know what you do to me?" he says, voice wrecked, barely a thread of control left.

He cups my breasts in both hands, molding me against the hard line of his body, his erection pressing hot and insistent against the small of my back.

I whimper, helpless, boneless in his arms.

"Imagine how this would feel inside you," he murmurs against my skin, hips rolling in the barest suggestion, enough to make my thighs clench tight.

My breath stutters. Apprehension and desire weaving together, low in my belly, sharp enough to ache.

Alex feels it—me tensing—and slows immediately, brushing a kiss over my shoulder like a promise.

"But *not tonight*," he whispers, echoing my words. He's toying with me.

He steps back just enough to guide me toward the bath, fingers sliding down my hips, hooking into the lace of my panties.

"One more thing." He's almost laughing under his breath as he drags the last scrap of fabric down my legs. I step out, shivering.

Alex's hands frame my hips for a beat, then trail lower, giving my ass a playful squeeze that makes me yelp softly, giggling and aching.

He guides me carefully up the steps, into the bath. The water is hotter than I expect, a searing kiss against my skin, and I gasp, sinking under anyway, letting it scald the night off my body.

Alex climbs in behind me, arms bracketing mine, pulling me back against his chest. His hands are everywhere—easy, slow, unrushed—tracing the slick line of my thigh, the curve of my hip, like he has all the time in the world.

I tip my head back onto his shoulder, feeling the wet slide of his mouth along my neck, my body melting against his in the heat and the quiet.

Alex pulls a cloth from the rack next to the bath, dipping it into the water, soaking it, before he drags it lazily over my shoulder, my collarbone, and the slope of my breasts. He lets the cloth float before reaching over to pump some soap from the dispenser and lathering it in his hands.

He rubs my shoulders, slick and wet, then my collarbone.

"You have no idea"—his voice is rough around the edges, almost to himself—"how fucking perfect you are."

He glides his soapy hands over the swell of my breasts, circling lazily around my nipples until they tighten into stiff peaks.

"Everything is so new to you," he says, and I hear him smiling, my body twitching and gasping under his touch.

"Alex," I moan. My cheeks flame.

Then he's gone, dispensing more soap into his hands.

Fucking tease.

He works it into a thick, silky foam and trails it down my torso, teasing along the hollow of my navel.

Then lower.

He pauses at the apex of my thighs, my back pressed into his twitching cock.

"May I?" he asks.

"Please," I plead, teetering on the edge.

He slides his hands between my legs, the lightest, slickest touch. Nowhere near enough pressure to satisfy the ache blooming there.

He hums low in his chest, the sound vibrating against the tile. "Fuck," he says softly "Your body is perfect." He continues to soap every inch of me. Thighs, hips, stomach, breasts. Methodically, almost cruel in how careful he is not to give me what I'm hungry for.

"I could make you come just from touching you like this." He drags the soapy cloth up the inside of my thigh, stopping just shy of where I'm throbbing for him.

"But *not tonight*," he murmurs, the words curling against my ear like a secret he's savoring. He says it with a smile in his voice, not anger, not disappointment, just pure, wicked patience. He presses a kiss to the side of my neck, slow and wet, teeth grazing lightly at the end, making me shiver.

A tease. A promise. A game he's far *too good* at playing.

———··———

ALEX'S BREATH is the only sound in the dark.

After our bath, we bundled ourselves into bed, clean and still flushed.

I was wrecked from the dancing, drinking, and teasing, and Alex was out within minutes, cock still hard, pressed thick and insistent against my thigh, a silent reminder of what I hadn't let happen tonight.

And yet, here I am, wide awake, staring at the ceiling that I can't even see.

Alex wants me. Makes me feel beautiful. Chosen.

So why am I thinking about Broderick?

His face tonight at the club.

Even now, curled against Alex, I see Broderick's fingers on my lip. The what-ifs that continue to haunt me.

I press my face into the pillow and try to block it out. My head starts to throb as sleep evades me and an inevitable hangover creeps in. I *need* comfort food. The thought alone makes my stomach protest loud enough to echo off the walls.

Carefully, I untangle myself from Alex's heavy arm and grab my purse from the chair. I pad out of the room barefoot, each step muffled by the thick carpet, and make my way downstairs to the kitchen.

The house is quiet, the echoes of tonight's shenanigans nothing more than a ghost now, secrets held by marble halls and too many closed doors. I'm not even sure what time it is—some ungodly hour where everything feels still.

As I round the corner toward the kitchen, the low hum of voices pulls me up short.

It's Broderick. Talking to someone.

"Do you think it's serious?"

His voice is low, tired.

"I don't know," the other man answers. It's Andrew, I think.

"What do you think she sees in him?" Broderick asks.

The realization hits me hard. They're talking about me.

A pause. Then, "Bro, do you *like* her?"

"No, no," Broderick says quickly. "I'm just looking out for her. She's Phil's little sister."

The words slam into me, cold and sharp.

But…he said he liked me.

Was that a lie? Or is he lying now, to Andrew?

Is he looking out for me?

Doubt creeps in, bitter in my mouth. I shouldn't even feel this way. I'm *with* Alex.

"Right," Andrew replies, the disbelief unmistakable in his voice. "It's been almost a year since Lauren."

Who's Lauren?

"Yeah," Broderick says. "Work's been…busy. Things are good. Momentum's good. Profits are strong. We're changing communities." He sounds proud—all the right words, all in the right tone—but underneath, I hear it.

That loneliness.

I didn't think someone like him would be lonely. It tugs at my heart. He lost his father, like I lost my mother. I can hear the sadness, I know it too well.

Andrew doesn't let it go. "Yeah, but when the work's done, Brody, who do you come home to?"

There's a soft sizzle, something dropped into a pan. Eggs maybe. Bacon. Whatever it is, the smell hits a second later, warm and mouthwatering.

"Alright, man," Andrew says. "I'll leave you to it. You and Elena did a great job planning everything. Thanks again. You're like the brother I wish I had."

"You know I got you."

Footsteps approach. I flatten against the wall, holding my breath as Andrew steps into the hallway, four water bottles cradled in his arms like precious cargo. Hangover insurance.

I wait until Andrew's footsteps fade, the silence swelling thick and heavy again.

Circling wide, I slip down the other side of the hall. If I come in through the second entrance, maybe Broderick won't suspect I heard anything I wasn't meant to.

I take a steadying breath before padding into the kitchen, heart pounding relentlessly against my ribs.

I'm not much of an actress—

"El."

I freeze.

Look up.

And there he is.

Shirtless.

Oh, dear God.

Every muscle on him is carved and golden under the low kitchen lights, skin kissed by the sun, a dusting of chest hair catching the glow. His pecs and abs ripple. I must look like a deer caught clean in the headlights. Where Alex is all lean and polished, Broderick is bulk and rugged edges.

"Oh," I stammer. "Sorry—I thought everyone had gone to bed." At least I don't have to pretend to be shocked, because at the mere sight of his perfect body, now I am.

Broderick chuckles, soft and rough. "You okay? You look like you've seen a ghost."

I laugh awkwardly, placing my purse on top of the counter and tucking a loose strand of hair behind my ear. "Something like that."

He tilts his head, studying me. "Couldn't sleep?"

"Yeah," I answer quickly, desperate to steer the conversation somewhere, anywhere else. "Whatcha making?"

"Grilled cheese," he says, flipping the sandwich in the pan with a lazy flick of his wrist. "You want one?"

My stomach answers before I do, grumbling loud enough for both of us to hear.

"Please." I huff, cheeks burning.

An easy grin spreads across his face. "Alright. Grilled cheese coming right up."

I lean against the counter, arms crossed, watching him move —the way his back flexes when he reaches for a plate, the low-slung waistband of his sweatpants teasing the edge of indecency. *Those dimples,* burnt into my memory.

His body is perfection. I bite my lip swallowing my desire.

I shouldn't be ogling him like this while Alex is upstairs.

"I'm sorry about *earlier*…" I say, the awkwardness of the situation of Broderick, Alex, and me, all entangled in my mess.

He shrugs. "We're good. You're with *him*, I'll get over it."

The thought of him getting over the idea of us doesn't quite sit well. It's selfish and fucked up of me. Am I so desperate to feel wanted that I'm greedy for it?

I sigh heavily. "I wish it wasn't so…" I can't find the right words.

Hard, confusing, frustrating? All of the above.

"Your fault for being so damn adorable." He's already assembling another sandwich, layering bread, butter, and three kinds of cheese like it's muscle memory.

"I'm a woman, not a bunny." I scoff. *Adorable.*

He chuckles, low and breathy, his eyes searing into me. I look away. Their pull is undeniable, and with me being pent up from Alex's earlier teasing, I'm not sure I can trust myself.

I shouldn't.

The sizzle of the sandwich he places in the pan echoes between us.

"You always look this intense making grilled cheese?" I tease, looking at him, now with his back turned. That back, *fuck.*

I'm trying to sound normal, trying not to drool.

Broderick shoots me a crooked smile over his shoulder. "Only when it's for royalty."

I snort, shoving his arm when he comes closer. He barely budges. Like trying to push a damn brick wall. But the small touch sends a jolt up my spine. He feels *nice.*

His forearms are corded with veins as he works the pan over the heat.

Desire tugging at something deep inside me.

He sets the sandwich down in front of me, slicing it neatly in half. "Here you go, your majesty."

I'm about to reach for it when he steps closer, towering over me in that way he always does, tall enough to make me tilt my head back to meet his eyes.

I can feel the heat radiating from his skin. He's close enough to touch.

I bite my lip.

He grins, slow and deliberate.

"You know," he says, voice low and rough with amusement, "you're gonna give me a crick in my neck if you keep making me look down at you like this."

Before I can fire back some smartass comment, his hands are on my waist. In one easy motion, he lifts me and sets me down on the counter.

I squeal, laughing, palms bracing against the marble for balance. "Brody!"

He steps between my knees, smirking up at me now, satisfaction written all over his face. We're not quite at eye level, but close enough.

I lick my lips, savoring the warmth of his hands still lingering on my skin.

"Much better." He rests his hands on either side of me, close enough that his heat seeps through the thin fabric of my dress. "Now I won't need a chiropractor tomorrow."

I roll my eyes, but my heart is racing so hard it feels like it might knock me clean off the counter.

I'm very aware of how close we are, how easy it would be to lean in, close the inches between us, taste the smile on his mouth. And make good on that almost kiss.

The sandwich sits forgotten between us, the air crackling, the space shrinking. Then he takes a step back, tutting. He's fighting the urge, sticking to the line I drew in the sand.

I try to recover my equilibrium and grab one half of the sandwich and take a bite, still trying to catch my breath from his touch, from the space that hummed between us. The cheese stretches, gooey and hot, and I have to tear it away awkwardly with my fingers.

"Mmm," I hum, mouth full. "God. That's actually amazing."

"Nothing beats grilled cheese." He's grinning as he takes a bite from his own.

"Thank you," I murmur, the words slipping out before I can second-guess them.

His gaze lingers on my mouth, steady and warm as he watches me take a few more bites.

"You've got a crumb," he says, his voice dipping low.

His eyes—dazzling green, sharp as glass, soft as moss— search mine, something unspoken threading tight between us. Then his thumb lifts, brushing the corner of my lip with a gentleness that makes my breath hitch.

Just a swipe.

Bare skin against bare skin.

But it tingles, sharp and electric, a spark that runs straight to my toes.

He doesn't move right away. His hand hovers close, as if he's caught between pulling back and leaning in, trapped in the same breathless space I'm drowning in.

My stomach flips violently, nothing to do with the grilled cheese cooling in my hands.

Broderick finally steps back, tearing another bite from his sandwich like he didn't just tilt my entire world sideways.

He leans against the counter, watching me like it's the most natural thing in the world.

"You know," he says, waving his sandwich vaguely at me, "this is kind of unfair."

I barely register it until I follow the line of his gaze.

Oh, fuck.

Me.

Perched on marble in the middle of the night.

Dressed in nothing but a silk negligee, nipples pert and feet bare, eating grilled cheese, while he stands there, shirtless and impossibly gorgeous in his own right.

Heat blooms under my skin, crawling up my throat, burning at the tips of my ears.

Broderick's still watching me like I'm something delicate and risky at the same time. Like if he looks long enough, I might disappear.

"You're testing this friendship," he growls, eyes dropping to where the silk clings to my skin. "You in that dress. Eating grilled cheese like a *fucking tease.*"

The sound reverberates through me, and I clench. I swallow a gasp.

I should laugh. I should say something flirty, something stupid. But I don't.

I can't.

Because all I can think about is the almost kiss.

Broderick takes a step closer, not much, just enough for his thigh to brush my knee. My breath stumbles.

His eyes flick down to my mouth.

For one suspended second, he leans in.

My lips part. I don't move.

I *can't* move.

I wonder…What if I'd met him first?

What if Alex wasn't sleeping upstairs in my bed?

Would he kiss me now? Fuck me on this counter?

Would I let him?

My heart slams against my ribs, so loud I swear he can hear it. But then he stops. Pulls back slightly, his jaw ticking.

"You're trouble, Elena," he says, almost gently. "You know that?"

My chest heaves, breathless.

I could say the same about *him*.

He lingers, close enough that I can smell the faint trace of soap and smoke and something else I can never name but always feel, and then he smiles wide enough to break whatever that was.

The moment I almost gave in. *Again.*

"Elena…I'd like my phone back, please," he murmurs.

I laugh awkwardly, his words cutting through the tension.

I nod toward my purse, sitting on the edge of the counter, trying to catch my breath.

He turns, grabs it, opens it, and takes his phone out before placing it back on the counter.

"Thank you." He starts to walk out, then pauses in the doorway, every muscle in his back pulled tight.

Doesn't look. Just stands there for a moment.

I wonder if he's fighting it too.

If he's thinking about my legs brushing his hips, my breath catching when his thumb grazed my lip.

If he wonders about all the what-ifs.

But he leaves.

And I'm still on the counter, too full of want, guilt, tasting grilled cheese and every *almost* that passed between us. Again.

I exhale—then drag in air and sense in the same breath. Slipping off the counter, I dart upstairs, desperate for release. Desperate to erase the lingering of what-ifs.

Pushing open my bedroom door, the hallway light spills across the bed where Alex lies flat on his back, mouth parted, chest rising, slow and deep with sleep.

Walking to him, my heart hammers, feet silent on the carpet. For a moment, I watch him, the way the sheets cling to his hips, the way one arm flops loose across the mattress.

I crawl into bed beside him, pressing my body into his, needing the warmth, the solidity, the *yes* I know he'll give me without hesitation.

"Alex," I whisper, lips brushing over his bare torso in soft, open-mouthed kisses. I'm tempted to ask him to fuck me—beg for it, even—just to drown out the thoughts of Broderick. But I won't. I know I'll regret it if I do it for the wrong reasons, if my heart isn't fully in it.

Still, I need Alex to make me feel good—in the way I know only he can.

He stirs, grumbling low in his throat, shifting toward me. My fingertips trace the line of his stomach, inching lower, finding him already half-hard under the thin fabric of his briefs.

I stroke his cock—slow, coaxing—and feel him swell under my hand.

"Elena," he rasps, voice thick with sleep and heat.

"Can I play?" I whisper, my voice trembling.

"I'm yours."

It's all the permission I need.

I tug the waistband of his briefs down, freeing him, greedy and eager to drown myself in something real and hot and now. Alex gasps, the sound sharp in the dark.

With the flat of my tongue, I drag a slow lick along the entire length of his shaft. His cock throbs against me, growing harder with every wet, hungry pull of my mouth. Between strokes, I pull back just enough to murmur, "Alex… touch me."

I grab his hand and press it between my thighs.

"*Now.*"

He lets out a low, amused laugh. "Bossy little thing," he says, his voice thick with approval.

His hand trails up my thigh, painstakingly slow, fingers slipping beneath the silk of my negligee. He hooks my panties with two fingers, pulling them down and tossing them somewhere into the dark.

Then he strokes the inside of my leg, slow at first, then firmer, the rough pads of his fingertips skating higher, closer, like he can feel how badly I need it, how close I am to unraveling already.

"Now, Alex…please," I whimper, the words barely audible, muffled around the head of his cock as I suck him slow and greedy.

Alex groans, hips twitching under me, his hand curling tighter around my thigh.

"Fuck, Elena," he breathes.

He tugs lightly, urging me up, pulling me toward him.

"Come here," he says, voice rough and lazy and full of heat. "Sit on my face."

My whole body jolts.

"What?" I gasp, mouth still full of him. "How…"

"Like this," he growls, grabbing my hips.

In one swift motion, I'm propped on his chest, thighs straddling his shoulders, my crotch and ass mere inches from his mouth.

I gasp, heart slamming against my ribs.

Panic flickers—what if I suffocate him, what if…?

But Alex just grips my hips tighter, steady, sure, grounding me.

"You're already so wet," he groans, voice rough with desire. He plants a kiss on me. "I want you gushing all over my tongue—drown me in it." He peppers kisses along my inner thigh before pulling back just enough to murmur, "Now, be a good girl and fuck my face."

Heat flashes through me, so fierce it borders on pain.

He eases me down, his mouth finding me like he's been starving for it. He licks the lips of my pussy so slowly it makes me sob, *finally*, lapping up my wetness before tapping my clit with the tip of his tongue. A sharp, wicked flick that makes my thighs tremble.

I *need* this.

Then he drags his tongue from my center all the way to my ass. Slowly, he swirls his tongue and licks.

Oh. My. God.

This wasn't in the manual.

He swipes his tongue over my backdoor in gentle strokes until I nearly shatter, the sensation sending ripples of electricity shooting through me. Every thought, every fear, every *almost* from downstairs wiped clean in a white-hot flood of sensation. This is something else.

I'm trembling, shaking with every kiss, every filthy, perfect move of his lips and mouth.

Alex grips my hips tighter, groaning into me like he can't get enough, like he never wants to stop. And I hope he doesn't.

My hips have a mind of their own, grinding into his face, taking his tongue deeper, harder against every point of pleasure he's got unrestricted access to.

His dick pulses against my palm—insistent and still begging for my mouth.

I lean forward, swallowing his cock, and we lose ourselves in each other. I spit and slurp on his head, taking him into the back of my throat, stroking his shaft, the saltiness of his precum coating my tongue. His hips thrust, meeting my every move.

Together, we're a tangled mess of limbs and mouths.

Alex's tongue moves with purpose now—slow, deep strokes, pushing in and out before teasing my clit with the flat of his tongue. Then he slips his tongue in my ass again, leaving no part of me untouched, every tender spot claimed. My whole body quakes above him.

His fingers dig into my hips, squeezing my ass, spreading me wide. He holds me steady, dragging me down onto his mouth—unyielding—while I writhe, overwhelmed by the sheer force of it.

I whimper around his dick, trying to keep rhythm, trying to hold on, but the fabric of my being is being ripped apart at the seams, with every stroke of his tongue.

"You taste so good," he groans against me, the words vibrating through my core. "Sweetest fucking thing I've ever had."

I moan helplessly, the sound vibrating down his shaft, making him buck up into my mouth.

"That's it, Darling," he murmurs, voice wrecked with need. "Use me. Fuck my mouth. Take what you need."

His filthy words make my hips jerk against his face.

Alex groans in approval, tongue tapping harder against me, relentless now, chasing my release like it's the only thing that matters.

I pant around him, my free hand clawing uselessly at the sheets, trying to anchor myself. I rock against him, grinding into him harder, the weight of me settling into him. He might suffo-cate. He might die like this. But in this moment, I don't think he cares. Neither do I.

"Talk to me," he rasps, voice ragged between licks. "Tell me how good I make you feel."

I pull off him long enough to gasp, "So good, Alex—Fuck! It's so much, you're making me—"

"Tell me what you want," he growls, teeth grazing lightly over my pussy. "Tell me how bad you need me."

His voice alone makes my pussy clench, wetter, needier, grinding down onto his mouth without thinking.

"I need you," I cry out, frantic now, thighs shaking. "Please, Alex—Please don't stop—I'm so close—"

His fingers scrape against my skin, pushing me deeper into him. The sound of his muffled moans, the wet slide of my arousal —it's all too much. It sends me over the edge.

With a strangled cry, hips bucking helplessly against his mouth, the orgasm rips through me like a tidal wave, blinding and violent, as my wetness runs down my thighs.

I shudder, collapsing against him. My legs tremble so much, he has to hold me steady.

He keeps licking me through it—slow, savoring every twitch, every aftershock—until I'm whimpering from oversensitivity.

When I finally ease down, boneless, and wrecked, I take his throbbing cock back into my mouth, yearning to give him the same undoing.

He's so hard now, leaking against my tongue, his hips jerking up without control.

"Fuck, Elena," he groans, voice strangled, hands fisting the sheets beside him. "Just like that. Don't stop. You're perfect."

I hollow my cheeks, sliding him deep, letting him feel all of it.

His groans grow louder, desperate, until with a choked gasp, he thrusts once, twice, and spills into my mouth, thick and hot.

I take him all, tasting the salt and heat of him, not stopping until he finally slumps back against the pillows, utterly spent.

For a long moment, there's only the sound of our breathing before we both drift off into a dreamless sleep.

Chapter 23

August

We were reluctantly up before sunrise. The children of some of Manhattan's finest, now reduced to a mess of clammy bodies and quiet regrets. The staff glide through the house with practiced efficiency—salty, greasy breakfast laid out across marble counters, intravenous drips humming quietly in the conservatory. The preferred cure for too much money and not enough sense.

But not all sins get erased so easily.

The moments with Broderick still cling to me—quiet, charged, too close.

Then what followed with Alex.

My head spins thinking about it.

I'm tangled, pulled in opposite directions, and none of it feels clean.

The girls and guys have split off, each group indulging in more civilized pursuits for the day. I'm thankful for the distance.

The girls begrudgingly start with an early morning yoga session on the beach, led by Natalie. While some of the women take it seriously, Riley spends most of the time making exaggerated poses and whispering hilarious commentary under her breath, sending me into fits of laughter. Philippa, ever the perfectionist, shushes us repeatedly while trying to hold her warrior pose. But I can see her quaking, trying to stave off the lingering effects of last night's excess.

After yoga, we board the Montgomery yacht for champagne and canapés, cruising along the Hamptons coastline. Sunhats and oversized sunglasses are practically mandatory, and the mimosa refills never stop. It's indulgent, glamorous, and very Philippa. At some point, a few of the girls jump into the water, squealing as the salty waves envelop them. Riley, of course, dares me to join, and after some coaxing, I cave, splashing into the cool ocean together, it feels good to let loose with the girls.

Meanwhile, the guys go jet skiing and deep-sea fishing, a combination that suits their rugged, adventurous energy. From the text updates Broderick sends, it seems like Andrew has been crowned 'King of the Sea' after catching the biggest fish, and Broderick dubs himself captain of the ship.

Alex spends the day with his own friends, who are also enjoying the weekend in the Hamptons.

By early afternoon, we've dried off, changed into our brightest summer outfits, and make our way to The Patio, a chic poolside bar. The place is quintessential Hamptons—white linen curtains billow in the warm breeze, turquoise pool water shimmers under the sun, and a playlist of upbeat tropical house music sets the perfect mood.

Philippa, stunning as ever in a white sundress and a 'Bride-to-Be' sash, holds court at the head of the table while we sip chilled champagne and indulge in fresh seafood platters. I sit next to Riley, both of us in bold, colorful summer dresses, matching the vibrant setting around us.

I'm mid-bite into my lobster roll, half-listening to the hum of conversation around me before one of Philippa's friends grabs my attention.

"So, Elena." Sienna leans forward, twirling her cocktail straw with a knowing smirk. "We need to talk about Alexander."

"You guys were all over each other last night—it was sickening in the best way," Avery says, her face full of mischief.

Little does she know how *all over* each other we actually ended up being.

Natalie practically swoons. "You guys are like…a dream. How did you meet? And don't give us the 'mutual friends' excuse. We need details."

Riley stifles a laugh into her mimosa, while I take a slow sip of champagne, giving myself a moment to collect my thoughts.

"Well," I start, setting my food down. "We met at a vintage store."

"A vintage store?" Sienna raises a brow. "That's so mysterious."

"It's kind of a long story," I admit, remembering how our first meeting had been anything but ordinary. How we collided into each other, how I ended up in the hospital, and how he later showed up at my apartment, charming as ever, with gifts and a teasing grin.

"Did you know who he was?" Natalie asks, resting her chin in her palm.

"Not at first," I confess, playing with the stem of my glass. "I mean, I knew he was ridiculously handsome, but I had no idea he was famous. I got to know him as just…Alex."

A collective sigh moves around the table.

"He's so much hotter in person," Avery gushes. "I saw him once at a fashion event, and I swear he looked unreal. It's not fair."

Sienna leans in, eyes alight with curiosity. "But what's he like? Off-camera, I mean."

I hesitate, feeling a flicker of warmth at the thought of him. "I don't kiss and tell." I wink at Riley, keeper of all my secrets. She laughs under her breath, chest puffed out and proud.

There's a round of giggles and cackles. Protests over me holding out on juicy details. Another jab about me being a tease— *and fuck, do I know it.*

I smile but say nothing, my thoughts momentarily drifting to Broderick last night. The contrast between them is undeniable. If Alex is a wildfire, Broderick is the heat that lingers on my skin long after. And yet, here I am, caught between being with Alex and the idea of Broderick.

Riley, sensing my shift in mood, nudges me with her shoulder. "Alright, enough of the love-life grilling," she announces, lifting her glass. "To Philippa, and her last few weeks as a free woman!"

The table erupts in cheers, the weight of the moment dissolving into laughter.

Riley and I excuse ourselves to the ladies' room, giggling about something stupid she said moments before. The champagne has me feeling a little lightheaded, my skin warm from the sun and the lingering high of conversation. But as we head back to the table, the air shifts.

That prickling sensation—the one you get when you're being watched. And then, there she is.

I recognize her immediately from the panel at Geek-Fest.

Walking toward me, every inch the blonde bombshell I've seen in magazines, is *Madison Walsh.*

She's devastatingly beautiful—the kind of woman who doesn't just turn heads, she *owns* the attention in the room. Her long, sun-kissed hair cascades in billowing waves. Her bronzed skin glows in the afternoon light. She's taller than me, taller than Riley, dressed in a crisp white dress that hugs every inch of her model-length frame, her legs on full display. She looks like she was born for this world.

And she's not alone.

Flanked by two equally stunning women—one a statuesque brunette with box braids, the other a dirty blonde—it's like a Hamptons fashion editorial walked off the page and straight into my reality.

I freeze. My heart lurches.

Madison smiles, slow and practiced, but it doesn't reach her eyes. "Hi," she says softly. Friendly. Controlled. Calculated.

I open my mouth. Nothing comes out.

I've imagined this moment before—what it would be like to meet her. But none of those scenarios included me standing here, completely frozen, purse clenched in white-knuckled fingers.

"Um…hi." It comes out weak. Pathetic.

Madison tilts her head, studying me like I'm something under glass. "You're Alex's friend, right?" she asks, putting an extra beat of emphasis on *friend*.

Her friends snicker.

We haven't defined our relationship yet. Definitely friends. Kind of lovers. Not *nothing*.

I nod, scrambling to collect myself. "Uh, yeah." My voice is steadier this time, but my pulse is not.

Her smile widens, like she's been saving the final blow—she lands it.

"I'm Madison," she says, voice sticky-sweet.

"Alex's girlfriend," her friend with the braids cuts in, sharp as glass.

The words slice through the air.

"It's nice to finally meet you," Madison adds, smile gleaming like she hasn't driven a stake into my chest.

For a second, all I can hear is blood rushing in my ears.

Girlfriend? Alex's *girlfriend*?

There's no time to process it. Not before Riley scoffs—loudly —beside me.

"Bullshit," she says, arms crossed.

That one word pulls me out of the spiral. If Madison's his girlfriend, why the hell is Alex staying with *me* this weekend?

Madison's expression flickers—for a second—before she turns her gaze to Riley, her eyes narrowing.

"Sure," she says, like she's humoring a child. "But this is what we do. On and off. Like a merry-go-round. I've been in his life for years now. We love playing this little game."

Her friends smirk again, nodding along like backup dancers to a lie.

Something in me hardens. He told me they were done. That there was nothing left between them.

But I hadn't asked if we were exclusive. Maybe I'm just a distraction. A convenient *something* before he inevitably goes back to *her*.

The thought churns in my mind.

Madison's calm, confident, and practiced. She's getting pushing my buttons, and she knows it.

I take a breath, pushing the mess of feelings down.

"I'm not sure what you're expecting me to say," I reply, tilting my head. "Congratulations?"

Riley lets out a sharp laugh beside me, unable to help herself.

Madison's eyes twitch—slightly—but she recovers fast. "I thought you should know," she says, her tone all fake innocence, "since you and Alex seem to be spending so much time together. I wouldn't want there to be any confusion."

I meet her gaze, squaring my shoulders. She might intimidate me, but I won't let her see it.

"Funny you should say that, considering Alex was in *my* bed last night," I spit back.

Her smile falters, fingers tighten around her purse strap before she gives a small, brittle laugh, like I'm amusing.

"For now," she adds, her voice soft but cutting. She gives me one final once-over, something flickering behind her eyes, and then turns. Her entourage falls into step beside her as they head for the bar.

I don't breathe until she's far enough away. My hands grip my purse like it's the only thing anchoring me.

Riley whistles low. "Wow. That was a level of bitch I haven't seen in a while."

I don't answer. My mind is spinning.

Alex said they were done.

So either he lied…

Or this is part of *her* game.

And I honestly don't know which thought unsettles me more.

Riley places a hand on my arm, yanking me back to the present. "Elena." Her voice is careful. "You do know that was total manipulation, right? She wanted to shake you. And I gotta say, you did a damn good job standing your ground."

I nod, though I'm not sure I fully believe her. Because no matter how composed I may have *looked*, no matter how well I played it off, Madison weaseled her way under my skin.

We finish lunch and enjoy the activities planned for the rest of the day—shopping in town, then heading to the spa for mani-pedis and massages. The thought of an afternoon wrapped in fluffy robes and lavender oil sounds perfect, exactly what we all need before the big night ahead.

And yet, even as I laugh along with the girls, even as I smile, try to stay present, I can't shake the tension still clinging to my chest.

The encounter with Madison leaves an imprint. One I can't quite brush off.

She was *too* confident. *Too* poised. Like someone who knows something I don't. Every carefully chosen word, every flicker of amusement in her eyes—it was all designed to make me doubt.

And damn it, it's working.

Riley, ever the perceptive one, nudges me with her shoulder as we stroll past boutique windows, her smirk knowing. "I can hear you overthinking," she teases.

I sigh, dragging a hand through my hair. "Something about her felt...off. Like it wasn't just about Alex. She was setting something up."

Riley hums, tapping her chin dramatically. "Yeah, well, the bitch is definitely calculating. But listen, babe, if she really had Alex, she wouldn't have needed to come up to you like that. That was an intimidation move. Plain and simple."

I want to believe her. I really do.

But my gut tells me this isn't the last I'll hear from Madison Walsh.

BY THE TIME the sun dips below the horizon, streaks of gold and violet stretch across the sky. We're back at the Montgomery Estate, where warm lantern light spills over manicured gardens.

The guys are already back from their adventures, looking spunky in relaxed button-downs and linen pants, lounging by the outdoor bar.

Alex's gaze finds mine before he pulls me into an embrace, arms warm and familiar. "Hey," he murmurs, voice low, dragging me out of the spiral. "How was your day?"

"It was good," I say, but the words come out flat.

His smile falters—just slightly. So slight no one else would notice. But I do.

We settle by the pool, sliding into the rhythm of the group. Andrew and Broderick are deep in debate with Philippa and Sienna, laughter rising above the music. The taste of champagne still clings to my lips.

I want to melt into it. I want Madison's words to vanish into the night air. But they cling to me.

Broderick throws a teasing remark my way. I don't bite. His brow lifts in concern, but I dodge it, eyes fixed on the water or my drink or anything that isn't him. Or Alex.

From the outside, the night is almost perfect. But under the glow of string lights and summer air, something simmers.

I feel it in the way Alex watches me between conversations, how his hand finds mine, squeezing gently, like he's checking I'm still here. I am, though not really.

He finally pulls me aside, guiding me quietly through the house and into the dim hush of the library.

I know this won't be sweet nothings.

The door clicks shut behind us.

"You've been weird all night," Alex says, his voice clipped. The usual charm fades into something sharper. "Are you going to tell me what's going on, or do I have to guess?"

I cross my arms, leaning back against the edge of the desk. "You really don't know?"

His jaw tightens. "Enlighten me."

I exhale slowly. "I ran into Madison today."

Something flickers across his face. Not shock. Not guilt. Irritation. Like he already knows what's coming.

"Let me guess." He rubs a hand along his jaw, eyes narrowing. "She fed you some bullshit story about us?"

"She said she was your girlfriend."

He lets out a dry laugh, shaking his head. "She's not."

"Then why does she think she is?"

He snaps, stepping closer. "Madison knows exactly what we were. She's messing with you."

"Then explain it to me."

Alex exhales hard, dragging a hand through his messy blond

hair. "We were never together. She was…someone I fucked around with."

The words hit like concrete.

My spine stiffens.

He throws it out like it's nothing. Like *I* could be nothing, too.

"She knew what it was," he continues, locking eyes with mine. "It was casual. No promises. No exclusivity. And trust me, Madison had plenty of other people keeping her occupied."

The bitterness in his tone slices through the air. I feel it lodge somewhere beneath my ribs.

"She made it sound like—"

"I don't care how she made it sound," he cuts in, sharp and fast. "She's toying with you, and you're letting her win."

I want to believe him. I do.

But doubt coils at the base of my skull—cold and persistent.

Because it's not just Madison.

It's the bruise he left when he lied before.

The one I keep pressing to see if it still hurts.

It does. And I hate myself for not being able to let go, move on. It's like I'm torturing myself. Maybe there's something wrong with me.

His gaze scans my face, and whatever he sees—whatever flickers behind my eyes—sets something off in him.

"Fucking hell, Elena." He backs away, pacing, dragging both hands through his hair now. "Are we really doing this again?"

"Doing what again?" My voice cracks despite myself.

"The trust thing," he snaps, stopping short. His eyes blaze. "I've told you the truth. I don't owe Madison anything, and I sure as hell don't owe you an explanation for something that ended before we even met."

"That's unfair."

"What's unfair is *you* calling me out over Madison while I've had to stand by and watch whatever the hell's going on between you and *that guy*."

My breath gets stuck halfway in. "What?"

"Did you invite me here to make him jealous or something? What is he to you?"

He's unraveling now. The anger is real, but underneath it—panic.

"A *friend*. He's just a friend."

Denial tastes sour the second it leaves my mouth.

And I know he hears it too because his expression twists, turning into something bitter.

"You don't think I see it, Elena?"

"See what?" I breathe.

"The way *he* looks at you."

"I can't control that." I take a step back. My hands are cold. My heart's thudding against bone.

"Are you giving him a reason to look at you that way?"

I hesitate. "No."

"Who's lying now?"

"This is all new to me, Alex. You know that."

He scoffs—low and hard. "I don't know how long that excuse is going to work for you."

I stare at him, my breath shallow. "This isn't just about Madison."

"Then what is it about?"

"I don't know." I sigh, exasperated.

The silence between us stretches tight. A breath away from breaking. His chest rises and falls in quick, shallow pulls. His jaw works like he's biting down on something cruel. "For what it's worth, I'm not lying about this."

"But you did lie to me before," I say. The words cut, sharp and brittle. "Maybe I forgave you, but that doesn't mean I forgot how it felt." He flinches like I've slapped him.

His hands clench at his sides, then fall loose again. He exhales through his nose—controlled. Barely. "And what am I supposed to do with that?"

I press my palm flat against my chest like I can hold myself together. "I don't know. But I don't want to be another woman you *just fuck.*"

That lands. His eyes narrow, then he looks away, jaw tight. A vein in his neck twitches.

Before either of us can say another word, Natalie knocks on the library door to ask about something trivial. The moment is severed clean. But the weight of it lingers.

Alex drags a hand through his hair, muttering under his breath before walking off. And the conversation stays unfinished.

But not forgotten.

Laughter and music float up from the party below, but they barely register. I'm too caught up in my own head, pacing the edge of the porch like I can outwalk the thoughts thrashing about.

The fight with Alex still clings to me—his sharp words, the frustration burning in his eyes, the way he looked at me like I'm slipping through his fingers and he doesn't know how to stop it.

I brace my hands on the railing, sucking in a breath of cool night air, trying to calm the storm clawing through me.

"Okay, what the hell is going on?" Riley's voice cuts through my spiraling. I turn to find her leaning in the doorway, arms crossed, one brow arched like she's already sifted through every thought in my head.

She steps closer, eyes scanning me carefully. "You've been MIA for an hour, and you look like you're about to throw yourself into the ocean fully clothed. Spill."

I let out a shaky breath, dragging a hand through my hair. "I had a fight with Alex."

Her eyes sharpen, the teasing edge slipping for a moment. "About what?"

"Madison," I mutter, eyes fixed on the dark waves crashing against the shore. "The conversation earlier with her. And when I asked him about it, he got…defensive. Irritated."

Riley stays quiet for a beat, her gaze softening. "Did he explain?"

I nod. "Yeah. Said it was nothing. Casual. Over before I even showed up. But…I don't know, babe. It's not just about her. It's everything. Me not knowing where I stand with him. Feeling like I'm always waiting for the other shoe to drop."

Riley leans her elbows on the railing beside me, bumping her shoulder into mine. "Okay, but let me ask you something."

I glance at her, wary. "What?"

She tilts her head, studying me. "Have you ever felt this way about anyone before?"

The weight sits heavy in my throat. "You know I haven't."

She smirks, but it's soft, understanding. "Exactly. I've never seen you like this."

I frown. "Like what?"

"*Alive*," she says, like it's the most obvious thing in the world.

"Elena, you've been sleepwalking through life for two years. You were practically dead with grief. And now look at you—pacing, feeling, fighting. Yeah, it's messy as hell, but that's relationships, babe. You're here. You're living again." Her words land hard, right in the center of my chest.

"But what if I'm setting myself up to get hurt?" I whisper.

Riley shoots me a look. "It happens, and sometimes it doesn't. It's part of the deal. But if Alex makes you happy? Chase that feeling. Ride that high. And honestly?" She grins, bumping me again. "You deserve to ride *that man*, too."

A startled giggle bursts out of me, the tension cracking enough. I cover my face. "Oh my God, Riley."

"What?" she laughs with me. "It's true! You've been all locked up like a nun, and now you've got a six-foot-something

Swedish snack who's clearly crazy about you. Why not let your-self have that?"

"Broderick," I say, shaking my head.

I see the realization wash over her face. "I get it. You weren't planning on Broderick. He came out of nowhere. But now it's a choice. Are you going to go with what's in your hand, or rush headfirst into the *what if?*"

She's right. I need to decide.

Because hanging in the balance between them, it's not fair. Not to them, not to me. And as much as I crave that validation—from *two* people, something I never thought I'd experience—I can't become my father.

I can't string people along because it feels good to be wanted. Chosen.

"You don't have to have all the answers right now," Riley says, her voice gentle, tugging me back. "But maybe it's time to stop running from what you want and run toward it instead. Head-first. Even if it's messy, at least it's sexy. And no matter what, I'll be here, whatever you choose."

I stay quiet. Let the words settle. Because she's right.

Maybe I don't know where this ends. Maybe it explodes. But Alex makes me *feel*. And isn't that worth something?

I let out a breath. "I think...I think I want to see where this goes with Alex."

Alex is the right choice. I've already let him in. It makes sense.

Riley grins. "Good. About time you admitted it."

I glance at her, squinting. "You always this smug when you're right?"

She laughs. "Always."

I smile, and for the first time all night, I feel a little lighter. "Thanks."

Riley loops an arm around my shoulder. "What are best friends for if not to encourage questionable life choices?"

I laugh again, tension peeling away. Together, we turn to face the house, lit up with guests and the hum of the party.

After our little heart-to-heart, I slip upstairs. My legs move on instinct, but my chest stays tangled.

The second I open the door to my room, I freeze.

Alex is lying on the bed, one arm thrown behind his head. His eyes find mine the second I step in.

"I couldn't find you," he says, voice low, unreadable.

I close the door quietly behind me. "I needed space."

His jaw ticks. "From me?"

I hesitate. Too long.

Alex sits up slowly, his eyes sharp. "If you don't want this, Elena, tell me now."

I open my mouth. Nothing comes out. His words disarm me.

He exhales hard, dragging a hand through his hair. "If you're with me, you're with *me*. Not running off and hiding every time it gets complicated."

My pulse thumps in my ears, but I step closer. "That's not what I'm doing."

"Then what are you doing?" His voice softens, but the fire in his gaze doesn't move.

"I'm scared," I admit.

His shoulders tense. "Of what?"

I stare into his eyes. "Of getting it wrong. Of believing this is something it's not."

Alex rises, closing the space. He reaches out, brushing his thumb along my jaw, so gentle it unravels me.

"This," he murmurs, voice rough, raw, "is real."

I let out a shaky breath. "Then say it."

His hands slip to my waist, holding me like I might vanish.

"I've wanted you since the moment you fell into my life. Not just for now. Not for when it's easy. I want all of you and *only you.*"

My heart pulls tight in my chest.

"And if you're mine," he adds, his thumb drawing slow, dizzying circles against my hip, "then you're mine." His gaze darkens, voice softening to something low and certain. "No doubts. No running."

Everything inside me leans into him. I let it.

It's not perfect. It's not certain.

But it's real.

I lift my chin. "I'm all in."

Something fierce flashes through his eyes, then he kisses me, hard and hungry, like he's claiming me.

When he pulls back, his lips curl into a smirk, but it's looser now. Like relief.

"Well, then," he murmurs. "Looks like I finally have a girlfriend."

The word knocks something loose in me. I laugh, breath catching. My cheeks flush. "Say that again."

He arches a brow. "What, that you're my *girlfriend*?"

I bite my lip, smiling. "Yeah."

His smirk deepens, tugging me closer. "*My girlfriend,*" he whispers against my lips before sealing it with a kiss, the confirmation I needed. We've slapped a label on it.

I feel the resolve settle into my bones.

And just like that, I let Broderick Schwartz fade to the back of my mind.

For now.

Chapter 24

Dancing With Myself

The stage lights gleam down on me as the music swells. The energy in the studio is inspired, a palpable current of anticipation and excitement. Wearing denim shorts and a white top with a sparkly silver jacket, I grip the microphone and let the first notes spill from my lips, my voice weaving a spell over the audience, an acoustic rendition of my first single 'Ignite.' The band behind me plays with precision, each note falling perfectly into place as I deliver a performance that is equal parts raw and refined.

The studio audience erupts as I hit the final note, the applause ringing through the room. All I hear is my own heartbeat, the energy of their cheers washing over me. I take it in, grounding myself before I smile and give a slight bow. It has been a long road to this moment, and standing on the *Rise and Shine America* stage feels like the beginning of something incredible.

As I step off the stage, Lara Spencer greets me warmly, leading me to the plush interview area. "Elena, that was phenomenal! You've had such a whirlwind year—returning to the U.S.

after being away for so long. I loved watching you on *Starstruck Australia*." She touches her hand to her chest in earnest. "Your mom's cancer battle, winning it all for her, I was in tears every episode. You know, I lost my mom to cancer, too. Your story really struck a chord with me and so many others," she says, her eyes glistening with unshed tears.

"Aww, thanks, Lara, that means so much. I'm a big fan of the show. Thank you for having me," I answer confidently, her sentiment hitting close to home.

"Oh my God, your accent is adorable. Isn't it adorable?" she gushes playfully to the studio audience, and they erupt in laughter and applause.

I laugh with her, feeling the jitters of nerves fading away.

"So, tell the good people what you're working on. What can we expect next for you?"

"My sophomore album is set to be released in September. I'm really excited about it, it's a completely new direction in sound, and I'm working with some incredible producers."

"I can't wait to hear it. Be sure to send me an advance copy! You came on the scene and had such resounding success back in Australia—your debut album and award nominations. I see big things for you here!" she exclaims.

I tuck a loose wave of hair behind my ear and smile. "Thanks, Lara. It's surreal, honestly. I feel incredibly grateful. This is what I've always dreamed of, and to have people connect with my music—it's everything. I put my whole heart into this album, and I hope the fans connect with it as much as my first."

"I have no doubt it will, Elena. You're such a talent—your voice, your songs really resonates with people," Lara says warmly.

I'm touched by her comment, warmth spreading through my chest as a mix of pride and nostalgia washes over me. I think of my mother, of the long nights spent dreaming about moments like this, and how surreal it feels to be here now. I simply nod, placing my hand over my heart in silent gratitude.

Lara pauses, taking a deep breath, before leaning in slightly, her expression turning more serious. "And, of course, you've been in the headlines a lot lately. Not just for your music. There's been quite a bit of buzz about your personal life. How are you handling all of that?"

I smile, keeping my expression poised. My fingers curl around the armrest, a small attempt to steady myself, but I hope to God my face doesn't show it.

"I focus on the music. People will always talk, but at the end of the day, I'm here because of my art, and that's where my heart is." I respond with the well-crafted response Kylie and I worked on in the lead up to this interview.

Lara nods approvingly. "We love a hard-working queen!" The crowd responds with a resounding applause.

"Well, we can't wait to see what's next for you! Thank you for being here today."

As Kylie, Mark, and I head back to the dressing room, Kylie is on her phone checking socials and reading out loud some of the comments coming through.

"One user says…" Her voice is steady and proud.

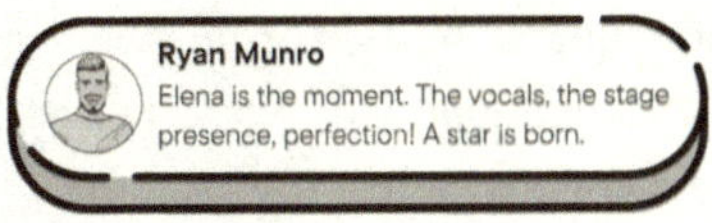

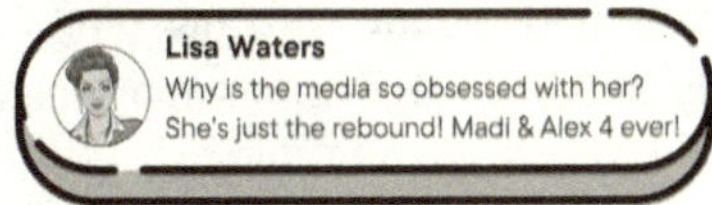

"Ugh, people are the worst," Kylie groans.

I roll my eyes, brushing it off. "Let them talk. They always will."

"I think overall, that was a resounding success," says Kylie.

"Okay, let's discuss next steps," Mark adds.

ONCE KYLIE, Mark, and I wrap up, I head back home to shed my performing persona and slip into my civilian clothes. This afternoon, Philippa has her final bridal fitting before her big day, and I get to try on my bridesmaid dress.

My phone dings with a text from Riley.

RILEY

You're a freaking Queen! So proud!

Another text I missed from earlier—from Broderick.

BRODERICK

I have some notes, LOL. Just kidding, you killed it.

I laugh, shaking my head. But as I scroll, my heart sinks.

Nothing from Alex? Maybe he's busy with work. I try my best to set aside the feeling of disappointment as I hurry out the door.

The bridal boutique is nestled in a quiet, upscale corner of Manhattan, all soft lighting and ivory fabrics. Philippa waits outside with Carole and my father.

They see me, and Phillipa and Carole both rush to embrace me, gushing over my performance this morning. My father stands to the side, simply nodding. His expression is unfamiliar—pride, maybe?

While Carole, Mortimer, and I sit on the plush sofa, sipping complimentary champagne, we wait for Philippa to emerge from the dressing room.

She steps out, and I'm momentarily stunned. The dress clings to her perfectly, the intricate lacework of the bodice catching the soft light like something out of a dream. Her gown drapes elegantly around her, the most glamorous veil cascading down with delicate lace details. She looks breathtaking.

I don't much believe in marriage—maybe I never have. But standing here, watching my sister glow in a dress meant for forever, I can at least appreciate the beauty of it, even if I don't believe in the promise it represents.

"Oh, Philippa," Carole gushes.

"Do you guys love it?" she asks.

"Wow, you look like Mom."

Philippa's eyes soften at my response. Carole hangs her head at the mention of my mom.

"Oh, Dad, please don't cry. If you do, then I will, and then I won't be able to stop," Philippa says, her voice thick with emotion.

My father sits silently, his eyes welling with tears. I try to ignore the sting of jealousy creeping in. The way he looks at her, the softness in his eyes—it's something I don't think I've ever been on the receiving end of. And that thought stings even more.

We all watch as the seamstress makes small adjustments to

Philippa's dress before she heads back to the dressing room to change.

"Elena, I just wanted to tell you again how proud I was of your performance this morning," says Carole, making small talk.

"Thank you."

I know she's trying to be kind, but being friendly with her feels like such a betrayal to my mother.

"Your voice is so wonderful, it always has been. Such a powerful gift to have," she adds.

"It's definitely something," my father adds, catching me completely off guard. "You handled the interview well."

Before I can respond, Philippa bounds out of the dressing room.

"Your turn," she sing-songs, snatching my hand and dragging me toward the back. In a flurry of fabric and impatience, she strips me down and shoves me into the bridesmaid dress she selected.

As she zips me into my dress, she lets out a low whistle. "Damn, sis, you look amazing."

I glance at my reflection—the champagne floor-length dress hugs my frame perfectly. It's fitted off-the-shoulder bodice exuding an understated elegance. Simple and sophisticated.

And yet, despite the warmth in Philippa's voice, despite the excitement of the moment, a thought that's been sitting on my tongue finally slips out.

"I know you probably only asked me to be your maid of honor because we're sisters." My chest tightens. Unable to meet her eyes, I keep my tone light, though there's a heaviness behind it.

Philippa pauses, her hands stilling on my shoulders as she meets my gaze in the mirror. For a moment, I brace for one of her classic, polished responses. The kind that keeps emotions neatly contained, that sidesteps anything too raw. But instead, she exhales, her expression softening.

"Yes, that's one of the reasons," she admits with a small smile. "But also, I asked you because I want this to be the start of us rebuilding what's been broken between us. We barely had time together growing up, always tangled up in Mom and Dad's mess. But their baggage isn't our baggage. It never should have been."

Her words land softly, but they hit deep. The weight of our family's history has always sat between us like an unspoken wall, built brick by brick by years of resentment, misunderstandings, and circumstances beyond our control.

Nodding, I take in her expression—the sincerity. This is Philippa, not the polished, put-together version that fits neatly into our father's world, but my sister, the girl who used to sneak into my room and braid my hair when I had nightmares.

"I'd like that," I say quietly, my voice barely above a whisper.

Without hesitation, she pulls me into a hug, and for the first time, I don't stiffen or pull away. I lean into it.

My big sister.

She smiles, a real one this time, before nudging me playfully. "Good. Because I need you to give one hell of a maid of honor speech, and if you embarrass me, I'll never forgive you."

I scoff, rolling my eyes. "Oh, I'm absolutely telling the story about how you snuck a wombat into the house when we were kids."

"Elena!" she gasps, shoving my shoulder.

The laughter comes easily, melting the tension that always seems to cling to us. Maybe this is the start of something new. Maybe, for once, we can just be sisters.

My phone dings, and it's from Kylie, a link to a story. I click into it, and my stomach drops:

The Daily Chronicle

BREAKING NEWS

Caught in the Crossfire: Alexander Westerberg's Sizzling Love Triangle!

Exclusive details: Alexander Westerberg heating up the Hamptons, and not just from the summer sun.

Exclusive photos show the international heartthrob getting cozy with former flame, Madison Walsh, during an intimate birthday dinner at The American Hotel, known Hamptons hotspot.

But notably absent from the celebration? His rumored new flame, rising songstress, Elena Montgomery.

But wait, it gets better!

Just hours later, Westerberg was photographed getting very cozy with Elena at Vanguard.

One source says they "couldn't keep their hands off each other."

They were spotted strolling the private beach at the Montgomery Estate, arm-in-arm, looking every bit the loved-up couple days later.

So what's really going on? Is Alexander juggling two leading ladies, or is someone about to get seriously burned?

375

A lead weight anchors in my gut, the blood draining from my face as I stare at the screen. The words blur, but I can't look away. Of course, they'd spin it like this. Of course, I'd end up in a tabloid-fueled mess with Alex. *Again.*

Photos of me in his lap at Vanguard, his hands halfway up my dress. Photos of us on the beach, me straddling him on the sand.

Fuck.

I set my phone aside, forcing myself to be present with my sister, though the headline lingers in the back of my mind, needling at me like a thorn I can't pull out.

Despite my protests, Philippa insists I step out into the main gallery of the bridal boutique to show Carole and Father the dress she's selected for me.

Carole's face lights up the moment she sees me, gushing about the fabric and the fit. "Oh, Elena, it's stunning on you."

My father, however, is silent, though his face has changed.

Philippa notices immediately. "What do you think, Dad?" she asks, her tone expectant.

He exhales slowly before setting down his drink. "I have some thoughts, but it's not about the dress." The disappointment in his voice is unmistakable.

I recognize it well.

"Dad!" Philippa gasps.

Mortimer sighs before pulling out his phone. "My team sent me this." He holds up the screen, and I don't even need to look. I already know.

The fucking article.

"And what of it? Celebrities get photographed all the time."

"Not with his hands up your skirt, Elena. Don't you care what people will think or say?"

"It has nothing to do with you or your precious empire," I snap, crossing my arms.

His eyes harden. "I could give a damn about that."

The bluntness of his response throws me off, but before I can recover, he stands, leveling me with a look. "You're going to allow yourself to be humiliated like this, reduced to a frivolous headline? Where is your dignity?" His voice is sharp, cutting straight through my defenses.

I'm stunned into silence.

"He has a reputation. Women come and go. He's not serious, Elena. I know the type—he *will* break your heart, mark my words."

There's something in the way he says it, something almost resigned.

And then it hits me.

Of course, *he* knows the type.

He *was* the fucking type.

Stepping out on my mother multiple times during their marriage. Cheating, lying, wrecking everything in his path. And now he has the audacity to stand here and judge me? To sit across from me with his mistress-turned-wife and pretend to be the moral compass of my life?

My fists clench at my sides as fury bubbles up inside me, white-hot and uncontrollable. "Of course, you know the type, *Mortimer*. You *are* the fucking type." My voice shakes, but it doesn't waver.

"Elena, please, calm down," Philippa whispers, gripping my arm as if she can physically hold me back.

But I'm past the point of being restrained.

"Who the fuck are you to dictate who I can and can't date? You sure as hell didn't rein yourself in when you were screwing half of Manhattan behind my mother's back. And then—then you had the audacity to fucking marry your whore just to rub salt in the wound!"

The words rip out of me, raw and jagged, slicing through the room like a blade.

"Oh my God, Elena—Carole, I'm..." Philippa gasps, her eyes wide with horror.

Carole's face falls, her hands trembling at her sides. She doesn't say a word, just stands up and quietly leaves the boutique.

A moment of silence stretches between us, thick and suffocating.

I inhale sharply, my chest rising and falling in ragged breaths. "I appreciate your fatherly concern. It's about eighteen years too fucking late, but I can handle my own relationships."

Mortimer's expression is unreadable, but his eyes flicker with something—rage, guilt, maybe both.

"Clearly, you can't. Otherwise, you wouldn't be in the middle of yet another scandal," he bites back. "And don't you *ever* talk to *my* wife like that again." His voice is firm and cold, slicing through me.

He doesn't wait for a response. He gets up and walks out, leaving the tension crackling in his wake.

The breath I'd been holding finally releases, but instead of relief, all I feel is exhaustion. My knees buckle, and before I can stop myself, I collapse onto the floor in a broken heap.

Philippa is beside me in an instant, wrapping her arms around me as I shudder against her.

She doesn't speak. She just holds me.

And for the first time in a long time, I let her.

After the heated exchange at the bridal store, Philippa and I return to my apartment, the weight of the day—one that started with such a high—now sits heavy on my shoulders. I peel off my heels, tossing them carelessly near the door before flopping onto the couch. Philippa follows, more composed, but I can tell she's still processing everything. She sits across from me, curling one leg under the other, her expression unreadable.

For a few moments, neither of us speaks. The only sound is the faint ticking of the clock on the wall.

Then, finally—

"What the hell happened back there?" Philippa asks, her voice quieter than I expected.

I exhale, rubbing my temples. "I don't know, Pip. He…set me off."

She studies me for a beat before tilting her head. "You said something…about Dad stepping out on Mom. About Carole being his mistress. That wasn't true, was it?"

I freeze.

The exhaustion in my body is drowned out by a cold realization. *She doesn't know.*

I sit up straighter, gripping the throw pillow in my lap, avoiding her gaze. "Philippa…"

She shakes her head, her brows knitting together. "No. Tell me. What did you mean?"

I hesitate. I could lie. I could brush it off, pretend I was lashing out, let her keep the version of our family she believes in.

But I'm tired. And I can't *unring* the bell.

"You really don't know, do you?" I murmur.

Philippa's jaw tightens. "Know what?"

I fight the lump in my throat—the kind that rises when you know the next words will shatter someone's world, and you're the one saying them. "Carole wasn't just some woman Dad met after the divorce, Philippa. She was the reason for the divorce."

She lets out a short, incredulous laugh. "What? No, that's— no. They got together *after*. I remember Mom saying—" She stops mid-sentence, her expression shifting, doubt creeping in.

I give her a knowing look. "What exactly do you remember her saying?"

Her mouth opens, but nothing comes out.

I push forward. "Did she ever actually tell you that? Or did she…not tell you the truth?"

The color drains from her face. She looks away, shaking her head. "No. That's not—Dad wouldn't—Mom would've—" She stops again, realization dawning, the cracks in her belief system widening.

She's piecing it together, whether she wants to or not.

I take a deep breath. "Carole was his mistress for years, amongst other women. Mom knew. She tried to fight for their marriage, but Dad gave her an ultimatum—stay and turn a blind eye, or leave and let him have full custody of you."

Philippa flinches like I've physically hit her. "That's not possible. Mom—Mom wouldn't have left me."

My throat tightens. "She didn't want to. But he made sure she had no choice."

She stares at me, eyes wide, glossy. "You're lying."

I shake my head. "I wish I was. But it's the truth. You were a kid, Pip. We both were. You didn't see what she went through after she left—the anguish, the resentment. The way she hated him for driving her away."

Philippa blinks rapidly. "Why didn't she tell me?"

I soften. "Because she didn't want you to hate him."

A beat passes, the weight of it all settling in.

And then Philippa does something I didn't expect.

She laughs.

But it's a broken, bitter laugh, the kind that barely makes it past her lips.

"You know," she murmurs, voice hollow. "I spent so many years feeling abandoned. Wondering why she left me. Why you left me. If I wasn't enough to make her stay."

Her voice cracks at the last word.

"Pip…" I start, my chest tightening. "She never wanted to

leave you. That was the hardest thing she ever did. But she thought she was protecting you."

She shakes her head, brushing back tears.

"Do you know what it's like to be nine years old and realize your mom isn't coming back? To go from having her tuck you in at night to being raised by nannies who come and go like you're some chore?" She swallows hard. "I spent so much time waiting for her to come back. Waiting for *both* of you to come back. Thinking maybe, if I was perfect, she'd change her mind. But she never did."

I inhale sharply, guilt slamming into me.

Because I had Mom. I had years with her. Philippa only had fleeting moments, a few weeks or a month here and there, when she visited Australia.

"And then there was Carole." Her voice wavers. "She wasn't Mom, but she was there. She showed up. Remembered my birthdays, my ballet recitals. Helped me with my homework. She became…something close to a mother to me."

Her gaze darkens. "And now you're telling me it was all built on a lie?"

I don't know what to say.

I hate Carole. I always have. But Philippa saw something different. She didn't see the woman who tore our family apart. She saw the woman who stayed when our mother left.

"I know you hate her," she cries, a single tear slipping down her cheek. "But I can't. She was there for me when our mother wasn't. In the same way you love Jack, I love her."

It's a gut punch.

I could never compare the love I have for Jack to Carole, but I understand. Carole was there for her. She was a source of comfort. The person who picked up the pieces when our mother left.

And that softens my resolve against her.

I don't have to like Carole. But I can appreciate what she is to my sister.

Philippa lets out a ragged, unrestrained sob.

And I hold her.

For the first time, I don't stop her.

Because what do you even say to someone whose entire world has just been rewritten?

I watch her go; my chest tight with emotions I can't even name.

For so long, I've held onto my anger. My resentment. I thought I was the only one who suffered from our parents' mess.

But now I see it clearly.

She lost something, too.

And despite everything, maybe…we're more alike than I ever thought.

After Philippa leaves, I sink into the lounge, wine glass in hand, staring out at the cityscape. The lights shimmer across the skyline, flickering like distant stars, but my mind is elsewhere, sifting through the wreckage of today.

Everything with my father is a fucking mess, but somehow, I feel lighter. Like a thorn has been plucked from my heart. Having Philippa know the truth—it's strangely healing. I've carried it alone for so long, assuming she was untouched by the same catastrophe that broke me.

I'm always so wrapped up in my own shit, and because Philippa appears to have it together, I forget that she's hurting too. We're both damaged by the same disaster.

The weight of it settles into me as a knock at the door pulls me from my thoughts.

Riley probably forgot her key again.

I sigh, setting my glass down as I pad over to the door. But when I open it—

It's him.

Alex.

My breath catches.

"Älskling," he murmurs, his voice warm, endearing.

I don't hesitate. I throw myself into him, arms around his neck, burying my face against him.

He didn't forget about me.

His arms tighten around my waist, holding me like he never wants to let go. "Congratulations on your performance this morning." He breathes me in, slow and steady.

"I thought—" I say, pulling back slightly. "I didn't hear from you all day."

He brushes a stray piece of hair behind my ear. "I know. Press was nonstop. Interviews, appearances. I barely had a moment to breathe, let alone pick up my phone. I wanted to be the first person to call you, but by the time I could, it was already late."

I nod, exhaling, letting the tension ease from my shoulders.

He tips my chin up, eyes searching mine. "I saw the article."

I stiffen slightly, but he shakes his head. "Elena, Madison means nothing to me. She was at my birthday dinner because she happened to be in town, and mutual friends invited her. That's it. There's no 'love triangle,' no hidden meaning behind the photos. Just you and me."

I bite my lip, feeling the weight of his words, of the certainty in them.

His fingers trail down my arm, threading through mine. "Let me make it up to you. Come with me."

My eyes snap to his. "What?"

"Let's get away from all this. Just us." His eyes burn into mine, a flicker of something reckless and enticing in them. "We can leave tonight. I'll take you to Sweden, to my family's cabin. It's remote, no press, no service, no distractions. Just you and me."

My breath catches.

No media. No outside world.

Just him and me.

A chance to breathe. A chance to exist together without the world watching.

"Tonight?" I repeat, like I need to make sure I heard him right.

He nods. "Pack a bag, Älskling. Let's disappear."

Chapter 25

Hypnotizing

I stand at the edge of the tarmac, my fingers gripping Alex's hand as I stare up at the sleek private jet. The weight of my decision presses against my chest, but when Alex turns to look at me—his eyes deep like the ocean glinting under the floodlights—a slow thrill coils through my veins. There's no turning back now.

I've left nothing but a hastily scribbled note for Riley, telling her I'll be away for a few days. She won't worry.

He reaches for my hand, his warmth anchoring me as we board the jet.

The flight to Stockholm is smooth, the hum of the engines a low, steady backdrop. Alex stretches out beside me, at ease in the plush leather seats. He pours us both a glass of wine, and as I sip, I find myself watching him—how the golden light casts soft shadows across his sharp cheekbones, how the corner of his lips tilts up every time he catches me staring. There's something exhilarating about sneaking away, just the two of us.

We land in Stockholm under a sky streaked with soft pinks and oranges. The air is crisp for early August, warm enough not to need heavy coats, but cool enough that I shiver when a breeze slips past. Alex notices, shrugs off his leather jacket, and drapes it over my shoulders before leading me toward our next stop.

The city buzzes with late-summer energy. We pick up everything we need—groceries, wine, warm sweaters, extra blankets. At one point, I get lost in the charm of a small bookstore, running my fingers along the spines of poetry books.

Alex finds me there, watching with that same unreadable expression he always wears when he thinks I'm not paying attention.

"You always get that look when you're thinking," he murmurs, stepping closer.

"What look?" I ask, arching a brow.

Alex traces a fingertip along my jawline, his touch gentle and slow. "Like you're carrying too much weight on your shoulders."

I swallow the lump in my throat, the intimacy of the moment catching me off guard. He never lets me hide—not from him, not from myself.

After packing up our car, we start the drive north, leaving the bustle of the city behind as the roads narrow, flanked by towering pines. Färnebofjärden National Park sprawls before us, the scent of damp earth and lake water filling the car as we pull up to his family's cabin.

It is beautiful in its simplicity. A deep red wooden and stone structure nestled among the trees, its large windows reflecting the soft ripples of the lake beyond. A small wooden dock stretches out over the water, the sun casting golden light across the still surface.

Inside, the cabin is warm and rustic, the scent of aged wood and pine lingering in the air. A stone fireplace dominates one side of the room. In front of it, a huge fur rug spreads across the floor. I run my fingers over the textured fabric, a small smile playing on my lips as I take it all in. There really is no cell service out here, just the crackling of the fire, the distant rustle of trees outside, and

Alex moving around the space with the ease of someone who fits into this life, his confidence so sexy and addictive.

He sets down the bags and turns to me, a mischievous glint in his eyes. "We have a family tradition," he starts, crossing his arms as he leans against the kitchen counter. "Every summer, first night at the cabin, we strip down to our underwear and dive straight into the lake."

"You can't be serious."

His grin widens, slow and teasing. "Dead serious."

I roll my eyes.

"Scared you can't handle a little cold?"

I shake my head. "That water is probably freezing."

"That's the whole point," he says, stepping closer. "It's exhilarating. A cleanse. And, you know, maybe I can warm you up after."

I narrow my eyes at him, crossing my arms. "Oh, I see. This is your sneaky way of getting me to strip down."

He smirks, running his tongue over his bottom lip. "I mean, I won't complain. But I also think you're bluffing. I don't see you actually doing it."

I scoff, heat curling low in my stomach. His challenge is like fuel to a fire. "You think I won't?"

He tilts his head, gaze raking over me. "I think you talk a big game."

I shove him playfully, my pulse racing. "Fine."

Alex arches a brow. "Fine?"

I kick off my shoes, pulling my sweater over my head. "You're not the only one who can handle a little cold."

His eyes darken with amusement—and something else—as he quickly follows suit. Within seconds, we're both standing on the dock in nothing but our underwear, and I have to take a second to appreciate the sheer perfection of him. His abs look like they're chiseled from marble, every muscle taut and defined, a masterpiece of strength and control. My gaze traces the sharp cut of his V-line, disappearing beneath the waistband of his boxers, and my mouth goes dry. The cool afternoon air prickling against my skin doesn't compare to the heat pooling low in my belly as I force myself to look away before he catches me staring.

"Are you ready?" he asks, taking my hand.

I simply nod, taking a deep breath, my heart hammering. Alex looks at me, his expression a mixture of challenge and admiration. Then, without another word, we take off running and leap off the dock together, the icy shock of the lake stealing the breath from my lungs as I'm plunged beneath the surface.

The water hits my skin like a thousand pinpricks, jolting every sense in my body. I have never felt so alive. It's such a thrill! We emerge from under the water, and Alex reaches out and pulls me into him. Before I can think, before I can fully take a breath, my lips crash into his, carnal, hungry. I've never needed a kiss as much as I need it right now.

We return to the cabin with the utmost haste, our underwear clinging to our damp skin, breathless laughter spilling between us as we burst inside. The lake's icy shock still lingers in my veins, but the adrenaline, the exhilaration of it, burns hotter. I can't stop smiling.

Alex shakes his head, water droplets flying from his hair as he grins. "You're insane."

"You challenged me," I remind him, arching a brow. "And I don't lose."

His eyes darken, that slow, knowing smirk curling at the corner of his lips. "I don't think you have a single idea what you started." The flicker of heat in his voice sends a shiver straight through me—not from the cold, but from the way he's looking at me now, like he's seconds away from devouring me whole.

He watches me for a moment longer before exhaling sharply.

"Go shower before you freeze." His voice is rougher now, strained.

I should go. I should move. But there's something intoxicating about the way he's barely holding himself back, how he's clenching his fists as if resisting the urge to reach for me.

I bite my lip, savoring that power for a second before turning on my heel, making my way to the bathroom.

By the time I step out of the shower, warmth has seeped back into my skin, but I can still feel the thrilling charge left behind from the lake, from Alex. The mirror is fogged over, but my reflection is clear in my mind—the flush on my cheeks, the brightness in my eyes. I've never looked like this before.

Alive.

When I re-enter the main room, Alex is crouched by the fireplace, coaxing flames to life. He's changed into dry sweatpants, but his torso remains bare, muscles flexing as he moves. The fire casts flickering gold across his skin, accentuating every defined ridge of his abs, the sharp lines of his arms.

For a moment, I can only stand there, watching him, my breath shallow. He turns his head, catching me mid-stare. I don't look away. His gaze drags over me, over the oversized sweater hugging my frame, and my damp hair curling over my shoulders. Something shifts in his expression.

"Better?" he asks, voice rough, edged with something deeper.

I nod, my throat dry.

He stands slowly, stretching to his full height, and I swear the air thickens between us. Neither of us speaks as I move toward the sofa, curling into the corner, my legs tucked beneath me. Alex joins me, pulling a blanket over us, but the warmth of the fire is nothing compared to the heat of his body beside me.

The silence isn't uncomfortable, it's charged, vibrating with everything unspoken.

His fingers find my knee beneath the blanket, tracing soft, looping rhythms along my skin with a featherlight touch.

"Tell me what you're thinking," he murmurs.

I exhale, my lips curving slightly. "At this very minute, nothing. My mind is quiet, probably for the first time in my life."

His hand stills, then slides higher, his palm warm against my thigh. "I like you like this."

I tilt my head, meeting his gaze. "Like what?"

He shifts closer, his breath fanning across my lips. "Unfiltered. Unrestrained." His hand drifts higher. "Carefree."

My pulse hammers.

That's what this is, isn't it? That's what he is. Alex is the first person to ever make me let go, make me stop thinking so much, and just feel.

From the moment we met and every moment since, we've been drawn to each other. Undeniably and inevitably.

Kismet. The word echoes in my mind.

I decide, it's time to let go, give in to what I want, what I've long wanted, since the moment I met him.

I want the way his fingers burn against my skin. I want the weight of his body pressing me into the fur rug before the fire. I want his lips on mine, on my throat, lower. I want everything he's silently offering, everything I've been too afraid to take until now.

So, I do.

I reach for him, my fingers threading through his damp hair, pulling him toward me. The moment our lips collide, it's not soft or tentative. It's a collision of heat, need, something raw and charged.

He groans into the kiss, deepening it, his hands gripping my hips as he pulls me onto his lap. I can feel him, hard and ready beneath me, and instead of hesitating, instead of thinking, I rock against him, savoring the low curse that rumbles from his throat.

"Elena," he breathes against my lips. His hands slide beneath my sweater, fingertips skimming up my spine.

I shiver, not from the cold, but from him. From the way he's looking at me like I'm something he's been starving for.

"Alex, I want it…I want you," I whisper, my voice steady, certain.

His grip tightens, his forehead dropping to mine. "If we start, I won't be able to stop."

My heart pounds.

"Don't stop."

That's all it takes.

The next moment, he's lifting me, laying me down onto the fur rug before the fire. The world narrows to the heat of his mouth tracing down my neck, the slow drag of his lips over my collarbone, the way his fingers tremble as he pushes the sweater up over my head.

And then there's nothing between us but firelight and the sound of our breath.

He pauses for a moment, hovering above me, his stormy eyes searching mine, asking me one last silent question.

I answer him with a kiss, with the way I arch into him, pulling him closer, pressing my body fully to his.

The fire crackles beside us, its golden glow dancing across Alex's bare skin, highlighting the tension in his muscles, the way his body moves with controlled, deliberate intention. He hovers over me, his breath warm against my lips, his hands bracketing either side of my head as he watches me—like he's waiting for me to stop him.

I don't.

Instead, I reach for him, my fingers sliding over the sharp cut of his jaw, down the ridges of his torso, reveling in the way he shudders beneath my touch. His body is a masterpiece—strong, sculpted, and undeniably his, the embodiment of the thrill and danger that drew me to him in the first place.

He exhales sharply when I drag my nails lightly down his abdomen, and in one swift movement, his mouth crashes into mine, and I meet him head-on—lips parting, teeth grazing, breath mixing hot between us. My fingers curl into his hair, dragging him closer, like I can't get enough. I kiss him harder, deeper, tilting my head. Every inch of restraint slips through my grip.

His hands roam my body like he's memorizing me, learning every curve, every dip, every soft gasp that escapes my lips. His mouth follows, pressing slow, open-mouthed kisses along my collarbone, across my shoulder, down, down—until he reaches the swell of my breasts.

His fingers work the clasp of my bra, and when the lace slips away, the way he looks at me makes heat pool deep in my core.

"You're so fucking beautiful," he murmurs, voice rough and adoring.

"Alex." His name escapes my lips, a breathy plea.

His lips brush the base of my neck. "So innocent...so perfect." His tone drops—dark, heady, almost possessive.

His mouth trails lower, his tongue flicking over my nipple before he sucks it into his mouth, rolling it between his teeth enough to make me whimper. My back arches, pressing into him, needing more, and he gives it, moving to my other breast, teasing, taking his time.

He nuzzles himself between them, his hot breath kissing and lapping up my skin.

"Touched only by *me*..." he murmurs, dragging his mouth down my stomach. "Fuck, you don't even *know* what you're doing to me." His breath is hot against my skin. "I think about it all the time—sliding inside you for the first time...stretching you open, so slow you cry for more. Teaching you how to take me. How to pleasure *me*." He kisses the inside of my thigh, eyes locked on mine. "No one else gets this. No one else gets *you*. I'm going to mark you so deep, you'll never forget who you fucking belong to."

I'm a mess of moans and shallow gasps, and he's barely even touched me. His words wreck me. I fist my fingers in his hair, yanking him up, kissing him harder this time.

"*More*," I pant.

He chuckles against my mouth. "Patience, Elena."

But patience is gone. Burnt out of me. I've waited long enough.

I shove at the waistband of his sweats, desperate to feel more. He's already hard—thick and straining beneath the fabric. He groans, low and guttural, helping me push them down.

He springs free, heavy and flushed, and I freeze, swallowing hard. The sight of him sends a jolt straight through me, making my thighs clench. All I can think about is how he'll feel stretching me open. How full I'll be. How I'll never come back from it.

My hesitation must show, because Alex lifts my chin, brushing his lips over mine.

"I'll take care of you," he murmurs.

His hands glide down my body, slipping beneath the thin fabric of my panties, and the moment his fingers brush against me, I gasp.

"You're so wet," he groans, his forehead dropping to my shoulder. "Is this all for me?"

I can't answer. I can barely think as he circles my clit, teasing, applying enough pressure to make my hips jerk against his hand. He watches me, his eyes dark and hooded, studying every reaction, every breathy moan that spills from my lips as he strokes me, slow at first, then faster.

And then he slides a finger inside me. Then another.

I gasp, my hands gripping his shoulders, my nails digging into his skin. He adds another, curling them just right, his thumb pressing tight, perfect circles against me, and I swear I start unraveling right then and there.

He rocks his hand back and forth in a steady rhythm, curling, stretching, in and out, then curling again.

Heat rises, deep within me, a current of electricity dancing across my skin.

"Come for me, Darling, give it to me," he whispers, his lips brushing against my ear.

And I do.

I feel the wetness dripping from my pussy.

Ecstasy rushes through me as my body trembles, rideing out each wave, my thighs clenching around his wrist. He groans, kissing me through it, consuming my gasps like he wants to keep them.

I'm still shuddering when he pulls back slightly, stripping away the last scrap of clothing between us. He kneels between my legs, stroking himself as he watches me, his expression pure hunger.

"Are you sure?" His voice is hoarse, edged with restraint.

I nod, but that's not enough for him. He leans down, pressing a kiss to my lips. "Say it."

"I want you," I whisper, my fingers tracing down his spine, over the taut muscles of his back. "Take me, claim me, fuck me."

His control snaps.

He lines himself up, tapping my clit twice, and I gasp as it tingles, sensitive post orgasm. Then he slides lower, his tip pressing against my entrance as he waits, giving me a moment, letting me feel the weight of him, the delicious stretch as he pushes inside. *Slowly*.

A sharp hiss escapes me, and my body tenses. He's big, and even though he's taken his time, there's still a slight sting as he fills me, inch by inch.

A mixture of pleasure and pain courses through me.

In that moment, I realize: *I like it.*

"Relax," he murmurs, pressing kisses along my jaw, my neck, my shoulder. "Breathe."

I exhale shakily, and as I do, my body adjusts, the ache giving way to something deeper, something that has me wanting more.

Desire.

When I finally look up at him, his jaw is clenched so hard it looks painful. "You're so tight," he groans.

Then he moves.

He starts slow, rolling his hips, pulling almost all the way out before thrusting back in, filling me completely. The stretch, the friction, the way he rubs against every single nerve ending inside me—it's overwhelming, breathtaking.

His mouth and hands grasp and ravage my breasts, his tongue artfully teasing and pulling my nipples.

"You have perfect tits," he growls, his breath against my chest, emboldening me.

I lift my legs higher, wrapping them around his waist, drawing him deeper. A broken moan rips from his throat, his grip tightening on my hips as he thrusts harder, faster, his control slipping.

"Alex," I gasp, nails raking down his back.

He groans deeply, his forehead pressing against mine. "I love the way my name sounds on your lips," he pants, his rhythm relentless as he drives into me over and over.

"Alex… Al…ex…Alexander," I cry out.

His cock throbs inside me. "Elena, you're my undoing," he groans, pushing into me again and again.

It's too much. It's not enough. I need *more.*

I shift beneath him, raising my hips to meet him.

He stills. "Oh, Darling, you want to drive?" he coos wickedly.

I bite my lip, unsure, then in one swift move, he flips us, pulling me on top.

I gasp as I find myself straddling him, my hands braced

against his torso, his shaft disappearing inside of me, and I feel myself stretch around him.

"Ride me." His eyes are dark and hooded as he takes in the sight of me. His hands grip my thighs, guiding me at first, but I take control, rocking my hips, finding a rhythm that makes stars explode behind my eyes. It feels different this way, deeper and fuller. I watch as his cock disappears inside me as I move up and down, taking the entire length of him. My head falls back as I lose myself to the feeling.

"That's it, Darling, use me." His eyes are ablaze as he watches me grinding against him. His other hand snakes between us as he rubs my clit, my slickness coating the both of us.

"You're so deep, Alex, you feel so good" I moan, my greedy little pussy taking every inch of him. Was this what I was missing out on all this time? Breathy grunts escape my lips as his hips thrust to meet mine.

He leans up, taking my breast into his mouth while I ride him. His hand grasps the nape of my neck, the other rubbing my most sensitive spot.

He lets me take him.

Use him. For *my* pleasure.

Losing myself completely.

And when I do, when the sensation crests again, crashing through me in waves so intense I forget my own name, he follows, groaning my name, our moans echoing through the cabin. His body tenses beneath me before a strangled grunt falls from his lips as he spills inside me.

I collapse against his chest, breathless and trembling.

For a moment, there's nothing but the crackle of the fire, the mad hammering of our hearts, the rise and fall of our chests as we come down.

Then, he laughs. Low and satisfied, his chuckle rumbles beneath me.

"What?" I mumble against his skin, still dazed.

"Fuck," he hisses, forehead pressed to mine. "We're gonna have to get you the morning-after pill when we're back in Stockholm."

My breath catches, and so does my gaze.

He grins, dark and breathless. "Didn't pack enough condoms for what I've got planned for you."

My lips part, pulse hammering.

"No condoms needed," I whisper, dragging my thumb along his lips. "I'm on the pill."

His eyes snap like I've said the magic words and unlocked something in him.

"Jesus," he mutters. "I'm going to have so much fun with you."

"Yes, please," I whisper

He chuckles breathlessly. "How was that? For you?"

I meet his gaze. Deep and quiet. He wants the truth, but more than that, he wants *confirmation*—that I'd remember this for the rest of my life.

"Incredible." I smile, wistful. My legs are still shaky, the tenderness between my thighs a quiet reminder of how deeply we'd been connected.

He smiles, chest lifting with a kind of quiet pride. "I told you," he murmurs, brushing his lips against my forehead. "I'm great in bed."

I snort. Smug bastard. "Great?" My voice is hoarse from moaning his name into the firelit room. "Bit of an understatement, don't you think?"

He chuckles, the sound low, pleased. "I aim to please."

And please, he did.

Because he wasn't just great in bed. He was great on the table. On the couch. On the floor. In the shower. Out on the grass under the setting sun. Over the next few days, we're a mess of limbs and lost inhibitions.

At one point, I half-jokingly mutter something about needing water for survival, and Alex—completely serious—carries me, bare-ass naked, to the kitchen, hand-feeds me strawberries, and makes me drink straight from his palm at the sink. While he helps himself between my thighs.

Another time, I tried to escape to the bathroom for a break, only for him to drag me back into the shower, murmuring something about how I'm too slippery to resist.

By the eighth—or is it ninth?—time, I accept my fate.

This man has no off switch.

And, apparently, neither do I.

I had no idea I was this insatiable.

I try to reclaim some semblance of dignity, rolling away for a moment of peace, only for him to tackle me back into the pillows, lips trailing down with a wicked grin.

"Alex," I groan, half-pleading, half-laughing. "I need a break. I need food. I need—I don't know—air?!"

He props himself up on one elbow, smirking like a man who has just discovered his new favorite hobby. "You're cute when you beg."

"I'm not begging," I whimper, even as I shiver under the lazy drag of his fingers up my thigh.

"You will be," he says simply.

And, to my complete and utter humiliation, he's right.

By the time we finally pass out, tangled in the sheets, the fire nothing but dying embers, I have never felt more exhausted in my life. Or satisfied. Or alive.

He shifts behind me, rolling us onto our sides. One arm draped on my waist, the other under my neck, drawing me tighter against his chest like I might vanish.

His breath is warm at my ear. "Why'd you wait?"

"Wait?" I ask, my brain still a mess of thoughts.

"For sex?"

Oh.

It wasn't a decision. Not really. I didn't draw a line in the sand or swear anything off. It just… never happened.

Between Riley's stories of *dud roots*, Mom's mistrust of men that stuck to me like a second skin, and then her cancer, wanting never felt like a priority.

I inhale, grounding myself in the warmth and weight of his arm as he drags his thumb across my skin.

"It wasn't a decision," I say slowly. "It…never felt right. Not until now."

He's silent for a beat. Then his fingers trail along the curve of my hip, thoughtful, almost absent.

"I'm glad it was me," he confesses. "I hate thinking about anyone else ever getting the chance." His voice rasps against my skin. "It's selfish, I know. But the thought of someone else touching you—someone else making you feel like this—would drive me fucking insane."

I don't move. Can't.

He brushes my hair back, presses a kiss just below my ear. "You don't even realize what you've done to me, do you?"

My pulse stumbles. His voice has that edge again—low, reverent, full of something I can't name.

"Elena," he breathes, voice wrecked. "You've *bewitched* me. Being with you—it's the only time I can be myself. It's freedom from the noise, the pressure, the past. I can't escape you. You're in my head all day—what you're doing, who you're with, if you're thinking of me. And then at night, in my dreams…"

"Your dreams?" I whisper.

He leans in closer, eyes burning. "From the moment you collided into my life, it's only ever been you. You're in all of them. I think of nothing else—being with you, touching you, holding you…making love to you."

His voice drops, almost a growl. "*Älskling*, I would burn the whole fucking world to keep you. To feel you beside me in the dark. To know you're mine—not just for now, but for whatever forever we can steal. I would give anything, say anything, *be* anything, if it meant you'd be mine forever."

My chest rises, tight and too full. Something turns inside me, something soft, like a key unlocking a door. My heart beats differently, and I don't think it will ever beat the same after this.

Is this what it feels like?

Is this…*love?*

"Alex," I breathe his name like a prayer. "I've never felt like this. You make me feel seen, you make me feel desired, sexy, confident, I…"

And I know my heart has leaped over the edge, falling, deeper and deeper. I want to say it, but my mouth goes dry. It's *too soon.* I'll scare him away.

"I know, Elena, I feel it too," he says, tightening his arm around me. "Too fast," he whispers against my shoulder. "But I don't want to slow down."

Neither do I.

And that's the most dangerous part of all.

Chapter 26

Lost Cause

I wake feeling blissful. Thighs sore, naked and tangled in sheets. I'm the happiest I've ever been.

Alex is already up—shirtless, standing by the window, hair tousled, coffee in hand. Better than the view outside. I'm absolutely addicted to the man.

The fire's burned down to embers, but the heat between us still lingers, slow and thick in the air.

He catches me watching and smirks.

"Morning, *Älskling*."

"Morning, *boyfriend*. I could get used to this," I murmur, stretching. My body aches in the best way.

"I like when you say that." He turns toward me and takes a slow sip, eyes dragging over my body like he's cataloguing every inch of the damage.

"Say what?"

"Boyfriend." He chuckles, taking another sip of his coffee.

"So, we've run out of food." He grins, unbothered. "And if I'm not wrong, today's your last pill. So, unless you want to stay up here and raise a brood of Swedish mountain babies with me, we should probably head back."

I groan.

He crosses the room and leans down, pressing a kiss to my shoulder, warm and tender, the smell of coffee on his breath.

"I could always swallow," I tease, licking my lips.

His brow lifts, eyes darkening, a low chuckle rumbling from his chest. "What have I done?"

"You've only got yourself to blame," I say, rolling onto my back, my breasts spilling out of the blanket. "You've spoilt me. I've never been hornier in my life."

His eyes widen as he takes in the sight, and groans—one of those helpless, wrecked sounds—and drags a hand through his hair like he's physically trying to hold himself together.

"Elena…" His voice drops. "It's fucking tempting to put a baby in you. Just to make sure you stay *mine* forever."

My heart skitters. My mouth doesn't care.

"Okay, put a baby in me, please," I joke sweetly, grinning like I'm high on him.

"You're far too young and I'm not ready to be a dad…*yet*." He pauses. "And I'm not ready to share you like that."

"How about you *fill* me up anyway," I tease, wickedly pulling the blanket down further, raking my fingers down my body.

He curses something in Swedish, tsks, and turns away, shaking his head as he walks back to the kitchen.

The drive back is pure agony—the kind where every glance turns molten, every brush of his hand makes my thighs clench. The number of times we have to talk ourselves out of pulling over and fucking on the side of the road…We lose count.

The only thing that stops us is the very real possibility of being arrested for indecent exposure.

We return to Stockholm still drunk on each other, caught in the high—untouched, reckless, intoxicating.

Just us.

After a quick stop for essentials—*condoms*—we barely make it through the door of his apartment before we're on each other again

"Welcome—" He doesn't finish before my lips are on his, silencing any attempt at hospitality. My fingers grip his shirt, fumbling with the buttons until frustration wins out and I rip it open, buttons scattering across the hardwood floor.

Alex laughs breathlessly, pulling back just enough to raise an amused brow. "You're eager."

"You didn't bring me here for sightseeing." I smirk, my voice teasing as I tug him closer by the waistband of his jeans.

He groans softly, his mouth chasing mine as he tries to regain control. "But I had a whole tour planned. The balcony has an amazing—"

"Right now, your dick is the only view I care about," I whisper against his jaw, teeth grazing playfully.

"Well, if you insist, Darling."

I shove him playfully, sending him sprawling backward onto the soft rug in the middle of his living room. His laughter is bright, and I'm loving this version of him. Fun and carefree.

I follow, climbing over him, straddling his hips, and run my hands over his chiseled torso before leaning down to capture his lips again.

His hands find my waist, squeezing gently as our kiss deepens. My fingers thread into his hair as I grind my hips against his hard cock growing beneath me.

"Jesus, Elena."

"You want more?" I shift again.

He gasps as I press into him, his eyes heavy and hungry. "I like watching you be greedy."

I giggle, heat pooling at my center as my hands slip between us as I tug his jeans open impatiently. "Then pay attention," I whisper against his ear. "I'll show you just how greedy I am for you."

He chuckles breathlessly, as I palm his cock over his underwear. His laughter melts into a deep groan as I give him a firm squeeze. His needy hands lift my dress clean off my body, eyes widening when he sees I'm bare underneath.

"No underwear?" he murmurs, voice thick with appreciation.

"You like that?" I ask, staring down at him with a playful smirk.

He nods. "You dirty little girl." His voice is raspy as he bites down on his lip, arching himself into me, his hard bulge brushes against my pussy. I moan softly, feeling the heat through the fabric of his briefs.

"I want you now." Alex's eyes darken, raw hunger flaring in their depths as he grabs me, flipping us swiftly and pinning me beneath the weight of his body. His mouth claims mine, hot and possessive, while he rocks his hips against my aching center. I grind into him shamelessly, desperate friction turning me into a feral cat in heat. Just as pleasure threatens to swallow me whole, he flips me again, forcing my body flat against the floor, his dominance leaving me breathless and craving more. "I got this rug in Morocco," he whispers wickedly. "How about we make a mess of it?"

I hear him put on a condom, then he squeezes my ass with both hands, yanking my hips up, before he slides into me slowly, inch by inch.

My mouth goes slack; of all the positions we've tried over the last few days, this has to be my favorite. Face down, ass up.

His grip tightens on my hips, holding me steady as he sinks deeper, finding that rhythm that makes my breath hitch. "Fuck, Elena," he rasps as he runs one hand down my back, grabbing the nape of my neck, his fingers running through my hair, and I melt at the feeling. "You feel incredible like this," he says as he snakes a hand around, toward my clit, rubbing it with each thrust. "Your pussy was made for me."

I moan shamelessly, fingers curling into the rug beneath us, sensations spiraling through me as he drives himself deeper. "Harder, Alex. Fuck me harder," I beg. Meeting him thrust for thrust.

Alex grunts. "So greedy." He picks up the pace, sending sparks of pleasure through my entire body, the sound of our skin slapping against each other echoes off the walls.

Tingles rise through me as I feel myself inching closer to orgasm.

"Alex!" I cry, coming apart as my arousal runs down my inner thighs, ecstasy rolling over me in waves. Seconds later, Alex follows, gripping my thighs tighter as he fucks my boneless body to climax, calling out my name before collapsing on me.

Breathless and spent, he presses soft kisses along my shoulder, making me shiver.

"I think we officially ruined the rug," I whisper, feeling the dampness at my knees.

"Worth it," he laughs.

———··———

LATER THAT NIGHT, Alex prepares dinner while I sit on the sofa with some tea. "I can't believe we have to leave tomorrow," I sigh.

I don't want this to end. I don't want to let the world back in.

"Don't tempt me," he says, wicked and low.

I smile, watching him power on his phone.

"Back to reality." I pout, grabbing mine from my bag on the table.

My screen lights up.

Calls. Texts. Notifications.

Riley. Philippa. My father. Mark. Kylie.

What the fuck is going on?

Every app is blowing up. I tap one. My thumb freezes mid-scroll.

Then I gasp.

What the fuck.

Flashing headlines.

My name.

Alex's name.

Everywhere.

ALEXANDER WESTERBERG'S NEW LOVE AFFAIR—WHO IS THE MYSTERY BRUNETTE?

ALEXANDER WESTERBERG EXPECTING A BABY WITH CO-STAR MADISON WALSH. SOURCES CONFIRM.

I blink at the screen as a cold weight settles inside.

Then: **MADISON PREGNANT—PREGNANT AND ABANDONED.**

My fingers tremble.

But it's the last headline that steals my breath: **THE OTHER WOMAN? FANS ACCUSE SINGER ELENA MONT-GOMERY OF HOMEWRECKING SCANDAL.**

I claw at my chest.

"Alex," I choke, shoving my phone at him with shaking hands.

His face pales instantly, his own phone vibrating violently in his grip. He freezes, eyes darting across the screen, reading every word in horror.

"No…no, no." His voice is sharp and broken, like he can't make sense of what he's seeing.

He drags a hand through his hair, pacing now, panic pouring off him in waves. "This can't—She's pregnant?"

It feels like the universe is playing a cruel joke.

Hours ago, we were tangled in bed, laughing about Swedish mountain babies.

Now there's the very real possibility he already has one on the way.

And I'm the punchline.

His voice cracks. "What the fuck?"

Alex's phone buzzes violently.

He answers it and barks, "What?" but the panic in his voice is unmistakable. Raw. Someone is shouting on the other end. His agent? Publicist? I can't tell.

Alex turns away, running his hand through his hair as he paces down the hall, voice fraying at the edges.

I stare at my phone, reading the comments, over and over.

> Slut.

> Homewrecker.

> How could she do this to another woman?

> Her dad was a cheater too—must run in the family.

The high of the last few days crumbles, crashing violently into cold, brutal reality.

This is why I never let myself get carried away.

Why I never lose control.

Why I never let myself hope.

My knees buckle, and I sink to the floor, head spinning, the phone slipping from my hand.

"Elena—"

Alex is beside me in a flash, dropping to his knees. His face is pale, like he's seen a ghost.

"I didn't know," he breathes, voice shaking. "Elena, I swear to God, I didn't know. You've got to believe me."

I shake my head, scooting back, hands trembling. "Don't—"

His eyes search mine, panic and devastation written across every line of his face. "I didn't fucking know. I ended things with her. It was over."

I stare at him, throat tight.

"When?" I whisper, the words barely audible.

His brow furrows. "What?"

"When did you end it, when did you stop fucking *her*?"

He looks confused, then hesitant, and I know before he says a word that I'm not going to like the answer.

"How long before you *met* me, Alex?" I press, voice raw and shaking.

His jaw tenses.

"Two days."

The air punches from my lungs.

Two. Fucking. Days.

I stare at him, It feels like I'm collapsing from the inside out.

I want to believe him, but it's so close. Too close.

There's a real chance this baby is his.

"Elena, please." He reaches for me, desperate. I flinch away.

"I didn't lie to you," he whispers, voice breaking. "I swear to you, I didn't know."

But it doesn't matter.

It still feels like the floor's been ripped out from under me.

"This is what I get," I whisper, voice hollow. "For thinking… for believing this could be something real."

His face crumples. "No—Elena, no, please. Don't do this."

I shake my head, tears burning in my eyes.

"This was a mistake." My voice cracks. "All of it."

Alex's eyes flood with panic, but I can't look at him.

Not when everything I let myself hope for is unraveling right in front of me.

Madison Walsh Confirms Pregnancy — Names Alexander Westerberg as the Father

Hollywood's golden girl turned heartbreak heroine?

In a raw, emotional interview last night, actress Madison Walsh confirmed she is pregnant and revealed international star Alexander Westerberg as the father.

"I never thought I'd be doing this alone," she said through tears. "I loved Alexander...I still do. But this isn't just about us anymore. It's about this baby."

Insiders claim Madison was blindsided by Westerberg's rumored romance with rising singer Elena Montgomery, with photos of the pair surfacing just as Madison discovered her pregnancy. "It's been devastating," a source shared. "But she's determined to move forward with her head held high."

Asked if Alexander has acknowledged the baby, Madison hesitated. "All I can say is, I hope he'll want to be part of our child's life. But if not, I'm ready to do this on my own."

Social media has erupted in response, with #TeamMadison and #JusticeForElena both trending. Westerberg and Montgomery have yet to comment, though sources close to the couple say they're "reeling."

Pop Queen Ava Edwards Dazzles at Sold-Out Madness and Mayhem Tour!

The Other Woman? Fans Accuse Singer Elena Montgomery of Homewrecking Scandal

Inside Elena & Alexander's Scandalous Love Affair – A Timeline of Passion, Lies & Late-Night Rendezvous

Leading Man Julian Vale Rumored for Another Oscar — Hollywood's Most Unattainable Bachelor Strikes Again

I SIT CROSS-LEGGED on my bed, a half-empty bottle of vodka balanced between my fingers, the room dimly lit by the soft glow of my bedside lamp. Rain batters the windows in an unrelenting rhythm, matching the anguish swirling in my chest. Riley is sprawled out beside me, taking a lazy sip from the bottle before handing it back.

"This is a disaster," she mutters, rubbing her temples. "Like, on a scale from one to 'your boyfriend might be having a secret love child,' this is a solid fifteen."

I snort, but it lacks humor. My phone buzzes. I don't need to look. I already know the lineup: Kylie, in full crisis mode, trying to contain the media wildfire; my father, who's left enough missed calls to drain my battery dry; Philippa, checking in every few hours; and Mark, his messages clipped but concerned.

I sigh, leaning my back against the headboard, dragging a hand through my tangled hair. "It feels like the walls are closing in. I can't even go online without seeing my name in the headlines."

Riley exhales sharply. "They're eating it up. Every gossip rag, every entertainment site, even mainstream media is covering it. Half are trying to figure out if Alex is the villain or the victim, and the other half are dissecting your every move."

I take another swig of vodka, letting the burn settle deep. "And what am I? The clueless girlfriend? The heartbroken singer? The stupid woman who got involved with the wrong guy?"

"None of the above. You're Elena, and you don't owe anyone a damn explanation."

"You're biased." I huff

And she laughs. "Ride or die till the very end, babe."

My phone buzzes yet again, and I glance over to see a message from Broderick.

BRODERICK

How are you?

Seeing his name, his words, feels like a life raft, keeping me from drifting too far from shore.

"Who is it?" Riley asks.

"Brody."

"Are you going to text him back?" she asks, nudging my leg.

My fingers hover over the keyboard, hesitating, not wanting to drag him into this mess.

"Go on," Riley says, tapping my leg again.

ELENA

I'm surviving. It's a mess.

Almost immediately, the three dots appear, flicker, then disappear. A second later:

BRODERICK

I'll bring a vacuum.

A laugh slips out before I can stop it, the first one in what feels like days.

ELENA

Better bring a mop too.

Riley raises a brow but smiles when she sees me smiling.

Broderick has a way of making things feel lighter, even when everything's falling apart. He can pull a laugh from me when I don't think I have it in me. But as the smile fades, that familiar heaviness creeps back in. For a moment, I wonder if I made the right choice.

If chasing the high that came with Alex, the rush of something wild and all-consuming, was worth it.

Because now, I'm collateral damage to my own bad decisions.

And as much as Broderick's words steady me, I know I can't drag him into this mess.

I chose Alex and everything that came with him.

Now, I have to figure out if I'm going to keep drowning in it or finally let go.

Broderick deserves more than what's left of me after this carnage.

So, for now, I'll keep my distance.

When I look up from my phone, Riley's staring at me.

She nudges me with her elbow. "So, are we going to ignore the fact that you disappeared with Alex?"

I groan, bringing the vodka bottle back to my lips. "I needed an escape."

"Uh-huh." She smirks. "And was it an escape? Or was it a *mind-blowing, I need to re-evaluate my life* kind of escape?"

Heat creeps up my neck, and Riley's eyes go wide.

"Oh my God. You had sex, didn't you?"

I bite my lip, but the way my body practically lights up at the memory gives me away.

She shrieks, grabs a pillow, and smacks me. "You totally did! And it was amazing, wasn't it?"

I let out a breathy laugh, covering my face with both hands. "Riley, I can't even put it into words."

She flops dramatically onto the bed beside me. "And you're being safe, right? Last thing we need is you running around with a love child of your own."

The irony isn't lost on me.

"Oh my God, yes," I groan, nodding more to myself than to her. "I put myself on birth control weeks ago, just in case. And Alex told me he's clean. *Afterwards*."

Riley makes a face. "Not exactly peak timing."

"Not exactly peak anything, but better late than never."

The last thing I want is to end up in some sister-wives arrangement with Madison.

"So…" She turns to me, eyes gleaming. "Did he, you know… make you *O*?"

I flush, laughing again. "Yes. I don't even have anything to compare it to, but my God, Riley. Had I known it could feel like *that*…"

She throws her head back. "Thank you, God! Because if a man that hot couldn't bring you to the peak, then honestly? Set him on fire. Return to sender."

I laugh so hard my insides hurt, clutching a throw pillow to my chest. For a second, the weight on my heart lifts. I'm just a girl with her best friend, confessing the best and only sex of her life.

"I mean, I didn't even know my body could do that." My eyes go wide.

Her mouth drops open. "Wait, like multiple times?"

I nod.

"Like, back-to-back?"

I nod again, face buried in the pillow now.

She shrieks. "Elena! Oh my God, this is not a drill. This is a sexual awakening. This is a spiritual reset. You had a whole-ass transformation."

"Stop," I groan, but I'm grinning now, warmth buzzing in my chest.

"Okay, but seriously. Give me the full run down," she says, stealing the bottle from my hand. "I want details. I want angles. I want scenery. *Paint me a picture.*"

I hesitate, biting back a smile. "It was…slow at first. Gentle. He took his time with everything, like he wasn't in a rush to get anywhere. Like he wanted to savor the experience."

Riley gasps. "Okay, I need to write that down." She holds a fake pen and scribbles on her palm like a notepad.

I laugh again, head falling back onto the pillows. "Yeah, except now I'm left dealing with the aftermath of it all."

"Yeah, well"—she shrugs—"at least you had the best possible distraction before the shit hit the fan."

I sigh, taking another swig of vodka. *Cheers to that.*

She nudges me with her foot, grinning. "Such is life, babe. So, are you gonna give me the rest of the play-by-play, or do I need to waterboard it out of you?"

Chapter 27

Breathe Me

Mark wants to talk before the crisis meeting at Pacific Records later this morning. My dreams teeter on the edge of something I can't hold steady, slipping further from my grasp no matter how tightly I clench. Alex is off dealing with his own fallout.

Mark shows up at my apartment, bagels and coffee in hand.

"Thanks for breakfast," I murmur, my fingers curling around the paper cup like it's the only solid thing left in the room.

Mark sinks into the chair across from me, a heavy sigh dragging out of him. The bags under his eyes are dark and deep, the kind of exhaustion that no amount of coffee can fix. He must've been up all night with Kylie, trying to put out fires I hadn't even seen catch yet.

"This is a mess, Elena."

I pull a bagel apart with shaking hands, the crumbs scattering across the table. "It feels like it's being blown out of proportion," I say, though the words feel hollow even as they leave me.

"I wish it was." Mark scrubs a hand over his jaw, rough and

415

unshaven. "But I think it's time I remind you about your contract."

"What do you mean?"

He levels me with a look, the kind he only uses when he's about to tell me something I won't like. "The morality clause."

The words thud between us, foreign and sharp.

Back when I won *Starstruck*, when everything fell apart after my mom died, my old manager walked away without a backward glance. Mark stepped in, assigned by the label, the 'fixer' they promised would put me back on track. He renegotiated the terms with Pacific Records, secured me a three-album deal. I had signed without reading it. I trusted him.

"What did you do, Mark?" I whisper.

He leans forward, voice low, like the truth is going to hit me like a freight train. "It was the only way Pacific Records would honor the deal. You disappeared for two years, Elena. You broke your obligations. They were ready to drop you, blacklist you. The clause was their insurance."

I bite my tongue, holding in what I want to say.

"If your actions—your personal life, your public image—if any of it causes reputational damage to Pacific Records, leads to poor record sales, public boycotts, media scandals, they can void the contract."

I stare at him, the coffee cooling in my hands. My career, my future, balanced on a knife's edge because of something I didn't even know I was carrying.

"What? Why wouldn't you tell me?" My voice cracks, too loud in the stillness of the apartment.

Mark exhales through his nose, pinching the bridge of it like he's holding back the urge to shake me. "I *did*. You just weren't listening. And it's partly your responsibility too. You have to take some blame."

"You're right, I'm…sorry"

"Is this guy really worth it?" he asks, his eyes searching for some sliver of sanity in mine.

"I don't know," I rasp, the words sticking in my throat.

"This all hangs on your album's ability to perform, Elena. If you want this—if you *really* want this—then you better fight for it. Because no one is gonna hand it to you."

"I know," I bite out. My nails dig into the side of my coffee cup. "But this feels like a fucking collar. There's got to be a way to renegotiate terms."

"Maybe." He leans back, folding his arms. "Once you prove yourself. Maybe then, you'll have some leverage. And maybe with your dad backing you—"

"I don't want him involved," I cut in fast, sharper than I mean to.

"I figured," Mark says, softer now. "But think about it. And maybe—maybe you should actually *read* your contract again. There's not just the morality clause…there's the abandonment clause too."

I drag a hand down my face. "As if this could get any worse."

"Both clauses together mean if you can't fulfill your contractual obligations, or if you abandon them for any reason, Pacific Records could sue you for breach of contract." His words land like blows, each one making it harder to breathe.

"Fuck, Mark. You really backed me into a corner."

"I'm sorry." His voice is tight. "I did what I had to. Because I believe in you. I still do. You needed a foot in the door. A push to get you going again."

My chest aches, guilt curling deep. "I'm sorry for putting you through this shit."

Mark laughs under his breath, dry and fond. "Wayward, tortured artists are part of the job. And for what it's worth, I think I'm right about you. Pre-release listening sessions are going well. Feedback's been resoundingly positive."

"That's good," I mutter, but the words feel weak, brittle.

"I'm gonna need more from you, Elena." He leans in, voice dropping low. "I can fight for you. But only if you fight for yourself."

"This album means too much to me," I whisper, the words scraping out raw. "I can't let it get buried over this."

"Good." He stands, tossing his empty coffee cup into the trash. "Then we better go."

The car ride is short, silent but for the low hum of the engine. I stare out the window, the city blurring past, my insides twisting tighter with every block.

When we pull up to Pacific Records, I climb out stiffly, my legs numb. Paparazzi clamor at the front, trying to steal the money shot. Mark and security shield me from most of it.

Once, this place had felt like a beginning, a doorway to something bigger than I could dream. Now, it looms in front of me, all glass and steel, cold and unyielding. A prison I've shackled myself to with my own signature, in exchange for my voice and my dream.

As I sit there in the boardroom, I feel like a kid in trouble, called into the principal's office. Everyone is talking at me, not to me.

I keep my eyes on the polished table, fingers curling tight around the guitar pick I found in my pocket, one I don't even remember grabbing. I dig it into my palm, harder, just to keep from screaming.

It's the only thing keeping me tethered, stopping me from going over the edge.

And still, the voices keep going, like I'm not even in the room.

Kylie stands at the head of the long table, her jaw tight, her voice clipped as she runs through crisis control plans. Mark sits beside her, his fingers pressing into his temples, while the rest of the table—label executives, PR strategists, lawyers—watch me like I'm a grenade, ready to detonate.

"This story isn't dying down," one of the execs says, flipping through a folder of tabloid clippings spread across the table. **ELENA MONTGOMERY EMBROILED IN HOLLYWOOD'S LATEST SCANDAL. SINGER CAUGHT IN A LOVE TRIANGLE? WAS SHE PLAYED?**

Kylie sighs. "We must control the narrative. The best move is to distance yourself as much as possible, focus on the music, focus on the album."

I know what that means.

Distancing myself from Alex.

My heart clenches at the thought of it.

The weight of the last few days still lingers on my skin—his touch, the way he looked at me like I was the only thing in the world that mattered. And then the headlines, the fallout, the chaos.

I can't even process my own emotions, let alone navigate this media storm.

"We need a statement," Mark adds. "Something clean. No emotion, no complications."

"Something that puts space between you and Alex," Kylie clarifies, her eyes scanning my face. "Elena, you understand what this means, right?"

I nod, but I feel numb.

"It means you can't be seen out in public with him," she says, crossing her arms. "No photographs."

I nod again. It doesn't matter what I want.

My obligation to my career, to the contract I signed.

The promise I made to my mom, to fight for the dream I wanted my whole life.

I don't have the luxury of choosing my feelings right now, not when so much is on the line. Not until I know where Alex and I stand. And right now, we're navigating a minefield.

———··———

BY THE TIME I get back home, the silence is a welcome relief. Riley is at work, and for once, there are no buzzing phones, no urgent meetings, no outside voices telling me what I should do.

Just me. And my thoughts.

I head straight to my music room, my sanctuary. Picking up my guitar, my fingers automatically find chords, and my voice slips into melodies as I let the last few days pour out of me.

The lyrics come in frantic bursts, scribbled across torn pages—raw and unfiltered.

He touched me—blazing, all-consuming.

His eyes, hypnotizing—a tidal wave, pulling me under.

Lips on mine, truth and lies tangled in heat.

My voice cracks as the lyrics spill out, breath hitching on the edge of something deeper. Then, the shift—anger blooming like a bruise beneath my ribs. Discarding my guitar, I claw my way to the piano instead, driving my fist into the keys, which groan under the assault.

Mashing into the keys again and again until my fingers find the chords to *Appassionata Sonata* by Beethoven. My own lyrics taunting me to the point of madness.

Did I fall for a ghost?

An illusion of something real?

I play until I'm sweating, chest heaving. Pressing my forehead to the piano, fingers hovering over the keys, I let the weight of it all settle into my bones.

I care about him. Maybe more than I'm ready to admit. I'm addicted to the feeling of being desired and wanted by someone like him.

But it doesn't change the mess we're in. I let out a shuddering breath, the last notes fading into the air.

I'm still lost in the haze when I hear it.

A sharp knock.

A chill moves through my ribs.

For a moment, I hope it's Alex.

But as I step toward the door, something tells me I'm wrong.

The second I open it, I feel instant regret.

There he is—*my father.*

Standing stiff and proper.

"Elena," he says, voice cool, measured. Like this is another business meeting.

"Why are you here?" I ask, my voice flat.

He adjusts his cufflinks, like this conversation isn't about to gut me.

"We *need* to talk."

I cross my arms, leaning against the doorframe. "Funny, is that what we were doing right before you tore me down in front of Philippa and Carole?"

His jaw twitches. "I'm here because you're in trouble. Whether you realize it or not."

I laugh. It's sharp, bitter. "Oh, so now you care?"

He frowns. "Don't be dramatic."

"Dramatic?" My voice snaps up, too loud, too broken. "You think *I'm* being dramatic? I'm the one whose name is being dragged through every headline. The one getting death threats. The one getting slut-shamed online. I'm the one on the verge of potentially being dropped by my label—or worse, sued for every-thing I'm worth."

I deadpan, ice in my veins. "And where were you when my life was falling apart before? Huh?"

His expression hardens, but he says nothing.

"You want to play concerned father now?" I shake my head,

tears stinging my eyes, blurring the edges of the room. "Where the hell were you for the last five years? Where were you when *she* got sick?" The words rip out of me, raw and shaking.

His mouth presses into a thin, bloodless line.

"Where were you when she fucking *died*?" My chest heaves, the air too thick to breathe. "You never came to see me. Didn't even have the decency to attend the funeral. Not once. Not when I was drowning in grief in Australia. Not when I was alone."

His throat bobs, but still, nothing.

I take a shaky breath, anger and heartbreak closing in, drowning me.

"You didn't want me," I whisper. "You made that abundantly clear when you forced Mom to choose between us. And *now*? Now that I'm splashed across the tabloids, *now* you want to play dad of the year?"

"Elena—"

"You don't get to come here," I snap, cutting him off, "on your high horse, like you didn't destroy our lives with *your* actions."

The words tear free, years of resentment finally breaking the surface, too hot, too heavy to hold back anymore.

"No." I step closer, my voice shaking. "What changed? What did I miss in those five years? What happened to the man who didn't give a damn if I was halfway across the world?"

His eyes flick away for a second, the first crack in his armor.

"Was it Mom?" I whisper, my voice breaking on the word. "Was it her diagnosis? Did the guilt finally eat you alive?"

His jaw tightens. "You don't understand—"

"Then *help me understand!*" I shout, the words ripping from my throat, too jagged to control.

"Because from where I'm standing," I spit, "you only care about how I make *you* look. You didn't care about me when you tossed me aside as a child. You didn't care when I was grieving.

When I was broken. You only care about *your* name. Your precious dynasty."

He exhales sharply, chest rising and falling with the effort to hold himself together. "This isn't about *my* reputation."

"Then what is it about?!"

Silence stretches between us, long and suffocating, before he finally speaks.

"It's about *yours*," he says coldly. "Alexander Westerberg is a liability."

"Excuse me?" I breathe, disbelief slamming into me.

"He's careless." His voice is bitter. "Scandal follows him like a shadow. And now, because of him, you're dragged into this mess. *His mess.* Your career, your future, everything you've worked for—*everything*—is on the line because you refuse to see what's right in front of you."

I don't flinch. I won't give him the satisfaction. "That wasn't a problem when you were being careless in your marriage, was it?"

His face darkens, a thundercloud rolling across his features. "Don't start."

"Oh, what? Too close to home?" My voice sharpens, slicing between us like a blade. Heat flashes across my skin. I feel the control slipping, leaking out through the cracks I can't seal fast enough.

"Alex may be a lot of things," I say, my voice rising, "but you know what he's not? He's not the man who abandoned me. He's not the man who discarded me when I needed him most. He didn't break my heart."

"Elena—"

I step forward, closing the space between us until there's barely a breath left. My heart punches against my ribs, the pounding in my ears drowning out the rest of the world.

"He's the first person to make me feel like I'm *worth* something," I choke out. "So don't you dare stand here and tell me he's not good enough for me when you never were."

Mortimer's eyes burn into mine, a battle cry he's too proud to voice. His jaw tightens until the muscle jumps.

"You've worked too hard to let this man destroy you," he says, every word hitting like a fist to my gut.

"Don't talk about him," I grit out, barely holding the line.

"You think he cares what happens to you?" Mortimer snaps, his voice cracking like a whip through the air. "You think when *this* gets worse, he won't run? Men like him, they run, Elena."

The unspoken fear I'd buried slips right out of his mouth.

A long silence stretches between us.

I wipe at my face, tears falling faster now, his words sit heavy in my chest.

"Maybe Alex is a mess," I mutter, my voice splintering. "But so am I. And he sees me and he still wants me."

Unlike you.

I don't say the last part out loud. I don't have to.

Mortimer's face hardens. "He's going to hurt you."

"Maybe," I whisper, my voice breaking. "But you hurt me first."

His gaze drops, hands twitching uselessly at his sides—but he doesn't reach for me.

After a long pause, he straightens his jacket, cold and composed again, like he can button up the wreckage he's leaving behind.

"If you won't listen to reason"—his tone is stiff, clipped—"there's nothing more to say."

A bitter laugh scrapes out of me. I turn toward the window, so I don't have to watch him walk away.

"There never was."

The door clicks shut behind him.

I stand there for a long time, my shoulders shaking as I try to breathe.

Because even though I tell myself I'm making the right choice, some part of me still feels like that little girl, waiting for her dad to show up.

But not like this.

And so, like always, I have to be enough for myself.

I turn back into the apartment, the silence pressing in on me like a weight.

The city lights flicker through the window, distant and cold.

I sink to the floor.

And for the first time since this nightmare started, I let myself fall apart. The sob that tears from my throat is ugly, raw—the kind that feels like it'll rip me open from the inside out.

I bury my face in my hands, my whole body trembling.

What am I even doing?

Holding onto a man who might break me?

Fighting for a career that feels like it's slipping through my fingers? Clinging to a family that has never really chosen me?

I press my palms harder against my eyes, as if I can hold it all inside if I push hard enough.

But it still pours out.

Feelings I've been holding back since the first headline dropped. Since my dad showed up at my door and spoke life to all the fears I had about Alex. Since I realized that I had let Alex all the way in—and that meant he had the power to destroy me.

God, I miss her.

Mom, what would you say to me right now?

The thought hits me like a punch to the chest.

She would know what to do. She would tell me I'm stronger than this.

But all I feel is tired. So damn tired.

Collide

I let my body crumple to the floor in a heap, staring up at the ceiling as hot tears streak down my cheeks.

"I don't know if I can do this," I whisper into the empty room.

I wish I had her here to say it to. Wish I could crawl into her arms, feel her warmth, smell her perfume, have her tell me that everything will be okay, even if it isn't.

But she's gone.

And I'm here.

Alone.

Chapter 28

Be My Mistake

While my PR team's approach was to deny, distance, and protect me, Alex's PR team had a very different strategy, launching a calculated attack with surgical, efficient, and merciless precision. Within hours of my team issuing a carefully worded statement, his team had conveniently leaked images of Madison in dimly lit bars, tangled up with men who were most definitely *not* Alex.

The narrative shifted, headlines morphing from speculation about Alex and me to brutal scrutiny over Madison's indiscretions. Watching it unfold was surreal—how a life could be rewritten with a few well-placed photos and salacious headlines.

And while the public heat was off us for now, the underlying reality remained—Alex could still be the father of Madison's baby.

I exhale, glancing up at Alex, who is leaning against the kitchen island, swirling whiskey in a glass.

"You okay?" he asks, voice low, watching me carefully.

I nod, setting my phone down with a shaky hand. "Yeah. I

think." The words stall, caught somewhere between my chest and throat. "It's crazy how easy it is to manipulate what people think."

Alex smirks, but there's something weary underneath, like the mask he wears is starting to crack at the edges.

"Welcome to my world, *Älskling*," he says softly.

I inhale slowly, trying to stay grounded.

His world.

A world I'm now fully entrenched in.

And yet, despite everything—the scrutiny, the turmoil, the gnawing uncertainty—I can't help but feel a flash of gratitude that it's a world he pulled me into.

"Alex, we still have a lot to talk about." I sigh, staring down at my hands, the weight of everything pressing down on my shoulders.

"Nothing's certain until I get that DNA result." His voice drips with the deluded confidence of a man used to bending the world to his will. "They can't do the test for another two weeks. I'd rather not stress about something that might not even be something to stress about."

I nod, even though the words taste hollow in my mouth. This is bigger than me. Bigger than anything I've ever known how to handle.

My silence doesn't go unnoticed.

Alex stands and crosses the small space between us, sitting down beside me.

He takes my hand in his, firm but gentle, grounding me with the heat of his touch.

"Talk to me. This only works if we talk, Darling," he coaxes, his thumb brushing slow, tender circles over my knuckles, grounding me and setting my nerves on fire all at once.

After Sweden—after that earth-shattering experience where I had never felt more alive—coming back to this whirlwind feels like being torn apart piece by piece.

A small part of me wants to get off the ride. Retreat. But a bigger part of me…God, a bigger part of me isn't ready to give this all up.

"Alex," I breathe, barely above a whisper, my throat dry, raw. "I feel like I'm in free fall."

His hand stills against mine, but he doesn't let go.

His eyes lock onto me—sharp, unwavering.

He sees it all.

The cracks in my voice.

The tension in my jaw.

The way I'm barely holding myself together.

He reads the storm I haven't even named out loud.

"Then let me catch you." His voice is quiet, steady. "Like I did the moment you fell into my life."

I freeze.

From the moment I stumbled into his world, I haven't been the same. And I hate how true that feels.

I'm always the one in control.

The one who stays grounded, who keeps her distance, who knows better. But Alex makes everything feel untethered. Out of rhythm. A song progression that makes absolutely no sense, and all the sense in the world at once.

I've been walking a straight line my whole life, and he came in and shook me awake from the catatonic state I didn't even know I'd been living in.

Until him.

I shake my head, barely clinging to what little control I have left. "It's not that easy."

"Maybe it is," he murmurs, brushing his thumb along the inside of my wrist, a featherlight touch that sets my skin buzzing. "If you'd let it be."

And that's the problem.

I want to.

I pull my hand away gently, standing to put distance between us, because if I don't, I might fall right back into him without a second thought.

"My PR team practically begged me to stay away from you, to distance myself, lay low until the storm passes."

I let out a sharp breath, pacing toward the window, staring at the city below.

"And my father—" The word feels foreign on my tongue, heavy and wrong, "had the audacity to show up at my door, acting concerned, claiming you're going to destroy me. Like he didn't detonate our entire family first."

I let out a hollow, bitter laugh, the sound ricocheting off the glass.

"They think I can just flip a switch. Walk away from this. Walk away from you. Like you're some phase I'll get over."

Alex leans forward, resting his elbows on his knees, watching me like I'm something fragile.

"And what do you think?" he asks, voice low, careful.

I hesitate, chewing my bottom lip, my heart pounding so loud I'm sure he can hear it.

Every nerve in my body screams at me to say what I feel, even if it ruins me.

"I don't know," I whisper.

"Elena," he says, his voice unraveling at the edges. "I would destroy the whole fucking world for you."

He stands, stepping closer, eyes locked on mine, daring me to look away.

"If it meant taking you back to that cabin, keeping you there —just us—I'd do it. I'd never let you leave."

My breath catches. My chest aches from how badly I want to believe him.

"For you, my Darling…I'd give it all up. The career, the fame, the spotlight, everything. Say the word, and we disappear."

His hand comes to my face, thumb brushing along my jaw like he owns it. Like he owns me.

The words hit me low and deep, cutting through all my defenses.

He's not just offering me an escape.

He's offering me devotion I've never known before.

And it hits me like a drug.

I lean into the touch I should pull away from.

"I think"—I sigh, my voice trembling but finding strength—"if you want me, then I'm yours, Alex."

His mouth brushes the word against my skin. "Mine."

His eyes darken, something wild flickering there.

Hunger, yes. But something softer too.

Like awe. Like I've just handed him my soul, and he knows it.

"Elena," he breathes, my name spilling from his mouth like a prayer.

His fingers brush my face, tucking a strand of hair behind my ear, lingering as they drift down to my jaw, coaxing it upward until my eyes meet his.

"You think I don't know what this is doing to you? To us?" he whispers, voice rough now, like every word scrapes its way out of him. "But I can't let you go."

His thumb strokes along my cheekbone, unbearably soft.

"You are everything to me." His confession slips out like a secret he can't take back. His touch burns and soothes at once, like he's trying to memorize me.

"Mine," he says again.

A shiver runs through me.

Not fear.

Something worse.

The terrifying anticipation of falling too hard, too fast.

"Say it," he murmurs, his forehead pressing to mine, his

breath warm against my lips. "Tell me you want this. Tell me you want *us*."

I tremble all over with the weight of it. I close my eyes, and the words slip out, unguarded.

"I do." My voice barely makes it past my lips. "If we burn, we burn together."

His mouth curves—wicked and tender all at once—as it brushes against mine like a promise.

"Then let's burn, *Älskling*."

His lips press into mine, sealing our fates in an instant. It might be a terrible idea. It might ruin everything. But neither of us cares.

I kiss him back with just as much fervor, hands tangling in his hair as he lifts me smoothly, my legs locking around his waist.

He carries me to the bedroom, the door swinging open with a thud.

I take him in—his need, his flaws, his fire.

I'm his. And he's mine.

Even if it ruins me.

A FEW DAYS LATER, it's all hands on deck at Pacific Records.

What had felt like a firing squad days ago—a cold, tense room thick with judgment—has somehow transformed into a sunlit haven where dreams are spun out of thin air.

It's all so *fickle*.

One minute, I was facing complete and total ruin because of Madison's news. Now, those same suits are riding high off a PR victory—one they had nothing to do with.

Alex's campaign flips the narrative. His team turns the scandal inside out and hands them a redemption arc they can repackage in time for my album launch.

I'm no longer a liability. I'm the story.

Mark paces at the head of the table, a wide grin stretching across his face as he flips through a stack of streaming stats and pre-release feedback. The numbers are up. They're all so pleased with themselves.

Around him, the execs buzz like bees, murmuring over their tablets, swiping through glowing headlines like they hadn't been sharpening knives just days ago.

I sit still, hands folded in my lap, pretending not to notice how quickly the tide turns when there's something to gain.

"Elena, your first album from two years ago is charting! You're on fire right now." Mark stops pacing long enough to beam at me. "We think it's time to move up the release date of your single from the upcoming album. Capitalize on the press while you're hot."

"Move it up? By how much?" It takes everything for me not to roll my eyes.

Kylie, sitting beside me, shoots me a quick, encouraging smile, though it doesn't quite reach her eyes.

"Release the single next week, then the album drops two weeks after that," Mark says, grinning like a kid on Christmas morning. "Your socials are exploding, radio's playing your old stuff. People are hungry for more."

The room hums with nods and half-muttered approvals, the energy crackling with excitement.

And for a moment, I let myself feel it.

The high.

That flicker of *finally*. Like maybe all the drama was worth it.

Was it? This is what I wanted...right? But the realization lands hard and cold.

Why does it feel so hollow? Like I've traded something sacred for a headline.

"That's...great." I force a smile. "Really great news."

"Damn right, it is." Mark claps his hands once, loud and sharp. "We'll have the marketing team start teasing snippets tomorrow. You ready for this, superstar?"

I bite back the nerves fluttering beneath the excitement. I nod. "Yeah. I'm ready."

The moment we step out of the conference room, Kylie tugs gently on my arm, steering me away from the others.

"Hey, can we talk?" she asks, her voice low, glancing around before guiding me into one of the smaller side offices.

Once the door clicks shut, she turns to face me. Folding her arms, her brow furrows.

"I'm really happy for you, Elena. You know that, right?" She treads carefully.

I nod, already sensing the *but* hanging heavy between us.

"But," I say for her.

She sighs. "Yeah. But." She runs a hand through her perfectly styled hair, the cracks in her calm, professional exterior starting to show. "I have to ask…did you end things with Alex?"

I stiffen, jaw tightening. "No."

Kylie exhales, frustration and concern flashing across her face. "Elena—"

"I have no plans to end things," I cut in, holding her gaze steady. "Just because he *might* be having a baby with someone else doesn't mean we have to end. People have babies all the time, it doesn't mean their lives or relationships stop."

Her eyes widen slightly, like she hadn't expected me to be so firm.

"I'm telling you this because I care about you—you need to think about what this could do to your career if the truth comes out. If he's the father, and you're standing by him publicly, it could ruin everything you've built before you even really get to enjoy it. You'll lose in the court of public opinion. You'll stand in the way of their 'happy family' ending."

Her words hit their mark, but still, I feel that stubborn heat rising in my chest.

If we burn, we burn together.

"I'm not going to pretend we're nothing just to save face." My voice wavers. "I've spent my whole life hiding parts of myself to make everyone else comfortable."

Kylie softens, but she isn't done. "I'm not saying hide forever. But at least keep this private right now. Please. For you. Protect yourself until you know where this is heading."

I look away, staring out the floor-to-ceiling window overlooking the city. The sky is gray—cold and distant.

"We can't control what people say," Kylie adds gently, stepping closer. "But we can control what we give them to talk about."

Her words hang heavy between us.

Finally, I turn back to her, forcing a small smile. "Thanks, Kylie. I'll think about it."

She searches my face for a moment, like she isn't sure if she believes me, but finally nods.

"Okay. Just…be careful. You've worked too hard to let it all fall apart."

She leaves, the door clicking quietly behind her.

I let out a shaky breath, pressing my hands to my face.

Because even though I don't want to admit it, a part of me knows she's right.

Chapter 29

I Fall Apart

When I return to my apartment, despite Kylie's warning, I feel lighter. For now, the label is happy, and my reputation has recovered.

Groceries in hand, I stop dead in my tracks. There, sitting on the bench outside my door, is Carole.

Her posture is perfect as always, legs crossed at the ankle, her hands folded neatly in her lap. But there's something in the way she's staring down at them, something small and almost fragile that catches me completely off guard.

What is she doing here?

She looks up as I approach, offering a tentative smile. "Elena."

I freeze, standing awkwardly in front of her. "Carole. I… wasn't expecting to see you."

She nods, smoothing an invisible crease from her perfectly tailored coat. "I know. I wasn't sure I should come. But I wanted to talk to you."

A part of me stiffens—the old resentment rising, sharp and familiar—but something in her tone makes me pause.

"I won't stay long," she adds gently, sensing my hesitation. "But I was hoping we could talk. Just for a minute."

Against my better judgment, I sigh and unlock the door, leading her into my apartment. Inside, she perches carefully on the edge of a stool while I busy myself with the groceries, silent, unsure of what to say.

Carole glances around the apartment, her eyes softening like she's taking in every detail. "You've made a beautiful home for yourself."

I offer a polite smile, arms wrapping tighter around myself. "Thanks. But I don't think you came here to talk about Philippa's decorating."

She flinches slightly but doesn't argue. Instead, she exhales slowly, looking up at me with a raw honesty that disarms me more than I want to admit.

"You know," she begins softly, "when your parents divorced, I became the villain. And I'm not going to stand here and pretend I was innocent. I wasn't."

I swallow, arms tightening even more around myself. What is going on right now?

Her voice shakes as she continues, "But what no one knew, what no one cared to ask, was that I was pregnant."

The air leaves the room, sudden and brutal.

"What?" I whisper, my throat scraping raw.

She nods, blinking fast, like she's holding herself together by a thread. "I was pregnant when the media tore me apart. When everyone tore me apart. And in the stress of it all"—she breathes out—"I lost the baby."

I stare at her, heart pounding against my ribs.

Her voice drops even softer. "The doctors said it damaged me so badly I wouldn't be able to have children again. So, if you ever wondered whether I paid a price for what happened…I did."

The silence stretches between us, thick, suffocating.

"I...didn't know," I manage, my voice barely a whisper, something painful shifting deep inside me.

"No one did," she murmurs. "Monty knew, of course. But what would it have mattered? To everyone else, I was the home-wrecker. No one cared if I was bleeding out on the floor."

She wipes her eyes quickly, pulling herself back together.

"I'm not telling you this to make you pity me." She squares her shoulders. "That's the last thing I want. I wanted you to know that I understand what it's like. To love someone and not know if loving them will destroy you."

My breath catches, tight and aching in my chest.

"Your father was my first and only love," she admits, pressing her lips into a thin line. "I won't lie, I enjoyed the life he gave me at first. But there are times I've wondered if losing my baby was karma for the damage I caused your family."

My throat burns, tears stinging the back of my eyes.

Carole looks at me, her expression soft, almost pleading. "I see what's happening to you, Elena. I see what you're caught up in, and I don't want you to go through what I did. Like I said before, the press loves nothing more than a scandal."

Her words slice into me, hitting a place I've been trying so hard to ignore.

I sink onto the stool beside her, feeling like my body might fold in half from the weight of it all.

"I don't even know what I'm doing," I whisper.

She gives a small, sad smile. "I didn't either. That's hindsight for you."

I shake my head, raking a hand through my hair. "Everyone's telling me to walk away from him, from Alex. But I don't know if I can."

"I understand, Elena. More than you know," she says softly.

Carole reaches across the small space and gently takes my hand in hers. Her hand is warm. Grounding.

"Sometimes"—she sighs—"when you love the wrong person, you don't see it until it's too late."

Her touch is steady. And for the first time, I see *her*. Not the woman who tore my family apart. Just a woman who loved the wrong person and carries the cost of it in her bones.

In some ways, I can relate.

"I care so much about him," I confess, voice breaking open.

She nods, squeezing my hand.

"Everyone wants me to give him up." The words crack free. "But does that mean sacrificing the one thing that makes me happy?"

"There's danger in being wrapped up in someone like that," she says gently. "You risk losing yourself altogether. And you have to ask yourself if it's worth it."

"I…" I hesitate, the weight of her pressing heavy on my chest. "I think he is. He wants me. He chose me."

Her face is soft, no judgment in her eyes. She sits there and listens—really listens.

In that moment, my heart softens. Not forgiveness. But maybe a step toward understanding.

"I always thought you didn't care," I whisper.

She smiles sadly, squeezing my hand tighter. "I care more than you'll ever know."

Silence settles between us, but it's not uncomfortable anymore. It's something else—something almost like peace.

And as I look into her eyes, I see it—the same fear that haunts me. The fear that loving someone could be the thing that destroys you.

My phone has been buzzing nonstop—texts from my team,

my family, people I haven't spoken to in years. The sheer volume of it all is overwhelming…but exhilarating.

But before I can even *think* about letting it sink in, there's a knock on my door. I open it and see him.

Broderick. *With flowers*.

Tulips.

He isn't supposed to be here. I know he's flying to Europe in the morning for a last-minute business trip that will keep him away for weeks. But still, here he is, leaning against my doorway like he owns the place, a small smile tugging at his lips.

"Didn't want to leave without saying congratulations. Here." His voice is soft, his eyes lingering on me as he hands me the bouquet.

I grin, trying to act casual even though my heart races. "You didn't have to come all the way here just for that."

He steps inside with a shrug. "Maybe not. But I wanted to. Before I left, anyway."

For a moment, we stand there, something unspoken thickening the air. His fingers twitch like he wants to reach for me, but doesn't.

"I'll be back in a few weeks," he murmurs. "Try not to take over the world without me."

I smile, about to say something back, but before I can close the door, another voice slices through the room like a blade.

"She'll manage just fine."

His voice stops me in my tracks.

Alex.

He stands in the hallway, leaning casually against the wall, but his eyes—those sharp eyes—cut between Broderick and me, his jaw tight enough to crack.

"Good to see you too, Alex." Broderick's tone is cool, like this isn't about to explode.

Alex rakes a hand through his hair, exhaling sharply. "Do you always show up unannounced at *my* girlfriend's apartment the night before you leave town?" he says, stepping inside.

Broderick smirks, but there's nothing friendly about it. "Elena and I are friends. Or is that a problem for you?"

Alex's eyes darken. "Not when that 'friend' constantly undresses her with his eyes, or were you hoping we'd broken up and you'd swoop in like a hero?"

Broderick's expression hardens. "If you're insecure, just say so," he retorts, sharp as glass.

My heart clenches. I quickly step between them, the air thick like a storm about to break. "Guys—"

"What the fuck did you just say?" Alex shoots back, voice quiet, lethal.

"You heard me," Broderick bites out, squaring his shoulders.

"Are you two seriously doing this right now?" I ask, completely flabbergasted that these two grown men are acting like cavemen.

"He started it," they both grumble at the exact same time.

"I don't care, seriously. This is so stupid."

From the kitchen, Riley's voice cuts through like a fire alarm. "Do I need to hose you two idiots off again?!"

Neither of them answers, still locked in that silent battle, testosterone practically choking the air.

I throw my hands up. "Are you done measuring dicks, or should I give you some privacy?"

Still nothing.

Riley stomps over, arms crossed, fully ready to save me again. "Enough. Broderick, go. Have a safe flight, mate. See you soon. Alex," she adds, glaring at him, "stop being a jealous prick. Come inside and see your girlfriend."

Silence.

Broderick finally turns to me, his eyes softening. "I'll see you soon, El."

Then he walks out, brushing past Alex without even glancing at him.

Alex doesn't move for a long moment, his eyes still locked on the door like he could burn a hole through it.

Finally, he turns to me, his gaze burning, voice low. "I don't like him."

I let out a breath, dragging a hand through my hair. "Yeah, I gathered that."

He steps closer, the heat rolling off him like a live wire. "Tell me you don't feel anything for him."

I hesitate, just for a second.

And he sees it.

My lips part, but nothing comes out, fingers tightening around the bouquet Broderick handed me as Alex takes another step closer. His frustration is palpable.

There's a wild desperation in his eyes, searching mine for something he's terrified is there.

"Do you?" he asks again, quieter this time. "Feel something for him?"

"No." The word scrapes out of me.

"Tulips," Alex says, his voice low, eyes narrowing at the bouquet in my arms. "Bold choice. You know they're a symbol of love, right?"

Suddenly, the flowers feel heavier, weighted with unspoken meaning, as I set them carefully on the counter. My hands betray me with the faintest tremble, and somewhere deep inside me, the lid of the box labeled Broderick begins to rattle.

His hand shoots through his hair again, that exasperated, gesture he does when he's coming apart at the seams.

I watch him carefully. "What's going on with you? You don't normally…act like this."

His eyes are in agony. "Can we go to your room? Just to talk —privately."

I nod, then turn, leading him down the hall and quietly closing the door behind us.

He stays silent for a long moment, staring out the window like he can avoid it. Finally, he says, "Madison emailed me this morning."

"What?"

He turns back to me, and all that anger from before is gone, replaced by something raw and broken.

"The baby. *It's mine.*"

The air rushes out of me like I've been punched.

"Oh."

"I got the DNA results in my inbox." His voice is hollow. "She wanted me to know. Like it was some…*victory.* I don't know what to do," Alex admits, his voice cracking in a way I've never heard before. "I'm going to be a father, and I don't want this." He breaks off, dragging his hands over his face. "Not like this, not with her. *Fucking* bitch."

My chest aches for him.

He looks at me then, his whole body trembling under the weight of it. "Elena, I don't want her. I never wanted her. You know that, right?"

I feel my throat tighten painfully.

"I…" He stops again, swallowing hard. "I see *him* with you. And I feel like I'm already losing you. And now this…I feel like everything's falling apart."

His eyes are glassy, and for a moment, all the sharp edges of him—the arrogance, the recklessness—are stripped away.

It's just Alex.

Vulnerable. Hurting.

Before I can stop myself, I move toward him, reaching out to touch his arm gently. "Hey, you're not losing me. I'm right here."

His hand comes up to cover mine, holding on like it's the only thing keeping him tethered to the ground.

"I don't know what to do," he whispers again. And this time, it's not about Madison.

It's about us.

I bite my lip, my heart thudding painfully against my ribs. "I don't know either."

We stand there, suspended in that fragile space between what we are and what we might never be again.

"Hey, if we burn," I say softly, meeting his eyes.

He gives me a small, broken smile. "We burn together."

Our promise. Our curse.

We cling to each other as if we can hold back the tidal wave bearing down on us.

But even as I hold his hand tighter, my heart twists painfully, because somewhere deep inside, I know nothing about this will ever be simple.

Because now, I finally understand what Carole meant—sometimes loving the wrong person doesn't just hurt.

It consumes you.

Chapter 30

Go Your Own Way

As I sit on my green velvet sofa, coffee cradled between my palms, I let my eyes dance over the collection of clothes, shoes, and accessories Rio couriered over this morning. The soft sunlight spills through the windows, casting golden patches on the floorboards, warming the room that has become my sanctuary.

Tonight.

It's probably the biggest night of my life. Not just because it's my twenty-third birthday, but because tonight, the world will finally hear my debut U.S. album. A culmination of dreams, heartbreak, and countless hours poured into lyrics that bare my soul.

I never truly got to enjoy the release of my first album. The ink was barely dry on the press releases when everything fell apart. My first single dropped, and then so did my world.

Mom took a turn for the worse.

We knew the day was coming, a shadow that lingered in every corner, but when it finally happened, it still hit me like a semi-truck—loud, unstoppable, and shattering. I cancelled appearances. Any plans for further singles or a tour were left to collect dust. I locked myself away from everyone and everything.

Grief consumed me whole.

It took me two years to claw my way out of that darkness, two years to find my voice again, not only musically, but as a woman who knew how to stand on her own.

And now, here I am.

Sitting in this beautiful apartment that still feels surreal to call mine, in a city that both terrified and thrilled me when I arrived a little over three months ago.

Back then, I was bitter and naïve. But hopeful.

Now?

Now, I get to share this dream with my best friend, watching hers unfold right alongside mine. I have Alex, my first boyfriend, who makes me feel alive in ways I never thought possible.

I have never been closer to my sister, as we slowly stitch ourselves back together from the broken pieces our parents left behind.

Carole, the woman I once hated on principle. Well, there's an understanding between us now. Enough to not hate her. Enough to see her less as a villain and more as a flawed woman like myself.

And my father…Well, he's still a work in progress. Some days, I believe we'll get there. Other days, I wonder if he'll ever truly see me beyond what he wants me to be.

But despite everything, despite the mess and the past, my old music is getting a new lease on life. Somehow, maybe because of recent events—the media storm, the drama, the unexpected spot-light—people are listening again. They want more.

And I'm ready to give it to them. Tonight, I get to stand in front of Alex, my family, friends, and the people who believed in me enough to take a chance on me.

"You're up early," Riley says, emerging from her room, a mess of frizz in an oversized shirt that has paint on it.

"Yeah, the couriers brought these over for us tonight." I smile, bringing myself back to reality.

Realization slowly creeps onto Riley's still sleepy face.

"Oh, BABE! Happy Birthday!" she sings, off pitch.

I can't help but laugh.

"Are you ready for tonight?" she adds, making her way to the coffee machine.

"Born ready." My heart flutters with anticipation.

A FEW HOURS before the event, Rio and his team sweep into the apartment like a glamorous battalion—garment bags hanging on every door, makeup cases exploding across the kitchen island, trays of canapés I'm definitely not touching thanks to the knot in my stomach.

Philippa joins Riley and me for an afternoon of pre-drinks, pampering, and all-out glamming, and for once, it feels like the three of us are just sisters and friends. No tension. There's an ease to it. A warmth.

"I'm so excited and proud of you." Philippa beams, standing barefoot on the rug, champagne flute in hand, admiring the lineup of shoes laid out like museum pieces. "Seriously, Elena. I don't think you realize how far you've come."

I smile, soft and unsure, that familiar tug catching behind my ribs. "I don't know…it still feels surreal. Like I'm about to wake up and—*poof*—this is all gone."

Riley, mid-hair curl and phone in hand, glances at me from the chair by the window. "Girl, please. You've worked your ass off for this. Own it."

She grins, but her eyes soften, and I know she sees me, really sees me, clinging tight to the edge of this moment.

"*Ooh*, social media is on fire right now," she adds with a smirk. "Want me to read some?"

I laugh—light, breathless. "Go for it."

She sits up straighter, holding her phone like it's a royal scroll.

I shake my head, smiling, a small laugh escaping.

"That's so sweet," Philippa says, glancing over her shoulder. "You've touched people, Elena. You should let that sink in."

Riley keeps scrolling, her grin growing.

My chest goes warm, tight and fluttering. That familiar hum of vulnerability before I step out and show the world something I haven't fully come to terms with myself.

"Here's another one—Oh my God, this one's too good." Riley snorts and reads it in the most dramatic voice she can muster:

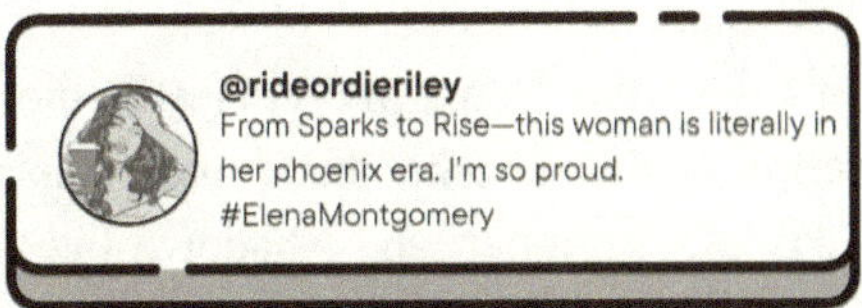

She looks up, grinning. "Oh, wait, that's me."

Philippa and I burst out laughing.

"Wow, subtle, babe," I tease, swiping under my eyes before any of the glam team notices I'm about to cry off my eyeliner.

"I mean it, though." Riley sets her phone down, all the playfulness gone. "Elena, I've watched what you've gone through, and now you're here, about to drop an album that's going to change everything. You deserve to rise. You deserve all of this."

Philippa nods, her expression softening. "She's right. I know I haven't always said the right thing—or known *what* to say—but..." Her voice falters, trembling beneath the surface. "Seeing you now, I wish Mom could see you tonight. She would be so proud."

The weight of it hangs between us. Heavy.

That hits me straight in the chest.

"I wish she could, too," I whisper as Philippa steps closer, wrapping her arms around me, careful not to smudge my makeup.

"I think she *does* see you," she adds quietly, voice shaky.

"Stop, Inga just did my mascara," I choke on a laugh, brushing my cheek as Riley throws her arms around us in a sloppy group hug, nearly knocking over Philippa's champagne.

"Look at us, we're a mess." Riley sniffles dramatically. "Who needs glam squads when we're emotionally glowing?"

We pull back, laughing, and for a moment, I let it sink in: how lucky I am to have them. My sister. My best friend. Standing by me when I feel both *ready* and *terrified* to show the world who I really am.

Rio claps his hands, breaking the moment with a bright grin. "Ladies, let's get our star ready to rise, shall we?"

They guide me into the chair, my girls still close. In the mirror, my reflection begins to take shape under their hands— foundation and lashes, shimmer and shadow, like layers of armor.

Once the glam team finishes weaving their magic, we're ready.

To my left, Riley radiates in a sapphire cocktail dress that hugs every curve. It's short enough to show off her long legs, with delicate silver straps that catch the light above us. Her wild red curls have been coaxed into glossy waves, though a few still rebel, because, of course, she would never be *too* polished.

On my right, Philippa is elegance incarnate. She wears a sleek black gown that drapes off one shoulder, her chestnut hair pulled into a low bun that highlights the sharp line of her jaw and the sparkle of understated diamond studs. Where Riley looks like the life of the party, Philippa looks like she owns the building—poised, composed, her signature resting-serious face softening only when her eyes land on me.

And me? My hair is swept into a sleek high ponytail, giving the illusion of height, of strength. I feel like I can *hold* something tonight. Like I can carry it.

Dangling from my ears are my mother's earrings—the ones she wore on that Miss Universe stage all those years ago.

Just knowing they're with me now…

It feels like a piece of her is, too.

I take a steadying breath, fingers smoothing over the fabric of my dress—a floor-length gown that starts as the deepest black, darker than midnight, but with every movement, it catches the light to reveal molten streaks of crimson and gold, shifting like liquid fire beneath the surface. The plunging neckline is softened by delicate sheer sleeves that cling tightly to my wrists. The way it hugs me feels like wearing fire itself.

Rio called it *a phoenix on the rise* the first time I slipped it on, and now, standing beneath the velvet city sky, I finally understand what he meant.

By the time we pull up to the venue, my nerves have morphed into a tight swirl of excitement and anxiety.

Riley squeezes my hand as the elevator glides silently toward the rooftop, her eyes wide and sparkling like *she's* the one about to perform.

Philippa stands tall beside me, radiating that graceful elegance she's known for, but when she catches my eye, she gives me a small, reassuring smile.

The elevator doors slide open, and soft ambient music greets us—a mellow acoustic mix underscored by the gentle hum of conversation and the clink of champagne glasses.

The rooftop is breathtaking.

Strung fairy lights crisscross overhead, casting a warm golden glow that flickers against the deep purple hues of early evening. Clusters of candles burn low in glass holders on tables wrapped in sheer white linens, surrounded by plush velvet lounge chairs. Tall heaters glow at the corners, warding off the early fall chill.

And there—set against the skyline that stretches endlessly beyond—is the small, intimate stage. A simple black mic stand. A wooden stool. And leaning casually against it, my guitar. Waiting.

My heart clenches at the sight of it.

Off to the side of the rooftop, I spot Mark deep in conversation with Kylie, both dressed sharply, champagne flutes in hand, faces bright with anticipation.

Near them stand two women I recognize instantly—Michelle and Sonia, the co-producers who stood by me through every high and low of making the album. They're deep in conversation with a few label executives, but when they spot me, they light up. Excited little waves, eyes gleaming with pride.

"Wow," Riley whispers as we step onto the deck, her eyes wide, sweeping across the view, the crowd, the stage. "Elena... this is your night."

"You did this," Philippa says gently, slipping her arm through mine. "All of it."

Before I can respond, the elevator chimes behind us.

Alex?

My heart flutters. Hope flares—sharp and immediate—before I can shut it down.

We all turn.

But it's not him.

It's Andrew, looking every inch the perfect gentleman in a tailored dark suit. He runs a hand through his hair, gaze sweeping the rooftop until it lands on Philippa. A grin breaks across his face, and he heads straight for her, pulling her into a hug so full of ease and familiarity it makes my heart ache in the best way.

I hear him murmur the word *sexy* and that's enough to tune the rest out.

Before I can dwell, I'm swept into a round of greetings—Mark, Kylie, a few of the label execs offering congratulations and toasting to the night like it's all effortless, like I'm not holding a thousand emotions in place with sheer will.

But my eyes keep drifting. Scanning the crowd. Catching on faces that aren't his.

Off to the side, I spot Carole and my father. She looks lovely, elegant in a sleek navy dress, a soft fur stole around her shoulders, grace touched with something more vulnerable tonight. Beside her, my father stands stiff, adjusting his cufflinks like the entire night is a trial he's been forced to endure.

Still, when I walk out, he looks up. His face is unreadable, all practiced restraint. But behind the distance, behind the detachment, there's a flicker of something softer. Like, for the first time, he's starting to understand what tonight means.

We haven't spoken since our fight. Since Carole's quiet revelation cracked open years of silence and resentment.

Because, of course, we're both too stubborn to make the first move.

But now, I watch him lean in, murmur something to Carole, then head toward me, his steps slow, measured, guarded.

"Elena," he says with a sigh, his voice even and polite, like we're strangers meeting for coffee. "Happy birthday. And… congratulations on your night."

I nod, my throat tight. "Thank you."

Small. Simple.

But maybe—for now—it's enough.

The rooftop starts to hum with more bodies, more laughter, more clinking glasses. I smile. I laugh. I let their joy wrap around me, warm and distracting.

But underneath it—beneath every cheer, every toast—I'm still scanning the crowd.

Where is he?

Every time the elevator chimes, my heart leaps.

And every time, it crashes.

Not him.

I try to brush it off. To stay grounded in what I *do* have—this moment, this celebration, these people who came for *me.*

But the longer the night stretches, the louder Alex's absence becomes. Before I can spiral too far, Mark's voice cuts through the rooftop, sharp and clear, pulling me back.

He stands on the small stage, champagne glass in hand, his signature grin lighting up his face.

"Good evening, everyone! Welcome, welcome!" he calls, beaming. "I want to thank you all for being here tonight to celebrate this spectacular young woman who, in such a small package, is an absolute *powerhouse* of talent."

Laughter and applause ripple through the crowd. My chest swells.

Riley leans in, gives my back a gentle pat. "Soak it in, superstar."

Mark's eyes find mine. His smile softens. "Elena," he says, lifting his glass slightly, "when we saw you compete on *Starstruck* two years ago, we *knew.* You were someone special.

And now, you've come such a long way—literally halfway across the world to be here with us tonight. And tonight…" He pauses, glancing around the rooftop. "Tonight, we celebrate your *Rise*."

A lump forms in my throat at the way he says it—not just the album, but everything it *means*.

"Happy birthday, Elena, and a toast to you!"

The rooftop erupts in cheers and applause. Glasses lift high, champagne flowing freely in every direction—bubbles catching the twinkling lights, sparkling like tiny stars in crystal flutes.

I force a smile, raising my own glass as faces turn toward me. But I can't help it, my eyes drift back to the elevator one more time.

Still empty.

"Okay." Mark grins as the applause fades. "Without further ado, the woman herself, here to give us an acoustic rendition of her brand-new single 'Sparks.' Take it away, Elena Montgomery!"

Another wave of applause breaks out, louder this time. All eyes swing to me.

Riley squeezes my hand. "You've got this," she whispers.

I smooth my palms over the shifting silk of my dress—as if I can ground myself in the feel of it—and will my legs to move toward the stage.

Even if Alex isn't here to see this moment, I'll still own it. Even if my heart aches.

The city glows behind me as I step onto the small stage.

I breathe in. Turning toward the crowd.

Warm faces. Familiar smiles. People I love. People who *showed up*.

My fingers brush the smooth neck of my guitar as I settle onto the stool. The dress pools around me, molten and alive.

The mic waits.

I lean in. My voice holds steady—steadier than I feel.

"Hi, everyone." I smile as the crowd quiets, a few faces

beaming back at me. "First of all, thank you. Truly. Thank you for being here tonight, for celebrating with me, for supporting me, and for standing by me in ways I can't fully put into words."

Soft murmurs ripple through the rooftop. Gentle applause.

"This album," I continue, glancing down before lifting my gaze again, "has been a long time coming. It's…pieces of me I wasn't always ready to share. Parts of my story I wasn't sure anyone would want to hear." I pause. Swallowing the lump that surfaces again. "But I hope tonight—and when *Rise* comes out— you hear not just heartbreak. But healing. And maybe even hope."

Applause swells, louder now. Riley whoops from somewhere in the back, and this time, I laugh for real.

I adjust the strap of my guitar and smile. "So, this is 'Sparks.' I hope you love it as much as I loved writing it."

The first soft chords rise into the night, curling through the rooftop air. Conversation fades into hush.

I begin to sing.

My eyes move through the crowd. Riley sways gently, wine glass in hand, her curls catching the candlelight. Philippa stands tall beside Andrew, pride practically radiating off her. Mark grins wide, like a proud uncle who knew all along I'd get here.

Then, during the second verse, my gaze lands on him.

My father.

He stands near Carole, no longer stiff or guarded. His face is open, watchful. There's something there I can't quite name.

Pride? Awe?

I hope maybe he finally sees me. Not the disappointment who chose melodies over mergers.

The weight of it nearly knocks the breath from me. I falter for a beat, but recover. *Keep going.*

Still no Alex.

By the time I strum the final chord, the note lingers like a held breath, and then the rooftop explodes into applause. Cheers, whistles, people rising to their feet, shouting my name.

I smile—real and wide—but it lands somewhere heavy inside my chest.

I stand. Bow slightly.

Then—

Crack.

A sudden burst behind me splits the night. I turn just as fireworks shoot into the sky, bursting into gold, crimson and silver, the light scattering over the skyline like glitter.

The crowd oohs and ahhs. As their gazes lift toward the night sky.

It should be perfect.

But even as I smile and tilt my face toward the sky, I keep glancing back at the elevator.

Still empty.

The realization creeps in—slow and cold.

Still no Alex.

As the fireworks fade, staff wheel out a towering cake, candles sparkling against the breeze.

"Happy birthday to you…"

Voices rise—off-key, joyful. Riley sings loudest, waving her arms like she's conducting a full orchestra. Philippa's voice is softer, steady, her eyes never leaving mine.

I laugh along. I play my part. But with every word, my heart pulls tighter.

The song ends. I blow out the candles. More cheers.

People turn away to mingle, to cut slices of cake.

Philippa slips in beside me, reading my face in a second. Her smile softens.

"Hey," she says, brushing a loose strand of hair from my cheek. "You were amazing."

"Thanks," I whisper voice tight, trying desperately to hold it together.

But Philippa knows me too well.

She leans in, her voice low and careful. "Where's Alex?"

The question lands like a punch.

My breath catches as the truth slams into me, undeniable now.

I shake my head, the words nowhere to be found. Like him.

Where *is* he?

Philippa's eyes stay on mine, searching. And when she reaches for my hand, I don't pull away.

I stare up at the sky—fireworks still streaking color across the black—and feel a tear slip down my cheek before I even know it's there.

THE APARTMENT IS SILENT.

The kind of silence that feels too big, stretching into every corner, pressing hard against my chest.

It's dark. The only light comes from the city outside, bleeding in through the windows—soft and flickering, like the world is continuing on without me.

I sit on the floor, dress pooled around me, heels abandoned by the door. My back rests against the green velvet sofa.

The only sound is the occasional soft clink of the champagne bottle tapping against my ring as I tip it back, drinking straight from the neck, because what's the point of a glass anymore?

Quiet tears slip down my cheeks.

The night was perfect.

Almost.

Riley left with someone. I didn't even catch his name. She kissed my cheek before slipping out, eyes dancing, murmuring something about not waiting up and enjoying my night with Alex.

And yet, here I am. Waiting.

I called as soon as the party ended.

Again in the town car.

Again, when I walked through the door, heels dangling from my hand, still half hoping I'd hear his voice behind me.

Each time, voicemail.

No call. No text.

The thought sinks deep, heavy as stone, as I sit curled on the floor, arms wrapped tight around my knees. The zipper digs into my back. The sequins scratch against my skin.

Did I do something wrong?

I whisper it aloud, just to fill the room.

My voice cracks on the last word.

I sound pathetic.

The champagne's warm now, but I drink it anyway, wiping at my cheek, mascara smudging beneath my fingertips.

And then—Buzz.

My phone vibrates against the hardwood.

My breath catches.

Alex.

His name glows on the screen like a flare. I stare at it too long, pulse thundering in my ears.

Then slowly, I press the phone to my ear.

"…Hello?"

Silence.

Just his breathing, low and ragged.

Not playful. Not teasing. Not his usual midnight voice that makes me feel like the only girl in the world.

It's tired. Pained.

"Elena," he finally says. His accent's thicker. His voice rough, like it hurts to speak my name.

Gripping the bottle tighter, I whisper, "Where were you? Are you okay?"

Another beat of silence.

Then—softly, so soft I almost miss it—he exhales, shaking.

"Elena, I'm sorry."

Relief sweeps through me. Sharp, quick, like air after drowning. He's sorry. That means there's a reason. Something happened.

He's here now.

"I can't do this anymore."

The room spins.

I sit up straighter, my chest tightening as the words hit like a cold slap. "What?"

His silence stretches, and that is somehow worse than the words themselves. Then, softer—almost like an apology—he says, "It's over."

I feel the breath leave my body. The champagne bottle slips from my fingers, landing with a soft, hollow thud against the rug.

"You're breaking up with me?" I ask, my voice shaking.

This isn't happening.

He sucks in a sharp breath on the other end, and for a second, I swear I hear something break in him, too.

"I'm sorry," he murmurs.

No. He can't mean that. Not tonight. Not after everything.

Tears blur my vision, slipping freely now. My throat is so tight, it physically hurts to swallow.

"Why?" My voice cracks. "Alex, don't—*please*."

"I have to go," he cuts in, his voice hollow, distant.

Please.

And before I can say anything else—before I can beg him not to do this—the line goes dead.

The phone slides from my hands, landing on the floor beside the abandoned bottle.

I stare at it.

The screen lights up for a second, long enough to flash my background.

That photo. Us, in Sweden. His arms wrapped around me. My head tipped back, laughing at something he said.

A reminder of everything we were before he blew it all up.

And then, for the first time all night, I welcome the loud, ragged sob that tears out of me.

I draw my knees to my chest, arms wrapped around them, trying to hold the pieces together as they begin to slip.

It's over. He doesn't want *me.*

The reality hits me like a truck.

Tears keep coming, relentless, until there's nothing left.

I'm hollow. Empty in a way that feels worse than crying.

Confirmation that I'm not good enough.

Peeling myself off the floor, I need out of this dress. It feels like a cage. The floorboards are cool beneath my feet. Jarring, like the night itself. I rise with the high, only to crash hard, left in tatters. The dress slips from my body, discarded like a second skin, pooling at my ankles as I walk away, leaving it crumpled and forgotten on the floor. A relic of a night that should have been perfect, but isn't. I feel sick.

The shower is scalding hot. Steam fills the room, fogging up the mirror until I can't even see myself. The heat burns against my skin, but it's almost comforting. If it stings enough, maybe it'll wash away the ache in my chest.

But it doesn't.

I stand under the water until my skin turns pink and raw, until my hands stop trembling, until there are no more tears left to cry. When I finally step out, I throw on underwear and Alex's T-shirt. It's soft and barely covers the tops of my thighs, but I don't care. Moving on autopilot, I pad barefoot back into the living room, water still dripping from my hair. The dress and half-empty champagne bottle are still there, abandoned on the floor.

Like me.

I don't even glance at them.

Instead, I walk straight to the bar cart, my fingers curling around a heavy crystal bottle of vodka.

No glass. No ice. No mixers.

I unscrew the cap with shaking hands and take a long, burning swig, the sharpness cutting through the numbness just enough to feel something real. The burn is a cruel reminder of a promise we made—and broke. I sink onto the couch, my damp hair clinging to my back, the T-shirt riding up as I pull my knees close to my chest.

I take another long sip, wincing as it burns its way down, but at least it's a pain I can control.

Cheers to me—numb, broken, and alone.

The city lights blur against the glass, smearing like watercolors, the world outside moving on without me.

My eyes burn, raw and swollen from crying, my body heavy with exhaustion and liquor.

The buzzer rings.

I freeze.

The bottle trembles slightly in my hand as my heart slams against my ribs.

Alex?

I sit frozen for a long moment, staring at the door in the dark like I can will him to appear.

Is he here?

Did he come to take it back?

Did he realize it was a mistake?

Then, a knock. Firm.

My breath catches.

Slowly, I set the vodka bottle down on the coffee table, my fingers trembling again as I stand, staring at the door.

I whisper a silent prayer. *Please,* let it be him.

Each step toward the door feels heavier than the last, my pulse roaring in my ears.

I reach for the handle, hesitating long enough to wonder if opening it will undo everything. If it'll fix what's been broken.

Then I pull it open.

Flowers and balloons greet me first, bright and colorful in the dim hallway light.

And then, a smile.

He came. *He's* here.

"Happy birthday," he says softly.

Before I can even think, I launch myself into his arms, wrapping my arms around his neck and kissing him hard, fierce and desperate, like I'm drowning and he's my only breath.

He tenses for half a second before his arms wrap around me, strong and steady. The balloons and flowers drop to the ground, forgotten, as he holds me like he'll never let go.

His scent fills me—mountains and amber, warm and familiar in a way that makes my chest ache.

I melt into him, clinging to his shoulders, my body trembling, lost in the moment.

Mountains. Amber.

No.

Alex smells like the ocean and citrus.

I pull back, breathless and confused, my heart pounding heavily.

His hands stay on my waist, grounding me as I blink, my eyes coming into focus.

When our gazes meet, it's green eyes I see.

Broderick.

Acknowledgments

Writing has always been my passion, books my sanctuary, and poetry the fuel for my soul. For too long, I let fear silence my creativity—but no more.

A journey's true worth lies in the friendships and memories forged along the way, and mine has been enriched by the incredible people who supported me when I finally shared my secret.

My deepest gratitude to the wonderful authors I met through Instagram—Anj Miranda, Kate Asher, Emme Goode, Rachel O'Rouke, Belinda Hamilton, Jordana Blake, Chloe Higgins, Jess McFarlane, and Arya Jacobs. Thank you for welcoming me with open arms into the bookish community, for your patience, thoughtful advice, and generous hearts. Your support has been a light in the chaos, and your friendship, a gift I will always treasure. You've been my safe landing.

To my brilliant editing team: Laura from Hummingbird Editing—there is no one I trust more with my manuscript. You encouraged me through every doubt, taught me so much, and made me a better writer. I truly believe fate brought us together—somehow, the universe made it happen even when your schedule was full. Vicky from Neon Galaxy Books—thank you for your enthusiasm for *Collide* and for being the best cheerleader a debut author could ask for.

Your meticulous care has polished *Collide* into something I am deeply proud of, and I am eternally grateful to you both.

Charles Manlangit—your extraordinary talent breathed life into my characters. Discovering your art at four a.m. felt like divine intervention. Maraming salamat for your heaven-sent creations.

To my amazing beta readers—Margaret Munro, Philippa Ryan, Stephanie Lambert, Brett Connerley, Amy Giles, Niesje Howie, Ashlee Adams, Diana Serinas, and Arabelle Urbano—thank you for taking a chance on me. Your laughter, tears, excitement, and relentless enthusiasm gave me the drive to finish this book. Your feedback and passion fueled my decision to self-publish. This would not have happened without you.

To my Barkada Babes—my street team, my ultimate hype queens—thank you for putting up with my antics, relentless flirting, inappropriate jokes, and for liking, sharing, and commenting on every post. You answered the call, and I adore you for it.

To my sister, Josephine—who doesn't even read but immediately asked, "Are you going to publish it?" upon hearing about my book—your unwavering belief in me has been invaluable. One day, I hope you'll experience *Collide*, perhaps as an audiobook made just for you, Sissy.

To my daughter, Evangeline—you are my greatest blessing. Though you're not old enough to read this yet, I hope it inspires you to follow your dreams, stand your ground, and be brave no matter what life throws at you. Everything I do is for you.

And finally, to my incredible husband, William—thank you for the late nights, for caring for our daughter so I could dive into writing and editing marathons, for tackling the laundry and dishes, and for enduring my wild plot ideas with unwavering patience. You are my everything, my rock, my biggest supporter, and the best book boyfriend anyone could dream of. I am endlessly grateful for you. *Mahal na mahal kita.*

About the Author

Alannah Roberts is a contemporary romance author whose books weave irresistible spice with compelling plots and captivating drama. Born in the Philippines and now residing in New South Wales, Australia, Alannah takes pride in crafting stories that highlight strong, vibrant women shaped by a rich heritage of resilience, hospitality, and passion.

Her debut novel, *Collide*, was over a decade in the making, sparked by a vivid dream during her daily train commute home while listening to Howie Day's song "Collide." From this fleeting inspiration emerged Elena's captivating journey—a tale of love, growth, and self-discovery.

Alannah balances her writing career alongside family life, sharing joyful chaos with her husband William, their daughter Evangeline, and an energetic battalion of Pomeranians, whom she occasionally showcases in exhibitions.

In 2023, Alannah faced a life-threatening ectopic pregnancy, a profound experience that crystallized her resolve to chase her dreams fearlessly. Determined not to live with regret, she set a timeline to begin the self-publishing journey once Evangeline turned one—a milestone she proudly accomplished, marking the beginning of her exciting new chapter as a published author.

The Rhapsody of Heartbeats Series

The journey has only just begun…Elena's story continues in

RUSH

Coming 2026

www.ingramcontent.com/pod-product-compliance
Lightning Source LLC
Chambersburg PA
CBHW051830180726

48283CB00004BA/1382